STOCKMAN'S SANDSTORM

THE STOCKMEN SERIES

MEL A ROWE

Also by Mel A ROWE

THE STOCKMEN SERIES:
Stockman's Sandstorm
Stockman's Stowaway
Stockman's Stormcloud
Stockman's Showdown

ELSIE CREEK SERIES:
The Art of Dust
Diamond in the Dust
Caked in Dust
Xmas Dust
Muster in the Dust
Rolled in Dust
Written in Dust
Doctoring Dust
Buffalo Dust

OASIS OF THE OUTBACK DUOLOGY:
The Station, Volume One
The Station, Volume Two

STANDALONE STORIES:
Avoiding the Pity Party
Unplanned Party
The Football Whisperer
Winter's Walk
Run Beautiful Run
The Sister Trip

Receive exclusive insights, and news on upcoming releases by joining:
https://melarowe.com/newsletter/

COPYRIGHT

***Caveat: As a courtesy, since there may be some sparse language choices in this story that may represent an obstacle for the reader, I am offering this warning. Please note this language and cultural references are purely for fictional purposes only and not designed to offend any individual persons, culture, or religions implied.*

The following is written in Australian English

For those who dared to find the courage
to try something new…

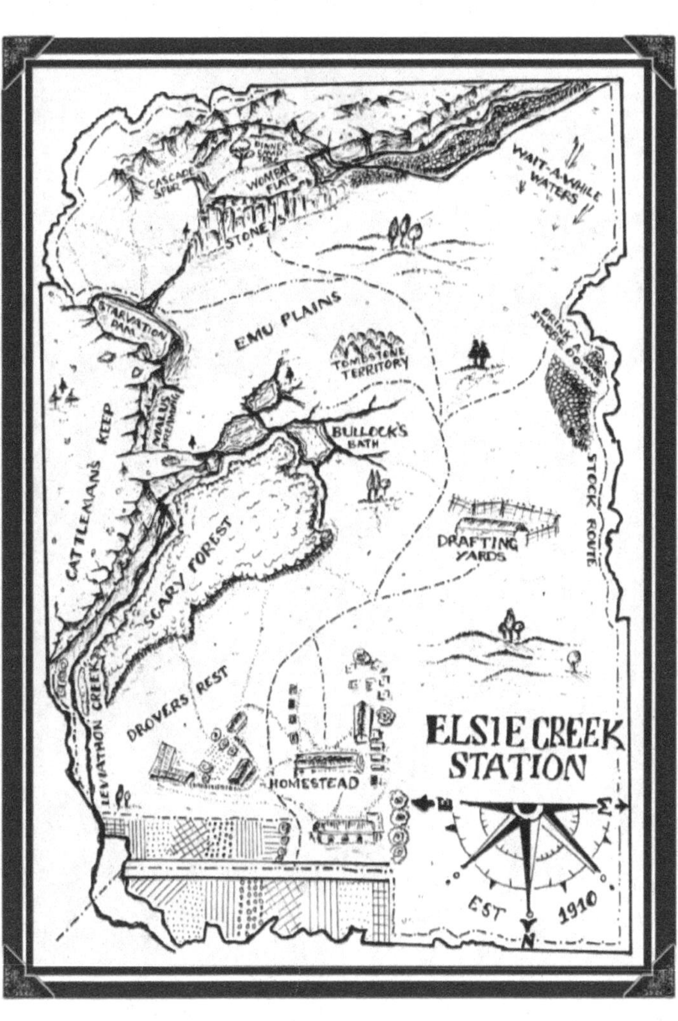

CASCADE SPUR
DINNER CAMP
WOMBAT FLATS
STONEY'S
WAIT-A-WHILE WATERS
STARVATION DAM
EMU PLAINS
TOMBSTONE TERRITORY
DRINK A STUBBIE DOWNS
CATTLEMAN'S KEEP
MALUS PADDOCK
BULLOCK'S BATH
STOCK ROUTE
SCARY FOREST
DRAFTING YARDS
LEVIATHON CREEK
DROVERS REST
HOMESTEAD
ELSIE CREEK STATION
EST 1910

Zero

Elsie Creek Station, November 1962

'H*arry! He knows.*' The hem of Penelope's skirt flicked up on her summer dress. Carrying her shoes in one hand, her small handbag in the other, she splashed through the mud, sprinting towards Harry.

At the stockman's shack, Harry slung on his hat, a prickle of fear brushing the hairs on the back of his neck. 'Pen? What's wrong?'

'We have to go, now.' Tears streamed down her face, one cheek red raw, with a visible handprint.

'Who hit you?' The fury was blinding.

'He knows.' Penelope's eyes were wide with fear. 'Jack knows.'

'Dammit.' Harry scowled at the farmhouse. This was not what they'd planned.

The screen door of the farmhouse kicked open, whacking hard against the weatherboard house, and out walked the head stockman, Jack Price, loading up a shotgun.

'He's going to kill us.' Penelope gripped Harry's shirt. 'We have to go, *now*.'

'Get in the car.' He hoped they could outrun the storm front, which was dragging along with it the possibility of flash flooding. 'Let's do as we planned, Pen. The rain will wash away our tracks.'

BOOM!

The gunshot blast made Harry and Penelope duck. Behind them one of the shack's windows shattered, sending shards of glass to scatter like glitter.

'Crikey! Let's go, now.' Harry grabbed Penelope's hand, and they dashed to the lean-to at the side of the shack, where his prized FJ Holden sedan waited. The front doors slammed shut, and the beefy six-cylinder engine purred to life. 'You can stay, Pen. He will forgive you.'

'I will never forgive myself if I stay. So I'm in this all the way, Harry Splint. I love you and only you. We'll be together forever.' She dragged off her wedding ring, tossing it out the passenger window where it landed in the mud.

He tenderly stroked her beautiful face. 'Together forever.'

'*Penelope Price, don't you dare!*' Jack ran towards them, his face full of fury as he loaded more shells into his shotgun.

'Go, go, go.' Penelope frantically tapped on the car's dashboard.

Harry planted his foot down, and the Holden sedan sped down the slippery dirt track as the heavens opened and thick sheets of blinding rain pelted down. Inside the car, the steamy air was thick with humidity. Adrenaline made his heart quicken as he tasted rain and sweat on his lips. They were finally doing it. 'Have you got everything, Pen?'

'I do.' She hugged her handbag to her chest. 'I found it.'

Another shotgun blast echoed in the air as a nearby tree trunk exploded, spraying bark chips and branches over the car.

Penelope swivelled in her seat, dropping a few shades of pale. 'He's coming.'

Harry pushed harder on the accelerator, as they barrelled down the dirt track heading deeper into the outback that made up Elsie Creek Station. 'We'll lose him at the river crossing.'

'But it's flooded, and there will be crocodiles.'

'We'll make it.' Or they would die trying.

One

Present Day

'*What sort of country is this?*' Harper Jamison stamped her foot in the red dust, gripping her phone. With no reception she couldn't call for a car service, she couldn't even google for instructions, and she couldn't find a simple how-to instruction card in the car's boot. She may as well have landed on the barren planet of Mars.

'*Augh.*' She kicked at the flat tyre that had stranded her in the middle of freaking nowhere. A land where sand and sediment had cemented together to create the scorched surface too close to the sun. With pockets of red dirt, scattered clusters of crumbly coffee rock, and towering ant mounds of dry mud, it was depressing for someone who'd never had an interest in the great outdoors.

Topping it off was an ocean of blue from a sky so big she felt like she was drowning under the smog-free atmosphere.

Only a single red dirt road ran down the middle of this whole lot of nothingness, making her feel like she was the only person to have survived a global apocalypse.

The scary thing was, this wasn't climate change, this was just the outback on a good day.

But now her foot hurt from kicking the dumb tyre, and there was some irritating dust inside her heels. But Harper Jamison refused to surrender. Not with her family name, and who she worked for. There was no such thing as surrender—

even if she was screwed.

Again, Harper raised her smartphone to the colossal sky, hoping to find some sort of mobile signal in this godforsaken dust bowl. Surely there had to be a satellite up there spying on her.

Sadly, no signal bars. Above her there was nothing but that sky.

Sighing, she used the back of her hand to wipe at the sweat beading on her forehead. She hated sweating. Hated being hot. Hated dirt in the shoes that were giving her blisters, because her favourite pair of shoes had been destroyed.

Determined, she dragged out all the tools she could find and laid them out neatly on a car mat she'd placed on the red, powdery dirt. She was clueless as to what tool went with what, let alone their names, or their purpose, but she had a brain that solved problems. She would figure it out.

She picked up a solid steel contraption, searching for a clue. A set of serial numbers ran down the side along with the word *Jack*.

Well, that was a start.

Harper knew a jack and a spare tyre were required, but what tool took the wheel off the car?

Removing her black suit jacket, she tossed it on the back seat where her suitcase rested. She clipped her hair into a tight bun, undid the top button of her white business shirt, and rolled up the cuffs of her sleeves, as she approached the boot of her car where the spare tyre lay taunting her.

Her tiny fingers gripped the fancy rim, but it was a struggle to pull it free from the tyre well. Determined, she gritted her teeth and dragged it out where it bounced with a thud in the dirt and rolled away from her.

'*Hey*. Come back!' She ran after it just as another vehicle approached, leading a trail of red dust to spread like a dusty firestorm across the sky.

She caught the runaway tyre, but the fear of being trapped in no-man's-land had her skin breaking out in goose pimples. Licking the gritty dust from her lips, she'd never felt more exposed in her life, with only a bunch of towering ant mounds to hide behind.

You'd think all her years of training, and the years of living under a constant level-four terrorism threat, would count for something, but here she went and did this to herself. *Silly girl.*

Those AFP Specialist Protective Service guys would roll their eyes if they could see her now. But, then again, if they were here, they'd gallantly change the tyre, while she kept working inside the air-conditioned car, well away from the burning sun.

But this trip had nothing to do with her job. And this wasn't a foreign country. Even though this was her first trip to the Northern Territory, it was nice to be back home in Australia.

The crusty white Hilux ute rolled to a stop, allowing its trail of dust to wash over her like a mini sandstorm. The dust was in her sinuses and the grit was in her teeth, with a fine layer spread across her skin like sandpaper. It was awful.

But that wasn't her biggest concern—it was the type of vehicle that sent a shiver of fear washing over her. It was the same style the villains drove in those vintage outback horror movies that forced you to never leave suburbia again.

Harper let the tyre drop with a heavy thud, stepping back from the ute as her heart hammered in her chest.

The engine coughed as if it was about to stall, and the window wound down to reveal a smiling, tanned, and gloriously beautiful cowboy.

Harper rubbed her eyes. She had to be hallucinating. Whatever her fearful, primal brain had been expecting it wasn't a man in a wide-brimmed hat that came with an even wider smile.

'Are you going walkabout with that tyre?'

'I'm what?' Harper struggled to pick up the tyre. 'Aw, come on.' Her white shirt was now smeared with black tyre marks and red dirt, even some of the dust was now rubbing inside her bra as if she'd nosedived to bathe in the dust.

The driver's door of the ute creaked open.

'Here, allow me.' He took the tyre with one hand, effortlessly carrying it like it was a handbag. But it was the sexy saunter in his dusty denim jeans that had her head tilting for a better look.

'You don't have to …' She rushed after that beautiful butt. She'd rushed a lot for paperwork, votes, time, but never a butt. Yet she had to follow like he was the Pied Piper.

'I'm doing it, aren't I?' He dumped the spare tyre in the dust, pushed back the brim of his cowboy hat, then crouched down in the dirt. He used a tool to loosen the tyre's nuts, then slid the jack under the car, and started raising the car in a matter of moments. 'Why did you take out all your tools?'

'I didn't know what was required.' She checked her watch. Did she have time to change? She certainly didn't have time for this unplanned delay. It was like someone was making her waste time, stuck on the side of the road like this.

'So, you've never changed a car tyre, then?' The beautiful man's grin was only brightened by his stunning set of white teeth that contrasted perfectly with the deep tan. But the way his biceps worked as he effortlessly pushed the handle of the jack up and down, like a guy in the gym, made it impossible to look away.

What did he say?

Did he just imply she was dumb?

Two

sh chuckled at the pretty lady in the tight black skirt and dirty business shirt. It was obvious she'd never changed a tyre in her life. Even if the frown wasn't that flattering, at least she'd stopped staring at him like a roo trapped under a spotlight, scared as if he was going to shoot her.

Ash had never seen a woman with smooth skin as pale as ivory. Not out here. She suited her slick Audi with its fancy rims and interstate plates.

She was something special, alright. A pretty, wealthy-looking woman, with her hair and make-up immaculately done, like a model for some business magazine, or airline hostess, just richer. Even the water bottle she drank from was fancy.

'Is there something I can do to speed up things?' She checked her wristwatch again.

Besides, standing there and looking pretty ... 'No. We're good.' Ash pulled off the flat tyre. 'You should get this tyre fixed in town before you go any further.'

'Why?' She arched one eyebrow at him as if he were telling her some tall tale.

At least she'd stopped looking at him like he was an axe murderer.

'Listen, the outback roads chew up city tyres like these in no time. Unless you've got another spare floating in the back seat?' He dumped the dusty tyre into the boot, noting the fancy suitcase on the back seat.

'Where is the nearest town? City? Or something that resembles a human species gathering in one central location.' Like a businesswoman, late and lost in a foreign country, she pulled out a map. The seriousness was hot on her. 'The GPS thingy didn't work.'

He struggled to not laugh. 'Why? Where were you headed?'

'Elsie Creek—'

'The GPS should've picked up that town easily enough. It's on one of the back roads to Kakadu.' Ash pointed to the road in the direction he'd come from, while his eyes travelled up and down her trim figure. 'You'll want to take the next right. Keep going until you hit bitumen, then turn left. The mechanics are just past the Elsie Creek Pub, they'll be able to fix your tyre. How did you get out here?' Because she'd passed the turn-off to the town of Elsie Creek miles back.

'Um …' She hesitated, as she tried to read the map as if it was written in a foreign language. 'I must have picked up the wrong map. It can't be that hard, right? You just go from point A to point B without that lovely, computerised airline-hostie voice saying *you are at your destination.*'

He grinned as he leaned in closer, inhaling her delicate aroma as he turned her map the right way up. 'That's north.'

'I would've worked it out, eventually. You know, it's paperwork. I'm good with paperwork.' She slipped on her sunglasses as if to hide the blush that bathed her ivory skin, highlighting her plump, kissable lips.

Honestly, she was stunning in a fragile, feminine way that was igniting all his inner nerve endings with the need to impress this woman.

She was not the normal type of female he'd expected to meet on the side of the road. A conservatively dressed female, in a tight black skirt that showed off the curves of her thighs and high and tight arse to perfection. She wore no rings, just that watch she kept checking, and a set of simple pearl earrings that looked real.

She was way out of his league.

Ash pushed the spare tyre against the hub flange on the car. Spun the lug nuts over the threaded studs until tight, then lowered the jack. Satisfied with a final tighten of the studs, he tossed all the tools back into her car. 'All done.' If he'd been smarter, he would have dragged this out to flirt with the pretty lady some more.

'Here, take this for your trouble.' She held out a fifty-dollar note. 'I was going to pay for a car service.' She peered at him over her sunglasses. 'Maybe use it on that vehicle you drive?'

His old ute might look ragged, but she didn't need to look down at it like that. 'All good. I'm happy to help a lady. You can buy me a beer at the pub later.' Then he'd buy her dinner, if she didn't mind a pub meal. Although she wasn't the type of woman who'd hang out in the pub, either. So, what was a woman who looked like some fallen angel on a business trip, doing out here?

Now that'd be a story worth listening to.

He dusted his hand and held it out to her. 'I'm Ash, by the way.'

'Harper Jamison.' Her tiny hand was soft, but her handshake was strong, like someone who was used to shaking hands in boardrooms. 'Ash is an unusual name.'

Was this the part where he told Harper her name was hot? 'It's short for Ashton. Ashton Riggs.'

Her pretty brown eyes widened to show specks of gold that caught the sun, and her dark hair was like shiny water.

'Me and my brothers run Elsie Creek Station. That's where I'm headed now, for a business meeting.' The smile grew as he stood taller, adjusting his hat. It was so new being his own boss, no longer some lackey the way Harper had been looking down at him.

He checked his phone for the time. 'If I wasn't running late, I'd show you the way to town myself.' Which sounded better than going to work.

Did he dare?

He could always shrug off another one of Ryder's

expected rants over responsibilities.

'That's perfectly fine, thank you. I'd hate to take up any more of your time. I'm sure I can find it.' Harper slammed the boot shut and raced for the driver's seat.

'Don't forget, first right, then follow it all the way to the bitumen, then left into town. I could show you —'

'I've got it.' The driver's door slammed shut, the engine started, and she was off, doing a U-turn to leave him standing on the side of the road where a wave of dust washed over him.

'The snooty thing.' He grinned. Again, he glanced at his phone. Dammit, Ryder was going to kill him for being late.

Three

'**W**hy do I have to be the bore runner?' Ash slapped his hat against his leg, facing his three older brothers seated at the table that took up the front corner of the porch. When they'd moved in a few weeks ago, the first thing they'd done, after they'd dumped their boxes into the farmhouse they only slept in, was to move the kitchen table outside to become their boardroom table for their morning meetings. That he'd missed again.

Ryder slid on his hat as he rose from the table. He was the oldest, and the biggest of the Riggs brothers. Part cattleman, part tough-as-nails ex-miner, along with a double dose of ex-military mean with a business brain. Even though Ryder had ice water in his veins, he was their bank, which made him the boss in the decision making. 'If you'd bothered to show up on time—'

'I was helping this lady change her flat tyre.' He hoped Harper made it to town.

Ash shrugged, looking to Cap for help. Cap was normally the peacekeeper, the animal rescuing eco-warrior who usually backed up Ash. But today Cap wasn't buying it either, giving a deep shake of his head.

'Sure, you were.' Dex rolled his eyes, which was a change from his permanent scowl. He was always scowling, always looking for a fight. Outside of the illegal fighting pits, the only one who'd take Dex on was Ryder—so those two were always bluing. 'Are you sure you didn't hit the snooze button to snuggle up to your date of the week?'

'Well…' Ash shrugged because that's exactly what happened. 'I'll stay home tonight.'

'Until the next buckle bunny catches your attention.' Dex drained the last of his coffee cup.

'So, what are you guys doing, then?' It had to be better than cleaning stinking cattle slobber from the water troughs.

'I'm taking the dogs and helping Ryder muster that small mob into the paddock we've finished fencing.' Cap's big team of cattle dogs were sprawled across the dead lawn that faced the sheds. Over on the other side of the house, on the front verandah lay the ex-police dogs—a lethal-looking shepherd, a labrador, and a beagle. Two packs, all of them rescued and loyal to one man, Cap, who preferred animals to humans.

'Are you riding, Ryder?' Ash could hoon around on the bike and skip doing troughs.

'Nope. Chopper. It's only a small mob. I want to check our water supply while I'm in the air. We're heading into the deep part of the dry season and I want to see the damage to that dam.'

'Starvation Dam, Charlie calls it.' Dex rocked back on his chair's legs. 'He reckons it got smashed during some summer cyclone.'

'It looks too clean to be storm damage.' Ryder's stern tone made Dex stop swinging in his chair. 'I'll know more today.'

'Well, I'll be fixing that truck we inherited to help haul our livestock.' Dex slid on his hat, tucking his chair under the table. 'And I'll check the grader, in case of dam repairs.'

Which copped a nod of approval from Ryder.

'Charlie said he'll give you a hand with the troughs today, and show you where they are.' Ryder's boots trod heavily down the front wooden steps. 'And Ash?'

'Yeah?'

'Listen to Charlie. He might only be the caretaker now, but he was this station's head stockman for decades. He knows his stuff.'

'*Ryder Riggs!*'

'Oh, man. Who upset the redhead?' Ash started backing

away as the caretaker's granddaughter stormed towards them, obviously in a rage.

'At least she didn't say *my* name.' Dex grinned, leaning his shoulder against the post to settle in for the showdown.

Bree stomped towards them from the direction of the caretaker's cottage. Her long leather welder's apron hung loose, where she slapped her thick leather gloves against her thigh. Her brimless, cooling skull cap barely contained her mass of red curls the colour of the fiery sun, and her green eyes were bright.

'Morning, Bree,' called out Ash.

'Are you still wearing the same clothes as yesterday?'

Ash grinned. 'You noticed me.'

'Don't flatter yourself, snowflake. You're obviously some poor girl's idea of a good time, just not mine, cowboy.'

Ash frowned at the insult. 'I'm not a cowboy.'

'You're not a cattleman, either. But you—' She swung around to point at Ryder. 'My grandfather is not your slave.'

'I never said he was.'

'We don't work for you.'

Ryder crossed his muscular arms. 'Your grandfather is the caretaker. I won't stop him, if he wants to work. And if he does, we'll pay him.'

'He's already being paid, remember? The caretaker's caveat, which includes that trust paying his *re-tire-ment*.'

'I'm not stopping the man if he wants to help, just because you say so.' Ryder leaned menacingly over her. It was a mean look.

You'd think she'd stop, like most people did, and back away from Ryder. Not Bree.

'Charlie has orders to fill.'

'You've just lectured us about overworking the man, and what are you doing?' Dex piped in.

Bree glared at him with those fiery green eyes. 'Do me a favour, Dex? Reinvent yourself over there, just not in my oxygen circle, buddy.'

That left Dex mumbling under his breath as Cap

chuckled.

Her sassy comebacks even had Ryder smirking—which was as close to a smile as you'd ever get from the man with ice in his veins. 'Charlie's just showing Ash where the troughs are. That's it.'

'Really?' She narrowed her eyes at Ryder for a long beat, then looked at the others, who nodded. 'Okay …' She stepped back from Ryder's shade. 'Just remember his age.'

'It'd be good if you remembered his worth.'

She whipped up her finger like a dagger aimed at Ryder. 'Listen, cupcake, if I—' She peered over her shoulder to spot the rising red dust coming down the long dirt driveway. '*Incoming.*'

'Who's that?' Ash trotted down the steps.

'Quick! Where's the shottie?' Bree jumped up the front steps, kicked at a loose floorboard along the verandah, and reached underneath to remove a shotgun.

'VISITORS!' Old man Charlie wolf-whistled out the front of the caretaker's cottage, waving his hat at Bree, who waved the shotgun at her grandfather. Signal received.

'What the hell are you doing?' Cap stepped away from the determined redhead.

'We don't like visitors.' Bree cracked open the shotgun's barrel to check its shell cases. Snapping it back into place, she headed down the steps. 'We got a lot of death threats before you boys bought this place.'

'Not on my watch.' Ryder reached for the shotgun, but Bree held it back.

'It's the cops. It's Porter.' Ash pointed to the police car.

'How do you know Policeman Porter?' Bree had her body turned to keep the shotgun well out of Ryder's reach.

'We met him when we were staying at Sandlot Station, helping Jonathan and Mandy out,' replied Ash, hoping somebody would calm down the redhead. 'We helped the police search for a kidnapped couple, that ended up being this treasure hunt. And Ryder's been mates with the town's top cop since he helped save that kid from a bomb exploding at the school.'

'Hero, huh?' Bree still didn't move, keeping her eyes on Ryder.

'Bree, give me the shotgun.' Ryder held his open palm to the woman.

'Nope. It's not your gun.'

'You hid it in my house.'

She jutted out her dainty chin. 'Not anymore. I'll just find it a new hidey spot.'

'What are the coppers doing out here?' Charlie rushed up to Bree. He then leaned over with his hands on his knees to catch his breath.

Bree glared at Ryder as if to make her point. 'It's okay, Pop. Take deep breaths. Tell me you took your heart pills this morning?'

Charlies nodded, wheezing, as he waved her hand away. 'I'm fine.' His grey eyes focused on the police car parking nearby.

'Hey, fellas.' Porter adjusted his police cap and gave a friendly smile. 'Everything all right?' Porter nodded at Ryder and Bree, stuck in their heated stand-off.

'All good. I'm just scaring off a few possums in the shed.' Bree swung the shotgun onto her shoulder. Then under her breath she muttered to Ryder, 'It's mine, registered to me, that Porter inspected for correct licensing. So hands off, cupcake.'

'We'll talk about this later, Bree. Including that story about the death threats your grandfather forgot to mention.' Ryder side-glanced at his brothers. It was the first they'd heard about any death threats. 'What can we help you with, Porter?'

'We're looking for Ash.' Porter pulled out a file, as the passenger door opened of the twin-cab ute with its chunky police cage on the back.

'What did you do, bro?' Cap arched his eyebrows at Ash.

'Me? Nothing. I'm innocent.'

'I'd doubt that very much,' mumbled Dex, rocking on his

boot heels.

'Do you guys know Jenny? She's the head nursing sister at our local bush hospital.' Porter did the introductions.

'I do. Hi, Jenny.' Bree waved.

'Hi, Bree. Are you okay, Charlie? You're looking a little flustered.' Jenny was a middle-aged woman opening the back door.

'You'll be happy to know Charlie did some cardio this morning. My grandfather ran all the way from the cottage fence to here.' Bree's light giggle had Ash grinning with Cap, as Charlie scowled at her while wiping the sweat from his brow.

'I'm looking for Ashton Riggs.'

That wiped the smile off his face. 'That's me.' Ash stepped forward, trying to think of what he'd done to warrant this kind of attention from the police.

Jenny grabbed something out of the car, then turned around holding a toddler in her arms. 'This is Mason Riggs. And he's your son.'

Four

ex's laughter carried across the compound. For a man who wore a permanent scowl, it was rare to hear Dex laugh. But this was a full belly laugh, holding his stomach with one hand, while slapping his denim thigh with the other as if it was the world's greatest joke.

'You're kidding, right?' Ash could only blink at the toddler. A full-blown, living, breathing little boy. And he knew nothing about kids.

'Your name is on the birth certificate, and it's requested in the paperwork.' Policeman Porter held up a file.

It was impossible. He didn't have a child. No way.

Ash looked at his big brother, Ryder, the man who had a plan for everything.

'Can I see that?' Ryder read through the paperwork, and there was a lot of it 'Why is the kid here?'

'We're instructed to deliver Mason to his father,' explained Jenny.

Everything slowed down. The way the birds flew, the dust stirred, the blink of the boy's eyes that stared at him. Ash struggled to breathe as the nurse and the policeman spoke about details, he just didn't hear any of it. This had to be a nightmare. 'What do I do?'

'Hold him.' Jenny put the toddler into his arms. The boy had that baby smell of baby powder and custard. 'Your son's gear is in the police cage.'

Son? Nah, he had to be dreaming. 'But ... A son.' He looked down at the boy to find his own eyes staring back at him.

'Paperwork's legit.' Ryder's shadow stretched over them as he peeked at the boy. 'Mason. Good strong name.'

'We have a nephew?' Cap smiled at the toddler as if he'd stumbled on another animal to save.

But it was Ash who needed saving. 'What? Why? How?'

'I guess we all know about the how, there, Ash.' Again, Dex cackled.

Bree giggled beside him. 'As my grandfather would say, if you're gonna sow your oats, you eventually have to deal with the harvest.'

'Yep. Sounds about right.' Charlie chuckled, as he scrubbed rough nails at his ruddy chin.

It set Dex off on another round of riotous laughing, wiping at the happy tears in the corners of his eyes.

'I meant ...' Ash cleared his throat, desperate to save face. 'Why is he here?'

'Mason's mother died.'

That sobered them up.

'How?' Ryder asked Porter.

'I'm not sure on the details, only that the boy is here at the request of his mother.'

'Aw, he's got the Riggs' eyes and nose. A proper little heartbreaker.' Bree held her hand out and Mason's little fingers gripped onto her finger and gave a toothy smile. 'Yep, another player, like his father.'

Didn't that make Ash wake up from his stupor as the heavy thud of responsibility landed across his shoulders.

Come on, Ash was the guy who ran from responsibility, preferring a carefree lifestyle and children only complicated that life plan. He passed the child to the nearest female, Bree. 'Nope. Not gonna happen. I take precautions.'

'Obviously not,' piped up Dex from the rear.

Ash scowled at his brother.

'Don't think you can fob him off on me. He's your son.' Bree passed him back to Ash.

'I don't know what to do with a child!' Again, he looked

at his older brothers for help. 'I don't even know the mother's name.'

'Gemma Fallon.' Ryder held up the birth certificate. 'Says here Mason's eighteen months old, which means you knew her—'

'Two years and three months ago,' said Dex, 'when you danced the sheets—'

'Oi, have a bit of respect for the kid's mother who isn't here, please,' urged Cap.

'Where were you two years ago, Ash?' Ryder asked.

'Forget asking him who he was with,' said Dex, 'because we all know he likes the chase but gets bored with the catch and goes through women like—'

'Like what, hmmm?' Bree practically bristled with an unsaid warning. It shut Dex up. 'I love how stupid looks on you this time of the day, Dex. And, with that, I'm leaving. Have fun, boys. See you at Charlie's next check-up, Jenny.' With the shotgun resting on her shoulder, she marched off towards the caretaker's cottage whistling some tune.

'Seein' as how we aren't doing the troughs today, I'll go give the girl a hand.' Charlie trotted after Bree in his bandy-legged walk.

'Yeah, I'd better go get the dogs sorted out for mustering.' Cap took off for the kennels.

'I've got a truck to fix.' Dex did a runner for the shed.

That left Ash holding a small boy as Jenny talked about sleeping schedules, night nappies, and other foreign words, while Ryder helped Porter unload the kid's gear from the cage at the back of the police car.

The police radio squawked, with Porter talking in the background, all while Ash just stood and stared at the small boy in his arms.

'We've got to go, Jenny,' said Porter.

Jenny slid a card into Ash's shirt pocket. 'Here are my numbers. Call me if you have any issues.'

'Oh, and I'll be back to do a welfare check in twenty-eight days,' said Porter.

'Why?' Ryder asked.

'It's a request that came in with the paperwork.' The policeman shrugged. 'It's just to check if there are any issues.'

'And if there are, I can give the kid back?' Did Ash have an escape clause?

Jenny gasped.

'If it doesn't work out for you, the child does have options. It was in the mother's will that the boy be with his father—and your name is on the birth certificate.'

Jenny stepped in closer, draping the baby blanket over his shoulder. 'Ash, I know it's a big shock—'

'Ya think?' Daddy day care was not on his to-do list. Cleaning troughs actually sounded really good about now.

'It will take time to bond, but when you do …'

Nope. Twenty-eight days was too long.

'But today I feel like a stork, you know. *Happy daddy duties.*' Jenny waved as Porter tooted the horn, driving the police car out of the yard.

'What do I do, Ryder? I've never changed a nappy or even held a baby before.'

'Well, you're about to get a crash course, aren't you?'

Five

It was just after midnight and a child's wails echoed like a tsunami siren screaming across the outback plains. Ash held the boy in his arms, desperate to keep him quiet as he paced the front porch.

'What's wrong with the kid now?' Dex stumbled outside in a pair of boxers, his bare chest showing off his many tattoos and scars.

'He's got a set of lungs on him, I'll give him that,' said Cap, in shorts and a singlet. 'My dogs aren't this loud.'

'Now I remember why I don't want kids.'

'Hey, I didn't plan this.' Ash held out the boy. 'What is his problem? I've given him a drink, changed his night nappy, offered him food —'

'You mean, I did.' Ryder strolled outside with a steaming coffeepot in one hand and a stack of cups in the other. 'Cut the kid some slack. He's in a new house surrounded by strangers, and he's probably missing his mother.'

'I should call Mum. She can look after Mason,' said Ash.

'I already tried.' Cap sat back in his chair, blowing at the steam curling from the fresh cup of coffee. The strong caffeine aroma filled the air.

'What did Mum say?' Ash winced as his eardrums copped the full brunt of another wail from Mason.

'Mum said it's time you grew up and she won't be visiting for a while to meet her grandson. But she promised to send a few packages and she wants photos.' Cap picked up his phone and aimed it at Ash. 'We all know Mum loves her photos, and she wants lots of them.'

'So, if we send Mum photos of Ash looking absolutely pathetic, it might change her mind.' Dex picked up his own phone.

Now both of his brothers were taking photos as the kid wailed in Ash's arms, while Ryder casually sipped his coffee, watching over the compound, which was normal for Ryder, who didn't sleep much.

Dex dropped into his chair, leaning his arms on either side of his coffee cup, practically inhaling the brew. 'Someone needs to work out how to stop the crying, or I'm sleeping in my swag in the back of my ute.'

'I think I'll build myself a humpy near the dog kennels,' muttered Cap.

'Oi. Here comes trouble.' Ryder nodded at the torchlight.

'Do you reckon it's Charlie?'

'Not at that pace.' Ryder inhaled deeply, as if to brace himself for it.

'Boys.' Bree came into the porch light wearing a nightgown showing off her curves, with her long thick hair flowing past her shoulders. In one hand she held a torch, in the other she carried a small cloth bag. 'Hey, sweetie ...' She put her hand against Mason's forehead. 'Look at you, screaming down the house.' She reached into her bag, then rubbed something over his gums, followed by a colourful stick of ice, and the toddler was instantly quiet.

'What did you do?' Ash asked Bree, as his brothers sighed with relief.

'Your son is teething. Cruellest thing every child goes through.'

'How do you know?'

'I noticed him drooling yesterday, chewing his fist. At his age it's probably a molar coming through.'

'What did you rub on his gums?'

'Clove oil. It's the best thing for toothache, but not so tasty. That's why he's got that ice block. Don't worry, it's just frozen fruit juice to numb his gums. It'll be messy, but it works. I suggest you get him some children's paracetamol from town tomorrow. Goodnight, boys.' And just like that, she walked off.

'I'll pay you to babysit, Bree,' called out Ash.

'I don't work for you boys. Find a nanny, and one you won't sleep with, Ash. Find one who can clean, to save the farmhouse from looking like some frat house.' She pointed at the boxes of empty beer cans and bottles of bourbon. Assorted boots lay in loose pairs, while shirts and jeans lay wherever they fell. Heck, they hadn't even unpacked, more focused on working the land than being houseproud.

'Bree?' Ryder stood. 'What's the story about those death threats?'

She stopped in the middle of the compound, her head dropping to her chest as a trillion stars shone above her.

'We can't help you and Charlie, if we don't know what the problem is.' Ryder leaned his shoulder against the post, while Ash paced the porch holding Mason sucking on a stick of ice.

Bree sighed, as she turned and reapproached the light. 'When Darcie passed, there were plenty of offers to buy this station—from corporations, foreign investors, and even a few mining companies. But with the caretaker's caveat in place, it gave Charlie the power to say yes or no on who bought the property. My grandfather was only following Darcie's wishes for what he wanted for this place.'

'Did you get a lot of threats for saying no?'

She nodded. 'One particular group wouldn't take the hint.'

'Who?'

'Your eastern neighbour, Leo, and his band of balding gorillas.' It was a death look of pure fury that made Ash stop pacing.

'What did they do, Bree?'

She looked back at the cottage hidden under starlight. 'Can't be proven.'

'Tell us,' demanded Ryder.

'Fine.' She plonked her hands on her generous hips and took a few steps closer to the light. 'Besides threatening to bash my grandfather within an inch of his life, they poisoned Charlie's dogs, wrecked the dam, and cut the fences. They also slashed the tyres on our bull catcher, the Razorback. Started a bush fire, and damaged the truck Dex is trying to fix.'

'Is that why you keep a loaded shotgun under our porch?'

Again, she nodded, with none of her sassy humour. This was a whole new side to Bree. 'The last time, I caught two men holding Charlie over the bonnet of their fancy car, determined to get him to sign some documents. They didn't stick around long, not after I let off a warning shot.'

'Jeez, Bree, why didn't Charlie say anything when we bought the place?' Nervously, Cap raked fingers through his hair.

'Because Charlie didn't want to scare you off. He really wanted you boys to buy the place. He believes you'll do the right thing by this station.'

'Bree, are you going to tell me if there are any more guns stashed on this property?' Ryder asked. 'As the owners, we're liable.'

'Charlie and I keep all of our registered firearms in a locked cupboard in the cottage. As for the others ...' She turned to walk away, then hesitated as she spoke over her shoulder. 'Just so you know, Charlie is here until he dies. It's what he and Darcie said they'd do together, just that Darcie went first. It's my job to look after Charlie. As I would dearly love to have that man outlive me, I'm doing everything in my power to make it so. But he has a tricky heart and won't let them operate. It's his choice, his life. So, lemme make this perfectly clear, I do *not* work for you boys, and I certainly do not work for this station. As soon as Charlie passes, the caretaker's caveat will be over, and I'll be gone.' Bree turned on her heel and disappeared into the thick darkness cloaking the outback.

'I'd really like that woman, if she didn't scare me so

much,' muttered Dex.

'Yeah.' Cap nodded, sipping on his coffee mug.

Ryder frowned in the direction Bree had disappeared, pushing away from the porch rail. 'I knew that damage to the dam looked suss. Tomorrow, we'll think about setting up some security. In the meantime, I'm going to get a few hours shut-eye while that stuff is working on Mason. Ash, tomorrow you go get that kid whatever it is Bree recommends. A nanny would be good, too. See you at sunrise.'

'Can we afford a nanny?' Ash asked Cap and Dex.

'Probably not,' said Dex, opening the screen door to the house. 'But if it means I get some sleep, I'll chip in.'

'Me too,' said Cap, following Dex inside, leaving Ash alone with the baby.

All day he'd been in a numbed state, fighting the tight grip around his lungs and the weight on his shoulders, every time he looked at the boy.

Fatherhood. It was the biggest burden that came in the smallest package. How was he was going to make the next twenty-eight days when he'd barely made it through the first night?

Six

Ash stumbled through the creaky front door, blinking at daylight while slipping on the T-shirt he'd plucked from the bedroom floor. Yesterday was a nightmare. Had to be.

'Morning.' Like every morning since they'd moved in, Ash found his brothers watching the sunrise from the table on the front porch, where the smell of rich, aromatic coffee greeted him. He dropped into the chair he'd claimed as his own, as Cap slid over a coffee cup. 'Smells strong.'

'It is. We all need it after last night.'

'Oh, man, tell me yesterday was just a nightmare.' Ash roughly scrubbed his palms over his face. Then he glanced back and there was the kid, seated inside a fly-netted contraption, playing with some toys.

'You can thank Cap for feeding Mason,' said Dex.

'And it was Dex who set up the toys.' Cap grinned.

'I don't believe it. You, Dex?'

'I'm not doing it every day.' Dex pointed at Ash. 'He's your responsibility.'

'I'm thinking of doing a DNA test.' Ash didn't sign up for this, so best to do it now and not get too attached.

'Save yourself some money, daddy,' said Dex, scrolling through his phone. 'Mum emailed us some photos this morning. This one in particular … It's you at the same age as Mason. You're the spitting image of each other.' He slid the phone across the table.

'I could have told you that,' mumbled Ryder in his deep

voice. 'I remember you at that age and when that photo was taken, too. It was Mum's new Kodak camera that came in the post with a bunch of knitting wool.'

'Yeah, well, Mum wants lots of photos to add to the wall,' said Dex.

Ash frowned at the phone's screen. Their family-photo-loving mother had put two images side by side. One was of Mason only yesterday, the other photo he recognised from the wall of photos at his parents' place. The resemblance was uncanny.

'Morning, all.' Charlie, the old caretaker, approached. 'How'd you sleep?' He grinned, with a sparkle in his grey eyes, as the men grumbled.

'Coffee, Charlie?' Cap asked.

'As much as I'd like to, the caffeine makes my ticker race too much.' Charlie patted over his heart. 'Well, Ash, you ready to go?'

'Go where?' Ash slurped on his coffee. It was thick and creamy, coating his tongue as the perfect kickstart to the day. Slipping on his boots, he vaguely remembered he had to go shopping. 'The shops don't open for hours.'

'The troughs, lad.'

'Huh?' Ash's eyebrows rose over his cup. 'But—' He pointed at the toddler, having a fat time with some blocks.

'The kid can come too. I used to give my beautiful Bea a break and take my baby girl out with me whenever I was boundary ridin'. The rock in the saddle, or vehicle, puts them to sleep every time. Bree said the baby seat will fit the Razorback, no problems.' Charlie's boots, with their thick Cuban heels, clomped up the porch steps. He squatted before the small boy inside the playpen. 'Well, look at you. You're a Riggs all right. Got that same nose and eyes, he has … You know what you have here, lads?' Charlie tossed his thumb at the boy. 'You've got your first cowboy at the station.'

'He's not a cowboy,' Ash muttered.

Charlie grinned, adjusting his big hat. 'Traditionally, Northern Territory cowboys were what we called young boys who'd start learning the trade as junior station hands. Then they'd graduate to stockmen. Jackeroos were usually sons of cattle station owners. Boys sick of their dads telling them what to do back home, so they'd get sent to work somewhere else for a bit.'

'So, that'd make Mason a junior jackeroo, cause I'm a station owner?' It was better than calling the kid a cowboy, which was an insult to a stockman.

'Whatever you call him, he's your legacy, and he needs a hillbilly hood.'

'A what?'

'Charlie means a hat,' said Cap.

'As an old-timer, I'm not gonna tell you what to wear on your noggin, that's a personal thing, for sure. But back in the day, you could tell where someone came from just by the way they bashed their hat, like you mob do.' Charlie pointed at the brothers. 'There's a Territory style to you, Ash. Same with Dex, but with a touch of Queenslander. Cap, you did time in WA and a lot of sheep in South Australia, I reckon. And Ryder, you were in the military.'

'You can tell all that by a man's hat?' Ash adjusted his own well-bashed hat that he'd picked up in Katherine years ago.

'If you've been in the game long enough, like I have, sure. Where did the little fella come from?' Charlie narrowed his eyes at the boy holding up one of his blocks.

'South.'

'Yeah, Bree said he's got that southerner's skin. Guess that's why she gave me her special brand of sunscreen to put on the kid.' He tapped his work shirt pocket. 'But you get this billy lid a hat, slop on the sunscreen, and his skin will toughen up in no time. Well, enough chinwaggin', where's this baby seat at? Stop looking, I found it.' Charlie pulled the child's booster seat from the pile of baby junk. 'Back in the day, if they didn't sit still, we'd strap them to the seat with rope. So, someone must be making money outta these fandangled contraptions.'

'Before you go, Charlie ...' Ryder cleared his throat. 'Bree told us about the threats to try and force you to sell this station.'

Charlie paused on the front porch steps, his hand gripping the baby seat, as he scowled at the dirt. 'I told her not to say anything. It stopped once you lot bought the place.'

Ryder's chair scraped across the floorboards as he approached the old caretaker. 'Did they wreck the dam?'

'Can't prove nothing.' Charlie squinted at the small, swirling willy-willy of dust dancing over the dry paddock. 'All I know was that it was working fine one day, then the next its sides were torn down, along with our fences, with a stack of tyre tracks coming from the eastern firebreak. Bree and I were busy busting our butts fighting this bushfire. It started on the same day, over on the other side of the property.'

'Sounds like they'd done that as a diversion,' said Ryder, as Dex's scowl deepened.

'It was.' Charlie slowly shook his head, staring at his boots as he spoke. 'We had to do a back-burn to stop it from taking off, which meant sacrificing the crops we were getting ready to harvest. That boss of theirs was clever.'

'How?' Cap asked.

'Coz in one day, they'd left us with no food or water for the cattle to get us through the Dry.'

'What did you do?' asked the animal-saving Cap.

'Bree sat in the saddle for months, playing drover with that herd down the long paddock until the rains came, then she brought 'em home.' Charlie nodded to the open country towards the rising sun. 'It's that same mob of scrubbers you lot put in that paddock you finished re-fencing. You'll find more scattered along the plains, where they've got plenty of scrub feed to keep 'em happy. The rest, well ...'

'How many cattle did this station run?' Ryder asked.

'In her prime, Elsie Creek Station could hold fifty thousand head. When I became head stockman we kept it to twenty-five to thirty thousand head to not overrun the place, right up until Darcie left us.'

'Where did they all go?'

'When Darcie's son learned he couldn't sell the place without my okay, he went and hired this mob of contract musterers to come in and sell the stock.' Charlie scowled as he readjusted his hat. 'But don't you worry none. I picked out a herd before they stripped the place bare.'

'Where are they now?'

'Down at Wombat Flats. You can't take no vehicles through there, that's sure-footed stockhorse country.'

'Why did you take them there?' Cap asked.

'Coz we knew no fancy mustering mob would dare go there. But don't you worry none, it's a place where the cattle are safe, for sure.'

Ryder narrowed his eyes at the caretaker. 'Are they still there?'

'Yep.' Charlie gave a firm nod. 'Last count, I reckon you've got a thousand head of self-sustaining stock. Bree and me have been babying that herd for a year now. Couldn't have done it without Bree.'

Ash arched an eyebrow. 'I didn't know Bree was a stockwoman?'

'She won't admit it, but I needed the help, and she only did it for me. Good kid, that one. She's afraid of nothin' and never backs down from a fight. Like the time that bloke had me in a chokehold, Bree fair shot him in the bum, she did.' The wrinkles around Charlie's eyes deepened as he chuckled.

Cap spluttered over his coffee cup. 'Bree said it was a warning shot.'

'Yeah, that's right. Bree warned them the next shot would be at their heads. You should've seen them two bullies skedaddle after that. Which is what we should be doing, Ash. Now grab the billy lid and let's go.'

'But …' Ash had barely finished his coffee, let alone had breakfast.

'Stop your sookin'. You're a single dad now. How ya gonna feed the bugger if you don't get paid? I'll put this kid-carrying contraption in the Razorback.' Charlie carted the child's car seat away.

'What do I take?' Ash didn't have a clue what a baby needed.

Ryder passed him a large bag. 'You'll find change of clothes, some snacks, and his special kiddies cup.'

'Cup. Drink.' The boy held his hand out for the cup. 'Ta.'

Ryder nodded with approval at the toddler's manners. 'Don't forget to go to the supermarket and find that kid a nanny later today.'

'Yeah, right? You seriously can't expect me to pluck some nanny off the supermarket shelf.' Ash remembered he needed to get the boy some medicine.

'When Ash gets back, we should use his drone to check out the property, especially around the house,' suggested Cap.

'Good idea.' Ryder reached up to the exposed beams on the verandah's roof and pulled down a large paper roll. It was the station's map, that Ryder used coffee cups to sit on each corner to keep the map flat on the table. 'I've got some solar cameras in one of the boxes somewhere. We can start setting them up. Cap, which of your dogs would be a good guard dog for the homestead?'

'The shepherd.'

Ash hoisted the bag onto his shoulder, with the kid to his chest. 'Can't I stay and help with the security?'

'Sure. After you've finished the troughs with Charlie because what cattle we do have needs water. We didn't do it yesterday, and we know those troughs are dodgy, and none of us want Bree on our backs for letting Charlie do it on his own,' said Ryder. 'But while you're working the troughs, make a list of what needs to be repaired.'

'We're going solar with the bores, right?' That was Ash's idea.

Ryder patted Ash's shoulder. 'That's why you're doing the troughs. You know what to look for.'

'Does that mean you listened to me?'

'We heard a teeny tiny ramble of something,' teased Dex, rubbing his index finger over his thumb as if rolling an imaginary grain of rice.

An engine roared to life from the shed. It was the beefy bull catcher, the Razorback.

Dex nodded towards the shed. 'Are you going to risk your life and limbs letting Charlie drive?'

'Not a chance.' Loaded with a boy and it's luggage, Ash dashed across the compound, with his brothers chuckling behind him.

The kid squinted at the bright sunlight, with a giggle that was stinking cute. But his skin was so pale and shiny under the harsh outback sun.

He removed his own hat to shade the child. 'If you're going to stick around, you need a hat. Every stockman needs a hat. Or should we call you a junior jackeroo? JJ?'

'J-J?' Mason squinted his eyes as if getting his mind around the word. 'J-J.'

No way. The kid beamed at Ash like he was the sun, the stars, and the moon. No one looked at Ash like that.

But the burden of owning a station and now a small child was too much to carry at once. With twenty-seven days to go, he would just look at this like a babysitting gig. Then his life could go back to normal.

Seven

It had to be the world's smallest supermarket, yet it was crammed with the most amazing selection of foods from fresh fruit and vegetables, to a deli filled with various cheeses and specialty meats. More importantly it stocked shortbread. In particular, Harper's favourite brand.

'Hello, my beautiful buttery friends.' Harper snatched up a fancy red packet, her fingers trembling, in desperate need of a sugar fix. Never mind she hadn't paid for the biscuits yet, but she opened the packet and took one out. Sure, she was eating her feelings, but this was an emotional time, for heaven's sake. Her boss wanted her back in the office, her staff were leaving her a dozen emails every hour, and her phone hadn't stopped beeping with message after message.

Couldn't they cope without her for a few weeks?

Sure, she loved playing superhero, averting political catastrophes, but to the world she was just a face in the crowd, the prop holding up the puppet the public came to see. Harper never wanted to be the face that wielded the power, like her father. She just solved problems and was known as the fixer.

But this was one problem she couldn't fix with a few phone calls and a dozen emails. No, this problem had forced her to take an unplanned holiday, fighting brain fog as she struggled with all this free time she had on her hands. Normally she was always busy, racing to beat time. But being on holiday was different. Worse, the Northern Territory had its own impression of time: slow.

Yet when the shortbread's buttery, delicately sweet, and deliciously gritty texture crumbled onto her tongue, she closed her eyes and sighed as time stopped for just a crystal-clear moment of blissful peace. Once again, all was good in the world, and maybe she was ready to deal with what came next.

With a grin growing, she eagerly snatched the other three packets from the shelf and filled her small basket and continued searching for something wonderful for her tastebuds. Normally she did this to fill her bottom desk drawer for midnight sugar rushes, when they raced against deadlines. No need for drugs, or other stimulants, just the job's latest crisis. A job she used to love, but now avoided.

She strolled around the corner and nearly smacked into another cowboy. They were everywhere, as if harvested from some nearby field, then delivered to populate the small town of Elsie Creek.

What's worse, the pub was full of cowboys.

Sadly, the Elsie Creek Hotel was the only place to stay in town. It's also where the cowboys congregated, all trying to chat her up.

Harper didn't do small talk, not when she was so busy working, and she'd had the luxury of an assistant, or a soldier in a suit, trained to keep the public away. But she was on her own on this little unplanned holiday, where loneliness had never felt so … lonely. It only revealed her social awkwardness and the depth of disconnect that had her poor, achy heart echo with emptiness.

Ever since she'd landed back in Australia, she hadn't been able to shake that layer of suffocating loneliness, nor clear that muddle of brain fog that stopped her from thinking straight.

At least this wonderfully quaint supermarket sold her favourite brand of shortbread. If she bought enough food, she could hide in her room and avoid everyone until she could pick up her car's new tyre. Then she could get back on track. Or, at least, work out a plan over dinner.

Harper was used to eating alone, eating meals she never tasted, and was very much used to the taste of cold coffee. All while her mind focused on the never-ending stream of documents, emails, and memos from other departments, with her phone glued to her ear. That's if she wasn't walking the marble floors of large, cold buildings, or getting in and out of vehicles that came with drivers that whizzed her to and from airports. She rarely saw her apartment.

Only the heavenly sweetness of shortbread made her stop and provide her full and undivided attention. It was her Achilles' heel.

But the butt in those perfectly fitted jeans of the guy taking up space in the supermarket aisle sure was cute. 'Excuse me.'

'Yeah, sure, Miss.' He stood with his back to her so she could scoot past. 'Hey, I know you. Harper, right?'

She stopped with her mouth full, desperate to wipe the crumbs off her face. Oh, no! She swallowed hard on the dry biscuit. It was that gorgeous, smiling cowboy who'd changed her car's tyre. 'Ash. With … oh.' At the sight of the boy, her heart literally came stuck in her throat, or was it the dryness from eating shortbread she struggled to swallow, as tears threatened to form.

'This is Mason. Hey, do you know of a decent baby medicine?' Ash showed her a shopping list, where baby paracetamol topped the list. 'He's teething.'

She couldn't take her eyes off the boy, who seemed excited to see her. 'Hello, gorgeous.'

'They say he takes after me in looks.'

She rolled her eyes as she spoke to the child. 'Hopefully you'll have a humble streak like your mother.'

'Er, yeah.' Ash roughly wiped away his cheeky smile. 'His mother died.'

Again, her heart squeezed, along with that sudden need to cry or eat more shortbread. She wasn't meant to be this emotional. 'The poor little guy.' She couldn't help herself and let his little fingers wrap around hers. 'Want some shortbread? It's good for the soul.' She handed Mason a piece of biscuit.

'I don't know if he does. I only got him yesterday.' Ash gave a meek shrug.

'How are you coping?'

Ash didn't say a word. But he had dark rings under his eyes, was unshaven, in a wrinkled shirt that had some odd-looking stains on it. But what tugged at her normally stony heart was when the handsome man's dark brown eyes revealed a deep level of worry.

'Are you looking for a miracle cure in the supermarket, like me?' She held up her packets of shortbread.

'And a nanny.'

'Sorry? Can you just pluck one off the shelf?' With arms like Ash's, he could pick up the entire shelf, even with a toddler on one arm. Since when was a man holding a baby sexy?

'I wish.' His smile revealed a dimple on one cheek, making her smile with him. Not fair.

'Hey, did you get your car tyre fixed?'

'I pick it up today. They had to get one in from somewhere else. Apparently they don't keep tyres like mine out here.'

'All four-wheel drives around here.'

'So, I found out.' She gave a soft smile to little Mason, who'd finished his biscuit, eagerly holding his hand out for more. 'Well, don't you have good taste, little man?' She broke off another piece and handed it to the boy, who looked like his father. 'Have you got something for your son to drink? Shortbread can be rather dry on the throat.'

'Um, I think so? In one of these pockets, somewhere?' Ash spun around. The bulky baby bag he wore on his shoulder knocked over some canned peaches that spilled across the floor.

'Stop.' Harper held him in place. His arm was nothing but solid muscle. Not too big, not too small, and just perfect. But this was not the time to drool. 'I see it.' She removed the small water bottle from the bag's side pocket. 'Can I hold him?'

She'd never dared such a thing, but Ash looked like he needed help.

'Sure. Knock yourself out.' Ash passed the boy over, then bent to scoop up the assorted tins he'd knocked over.

The boy was so soft and squishy, instantly dampening that empty ache of loneliness as she held him to her chest. He smelled so good—citrusy sweetness and fresh soap.

'Mason, this is shortbread.' She held up the treat to the boy who fit perfectly on her hip. 'It's the food of the gods that will cure tummy upsets, bad hair days, and break-ups. If I give you another piece, this will make us friends.'

The boy was positively drooling, his brown eyes wide and focused on that piece of shortbread. The biscuit never looked like much, but the flavour was buttery heaven on the tongue. It was the taste of home.

'You and the boy get along.'

She ignored the father. Even if he was gorgeous, her focus was on Mason. 'Why are you looking for a nanny?'

'My three brothers and I are bachelors, and having a baby with us … We're not sure about keeping him, or looking after him, you know?'

She narrowed her eyes at Ash, as a heated protective wave washed over her. She held the child closer to her chest. Was Mason safe with his father?

Eight

Harper glared at Ash like he was some axe murderer. 'Stop looking at me like that.' Ash snapped at her. 'I wouldn't hurt Mason, or any child.' He wasn't an animal. 'Look, my older brothers do know what to do when it comes to taking care of a kid.' They knew more than Ash did, anyway. But he would never hurt a child, not the way Harper accused him with that glare. 'They just don't want to because we're busy working on the station.' He had a life.

'I see.' Harper sighed as if she'd been holding her breath, even relaxing her protective grip on the child.

Whoa. She was protecting the child!

Ash tilted his head at Harper, as she shared a sweet smile with the boy, which lit up her eyes.

But the boy's giggle did something to Ash. It made him lean against the shelf and listen, getting all warm in the chest. Or was it the pretty woman with skin as pale as Mason's? 'Mason likes you.'

'I like Mason.'

That was obvious, if she was ready to protect a kid she'd just met.

Ash grinned as he adjusted his hat. 'So, may I ask, what are you doing out here? I saw the suitcase in your car with its interstate number plates.'

'I'm on holiday.'

Some holiday if she was dressed to go to work in that

tight skirt, shirt, and heels that showed off her lean legs. She was mouth-wateringly stunning—in a conservative secretary kind of way—with her hair and make-up flawless. 'For how long?'

Harper shrugged. She didn't even look at Ash, concentrating on the boy she carried effortlessly on her hip, now playing some game of hide-and-seek for the biscuit.

Ash had never been so ignored. Especially by a woman—and a snooty one at that.

'Here's a long shot ...' He rubbed his hat on his head. 'How about we hire you ... I mean me ... I hire you to be Mason's nanny?' He had nothing to lose, and the lady seemed protective over the kid.

'Excuse me?' Harper gave him a slow blink, distracted enough for the boy to snatch the piece of biscuit out of her hand.

That's my boy. Wait. No, he's not.

'Hey, you. Don't snatch.' Harper playfully tapped a polished fingernail on the toddler's nose.

The biscuit was long gone, replaced by a shine in the boy's eyes.

'I don't know much about children,' she said. 'But if you have internet, I'm not shy about searching for answers.'

His jaw dropped, wondering if he'd heard right. 'Are you saying you'd take the job?'

'Only temporarily.'

'Great.' The relief was enormous. 'I'll take whatever time you've got. That'd give us time to advertise properly.'

'As long as you stop flirting with me.'

'Say what?' Asked the man who flirted with females for fun.

'We need to set some boundaries. I know what you are: you're a player.'

'I play games. As a gamer.' He exhaled heavily, letting his eyes crawl all over her from head to toe, taking in that trim figure of hers, and that fine soft skin.

She twitched her nose at him as if he smelled of rotten

fruit. 'I will not be some sordid cliché where the boss does the babysitter. I don't like things being messy and complicated in the workplace.'

Ash shrugged. Should he warn her about the station being nothing but a messy dust bowl?

'But I will help you, if you agree to keeping boundaries, that this is a strictly business-only relationship.' She jutted her chin out, the supermarket's light highlighting the simple pearl earrings, while she looked him over with clear disdain. The snooty thing.

He didn't care, as long as Harper took good care of Mason. Ash would do anything for a decent night's sleep or to just make it through the next twenty-seven days. 'Agreed. So, will you take the job?'

Nine

How did Harper let herself get talked into this? This wasn't part of any work schedule that came with a memo or emailed request as part of the paper trail. No, this was a handshake deal that had her following the dusty trail of someone she'd just met, to become a nanny.

Harper had had little to do with babies, except smile at photos of influential people's offspring and pretend she cared. How was she going to do this?

But Mason was different. His squishy hugs pushed away that deep-seated loneliness she hadn't been able to shake since landing back in Australia. His little giggle and gummy smile lit up the room, warming her heart.

Plus, they shared a love for shortbread, so the kid must be okay. Right?

But where Ash was leading her didn't feel right.

Harper searched for signs of life. There were none, just a red dusty road, with a rambling fence line that enclosed dry paddocks dotted with scraggly looking trees with crooked, spindly black trunks. Patches of pink wildflowers scattered like paint spilled on a red dusty floor, broken up by towering cone-shaped pillars of dirt that reminded her of stalagmites you might find on Mars.

She'd always had a dislike for space, planets, and stardust. Sure, she was nerdy—but she was the type of nerd who didn't like space or the outdoors.

And this place looked like she'd landed in a deserted galaxy in a land where horrendous heat waves shimmered across the dirt road, distorting the landscape ahead of her. Behind her it was the same picture, only marred by the plume of dust caused by her own car, turning the sky red.

How did she get talked into this?

She kept her eye on the GPS that recorded her path, as they passed the place where she'd had that flat tyre, only yesterday, then up the small hill that opened to a vista of nothing but land. Her eyes widened as her heart squeezed, because there was so much open country she could get easily lost, with no hope of anyone finding her.

She wasn't an explorer or an adventurer. Harper was a girl who managed time behind a desk in air-conditioned comfort, with the occasional field trip to meetings held in places of sand dunes and workman's rubble, to marble-floored buildings, and boardroom tables full of top brass and stuffed shirts.

But this …

Harper tried to force down the lump in her throat, gripping the steering wheel tighter. She glanced at her silent phone, well out of range now.

At least she'd had the common sense to email her assistant to tell her where she was going. But was she doing the right thing?

Following the trail of red dust from Ash's ute, she passed through a broken gate, with a towering archway where the intricate metal sign above said *Elsie Creek Station.* It led to a long and straight track full of potholes and thick pockets of red sand. Her car struggled to get through.

When she finally drove into the clearing, a simple weatherboard house stood on the right. On its deep front porch, a large wooden table occupied the far-left corner where five people sat, watching her.

Before she could put the car into reverse and stop playing Bambi who should have never left her mother, her job, or her world—Ash opened her door.

'Looks like we'll have to grade the track so you can get in and out of the place easier.' Ash gave such a boyish grin with that hinted dimple, stopping all her panic. Ugh, it was that grin of his that had her going through with this idiotic plan.

The hostile heat hit her in waves as she got out of the cool, air-conditioned car. Who knew that the extreme change in temperature would cause her sunglasses to fog up.

'Here … you're on the clock.' Ash pushed Mason into her arms. 'Come on, meet my brothers. I'll take your suitcase.'

Mason drooled with his fist in his mouth, rubbing sleepy eyes, wincing in the bright outback sunshine that was harsh, even for her. At least she had sunglasses. 'Mason needs a hat.' Or should she drag out her umbrella?

'It's on the list.' Ash loaded himself up with shopping bags from the back of his ute while dragging her suitcase to the house, where bickering voices greeted them.

'Everyone …' Ash dumped the shopping bags at his feet.

Harper's eyes took a moment to adjust to the cool verandah's shade. No wonder they were all out here. Nearby, boxes of empty beer cans and bourbon bottles rested against the wall, while dirty coffee cups and glasses covered the table.

The other side of the spacious verandah was full of baby gear. Her suitcase sat next to a portable cot filled with toys that Mason was reaching for. Harper put Mason inside the portable playpen and gave him his water bottle.

'This is Harper Jamison, the nanny.'

Harper cleared her throat at Ash, straightening her skirt, fronting for an inspection of the troops of a different kind.

'Oh, yeah, sorry. I'm tired. And this is all new to me, too.' Ash gave her a shy grin. 'Harper has agreed to help until we can hire a proper nanny.' Ash then pointed at the seated men. 'That's my brother Cap in the baseball cap. The one scowling is Dex, and the guy in the black hat is Ryder.'

'And we're chopped liver, apparently.' The woman, with a massive mop of red hair, tilted her head and narrowed her eyes at Harper as if to see right through her. It was unnerving.

'That's Bree and her grandfather, Charlie,' said Ash. 'They

live over there in the caretaker's cottage. Everyone, this is Harper. Do I call you the nanny?'

'No, thank you.' Harper raised her chin to face the outback committee at the bush basher's boardroom table. 'Where will I be staying?' *Please don't say the stables?*

'You'll have my room.' Dex crossed his arms over his chest. He had muscles on muscles, along with a mean dark look.

She nearly choked on air, looking to Ash. 'Remember those boundaries we talked about.' Keeping open the lines of professionalism.

'I moved out.'

'To where?' Ash asked Dex.

'I'm bunking in the old stockman's shack.'

'I'll be moving out, too,' said Cap, patting the cream-coloured labrador that leaned against his leg. 'I'm going to fit out that demountable near the kennels. What do you call it, Bree?'

'The dogbox.'

'Yeah, that. Infrastructure's there for the kennels. It just needs a bit of TLC.'

'Bulldozer would be quicker,' mumbled Dex.

'When did this happen?' Ash asked his brothers.

'Today. While you were out, bro,' replied Cap. 'We guessed you'd need the room for Mason and the nanny.'

'So, what were you arguing over?'

The men turned to frown at the elderly man.

'Charlie has our brand.' Dex jabbed his finger in the air at Charlie. 'Why can't we have it?'

'Coz it's mine. It's always been mine,' grumbled the old man. 'You tell 'em, Bree.'

'Hey, that's between you and these boys.' The redhead approached. 'Did you get the medicine, Ash?'

'We did. And this other woman recommended some rusks to try in the supermarket. But I got everything from your list.' Ash seemed proud of himself.

'You didn't get your son a hat, I see.'

'It's on a different list.' Ash shrugged.

'Yeah, I've heard that before … So, I made you some more of those frozen fruit sticks for Mason. They're in the freezer in that hovel you boys call a kitchen.' Bree turned to the table as she spoke, 'You boys do know a fridge is for food, not just for beer and bourbon? And it's a good place for keeping water cool, too.'

'None of your concern, Bree,' grumbled Ryder, his voice deep and stern. 'Butt out of our business.'

'Wait. Let's take a moment to grieve, and remember you said that, cupcake.' Bree playfully winked at Harper, obviously unfazed. 'Where did Ash find you?'

'In the supermarket. I was buying shortbread.' Her plan had been to eat in her room and not end up in the middle of Woop Woop.

'Did Ash sweet-talk you into this? He thinks he's a god to women.'

'No, it was Mason who did the sweet-talking.' Harper smiled down at the boy, to tenderly stroke his soft hair. 'I assure you it had nothing to do with his father. Ashton Riggs is not my type.' Not that she knew what her type was when it came to men.

'I'm standing right here, ladies.'

'Good.' Bree grinned, ignoring Ash. 'Welcome to Elsie Creek Station, Harper. If you need me, I'm over at the caretaker's cottage, just walk around the back. Come on, Pop, let's hit the mute button and move on from this argument. I've got a hot date with some hockey players, and a new batch of gin to try.' Bree skipped down the steps.

'I'm Charlie.' The old man removed his enormous hat before shaking Harper's hand. 'Welcome to Elsie Creek Station, missy. You need anythin' you let us know. I'll give you a tour in the Razorback once you're settled in.'

Oh, that sounded safe. Not.

'Not tonight, you won't, Pop. You've been drinking,' said Bree over her shoulder.

'Yep, reckon a hot shower and a decent spot of tucker and

it'll be lights out for me, for sure.' Charlie slapped on his hat and winked at her, only to scowl at the brothers as he hoisted a metal rod over his shoulder. 'I'll be taking my property with me and putting her under lock and key. When you're ready to do the branding, I'll bring it out, but not until then.'

'It's supposed to be our brand,' called out Dex. 'We own the station now.'

'You don't own the brand.' Charlie shuffled a little quicker towards Bree, where they hooked arms and began singing as they headed for the cottage.

'How much have they had to drink?' Ash pointed at the beer bottles covering the table.

'Charlie had a few. He was helping us with the security details. Bree, nothing. She wasn't here long. She brought over a cot and highchair that were stored in one of the sheds.' Ryder was a big man, with dark eyes narrowed at Harper, full of mistrust, the way soldiers used to look at her in foreign lands.

'Bree never stays longer than ten minutes. She just says her piece and leaves.' Dex gripped the roof's railing and stretched out his spine, his shirt coming loose from his jeans to give a peek at his chiselled abs. 'That brand is ours.'

'What brand?' Ash asked.

Harper peeked at Ash. Did he have a set of abs like Dex, like some family trait?

'The Elsie Creek Station branding iron.'

'Is that what Charlie was carrying?' Ash pointed towards a small house, with a long corrugated fence along the side, but the front fence had tiny white fairy lights weaved around the edges. Faint rock music and the smell of a wood fire came from that direction.

'We just found out that Charlie makes them.'

'Who does, what? I'm sorry, I'm confused.' If it wasn't for little Mason, holding her hand from his playpen, Harper would have bolted from this bizarre scenario.

'Have you ever worked on a cattle station?' Ryder narrowed his cold, black eyes at her. His icy glare had her shivering.

'No. Never.' She never lied. But she knew how to play politics and hide the truth, and Ryder looked like the type of man who could tell if anyone was lying, and would waterboard you for information.

But how could she lie when she didn't understand the context of their argument?

'Hmm …' Even Ryder's voice was deep and cold. 'Cap, give the boy his new toy.'

'I bet twenty this nanny doesn't last the week.' Dex slammed twenty dollars onto the table while grinning evilly at Harper. 'Any takers?'

What an arsehole!

'Stop betting in front of the girl, it's rude,' said Cap as he approached, with a dog following him. 'A brand is a combination of letters or marks we use on the cattle. Each station has their own registered brand that makes the cattle recognisable, so we can claim ownership over them should any wander. It's just that, somehow, Charlie owns the Elsie Creek Station brand and has it registered under his name.'

'Can't we just design a new brand?' Ash asked. 'Being new owners and all.'

'Elsie Creek Station's brand is the same one created back in 1910. It's a rare, legacy brand.' Ryder snatched up his beer bottle with a snarl and drank deeply. 'We just have to convince that old sod that brand is ours.' He sat at the head of the table, as if the man in charge. 'Whose turn is it to cook dinner?'

'Mine.' Cap gave Harper a soft smile. 'Hope you like steak.'

'Sure. When in Rome, right?'

'What do you think about dogs?' Cap nodded at the labrador, wagging its tail as it sniffed at the baby pen where Mason was trying to pat the dog. His squeals of excited laughter eased the tension in the air.

'I don't have a problem with dogs. I've always wanted one, but I was travelling too much with work to get one.'

'I get you on the travelling.' Cap patted the labrador. 'This is Mason's dog, Ruby. She's a nanny dog.'

'Cool.' Ash nodded with approval.

'I'm sorry, but aren't I the nanny?' Was she being replaced by a dog?

Cap crouched to pat the pale-coloured labrador that was watching Mason. 'Ruby's job is to watch over you both, in case of snakes and stuff.'

'*Snakes!*' Harper swallowed hard, her eyes darting to the exposed beams in the roof, covered in thick cobwebs.

'Nah, I changed my mind. I'm only betting ten that she won't make the next twenty-four hours.' Dex grinned, swapping the twenty-dollar bill for ten.

Harper glowered at the ingrate, so tempted to make that bet on herself.

'Ruby will stay in the house and under the boy's cot,' Ryder commanded. Leaving her no choice but to accept the dog.

She'd never had much to do with dogs. The ones she saw sat in doggy handbags carried by rich socialites in restaurants. But they seemed so happy, like Ruby with her wagging tale and smile, who made Mason smile—the same smile as his father.

Mason was so cute he should be paid to endorse nappies or sit alongside puppies and sell toilet paper.

'Do me a favour, Harper?' Cap pointed to the mean-looking black shepherd chained to the verandah's far corner post. 'Keep Mason away from the shepherd, until I get the dog assimilated.'

'You have an attack dog?' Was this place a dog kennel?

'Sarge is an ex-riot dog.'

'On a cattle station?' She then noticed the rifles leaning against the wall. A few surveillance cameras lay beside some shotgun shells, spilling over the map spread across the table. She recognised the assorted paraphernalia to show a war-room's battle in progress, a disorganised one at that.

A tingle of terror crept up her spine. She scooped up

Mason and held him close, with Ruby, the dog, watching her every move. Was the boy safe? Was she? 'Are you going to war?' What sort of hillbilly outfit was this?

'Nah, we're good. Aren't we, brothers?' Ash glared at his older siblings, then put on a fake smile for Harper. 'Come on, Harper, I'll let you pick a room.'

Ten

Dear Diary, welcome to hell.

It was a full thirty-seven hours and twenty-nine minutes since Harper had arrived at this soulless desert of dust, living on nothing but sheer teeth-gritting determination to beat Dex's bet. Only made worse by the prick reverting to his original twenty-dollar bet, that she wouldn't last the week.

He might win that bet.

Harper sat heavily in a kitchen chair in the large empty kitchen, where she fed Mason breakfast in his highchair. It was the only furniture in a house she'd class as a hovel filled with boxes.

It had taken Harper all of yesterday to clean and sort out Mason's room, next door to hers. Then she attacked the bathroom that should've been declared a toxic war zone. But Mason enjoyed playing in the enormous bathtub like it was a private swimming pool, while she got soaked to the bone with raw hands and broken nails from cleaning.

She was the nanny. Not a cleaner.

Even though she had no clue what she was doing as a nanny, at least she had wi-fi, which allowed her to play music and scour social media for tutorials and tips.

Today, she was exhausted. Who knew cleaning was more physical than taking five spin classes with her Swedish spin master, urging them to train for the ski season? She hated that man. Right now, she hated cleaning more.

But boredom drove her to contemplate cleaning the

kitchen with its long wide benches that only held a coffeemaker, and lots of cupboard space because it was a kitchen with no food!

They had plenty of baby food, beer, and bourbon. But there was nothing resembling any form of vegetable. The empty pantry had a few tins of beans that had long since expired, and were likely toxic.

Food for these savages was slabs of barbecued meat, slapped between slices of bread, smothered in tomato sauce, then washed down with a deep guzzle of beer.

Let's not forget the volume of coffee they drank, because she'd never seen one of the Riggs brothers drink water.

The coffee she approved of. She'd never been picky over her coffee, which she needed to keep her eyes open from lack of sleep. Especially when Mason and Ruby, the labrador, had moved into Harper's room at two in the morning.

But she needed food. She couldn't live off coffee, beef, and bread, and she was not about to steal the processed toddler food.

Mason pushed away his cereal bowl, upending it to land with a splat on the kitchen floor, where Ruby the labrador was eager to lick it clean.

She left the dog to it. She was over cleaning.

She was also over doing laundry.

Oh, how she missed her local laundry. The magical store where she dropped off her laundry in a white sack, to return a few days later to collect her suits and shirts all perfectly pressed.

Now she had to fight with an old washing machine that you had to hold on to during the spin cycle, or it'd walk off the verandah. And then it was drip drying.

D-d-d-drip. Drying.

On a metal wire that made up the clothesline already filled with assorted long-sleeved work shirts and jeans, starchy and faded from the harsh outback sun.

They were Cap's, Dex's or Ash's clothes. She knew this because yesterday, she'd watched in horror, as they dumped their clothes in a pile beside the washing machine where they had undressed, on their way to the outdoor shower. Then they'd tugged a set of clean clothes off the clothesline, dressing as they snatched a cold beer on the way to the table that lived on the front porch, where they sat around and argued over whose turn it was to cook dinner.

They were animals.

But all this baby talk and one-sided conversation was mushing her brain.

What she'd give for a trip to town to see people and asphalt roads and buildings that weren't covered in red dirt. She missed concrete, and the noise of traffic. She missed the smell of coffee shops and bakeries and the taste of buttery rich croissants in the morning on her way to work. Oh, and how she missed a man in a decently cut suit and tie.

She also missed her job, that didn't involve conversations about cattle, toddler talk, toddler toilet reminders, toddler food, night nappies, fixing dams, musters or beer. A job that didn't involve getting covered in toddler teething slobber and dog hair, stuck in yesterday's clothes with her hair in desperate need of a good wash and a blow dry. If someone dared mention the term toddler tantrum she was going to curl up in the corner and give herself a time out.

How women did this job for free had to be a joke. They deserved a dozen medals, a massive pay rise, and two months' annual leave just to catch up on some sleep!

But there was no way she was letting Dex win his bet.

'Knock. Knock.'

'Bree?' Harper bounded to the back door, blinking at the other female. 'Hi.'

'Oh, you poor thing.' Bree pointed at Harper as she stepped inside the kitchen.

'What do you mean?' Harper tried to tidy up her hair that she hadn't even brushed, with her shirt covered in breakfast mush. Or was that last night's dinner? 'I'd offer you a chair, but they all live outside. And I'm not touching that table they congregate at.'

'I wouldn't either. I brought over some more frozen fruit pops for Mason's teeth.' Bree slid the bag of goodies into the empty freezer. 'Haven't those boys gone shopping yet?'

'Not unless you like baby food. If I knew where Mason's car seat was, I'd go to town myself.' *And never come back—* which was possibly why they were hiding the toddler's car seat.

Bree poked her head into the empty pantry. 'Jeez, they're like cavemen. I bet they're hoping you'll cook and clean for them, too.'

'Well, they'll be waiting a while if they expect me to cook.'

'Why is that?'

'I can't cook. At least Mason's food comes with instructions.' Harper pointed to the empty packet on the kitchen sink, piled with dirty dishes. 'Besides, it wasn't part of the job description to cook and clean when I got talked into this.'

Bree giggled. 'Well, they're screwed, aren't they? So are you.'

'That's just great.' Harper collapsed heavily in her seat. She'd never felt so helpless.

At the sinks, Bree ran the tap and rinsed off a face washer then cleaned Mason's sticky hands and face, then carried his breakfast bowl to the sink. 'Well, come on then.'

'Where are we going? Please tell me we're going to a day spa, where we get waited on by a body-building Scottish man, in a kilt, who gives the best neck and shoulder massages.'

'Ooh. Now that sounds like my kind of heaven. But we'll be going a few hundred metres that way.' She pointed out the screen door.

'Why?'

'It's where I live, and where I can guarantee you won't need a tetanus shot to eat the food.' She picked up Mason from the highchair. 'Come on, toddler, let's get you toddling.'

'Play, Arper?'

'H-H Harper.' She corrected him.

'Play?' He held out his little hand to Bree.

'I'd like that very much.' Bree gave such a sweet smile, with shiny eyes as she let the little boy grip her finger.

Harper had to admire Mason's unbridled joy to find the adventures in his day.

'You'll need to tell Ash to put childproof locks on all the doors, because there is no fence out there to keep this little one contained.' Bree held Mason's tiny hand, his little shoes taking eager steps for the door, with Ruby's pitter patter of paws following.

'I don't know what I'm doing.' Harper couldn't even find the energy to move from her chair.

'Nobody does, blossom. We all pretend that we do, which is just part of being in the grown-up game. But you look like you've been attacked by thirteen spiders and a koala.'

Harper touched her hair, which felt like a webbed nest of sorts. It was a shocker, especially when she'd been brought up to always have her hair and make-up done. 'I guess I do.' It was easy to avoid mirrors in this place, because they had none.

'How about you go and take a long shower and get into some clean clothes?'

'Really?' Because that sounded like heaven to Harper.

'Take your time, and then come over to my place and we'll have some lunch.'

Harper's stomach growled at the prospect of real food. 'I— Thank you.'

'All good, blossom.' That beautiful redhead gave a knowing smile and a nod. 'Come along, Mason, let's give the nanny a break while we go on an adventure.' Bree opened the screen door and walked the toddler outside with the nanny dog Ruby following.

Harper leaned back in her seat and watched them. The opportunity to revel in the bliss of five minutes alone was heavenly. One week. She could last a week. Right?

Eleven

air washed, a light make-up applied, and in clean clothes, Harper felt normal again. Well, as normal as possible when her surroundings were anything but normal. Here the sun was so bright, she could feel it biting into her skin, and the floating dust particles landed like gritty sandpaper against her damp skin. She wanted to hide indoors, like she normally did, and not deal with the *Great Outdoors*—which wasn't really great at all. Whoever came up with that catchphrase should be sued for false advertising.

She strolled towards the caretaker's cottage that sat on the far left of the sheds. At night, you could see the fairy lights, and hear music and laughter that sounded so much more inviting than the farmhouse with no furniture, but a lot of boxes. It was a place that echoed of rattly air conditioners and snoring men, with a mean-looking shepherd who watched over them.

The caretaker's cottage was a rustic, squat-looking building made of river stone. She pulled back the metal rail that opened the wrought iron gate that matched the chest-high fence, hemming in a gloriously vibrant display of cottage flowers—gardenias, roses and fragrant lavender that grew among large clusters of daisies, globe-shaped purple alliums, cosmos, and so much more. It was a feast of flowers crammed into one location, where their sweet floral fragrance was heavenly. It was enough to raise her spirits as she dared to venture further.

She followed the wide stone path that weaved its way to

the sturdy front door. Old windows made of stained-glass squares stood on either side of the wooden door, while wind chimes hung from the verandah's roof, with not one cobweb anywhere.

The short verandah held a comfy cane chair, perfect for a reading nook. She was so tempted to collapse into that cane chair, to watch the flowers shift with the breeze, while listening to the delicate wind chimes, as they hypnotised her to sleep.

But Harper never sat still and did nothing, it was unheard of for her to waste time like that. Glancing at her watch, she pushed on.

'Hello?' Harper knocked on the wooden door. 'Anyone home?'

Bree called out, 'We're around the back.'

Harper followed the stone path to the right side of the house, where a thin corridor ran between the house and a high corrugated fence that hid the outside world. It opened to a large area, where she stood, dumbfounded, staring at the backyard.

It was an entire universe of green.

Considering the dust bowl that surrounded the farmhouse, this place was loaded with assorted plants growing from raised beds made of corrugated iron and more rock paths. Amongst it was Bree, wearing a big straw hat and gardening gloves. Beside her, Mason wore a hat like a bonnet, happily digging in the dirt with a trowel. While Ruby, the labrador, wagged her tail, sniffing at everything with a big smile on her face as if in doggy heaven.

'What is this place? Paradise?'

'It's a veggie garden, blossom. What do you think it is?'

'I've never seen one this big.' And she hadn't expected to find it out the back of the cottage hidden behind a corrugated fence. 'Do the brothers know this garden is here?'

'Probably not. Their focus is on fencing and cattle.'

'You have lettuce.' Lush, plump lettuce heads grew among purple kale. Bright orange and juicy red cherry tomatoes grew like Christmas lights on a leafy vine, beside some deliciously vibrant capsicums and chillies. She pinched at a leaf and sniffed. 'Spinach?'

Bree nodded. 'I'm guessing you're sick of the meat-only diet the boys have?'

Harper nodded. 'Hell, yeah.'

'You're welcome to help yourself. I have plenty to share.' Bree held out a plump tomato to Harper. 'Try it.'

It was like forbidden fruit, tempting her growling stomach.

'Thank you.' Harper's eyes closed as she bit into the tomato like an apple. Its firm flesh released a burst of sweetness, married perfectly with a tanginess and pulpy seeds to create a complex combination across her tongue. It was the best tomato of her life. 'I've never eaten a tomato like this.'

'City girl.' Bree filled her basket with radishes, shallots, moving on to the strawberries and passionfruit that grew near a massive banana plant loaded with baby green bananas.

'I'm from the land of dial-up deliveries. But this place, I'd never ...' Harper wandered around the yard devouring her tomato. No lawn grew here, just raised beds and the curvaceous stone paths like a secret garden. There were arched trellises that created shady walkways where beans and snow peas dangled like Christmas tree ornaments, along with butternuts and melons too.

'How come you can't cook?'

'Um ...' She wiped the tomato juice from her chin. 'I just never had the time to learn. May I?' She pointed to the cucumber. 'I've never seen them grow like that.'

'That one's not ready yet. I've got some in the fridge. Come on, I've had enough vitamin D for the day.'

'How do you not burn?'

'Sunscreen. Wide-brimmed hat. Long-sleeved shirts. Don't worry, I've put plenty of sunscreen on Mason, too.'

Who was having a fat time digging up a dirt bed with the

dog.

'I must add sunscreen to my shopping list.'

'I make my own sunscreen. You're welcome to try it.' Bree put a small tin on the quaint mosaic table, shaded beneath a pergola covered in grapevines. It created a wonderfully dappled shade over the unique crazy stone paving that ran along the back of the house, leading to an entertainment area containing an outdoor kitchen, complete with a sink, pizza oven, and a built-in barbecue. 'Take a seat. I'll get our brunch together. Nothing fancy.'

'This is fancy, believe me. It's like we're in Tuscany …' Harper waved her hand at the yard where tall cornstalks and large sunflowers gently waved on the breeze. They hid the corrugated fence line that barricaded two sides of the yard like a windbreak that cleverly concealed this wonderland.

But the open country view beyond the garden was divine. It was a lush green paddock that ran to a thick cluster of trees, overshadowed by an enormous rocky red escarpment.

The caretakers definitely had a better deal than the brothers with their farmhouse.

In the outdoor kitchen, Bree effortlessly worked on their lunch in between checking on Mason, who was still playing garden gnome. A rich fragrance of fresh basil filled the air as Bree sprinkled the herb over luscious slices of red tomatoes and cucumber. It was an effort to not drool with hunger.

'You're in luck. We made a stack of stone baked panini bread rolls this morning.' Bree placed a bread basket on the table.

'You make your own bread?' She was salivating at the crusty rolls.

'Charlie does.' Bree pointed to the pizza oven. 'He makes a mean pizza too.' Bree served up a platter of assorted cheeses, sliced Italian sausage and tender chicken strips, along with her sliced salad and herbs. 'Help yourself. I've got some wine somewhere, we could really make a day of it.'

'Do you know how tempting that is?' Harper practically wolfed down her food. 'I can't remember when I sat and ate a meal and actually looked at what I was eating. And how amazing this food tastes. And this yard.' She pointed her thick cucumber slice at the scenery. Cucumber and salt, and she was in heaven. How simple did life feel right now.

'My grandmother built this garden with Charlie. They were into permaculture long before they called it that.' Bree poured a tall glass of iced tea and passed it to Harper.

Harper sipped the tea, enjoying the vibrant peach flavour, delicately blended with black tea and vanilla, it was like summer spooling across her tongue. 'This place is so civilised.'

'Not after sunset, it's not.' Bree gave a wry grin with a devilish shine in her green eyes.

'I've heard you partying. Who with?'

'It's just Pop and me. We have the TV out here, where we cook, dance, and sing like morons at the moon some nights.'

'I've heard the singing. You know, I rarely see a sunset.'

'Sunrise?'

'I hardly ever saw the sky until I came back to Australia.'

'Where have you been?'

'Belgium.'

Bree arched her eyebrows. 'Doing what?'

'I work for the Australian Ambassador to Belgium, who was previously the Deputy Secretary for National Security and International Policy for the Australian Government. Before that I worked for the Minister for Defence.'

Bree lowered her cutlery onto her plate and leaned back in her chair. 'Now what is someone like you doing out here?'

'I've been asking myself that same question.' Harper stabbed at the lettuce that was so crunchy, the red onion peppery, mixed with a lush dressing. She'd be content to act like a goat, and munch on the food in this yard all day.

But Bree waited for an answer.

'I needed a break. I just didn't expect this kind of a break or that I'd end up here.' Harper waved her empty fork at the garden bed, where Mason was happily playing in the dirt. 'Is that dirt safe for him to eat?'

'Trust me, they don't eat it for long.' Bree giggled at Mason, spitting it out, then wiping his mouth, creating a clown-like mask complete with a massive smile.

She'd never seen the boy so happy. Or Ruby, furiously digging a hole into the rich soil, showering Mason with dirt where his laughter echoed around them as if it was the best game on the planet.

'He's getting so dirty?'

'Well then, Mason will fit right in with the rest of the Riggs brothers.' Bree smiled at Mason, but then turned in her chair to face Harper. Her undivided attention was unnerving. 'You were saying how you ended up out here?'

Harper dabbed at the crumbs left on her plate.

Yet, Bree's silent treatment made her want to talk. 'Sadly, due to Belgium's homegrown terrorism and violent extremists, I've been living under a level-four terrorist alert for five years now.'

'In Belgium?' Bree arched her eyebrow. 'Home of chocolate and waffles.'

'The Australian Government constantly issues travel warnings for those visiting Belgium. And Brussels is headquarters to NATO, that is sixteen minutes away from the Australian Embassy.'

'So, with you working for an ambassador—'

'It makes us targets.' She tried to make her shrug casual, but there was nothing casual about this topic. 'All embassy staff are told the day they start that they are targets for terrorism. And we had a scare, a big one. My work colleagues were killed by a car bomb—the car I was supposed to climb into.' Harper stared at her hands, so raw from cleaning. 'The blast blew me out of my favourite shoes, ruining them.'

'And you?'

'I, um, was slammed into the side of the building and ended up with six stitches in my head, and a severe concussion.' She still had a bald spot where the medical team had shaved her head, and she dropped her head to show Bree the scar. She'd never showed her war wounds to anyone before.

Honestly, she hadn't been the same since she woke up from that bomb blast, living under a thick cloud of brain fog. She needed to talk about something else. 'Ugh, what I'd give for a decent shampoo and conditioner. I ran out. I doubt the hairdressers in town would stock my brand.'

'I haven't bought shampoo in years.'

'So, how …' She pointed at Bree's impressive mop of healthy red hair.

'I make my own. I have a friend who makes organic soap that is positively to die for, I could just eat it.'

'So you make things?'

'Is that weird?'

'All I use my hands for is to shuffle papers or reply to emails. But now they're …' She held up her poor, sore, dried out, bleached fingers.

'Here …' Bree reached over to the side and pulled out a small tube. 'I swear by this hand cream.'

'You make this too?' Harper sniffed at the bottle, dabbing a small blob onto the back of her hand, and proceeded to rub it in. The cool relief was instant.

'No. But I do stock up. Living on a remote cattle station, you learn to make do with things, and to stock up or become self-sufficient. You have to, especially when Leviathan Creek cuts off the road to town in the wet season.'

'I can't imagine this place in the rainy season.'

'It's pretty. And then, my friend, this place is one long summer holiday where you can sip on a jug of gin, while wallowing in an ice bath to watch the rain fall.' Bree waved to the left of the paved area, where a long tin tub sat before the wide-screen TV with a superb view of the countryside.

'You have a pool?' Harper sat taller, thinking of Mason.

'Don't worry, the tub is empty.' Bree nodded at Mason obsessed with digging another hole in the dirt. 'Actually, it's a cattle trough. But I own a brilliant ice machine and love my freezers that allow me to indulge in ice baths while I'm watching the ice hockey. You should come over.'

'I know nothing about hockey.'

'What's to know? The players are hot, the game is fast, and its brutal fun. I also like to imagine how cold it is to go to an ice hockey match, especially when it's sweltering here in the outback summer.'

'So, um … Favourite team?' Harper struggled to make small talk, considering she came from a world that didn't do small talk. It was so much better than baby talk.

'I have none. You?'

'I don't do sport. Or small talk.'

'You're doing okay.' Bree unleashed a smile. It wasn't a mean one, it was the smile of a friend. And Harper needed one.

'So, you're Charlie's full-time carer?'

'And business partner.'

'Doing what?'

'How about, when you're ready to tell me the real reason you're out here, I'll share.'

Harper slammed back into her chair. No, it couldn't be that obvious. Could it?

But Bree's eyes saw everything. 'Don't stress, blossom. Eat up, and then I'll give you a cooking lesson for your dinner.'

'I'm happy to pay you to cook.'

'Why? When you now have the time to cook.'

'I never did, before. I lived under strict time schedules, racing to meetings, scoffing down whatever my assistant brought me, sipping on cold coffee. This is all new to me. Even conversation that isn't part of a negotiation.' Her shoulders sagged, tears suddenly forming. She sniffed hard, straightening her dress as if to compose herself. But it was a struggle. 'I've never—'

'Hey …' Bree leaned over and squeezed her hand. 'Just take it day by day. Especially after your horrific experience with a car bombing. That's not normal, blossom, so you're doing okay. Just know you're safe out here.'

'Why are you being so nice to me?' What was Bree's angle? Harper was so used to people bartering with her for political favours, with everyone having a hidden agenda.

'It's more pity than anything else.' Bree snuggled back into her chair and gave another one of her devilish grins.

'Excuse me?' Harper didn't want anyone's pity.

'You're living with the Riggs brothers.' Bree laughed, instantly lightening the mood.

'They haven't even bothered to connect a TV, and they have four of them.' She pointed at the wide-screen TV attached to the wall. 'They only use the inside of the house to sleep.'

'If they did, they'd argue over what to watch.' Bree playfully rolled her eyes. 'Can you imagine it? Ash would hog it to play his computer games. Cap would have it on some wildlife documentary. Dex would have it on a boxing bout, the bloodier the better. Ryder would have a split screen, watching the news, the stock market and the business channel all at once.'

'They're so different.'

'And they have a baby brother, Jonathan. The locals call him Rigsy. He's got a little bit of all of them, and he's a nice guy.'

'Why isn't Jonathan here?'

'Jonathan lives with his future bride, Mandy Must, on Sandlot Station. They're our neighbours to the west.' Bree pointed to the side, Harper had no idea which way was north, south or west. 'That's why the Riggs brothers came to town—to help Jonathan with his first muster.'

'Where were they before that?'

'No idea. But Jonathan told me it was the first time they'd been together in ten years.'

'That's a long time to be away from family.'

'Guess so?' Bree shrugged.

'So the family reunion must have been good?'

Again, Bree shrugged. 'I think watching their youngest brother, Jonathan, buy Sandlot Station made them want to work for themselves, too. Jonathan wanted them to stay close, he was the one who was keen for Pop to agree to meet the boys. Which Charlie did, and those four brothers bought Elsie Creek Station almost a month now.'

'Did they factor in their constant arguments?' It was relentless, the snarls, grunts, and snarky snaps she'd hear from the outdoor table.

'Dex and Ryder, right?'

Harper nodded. 'I ignore them. Or they ignore me. But right now, I don't care about the Riggs brothers ... Is that wrong?' She'd never talked badly about her boss to someone she'd just met. Where was the filter for her mouth? She was usually good at keeping secrets and being guarded with her reactions.

'No.' Bree giggled. 'Listen, what's said in this yard stays in this yard.'

'Thank you, Bree. For everything, the shower time, lunch, conversation and just ...'

'Settle, petal. It's obvious you've been living a pretty stressful life for a long time. Take a beat while I clear the table.'

'I should—'

'Sit and finish your iced tea and see how long you can sit still without doing anything.'

'I've never ...' Harper stopped at Bree's knowing expression. It was if Bree could see right through her, dishing out whatever Harper needed, even if she was clueless about what she needed for herself.

Bree swiftly cleared the table, leaving Harper to nestle back in her chair. She admired the large sunflowers bigger than her head swaying in the breeze. It was like she was enjoying a European summer, not the outback's winter without a cloud in the sky that was so endless it was like looking into a deep ocean that floated above her. She'd never seen a sky so big and so clear.

Bree returned with a fresh jug of iced water with cucumber slices and a plate of sliced fruit and assorted nuts. Pouring a tall glass of water she handed one to Harper. 'Did you meet the prime minister?'

'Not the current one.' The water was so crisp and the cucumber refreshing. It was the perfect palate cleanser. 'Do you know why Cap is camping on the verandah?'

'He's training Sarge to be the guard dog. Cap's demountable is airing out, and he wants to paint it before he moves in. Unlike Dex, who is squatting in the stockman's shack, sleeping on his swag inside his tent.'

'I'm glad Dex is out of the house. He's betting on me to not last the week. Arsehole.' She slapped her hand over her mouth. 'I shouldn't have said that.'

'Listen, cucumber, just so you know—I've bet a hundred against Dex on you to make it.'

'What? Why?'

Bree leaned in closer, her green eyes so clear. 'Because I know you will.'

'You don't know me.'

'No. But I can see it …' She tapped on her ears.

Harper remained perfectly still, desperate to not react or give her situation away.

'I won't ask, and I won't tell. Especially since Ryder told me to butt out of their business. And really, that's your secret to share.' She sipped her water, keeping her eyes on Harper. 'The Riggs brothers are not dumb, so don't ever underestimate them. Especially Ryder. He's already suspicious of you.'

'Ryder doesn't talk to me. None of them do.' She fiddled with her fingers in her lap. 'I don't know what to talk to them about.' So maybe it was her fault, too. 'I suck at this— conversation.'

'No, you don't.' Bree scooped up her cane basket, sliding on her hat and gardening gloves. 'In the meantime, let's go shop for dinner, then we can go find you a dining table and some chairs to set up the farmhouse kitchen.'

'Where? Not like there is a furniture warehouse out here.'

'Close. We've got sheds. But you should take a hat, I have a spare one inside for you to try.'

'I-I-I'm just helping them out.'

'Who?'

She shrugged, unable to answer Bree.

'Sometimes, keeping a secret can be good, which you'd know from your world.'

'It was full of secrets.'

'So don't beat yourself up struggling to share. But if you ever need to talk, blab, dribble, or stumble over words and have someone to listen, I'm here.' Bree gave a tender squeeze of Harper's arm. 'You should hear me after I've had a jug of gin, it's not even English.' She winked at her.

Such genuine kindness had tears blurring her vision. 'I'm sorry, I'm not normally like this.' Using the back of her hands, she brushed them away. 'Thank you for coming and checking on me, and for lunch.'

'All good. Honestly, I dropped off the fruit blocks for Mason more for my selfish need to ensure he didn't scream down the place at midnight. He did that on his first night. Where is Mason sleeping?'

'In the cot, supposedly, but he ends up with me. And Ruby.' Her bed got crowded, but having them there stopped the loneliness and the nightmares.

'You know why you have a nanny dog, don't you?'

'For snakes?' She shuddered at the thought, with her eyes darting to the shadowy corners of the garden.

'To protect Mason from you.'

'What? I'd never—'

'Petal, you're someone who Ash picked up from the supermarket, driving a sleek black Audi, looking after their nephew.'

'I'd never hurt Mason. I swear it.' In her heart she'd protect the child at all costs.

'I believe you. It's the rest you need to convince.'

'Then why hire me?'

'Because they're desperate.'

That hurt. Especially when Harper was in high demand, with plenty of high-paying jobs offered to her all the time.

'Chin up, petal. There's nothing I'd love more than to

prove those boys wrong and win that bet from Dex.'

'Got my vote.' Pushing up from the chair, she straightened her dress. She was never afraid to work hard. But this job, this place, was way out of her comfort zone. 'Do you know if Ash has advertised for a nanny?'

'Why would he? You're here now.' Bree laughed as she opened the back door of the cottage.

'I'm not a nanny.'

'Well, what are you then?' Bree returned with a hat for Harper.

'Good question?' But for now she was determined to beat Dex's bet.

Twelve

It was the middle of the night when Harper stumbled out of bed, in desperate need of some water. The farmhouse was so dark, she hit her shoulder against a doorframe. The sharp pain was excruciating. 'Ow.'

'Are you okay?' The light in the pantry was flicked on by Ash, who was holding a milk bottle, dressed only in a towel.

'I, um …' She gulped, forgetting all about her shoulder. Ash must have come from the shower with his hair dripping wet. Water droplets rolled down his straight shoulders, sliding between his perfect pecs, to trickle down the smooth ridges of the most perfect set of abs she'd seen in her life.

'Can I help you?' As he put the milk bottle away, the light from the fridge only highlighted his abs with that towel wrapped low around his hips.

She shook her head, unable to tear her eyes away from his perfect body. Or was she nodding?

'Harper?' The way he said her name in that husky whisper made her body tremble.

She had to be dreaming about this man stalking towards her. 'Water,' she croaked.

'Sure. I'll get you some.' His lips shifted into an easy grin. Not the wide smile that showed off his dimple, but one of amusement.

He turned his back to reveal a wall of muscle. It was so much worse than the front. She fought a sudden urge to scrape her fingernails down his beautiful back, to leave her mark on something so perfect, surprising herself at the savage thoughts coming from her normally conservative mind.

The tap at the kitchen sink turned on and off. 'We should put water in the fridge. But we don't have any bottles to keep it in.'

'List it.' Did that make sense?

'Good idea. I should pin a big shopping list to the fridge.' He held out the glass.

It took all her effort to lift her heavy arm to collect the glass. But then her fingers brushed against his and a heated tremor squirrelled down her arm, as if lighting up all her nerves inside. 'You, tank …' The glass hit her teeth as she guzzled the water, her eyes averted from the man who made her thirsty.

She wiped her chin to check she wasn't drooling. 'I meant *thank you.*' Where was her grasp of the English language?

'Ah huh.' The man stood in front of her with eyes so dark they were almost frightening, but steady, and locked on her.

She studied Ash in this soft light. He kept his hair trimmed short on the sides, with longer strands on top that were wet and glistening from the shower. With a straight nose, chiselled, smooth jaw, his delectable mouth barely shifted into a smile.

Normally he dressed in dusty denim jeans that hugged his thighs, and a long-sleeved work shirt that only hinted at his muscular arms. Now all of him, except for one part, was on display.

What would she give to let that towel drop so she could stand back and just admire his beautiful body in its entirety?

Even his scent was a potent combination of soap, shampoo, and rugged masculinity. Ashton Riggs was the perfect specimen of a hard-bodied, suntanned male.

'Can I help you with anything, Harper?'

How dare he say her name in a way that made her toes curl.

Why couldn't she move away?

His eyes slowly roamed over her body. The attention

made her press her back against the wall, where she held her breath and licked her lips.

Tilting his head to the side, he dropped his eyes to follow her tongue as it ran across her lips.

Then his eyes dropped to her chest, continuing down over her stomach and bare legs. Slowly, taking in her simple nightgown, now wishing she was wearing full-body armour.

But the way Ash looked at her, he had to have X-ray vision to see beneath the simple cotton nightgown. She'd never felt more exposed.

She should have listened to her mother and worn a dressing gown. But she didn't pack one, and why should she when it was so hot right now in this room. And why was she thinking of her mother when she had a near-naked man standing before her?

Could she blame those tall glasses, containing Bree's delicious gin mix, she'd had over dinner that carried over from her long lunch yesterday, as the cause for her body and mind's reaction to Ash? Standing in just a towel. Alone. In the dark.

'How's Mason?'

The boy!

Boundaries.

She sidestepped him, rushing to the sink to refill her glass. 'Good. Asleep.' Now that they had some distance between them, she found the courage to face him.

Why did they ever create a man who looked like Ash, to tempt her when she was only here for…

He walked towards her with such ease, as if he had all the time in the world to get where he needed to be. While she was the moron glued to the floor.

Plucking a glass from the sink, he stood so close to her she could feel the heat from his bare skin.

She scurried to the other side of the room. 'Are you avoiding your son?'

The tap gushed with water, filling his glass. But he didn't drink it, he just left it on the sink, his eyes staring at her reflection in the window.

She was trained to know her subject, to gather data, and to think of every scenario that gave her the advantage of winning over the opposition, yet nothing had prepared her to be one on one with someone like Ashton Riggs.

He turned around to face her. The corners of his lips turned up, giving her a sinful smirk, more playful than before.

Why couldn't she speak? Why was she helpless to fight this chemical attraction drugging her bloodstream? Why did she get out of bed?

It took only a few steps before he stood in front of her, to place both hands on the wall beside her, caging her in. 'No.'

What was the question? Why couldn't she move? Did she want to?

'Ash …'

'Harper.' He stepped closer, his body now breaching her personal space. It was a space she'd cautiously protected all these years, yet this man had entered it so easily.

She sucked in a sharp breath as he reached out to take a strand of her hair and gently tuck it behind her ear, sending shivers across her skin at the simple touch.

The corners of his lips slowly turned up, before showing his gorgeous smile, the one with the dimple that normally made her sigh. But this time it sent alarm bells screaming in her head, as a wave of heat washed over her, making her mouth water with lust.

Then her sanity finally showed up.

This man knew exactly what he was doing to her.

The flirt.

She shoved him away. 'Boundaries, Ash. You may be my boss, but I'm not here for you. I'm here for your son, the little boy you're avoiding.'

She scooted back to her room. There, leaning against the cool wooden door, as the air conditioner rattled to fight the heat, she forced herself to take deep breaths to slow her hammering heart.

Ash was a player. And Harper didn't trust players. They were as bad as politicians, who only played nice when they wanted something, or were racking up favours to exploit later. And a man like Ash could easily exploit someone like Harper.

She was here for Mason. And only for Mason.

Thirteen

Wearing thick goggles for his drone, Ash flicked the dials on the handheld console, and his favourite toy was up and in the air. Sounding like a swarm of bees, it followed the red dusty track to the fence line where the view was simply *epic*. It was like something straight out of a Hollywood movie, where he was the cameraman panning for the perfect shot.

He steered the drone to swoop low between the gaps of the metal gates. Spun it around to dance over the barbed wire fence, then dashed across to check over the cattle milling around the large bale of hay.

'Oi!'

Ash lifted his goggles to find Ryder, covered in red clay from fixing the dam, glaring at him. They were all filthy, but the job was done. 'Why aren't you out checking those troughs?'

'I am.' He slipped his goggles back on. 'I'm saving fuel by using the drone. Stop stressing. If I need to clean them, I'll add it to my list.' He steered the drone along the dusty paddocks to the water tank. 'Tank's full on the northern edge of Emu Plains. Hey, do we get to name any of the places on this station? Jonathan and Mandy are naming their paddocks at Sandlot Station.'

'We have names for the paddocks already. Where's your kid?'

Ash shrugged as he steered the drone, grinning at the roos running from the noise as it skimmed over treetops and headed for the next trough. 'He'd be with …'

'Harper.'

'Yeah.' Sweet little Harper. He didn't know what came over him last night, to stalk her like that, especially when they'd agreed on her terms of employment as the nanny. But she was also a female who'd taunted him in her nightgown last night, alone in the dark.

He had to have another shower—a cold one—after their encounter in the kitchen last night.

But he'd make sure to leave the pantry light on at night from now on, so Harper never had to stumble around in the dark again. He even found some water bottles, which he'd left inside the fridge for her to find, too.

'Have you seen your son today?' Ryder's voice was like cold steel, grating through Ash's thoughts.

'Nah. You told me to do the troughs, so I'm doing the troughs.'

'I also asked you for that list about the troughs.'

'I'm getting there.' He was lucky they only had a few troughs to check, because they didn't have that many cattle. Then he caught a plume of dust rising on the corner of the camera lens. He steered the drone around to discover it was a four-wheel drive coming down the track. 'Hey, Ryder, we've got a car coming.'

'Who?'

'No one I know.'

'I'll check the cameras are working.' Ryder's heavy boot tread moved to the porch table where Dex was throwing back a beer as he rocked in his chair, while Cap sorted out water buckets for the dogs. 'Cap, it's testing time for Sarge. We've got an incoming car.'

The thick dog chain rattled and clanged as it hit the cement, with the lethal-looking shepherd whining with eagerness to be free.

'Where's Mason?' Cap asked.

Ash shrugged. Harper was right, he was avoiding Mason. But every time he saw the boy an invisible weight crushed his shoulders, making it hard to breathe. Only twenty-four days to go.

Sarge leaped off the verandah and started barking. He was a mean-looking dog with a deep bark.

'We can presume the boy is with the nanny.' Ryder picked up his tablet and tapped on the screen. 'It's a driver only. Not a cop.'

'It's got some government emblem on the sides.' Ash focused on the small screen in the centre of his handheld controls. He steered his drone to follow the car down their driveway that was as long and straight as an airstrip, filled with deep pockets of bulldust and jagged rivets washed out from the wet season.

'Hey, can that grader fix the driveway?' He remembered how Harper's car had struggled when she'd first arrived. He'd made sure she had her fancy car parked in the shed to protect it from the sun, right next to his ute.

'The grader would level that driveway like butter. But one job at a time, brother.' Dex leaned in closer to Ryder, watching his tablet, while Cap watched over his dogs, especially Sarge, who stood in a tough stance in the centre, bristling with muscles. 'Can you tell what department the car is from?'

'Nah.' Ash worked the drone's dials to zoom in for a closer look. 'It's got government plates, too.'

'Take that drone higher and see if there are any other cars in the area,' commanded Ryder, sounding like an army sergeant. Ryder had never said what his rank was, or ever talked about his time in the military. He didn't talk much about anything other than work, rarely sleeping. But without Ryder, they'd never have this place.

'Will do, boss.' Ash grinned, pulling back the dials and increased the speed on the drone and it powered over the property. He could hear it now, the bee-like sound growing louder as the drone gave him a superb view of the entire homestead. 'No way! Did you know there's a massive vegetable garden at the back of the caretaker's cottage? And a pizza oven and an outdoor TV.'

'VISITORS!' Charlie's voice carried over from the long shed that stretched out from behind the caretaker's cottage. The place was deceiving, with that corrugated fence running along two sides.

'*We know, Charlie.*' Ryder waved to the elderly caretaker. 'Charlie is going to give himself a heart attack if he keeps running like that.'

'Hey, I found the kid.' Ash smiled at the image projected through the goggles. 'He's with Harper and Bree ...' He sighed at the sight of Harper, in her summer dress, shading her eyes as she pointed at the drone, saying something to Bree. Harper was so pretty with her dark hair shimmering like water. Zooming in on the camera lens he panned over her figure.

Then something caught his eye.

'Oh, no. Bree just pulled out a rifle with a scope.' He steered the drone out of there fast, while ripping off his goggles to shout from the corner of the verandah. '*Don't shoot the drone, Bree! It's mine.*'

Dex chuckled. 'I'd really like that woman if she didn't scare me so much.'

Between the barking dogs, the drone's noisy whirl, it was chaos when the troop carrier arrived.

Cap approached the vehicle, holding on to Sarge's collar. 'Can I help you, mate?'

'I'm a government courier with a delivery for the owners of Elsie Creek Station.' He held out a large manila envelope.

Ash zoomed the drone's camera towards the back of the vehicle to find it full of open office crates holding assorted manila envelopes.

'That'd be me.' Cap took the envelope.

'Have a nice day.' The courier turned the vehicle around and headed back the way it came.

'What is it?' Dex asked as Cap ripped open the envelope.

'You should lock that front gate.' Charlie huffed and puffed, dragging his boots up the porch.

'We need to fix it first. And I think we should only lock it when no one is home.' Ryder tapped away on his tablet. 'But I'm adding the repairs to the list.'

'You're sounding like me, Ryder.' Ash grinned as he steered the drone high to watch the courier's dust trail, leading to the main road.

'No freaking way.' Cap scowled at the paperwork.

Dex snatched the letter. 'What the flip! Those mothers—' He let off a load of expletives.

'What's going on?' Ryder put the tablet back on the table.

Ash landed the drone safely on the dead grass. Scooping it up, he went to join his brothers as they gathered at the table.

'We've been served for water violations and ordered to produce an environmental impact study on the property.' Dex passed the paperwork to Ryder.

'What?' Ash asked.

Charlie pushed back the brim of his hat. 'You fixed the dam, that's what.'

'Now we know why they wrecked it.' Dex scowled. 'It's for the mine.'

'There is no mine on this side of the highway,' said Charlie. 'There's one on the other side of the highway. But not this side. It's all cattle country out here.'

'Well, according to this letter from the government, we're encroaching on the water rights of some mining lease.' Ryder dropped the paperwork onto the table and tapped away on his tablet. 'It's a new lithium mining lease.'

'What's that, a new gold?' Charlie asked.

'They use lithium for lithium-ion batteries,' explained Ash. 'You'll find those batteries in nearly all of today's tech, from phones, computers, electric toothbrushes and power tools, even electric cars. Almost everything that can get recharged has a lithium battery, like Ryder's tablet there, and my drone.'

'Please tell me we don't have a mine setting up shop at our back door?' Cap dropped into his seat, as the fear grew in his eyes. 'Mines destroy the land, poison the water, they create a horrible impact on the environment, and on the wildlife—'

'Calm down, Cap.' Ryder dragged out his phone. 'I'll make a few phone calls and see what we can do.'

'Well, brothers, we only have a few weeks to comply. Or we'll be copping fines up to one million dollars or two-thousand dollars. Per. Day.' Dex tapped on the paperwork.

'For our own water? You're kidding.' Ash snatched up the letter and tried to make sense of the mumbo jumbo. He didn't read government documents, he read instructions for tech tools. Not this. But he understood it was official, with a very threatening undertone to show they meant business.

'So now we know who wrecked the dam,' said Dex. 'And they're coming for us.'

Fourteen

Ever since the government had served notice over the water rights, the tension on Elsie Creek Station hung like a thick and cloying blanket, smothering the oppressive outback air.

With a heavy boot tread, Ryder constantly paced the verandah while speaking to lawyers over the phone. Dex just wanted to kill something. Cap shook his head, full of doom and gloom while going on about the impact on the environment. And Ash tried to pretend everything was okay as he played with his drone.

If Harper didn't dislike them so much, she might have felt sorry for them.

To be honest, they hadn't told her anything. It was only from their arguments that Harper had been able to piece together what was going on.

It was also none of her business. After all, she was just the nanny, doing her best to avoid them all. Lately she'd even been ensuring she took a water bottle to bed, so she'd never bump into Ash alone in the dark again. She was only here for Mason.

Who was gone, *again*!

'Mason?' She peeked down the corridor of closed doors that led to the bedrooms and bathroom. The lounge room was a maze full of boxes, but the small boy was nowhere in sight. 'Ruby?'

The labrador gave a short sharp bark, but it was coming from outside.

A tremendous crash of aluminium cans splashed across the verandah, followed by a boyish giggle.

Mason.

She pushed open the kitchen screen door that led to the side verandah, which faced the sheds. Ruby wagged her tail as she sat on the verandah where Mason was happily pushing over another box of empty beer cans that spilled everywhere.

'Ash?' The first words she'd spoken to him in days.

'Yeah …' Not even a few metres away, Ash stood on the dead grass wearing thick goggles, holding the controls for his drone that was nowhere in sight.

'You need childproof locks for the doors in the house. And can you please find somewhere else to leave the garbage? I'm not cleaning that mess up.'

'But—'

'I'm not a housekeeper. It's your beer. Your problem.'

He didn't even bother looking at her, his eyes hidden behind those oversized goggles.

'You can help yourself if you want one, then it'll be your beer, too.' He shared a grin while focused on something else.

'I don't like beer.'

'Maybe you should. It'd get rid of that stick up your—'

'What did you say?' She crossed her arms over her chest, tapping her foot on the verandah's floorboards.

Finally, he peered over the goggles. But only for a moment, to pin her with a look that was full of annoyance. 'Leave me a note for whatever it is you said.'

'Childproof locks. Mason is getting into the fridge—'

'Okay, okay.' He ripped off his goggles. 'You don't need to *harp* on it, Harper.'

'Finally, someone said it.' The evil chuckle came from Dex, pulling out a beer from the nearby beer fridge. 'I'd shout you a beer, Harper, but then you don't like beer. And we don't do wine for whiners.'

'I've had enough of you!' She pointed at Dex, sick of his constant snide remarks, and the way he kept betting against her. She'd made it through the first week—barely—and now he'd extended the bet to the end of the month.

'Just who do you think you are?' She snarled at the bully.

Dex leaned against the fridge, wearing that smirk she wanted to slap off his face. 'Why don't you tell me? I'm all ears.'

'Whoa, whoa, whoa … Easy, Harper.' Ash rushed to put himself in between her and Dex.

'Are you defending him?' She stabbed at the air over Ash's shoulder, aiming at public enemy number one.

'No. I was just trying to protect you from Dex.'

That made her blink.

Dex just chuckled as he walked away.

Arsehole.

Ryder kept pacing back and forth. His constant heavy boot steps were driving her insane as he remained oblivious to, or uncaring of, Dex's smugness and her anger.

'Harper?' Ash lowered his voice, as his callused palm gripped her arm to drag her further away from the brothers. 'Dex is doing that to tick you off on purpose.'

She pulled herself free from his grip. 'So he can win the freaking bet?'

Ash's brow ruffled, keeping one eye on the drone's handheld monitor. 'I told him it was wrong.'

'Did anyone else make a bet about me?'

He shrugged. 'They're not discussing it in front of me.'

'Why should you care?' She narrowed her eyes at him.

His side glance was like a shot of heat to the heart. It made her swallow air.

'Mason likes you. He's happy and …' Raking fingers through his thick hair, his eyes darted to his brothers, before returning his focus to the drone's controls. But his voice became soft and low. 'I haven't got a clue what I'm doing when it comes to …'

'Your son?'

The nod was so minimal she'd almost missed it. But his admission had her heart aching for him, and for Mason, the little boy who needed his father.

'I don't know what I'm doing, either.' Especially these feelings she had for Ash, who now had his back to her. She had to admire his straight shoulders and strong back, and how it narrowed to the waist of his dusty jeans that cupped his butt beautifully.

'You're doing a helluva lot better than me.' He expertly steered the drone to buzz over their heads, where it slowly descended to land on the dry lawn.

The cans clanged loudly as Mason rushed towards the drone, just out of her reach. 'Mason?'

'Gotcha.' Coming from the laundry end of the house, Cap nabbed Mason by the back of his tiny jeans. 'Look at you, making a racket out here.' He scooped up the boy to tickle the toddler's tummy. Mason's laughter filled the air. 'Watch those blades on that drone, Ash.'

'I know.' He picked up his drone to make sure it didn't end up a child's toy.

'Come on, Mason. You can help me clean up these cans and we'll find somewhere to store them, until I go to the recycling centre.' Cap crouched beside the small boy and started throwing the cans like a game.

Finally, someone was doing something about the rubbish, as well as bothering to spend time with the boy.

'Ash, you need childproof locks for the house. Please.' Harper felt like she was nagging and hated how she sounded. Dex was right, she had become a whiner.

'Did Bree suggest it?' Ash put his drone on top of the outdoor beer fridge to recharge.

'Yes.' Bree knew everything about children. But right now, she needed to plead her case. 'Look, Mason is crawling into everything. Even though there is nothing in the kitchen cupboards, it's the fridge I'm worried about the most.' She pointed to the beer fridge. 'Mason is small enough to climb inside the fridges and hide, where we won't be able to hear him if the door closes. He could suffocate.'

Ash and Cap stopped what they were doing. Even Ryder

had stopped pacing. And for the first time she had the rare attention of all four men. They looked at her, then at the boy, then at the rattly beer fridge. She could hear them thinking.

'Ash, there's a small gate latch and some plywood in the shed you can use to block the kitchen door,' said Ryder. 'We'll keep the front glass doors shut from here on out.'

'I spotted some old lock hasps in the shed. I'll pop rivet them to the fridges high enough that even if that kid climbs on a chair, he won't open those fridges for a few years.' Dex jumped off the porch with dust kicking up behind his boots. 'I'll find the drill for you, Ash.'

Ash, Ryder, and Dex had scattered, leaving her with Cap and Mason, who were still picking up empty cans. It was crisis management in a whole new way.

At least they were doing something for the safety of the boy, but it also showed how much they cared. Finally.

'I'll help.' Now that Ash had gone, she felt foolish for her dummy spit. At least she got a reaction out of them.

'How are you doing?' Cap asked, as he dumped the empty cans back into the box.

Harper shrugged. 'Honestly, I'm not used to living with anyone.'

'Me neither.'

'Didn't you grow up with a stack of siblings?'

'As kids, sure. Having four brothers and two sisters made for an interesting childhood. But I've been out of home for a long time. It's usually just me and the dogs.'

Scout, the beagle, pushed its way through the cans to sit on Harper's foot, leaning into her for a pat. The beagle always came up to her for a pat, just like Ruby did. Unlike the muster dogs that lay on the dirt in the shade, who kept their distance. But they were all working dogs, not pets, so she'd been told.

Still, it didn't stop her from sneaking treats to Ruby and Scout. When home alone with Mason, she'd even use a broom to slide a bowl of goodies across the old floorboards to Sarge, where the regal-looking shepherd stayed at the corner of the house, keeping watch. But he'd wag his tail at her, even though he never left his post, like a good soldier.

'Is it true this beagle was a police dog?' She couldn't imagine it, especially when the beagle was so friendly.

'Scout was a drug dog, who worked for the Federal Police and Customs. She did the airports.'

'How did you end up with her?'

'Scout got hit across her nose during a drug bust.'

'Is she okay?' Her heart squeezed for the poor thing, who only leaned into her leg for a cuddle. It was like the dog could read her moods, making her a wonderful companion for keeping the loneliness away.

'Scout's fine. She's a little gun-shy, and she's not good with crowds anymore, like crowded airports. But her sense of smell did sustain some damage. Or she's faking it so she could quit the job.'

'What do you think?'

'Scout can still follow a scent. She's helped the local police with a kidnapping case.'

'How did it go?'

'It was a happy ending.' Cap patted Scout. 'Like Scout, here. She's living the dream, now.'

'Are you?' So where was her happily ever after? Why couldn't she live the dream where her true love saved her from cooking disasters and bad hair-days, while living in a world free from fear and only filled with love?

Cap smiled at the area of dead grass with a view of the sheds. It wasn't much, but the way he looked at the place, you'd think he was looking at paradise. 'I am. Let's just hope we get to keep it with the mine wanting our water.' He stood, brushing off his jeans. 'Come on, little fella,' he said, scooping up Mason. 'Let's go pinch your dad's ute and load up these empty cans. Where do you think we should put the cans?'

'Can you dump them all over Dex's bed?'

Cap chuckled as he lifted Mason to sit on his shoulders. 'That's a good idea. We can just blame Mason.' He then paused. 'Hey, Harper?'

'Yeah?'

'You're doing a good job. We might not say it, but we appreciate what you do.'

She clutched her throat as her wounded soul filled with gratitude. 'Thank you.' Cap was such a sweetie, it was hard to believe he was from the same bloodline as Dex and Ryder.

'I'm glad you found us some salads for tucker.'

'I can't burn a salad, can I?' But she was having cooking lessons with Bree, who had escaped into town with Charlie today.

Harper wanted to go to town, too. But she didn't know where the child's car seat was or how to even fit one in her car. It felt like a ploy to keep her here as the ageing fairy princess, dumped by political garden elves who'd moved on to greener pastures, leaving her in this dust bowl of day-to-day drudgery. But she had to remember she came here by choice.

'Can you tell Ash it's his turn to cook dinner?' Cap nodded, carrying an excited Mason over his shoulders, while the dogs followed him like he was the Pied Piper.

The brothers were all so different. But they all cared for this country and for their family. She just didn't get the bit about the country, it looked like a barren wasteland to her—except for the view from Bree's backyard.

Just then she spotted another vehicle coming down the long dusty driveway. With no one else around, Sarge gave out his deep warning bark. Did she dare?

'VISITORS!'

Fifteen

Ash rummaged through the workshop's containers of nuts and bolts to find the sliding locks. Now all he needed was the screws. 'Hey, Dex?'

'Yeah.' At the other bench, Dex grabbed the drill.

'Can you do me a favour and get off Harper's back?'

Dex turned around, wearing a cheesy, know-it-all, smart-arse grin. The kind of grin he used to stir up his opponents in the illegal fighting pits. 'You're not, are you?'

'What are you on about, now?'

'Falling for the nanny.'

'I am not.' Ash jutted out his jaw. 'I think she's snooty.'

'That's a nice way of calling Princess Harper a toffee-nosed—'

'Stop. Right now.' He scowled at his older brother, the professional bare-knuckle fighting champion. But the protectiveness he had over Harper was strong. 'I mean it.'

'Why?'

'For Mason's sake. The kid adores her, more than me.' He sighed, hating to admit that Mason preferred Harper, even Cap, over him.

'Maybe if you'd bothered to spend time with the kid, he'd like you too.'

'I don't know how. He's a kid.' He still got that squeezing sensation around his rib cage, whenever he looked at the boy. It put him off.

'You're the biggest kid I know, I don't see any problem.'

'I do.' Eighteen days and counting.

'Listen, brother, at his age, Mason will look up to you no matter who you are. And if you don't stuff it up, he'll look up to you for the rest of your life.'

'Do you look up to Dad?'

'Dad's Dad.' Dex shrugged as he flicked through a toolbox searching for the drill bits. 'Dad treated us well. He took the time to hang out with us and teach us things. Now it's your turn. You've got that drone, put the goggles on the kid and let him see. Or do what Cap's doing, just taking the kid for a walk, or let him help by picking up cans. Kids don't see our faults. Not at that age.'

'How come you know all about this? Have you got some child hidden in the closet we don't know about?'

Dex's face was sullen. The cocky shine of mischief in his eyes was replaced by a deep, deep sadness. 'I know, okay. I just do. That kid is your son, and it's about time you stepped up and started being his father.'

'VISITORS!'

'Was that Harper?' Ash spun around to face the farmhouse. His heart skipped a beat, worried for her. But she was okay, pointing down the driveway.

'What is this place, flipping Grand Central Station?' Dex mumbled, carrying an assortment of tools.

Ash jiggled the tools and the sheet of plywood under his arm. 'Hey, Dex?'

'What?'

'Leave Harper alone.'

'I moved out, didn't I.'

'You know what I mean. Harper knows about the bet.' Ash grabbed his older brother by the upper arm that was nothing but solid muscle. 'I mean that. Leave. Harper. Alone.' The depth of his warning echoed around them.

'I'll steer clear of the nanny. But I'm not cancelling that bet, it's up to two hundred now.'

'Who with?'

'Obviously not with you.' Dex grinned over his shoulder as they approached the house, just as a stocky work ute parked in the yard.

Cap carted Mason on his shoulders back to the farmhouse, where the boy was greeted by the nanny. Harper gave the small boy his own special smile, before she carried him into the house for dinner.

For the first time Ash felt a different twinge in his ribs, as if something was fighting against the pressure. It had him wanting to walk across that dead grass to go hang out with Harper and Mason in the kitchen. But that was impossible.

Especially since Harper was doing her best to avoid him ever since he'd stupidly hit on her that night. She was here for Mason. Anyone could see that. And Ash also noticed how attached Mason was to Harper.

Did he want that same kind of attention? But from who, Harper or Mason? Or both?

'What's got you shoutin' at me for, old fella?' The middle-aged man climbed out of the cab of his work ute. Sliding on a well-worn stockman's hat, he casually patted Sarge like he was a puppy.

'Some killer guard dog, that is,' mumbled Dex.

'It's Jonathan.' Ash pointed at their baby brother climbing out of the passenger side of the ute, hoisting a beer carton over his shoulder before leading the big man in the bigger hat to the verandah, where Ryder was there to greet them.

'Everyone, this here is the Station Hand.' Jonathan pointed at the man with grey flecks in his hair, and suntanned skin like leather, dressed in dusty jeans, and a pair of crocodile-leather boots. It was *the* Station Hand.

Everyone knew about the Station Hand. He was a legendary stockman, one of the best mustering contractors in the country, who'd taught thousands the trade of running cattle.

'Ron's the name.' Ron's hands were huge, full of calluses, giving them a firm shake. He was as big as Ryder, with an air of authority around him, as he cracked open a beer. 'I hear there's some new mine after your water?'

'I told him.' Jonathan handed out a round of beers. 'They

haven't hit us over our water yet. Our cousin, Monet, is going to do a flyover to suss out the mine to see who it'll affect.'

'Your station won't be affected.' Ryder shifted the many maps that covered the table. 'Sandlot Station gets the river run-off from Elsie Creek herself. So do all these stations, here. We don't. Our land has the headwater that runs into Elsie Creek with another river that runs all the way to the sea.'

'Which is why you lot got the name,' said Ron. 'You've also got the river from the run-off, courtesy of the escarpment and Cattleman's Keep. Pretty spot that peak is.'

'The reason I've asked Ron to visit is because he was my consultant when Mandy and I invested in Sandlot. Ron knows Elsie Creek Station.'

'You've mustered here?' Ryder asked the Station Hand.

'I did. With Darcie, the old owner, and ol' Splinter. Where is Charlie Splint?'

'Gone into town with Bree,' said Ash.

'Pity it's not Saturday, Charlie would have his pizza oven happening. Have you been to one of his pizza nights at the caretaker's cottage?'

'No. We've been busy trying to get the place sorted out.' Ryder's frown was filthy as he sat at the head of the table. 'Do you know anything about this mine?'

'No one does, it's that new. But when Jonathan told us what was happening, it got a lot of other local cattlemen worried that their water may also be under threat, too. We don't want to be like them southern farmers who pay for water from a river that runs right past them.'

'But we have a river that starts here. At this station,' said Dex. 'What I don't get is how they can claim we're infringing on their water rights.'

Ron shrugged his beefy shoulders. 'What did you boys do differently?'

'We fixed the dam they broke.' Dex scowled, crossing arms over his toned chest.

Ron narrowed his eyes at Dex. 'Can you prove it?'

'I wish. What's stopping them from wrecking it again?

Think about it, we've just fixed the dam, which Charlie said hasn't been working for six months. We've reduced the water flow.'

'When did the mining lease start?' Jonathan asked.

Ryder shuffled through the paperwork. 'Nine months ago.'

'How long was Elsie Creek Station up for sale?'

'A year,' replied Ron. 'Not long after Darcie passed. Elsie Creek Station might be on the smaller scale where land mass is concerned, but she's pristine cattle country with plenty of good Mitchell grass plains.'

'Not without water.' Jonathan sighed, dropping his elbows onto his thighs. 'I know the issues we had about water at Sandlot Station. Hey, I should bring Flo out here to do some water divining for you guys.'

'Elsie Creek Station has plenty of water. Always has,' said Ron. 'But if you've got a mine nearby, they could tap into the underground artesian water basins, which is what runs everyone's bores.'

'Oh, no.' Cap moaned, dragging his palms down his face as if living some horror story. 'Mines drain water basins, or contaminate them, rendering them useless. I can give you the data to prove this. It's a well-known fact.'

That quietened them down.

'Do you have any cattle?' Ron asked. 'I know Darcie's son stripped the place bare.'

'Were you in on that?' Dex asked bluntly.

'Absolutely not.' Ron crossed his arms over his beefy chest. 'We all knew what Darcie wanted for this station's future and have a lot of respect for Charlie sticking to Darcie's wishes. None of us locals took part in Darcie's son stripping the place like that.'

'To our advantage, it lowered the buying price,' said Ryder, as the money man.

'Brother, we bought a cattle station with no cattle,' said Dex, wearing his typical scowl. 'So, Ron, if you didn't muster the cattle, who did?'

'Darcie's son hired a mob of musterers from Queensland.' Ron slowly shook his head with sadness. 'Darcie would've rolled over in his grave for that.' He took a long pull of his beer, wiping his mouth with the back of his hand. 'Didn't that mob leave you with any cattle?'

'We've got a small herd we've paddocked here ...' Ryder tapped on the station's map. 'But we've just learned there's *maybe* a thousand head in this place called Wombat Flats.' None of them were letting their hopes get too far ahead until they saw it for themselves, and the condition of the cattle, too.

Ron adjusted his hat that hid his raised eyebrows. 'Sheez. What are they doing out there?'

The brothers said nothing, for Charlie's sake.

Ron gave a deep chuckle. 'I get it, I do. I bet Charlie hid some cattle out there, to not leave the place bare. It's what I'd do if I was in that situation. And I bet that bugger picked the best stock too.'

'Are you sure about the quality of that cattle?' Ryder narrowed his eyes at Ron. 'Charlie said they were scrubbers. Ferals.'

Ron grinned. 'Listen, fellas, Charlie is an old-school stockman who always talked down his herd's quality, like poker players who don't like to reveal their hand in a game. Trust me, Charlie would have kept a prime herd out there. He's been breeding the stock on this property for over fifty years, he knows quality, and would do his best to make sure he kept the best.'

Ash looked at his brothers. They had a herd. A good one. He could feel the hope building, not only in himself but in his brothers, too. 'This is good news, right?'

Even Ryder nodded.

'Do you know who helped Charlie muster that herd?' Ron asked.

'His granddaughter,' replied Ryder in his deep voice.

'Bree. Good kid. Helps my daughter out.'

'How so?'

Ron looked at them for a moment. 'Do you know

anything about the caretakers, and who Charlie is?'

'We know he was head stockman before he retired, but I'd guess he did some rodeoing from the way he walks,' replied Ryder.

'You'd be correct. Charlie *Splinter* Splint was a champion bull rider.'

'No way.' Ash and Jonathan spoke with wide eyes.

'Charlie started as a kid, following his old man and their family trade, where he used to blunt the horns on a bull for the rodeos, to not hurt the beast or its rider. And he was good at it. Quick, painless, and done in record time. Wasn't long and he was riding the things, following the rodeo circuit, until he got the wrong end of a bull one day.' Ron sat back. 'Darcie gave Charlie the caretaker's cottage when Charlie got hurt. Charlie's wife, Bea, nursed him back to health so he could ride again. He never rode another bull, but he was a damned good stockman. Still is. And when Charlie became head stockman here, the place flourished, giving this place a good name in the cattle industry. I know from firsthand experience how good Charlie is. He taught me a trick or two in my time, especially with branding.'

'Yeah, well, he's got our brand and holding it for ransom.' Dex snarled behind his beer as he rocked in his chair.

Ron chuckled. 'And that ol' bugger will probably keep it until he dies. Unless you come up with an offer he can't refuse.'

'How can he keep my brothers' brand, Ron?' Jonathan asked.

'Because back in the day, a cattle brand was a family keepsake. A legacy brand is what you hand down from generation to generation, and Charlie's father was a master brand maker.'

'For real?'

Ron nodded. 'Charlie and his father made all the brands for the entire North. And now Bree does it too, when she's not concocting a batch of witch potions for my daughter.'

'What?' Ash blurted out as his brothers raised their

eyebrows. 'Bree's a witch?'

'Bree distils herbs and makes cooking oils that my daughter sells online. Bush herbs.'

'Any other herbs?' Dex's mischievous grin grew.

'Bree does make a wicked green ant gin. My wife, Queen Elizabeth, loves Bree's rosella gin. I always order a crate when she makes a batch.'

'Bree's been holding out on us.' Ash looked back at the distant caretaker's cottage.

'That's a lot of grog. Is that legal?' Dex asked.

'Since when do you care if it's legal?' Jonathan playfully punched Dex's shoulder.

'If we're looking at legal action, I want nothing that could affect us.' Ryder stabbed at the map spread across the table. 'The caretakers don't own this place, we do.'

'Well, if there's an issue with the dam and the water rights, you'll wanna get that herd of cattle out of Wombat Flats, pronto.' Ron peered over the map. 'Because if that dam is now refilling, and if those mongrels decide to tear it down again, it's going to cause a flash flood through the Stoneys and out to—'

'Wombat Flats.'

'It looks like you mob are about to do a muster. But be warned fellas, that's stockhorse-only country. I hope you've all got decent saddles and know how to whirl a stockwhip.'

Sixteen

It was two in the morning when Harper woke to a faint cry. She bounded out of bed and rushed into the next room. Inside, under the faint glow of a night-light, lay Mason in his cot, thrashing around, having a nightmare.

'Shh, little one, it's okay. I'm right here.' She rubbed the boy's back, as Ruby pressed her nose against Harper's leg. Concern filled the sensitive dog's eyes.

'You too, Ruby. Everything will be okay.' She patted the dog's head.

'Is he okay?' It was Ash at the door. Thankfully in jeans and a T-shirt and not a towel.

She nodded, turning back to focus on the boy.

'What's wrong with him?'

'Nightmare.'

'How can someone that young get nightmares?'

'I don't know.' She shrugged. 'Nightmares can come for no reason.'

Ash stared at her for a long second as if trying to read her. 'You have nightmares.'

She did, ever since the bomb blast. 'Don't you?'

'No.' He shook his head. 'Maybe stress attacks.' Shoving his hands in his pockets, he lifted his shoulders high in an awkward shrug. 'Forget I said that.' He went to leave.

She grabbed his arm. 'What are you stressed about?'

He shook his head, looking at her hand on his arm.

She let go, but she wasn't letting go of this conversation, especially when conversations were so rare these days. 'Is it about the station?'

'No. Normally, I'm never stressed over anything.'

'So, what is it then?'

His dark eyes left hers to focus on the cot, he stepped back as if to keep his distance.

'Your son?' She'd never heard Ash call the boy that.

Ash gave a curt nod as the apple in his throat worked as if trying to fight the words that gushed out, 'It squeezes my rib cage so bad it hurts to breathe. But it's getting better.' He rubbed his lower chest as if suffering with a bad case of heartburn.

'Is that why you're avoiding your son?' She'd thought Ash was avoiding her, but apparently it was Mason.

He rubbed a rough hand over his face as if to rewind this conversation. 'It's stupid. Forget it, okay?' Again, he went to turn away.

'No.' She grabbed his hand, forcing him to stand beside her. 'Look at him.'

'I don't want to.'

'Why not?'

'I don't want to mess him up.'

'What do you mean?'

'I'd never own this station without my brothers. I suck at responsibility and that,' he said, pointing to the sleeping child, 'is the biggest responsibility a man can have. I didn't ask for it, Harper.'

'I know. Most new fathers have nine months to prepare for the responsibility. How much time did you get?'

'I didn't get any.' He rubbed the back of his neck, the burden evident in the bend of his shoulders. 'So, I'm not overreacting?'

'No. You just never had time to prepare.' She rubbed his back in slow circles like she did for Mason. 'The thing is, Mason didn't ask for it either. I bet his nightmare is about his mother not being here and how much he misses her. When he could be having happy dreams, discovering the pure joy of what it's like to have a father.'

'How was your dad?'

'The best. I was a total daddy's girl.' She gave him a shy smile. 'You?'

'I was closer to my mother. She had to keep me in line.'

Harper arched an eyebrow at him.

'Don't you judge and get all snooty on me, missy.' He playfully tapped her nose, surprising her so much she gave a girlish giggle.

'I let my mother control my bank accounts for my wage, so she'd put some of it away for me to save.'

'Nothing wrong with that. My mother did the same for me until I got used to doing it myself.' Harper then admitted, 'Sometimes when I'm shopping, I still hear my mother's voice telling me to put down that pair of shoes and back away from the store.'

'I get that sometimes when I'm buying computer games.' They shared a grin. He then looked at her. Like really looked at her, with none of that sleazy flirtiness from the man whose own brothers said he went through women in droves.

But when he lowered his head, his dark hair fell across his forehead in an oddly endearing way, exposing a whole new side to Ash, and it was hot.

She curled her hand into a fist, to stop herself from reaching out to run her fingers through his hair. The blood rushed in her ears, and electricity seemed to build in the air. But she wasn't here for Ash.

'Stay for a while.' Gripping his wrist, she placed his hand on the cot's side rail.

'And do what?'

'Nothing. Just look at him. He's your son. You need to accept that, because once you do, I promise you, it'll be one of the greatest gifts that life offers.'

'How do you know that?'

'Because it's what my father used to say about me, and I've heard other parents say that about their children. Mason doesn't need much, all he wants is your time. And the thing is, time moves so fast, one day you could blink, and they're gone.' She stared at the slumbering child, so small and peaceful, her heart ached to hold him. 'Moments like these, we don't know how precious they truly are.'

She gazed up at him, trying to control her own emotions, but it was a struggle. Time had always been her enemy, where there was never enough or she was too busy trying to recapture what time had stolen from her. Yet being on this station was like living in a hidden world that created its own rules about time, spending time with Mason and Bree, learning a whole new way to use time.

'Now I'm the one rambling.' She exhaled heavily, feeling heat brush over her cheeks.

'No, you're not rambling, Harper.' The way he said her name—a little deeper, with a little more gravel in his tone—made her heart quicken.

She focused on Mason and not the dreamy guy with dark eyes watching her.

'You know, all this little boy wants is to be part of a family, and you need to welcome him, Ash.' Unsure if she was saying the right thing, but she was hoping to convince him to bond with Mason for both their sakes.

'How?'

'Simply by spending time with him. Don't be like me, where you suddenly wake up in a place and feel like everything is gone because you were chasing time. Time spent with family, and with friends is more precious. The memories you create will last a lifetime.'

'You have a thing for time, don't you.' He tapped on his wrist. 'I noticed you're not wearing your watch anymore.'

He noticed her. Why did that make her tummy swirl with giddy glee? 'Bree made me take it off. I still keep it in my pocket.' They mirrored each other's grins. Only this time it came a little easier.

He was so close his manly aroma filled the air. He smelled so heavenly, like someone had taken every one of her secret dreamy desires, to then bottle it into an exclusive cologne that only her perfect dream guy would wear. Ash was that guy.

The only thing was, he knew he had some power over women and her. Especially the way his eyes dropped to her lips then rose back up to her eyes.

She headed for the safety of the door, but could feel his eyes tracking her across the room. 'And Ash?'

'Yeah?' He tilted his head, the soft light highlighted the bristles on his chin, accentuating his cheek bones. But his eyes were intense. Almost hungry.

'You will make a good father.'

He frowned at her, like she'd lost her marbles, instantly dousing that hunger in his eyes, as he stood straighter with hands in his pockets. 'How can you say that?'

'Because you still know how to play. You play on your drone, or your computer games. But you also understand what adult responsibility means.'

'Are you sure?'

'It's why you've been getting that constricted feeling in your chest. It's stress. And if you didn't care, you wouldn't be stressed with worry for your son, which is completely normal.'

Ash stared at her with widening eyes and slack jaw. He then cleared his throat. 'You won't say anything to my brothers about what I just said?'

'No. They don't talk to me.'

His frown shifted as if embarrassed for them.

'Hey, you must remember, they're not fathers, they're uncles. You're the father. And I know, deep down in my gut,' she said, patting her own stomach. 'You'll do great at it, too. You just have to try.'

'What if I fail? Make mistakes?'

'Every father does. My dad did. Didn't yours?'

Ash nodded. 'I like the man, but I don't want to be like him. Is that wrong to say?'

'No. It's the most honest thing I've heard you say.'

He reached out and gently stroked her hair, she almost sighed at the tenderness of his touch. 'I know.' He pulled his hand back fast. 'Boundaries.'

'Yeah, boundaries.' The boss-to-employee kind of boundaries, that were getting harder to maintain.

'Thank you, Harper.'

'You might hate me later, so hold your thanks for now, and focus on you and Mason.' She closed the door behind her, hoping, just hoping, he'd connect with Mason before it was time for her to leave.

And then she'd come clean with her secret.

Seventeen

Sitting on his bed, as the first sign of sunrise barely breached the escarpment, Ash slid on his jeans, then his boots. He stamped the floor, a lifelong habit to ensure they were on tight, and grabbed his shirt lying over his gamer's chair. He sniffed at it. Meh, it was clean enough to wear another day.

His computer screen came on with the movement, and he scanned over the emails and messages. He'd been up late last night, watching his kid sleep. His. Kid.

He shifted the mouse and put the PC to sleep. He was lucky if he'd had a few hours' sleep himself. Of course, he could play all night, and he'd still show up for the job he loved as a stockman, with the hope of sneaking in a nap sometime during the day.

But his brothers were having a meeting with Charlie this morning, to prepare for their first muster as the new owners of Elsie Creek Station. It was enough to create an excited energy to bristle through his veins like the ultimate sugar rush.

Talking about sugar, he opened his desk's bottom drawer, which was filled with assorted snacks perfect for late-night gaming sessions. He even had a small bar fridge next to his desk, stacked with more snacks and energy drinks. He wanted to make sure he was stocked up for the muster.

He dug through the goodie drawer filled with packets of red liquorice sticks, energy bars, and mints, when his fingers brushed against a red packet. It was shortbread.

He didn't eat shortbread, but he knew someone who did.

Kicking the drawer shut, he snuck across the hallway into the kitchen, where a coffee cup sat on the table. It was Harper's, who strangely enjoyed drinking cold black coffee.

He washed her cup out at the sink, dried it, then put it on top of the shortbread packet on the table.

He then grabbed his own mug and poured a hot cup from the coffeepot made earlier, by Ryder no doubt. Ryder rarely slept, but he drank a lot of coffee, then he'd pace the verandah with his heavy boot steps.

But then Ash didn't sleep much either, playing video games most nights.

He straightened the packet of biscuits, hoping she'd see it when she came into the kitchen.

'Morning.' It was Harper, dressed in a summer dress, slipping her hair into a ponytail.

'Uh …' Damn, she was pretty. 'Morning.'

Her pretty brown eyes dropped to the table. He pulled his hands away and stood straighter.

'Is that shortbread?' The shine in her eyes was like she'd swallowed the sun as she picked up the biscuit packet. 'Did you do this?'

He shrugged.

'Why?'

'At the supermarket when we were both looking for a miracle cure, you said shortbread was good for the soul.' He also remembered she'd called shortbread the food of the gods to cure tummy upsets, bad hair days, and break-ups.

'Why?' she asked again.

'Um …' He felt like an idiot, but the words spilled. 'I saw it on the shelf when I stocked up for my sugar stash in my desk. And, well, you said last night that you suffered with nightmares, too. And I thought it might help.' He enjoyed doing these little things for Harper to make her time easier at the station.

Her hand clutched her delicate throat, and her eyes got all glassy. 'Thank you.' She may have whispered it, but he felt it hammer deep into his soul. Gratitude on this woman was stunning.

He had to turn away, using the excuse of pouring her a cup of coffee. 'I bet it tastes better with hot coffee, too?'

'Thank you.' She dragged out her chair. 'Is it wrong to eat one for breakfast?'

He didn't need to reply. She'd already expertly torn open the package and was offering him some. 'I bought them for you.'

'You have a sugar stash. And this is buttery sugar. Take one. I don't mind sharing.' But then she wrapped her kissable lips around the butter-coloured biscuit, her eyes closed, and she moaned with pleasure.

It punched straight to his groin. He dropped into the nearest seat, just to watch her eat. The coffee was too hot, but he didn't care as he took a deep mouthful to stop his mouth watering as she took another bite. She brushed the crumbs from her lips, that he wanted to lick off before crushing her lips with his.

Back off, brother, the lady has boundaries.

'So, what was your nightmare about?'

Didn't that kill her joy? Swapping it with a thick layer of sadness.

'Sorry, I shouldn't have … I just thought that …' Ash had no idea what he was doing. Which was unusual, when he always knew what to say to the ladies.

Yet, conversations with Harper were unlike anything he'd come across, that only fuelled his need for more. 'What you did for me—last night—I don't feel like such a mongrel for what I've been feeling about Mason.'

'So I made sense?'

He nodded. 'I may be a lot of things, but I keep a lot of stuff private. Especially from my brothers, who treat me like I'm still the little kid who raced after them back home.'

'I can keep secrets, too.' She sipped on her coffee. Then reached for another shortbread, pushing the packet across the table as if to stop the temptation. 'I don't know what it's like growing up with siblings. Must have been nice.'

'It was chaotic. I used to idolise my oldest brothers, Dex and Ryder. They were like the cool kids at school, and I'd chase after them, wanting to be like them. But now, as adults, the only thing we have in common is the station and that we're stockmen with a different set of skills.' He had no idea why he'd confessed that to her.

But the look she gave him wasn't a snobby, judgy one. It was a look of concern.

Or was he confusing that with care?

'If you want to share …' He shrugged. 'Like that nightmare?'

She sipped on her coffee, her dainty fingers toying with the handle of her mug. 'It's the same one … I, um …' She inhaled heavily.

Ash didn't move. He wanted to hear this story.

'I'd survived this car bombing—'

'Where?' He sat straighter, leaning towards her, his stomach twisted in worry for her.

'Belgium. Just before I came out here …' She looked so frail, so vulnerable, staring at her fingers. 'My nightmare keeps replaying those final few moments. I hear my heels on the pavement, passing this small store, and through the window I spotted these biscuits on the shelf.' She tapped the red packet of shortbread. 'My work colleagues teased me for wasting time when they climbed into the car to wait for me. I told them I'd only be a quick minute, ducking into the store to buy a packet of this shortbread.' She held up her half-eaten, creamy-coloured biscuit in her slender fingers.

Ash reached over and gently covered her other hand with his. His thumb brushed over the back of her hand, as he gave her a nod to continue.

'The bell over the shop door tinkles. A guy whizzes past on his pushbike. A motorbike starts. Our work car's back door is open, my work colleague scoots across the seat to give me room to climb inside. And then …' Her voice dropped as her bottom lip trembled. He squeezed her hand to help soothe her. 'The driver turns the key, and there's this click, and it's like time stops ...'

Her voice became a whisper, 'I feel this invisible wave of power hitting me, it lifts me out of my shoes from the blast. I never heard the explosion, just this ringing in my ears. But then the wind slams me against the shop's wall as dust and glass rains down on me ... And that's when I wake up.' She bit on the biscuit, staring at her cup of black coffee, thoughtfully chewing.

'Were you hurt?'

'Concussion, stitches, and this ugly bald patch ...' She tapped the back of her head. 'I don't know if it's PTSD, or shell shock, but ever since I woke up in the hospital, the nightmares began.'

'Do you get them every night?'

She peered past him to the open kitchen screen door with a view of the soft, shell-pink skyline, announcing sunrise. 'Coming out here, they slowed down. Time, right? Heals all wounds.'

'You would mention time, being a clock-watcher.' He winked at her and was rewarded with a soft smile, the heavy mood lifting. 'Talking about time, have you got a minute? I'd really like to run something past you.'

'About what?'

'This way.' He led her to his bedroom, then thought twice about it. His crap was everywhere. 'Excuse the mess.' Shifting one pile of clothes to the other.

She giggled, and it was such a sweet sound. 'Maid's day off, huh?'

'We hired a nanny, hoping she'd do that.'

'This nanny would willingly chip in to pay for a maid. Cleaning is so brutal.' She held up her small hands, bleached clean. 'Wow, is this your sugar stash?'

Ash must have kicked the drawer too hard because it stood open. 'I play games late.'

'I had one too.'

'For what?'

'Work. Chasing deadlines, sometimes we couldn't go home. This is impressive. Oh, I love those.' She pulled out the caramel chews.

She had a taste for such old things, like shortbread and caramels, dressing in a timeless wardrobe, but one of quality, that made her look polished but pretty, too.

'Help yourself, any time.'

'No. Shortbread is enough.' She pushed the drawer shut. 'What do you want to ask me?'

'You know I play games?'

'I can see that.' She tapped on his gamer's chair.

'I want to gamify the station somehow.'

She arched her eyebrows at him.

'The reason I'm talking to you is I need a sounding board over this idea, and if you've been to Belgium, you know what goes on out there in the world. My brothers, they're ...'

'Set in their ways?'

He nodded. 'Ryder wants to put in security cameras, and I was thinking about using those security cameras for the cattle.'

'Sounds fair.'

'But I want to create an in-house system accessing each paddock using those cameras.'

'You want to create an intranet?'

'We don't get internet access past the homestead.'

'No, in-*tra*-net. It's a private network companies use to securely share in-house data. I don't know how much information you'd need to store for a cattle station, but I know government departments have been effectively using intranets for decades.'

'So you've used intranets before?'

She nodded. 'If you want to gamify the station, having an intranet would allow for in-house wi-fi access to your cameras, making it a smart investment in the right direction.' She tapped his gaming chair. 'I've seen security teams watch large buildings all from their air-conditioned offices. To lock and unlock doors—'

'Like paddock gates?'

'To adjust the temperature in rooms.'

'Like adjusting water heights in water troughs, so I don't need to check on them all the time, especially if we're getting more cattle.'

She squinted up at him with a coy grin, but the shine, that spark was playful. It was a good look on her. 'You really hate that job, don't you?'

'Do you even know what that job is?' He smirked at her.

She shook her head, where her grin grew into a cheeky smile. It was adorable. It had to be in the top ten of her file of smiles.

'Thank you for your opinion, and for giving me a good idea of what I'm looking for.' And for smiling at him. What else could he do to get her to smile?

'I'm not a tech genius. I wouldn't know where you'd start setting up something like that, but I know how to use them.'

'I do. I enjoy playing with tech, and I've been thinking about it ever since Ryder wanted to put in cameras. There has to be a way we can use them for the station, to cut down on the need for burning fossil fuels to do the simple task of checking troughs. I'd estimate it'd save us thousands on diesel costs, wear and tear on the vehicles, and saving time—'

'I'm all for processes that save time on things.'

'Well, I'm hoping to use that time for other things.'

'Your drone would play a big part in that, too.'

'Exactly.' He nodded, relieved someone else could see it.

They shared a smile for a long beat, but she turned away and looked over his computer desk and its silent screens. It gave him a chance to admire her dainty profile, her delicate chin, slender jaw, and slightly upturned nose. Her ivory skin was so soft, he wanted to gently brush his knuckles over her cheek, to sweep his thumb over those plump lips.

Then the small boy stirred next door.

'Mason's awake.'

He peered at the wall that separated them from the child.

'Do you want to get your son?'

Ash shook his head. 'I have a meeting with my brothers. We're planning a muster this morning.' He was keen to see how he could gamify the station, and to prove to his brothers that his ideas would be a valuable contribution.

Yet he felt guilty for not going to see Mason, especially after last night.

'Hey, that's why I'm here.' She paused, catching the doorjamb on her way out into the corridor. 'Thanks for the shortbread, Ash, and for not flirting with me.'

'Boundaries, right?'

'Boundaries.'

Yeah, well, right now, those boundaries of hers were beginning to suck.

Eighteen

'Charlie, you need to ask her,' urged Dex, seated at their outdoor table on the porch. Ash cradled his coffee mug, alongside the rest of his brothers, for their morning meeting.

The old stockman scowled. 'I don't need my granddaughter's permission to go on a muster, not when I've been flamin' managing musters long before any of you lot were born.'

'We know Bree won't let you go,' said Cap.

'Hey, does Bree have an illegal still?' Ryder took a deep mouthful of his coffee.

'Who told you that bulldust?' Charlie narrowed his eyes at them.

'The Station Hand visited last night. He also mentioned you and Bree are brand makers.'

'Dying trade, I'm afraid.' Charlie thumbed up the brim of his old Akubra. 'But we make 'em for sheep, pigs, even some alpacas, but mostly cattle right across the country. Bree takes care of the register, makes sure no two brands are the same. I've got a clever granddaughter, for sure.'

'And you'll need her approval to come on this muster?' Ryder leaned closer to the old man. 'We can't do this without you, Charlie. You're the only one who knows the path through the Stoneys to Wombat Flats.'

'Bree knows it, too. She's been up and back plenty of times to check on the cattle. They're safe enough, getting fat out there.'

'But if we don't move them and they decide our dam isn't legal …'

Charlie's grey eyes flared open. 'Cor blimey, it'll be a flash flood. They'll either drown or get cut off for good. And that's a bloody fine herd you don't want goin' to waste.' Charlie shifted to rest his forearms on the table. 'Have you lot got stockhorses? You'll need two per man, and then a couple of pack horses for your gear.'

'The Station Hand and our brother are finding us some,' said Cap. 'I'm taking the dogs, too.'

'Long, bloody walk for them dogs, you know. That beagle won't make it.'

'Long walk for cattle, too. But I'm only taking the cattle dogs.'

'What about Sarge, there?' Charlie nodded at the regal-looking shepherd that lived on the far corner of the porch.

'He'll stay to guard the property. Don't worry, I've got special feeders for the dogs that are staying.'

'We'll be locking the front gate, which we plan to fix ASAP, and we're putting up some more cameras, especially around the dam, along with these signs.' Ryder held up a tin sign stating *Private Property, under 24-hour surveillance.*

'You should hang signs that say *Trespassers will be shot.* That'll make 'em think twice.' Charlie chuckled. 'Hey, what's stopping them from smashing the cameras? They broke the fences and didn't care about hiding their tracks the last time. Have you got many cameras?'

'Not yet. We're making fake ones until our next order arrives.' Ash showed off his latest creation. The top of a glass beer bottle sat on a plastic container, cut down to size, painted white. It even had some shiny foil on top to look like a solar panel.

'What the flamin' heck is that?'

'A fake camera. If we make enough of them, they won't know what's real and what's fake.' Ash held up two clunky security cameras side by side. He was going to enlist Harper's help to make more with him, and maybe talk more about gamifying the station.

'I've gotta hand it to you lad, that's clever.'

Ryder sipped on his coffee and cleared his throat. 'Charlie, we want you to ask Bree to come with us.'

Charlie spluttered out a laugh. 'Fat chance that's gonna happen.'

'We need an extra pair of hands,' said Cap. 'The dogs can only do so much on a herd that size.'

'We also don't want anyone to know where we're going and that you've stashed the cattle out there.' Ryder pointed at Charlie. 'Technically, that herd of cattle wasn't your property to hide.'

'I did that for the new owners. You lot. It's your cattle, most are branded to say so.' Charlie crossed his arms over his chest and stared at the map for a good while. 'You'll have some ferals in that mob, for sure. But it's prize stock, that's been out there a year in that valley that's thick in pockets.'

'Which is why we need you and Bree.'

Charlie leaned back in his seat. 'Yeah, you'll need Bree to come. She's a damned fine stockwoman and a brilliant muster cook, too.'

Ash leaned forward. 'Is it true you guys have pizza nights on Saturday night?'

Charlie squinted, deepening the crevices around his eyes. 'You'll have to speak to Bree about that, she's the party coordinator.'

'But will she work for us?'

'You boys? Never.' Charlie's laugh echoed around the verandah.

'That's why we need you to ask her. We'll pay you double to cover her wages,' said Ryder. 'We need both of you on this muster, with you leading it.'

Charlie sat straighter, giving them a curt nod. 'Fair enough, then. I'd better get cracking.' He stood from the table. 'You'll wanna do a deep clean of the troughs before we go, Ash. None of that flyover business with that toy, either. Get into your ute and get ya hands dirty. I found algae choking up the trough on the east side.'

'It's on my list.' He hated being spoken down to, especially in front of his older brothers.

Charlie hobbled down the front steps. 'Who's watching the homestead while we're away?'

They all looked back at the house.

'You can't leave that city girl here. Not on her own.'

'Why not?' Dex said. 'The nanny will stick to the house like she does now.'

Charlie shook his head. 'What's wrong in lettin' that girl come with? That poor kid has been nowhere, all locked up in the homestead. And Wombat Flats is paradise, fellas. She's pristine country, that's worth the stickybeak.'

'No!' The stern word echoed across the verandah, matched by Ash's frown. 'They're not going. I will not risk their safety out on a muster.' His protectiveness over Harper and Mason flared like fire inside him.

Oh no, had he already gotten too attached?

'I can't see Harper climbing into a saddle. Not unless it was for some country club,' mumbled Dex.

'Oi.' Ash frowned at Dex. 'Leave her alone.'

Dex held his hands up in surrender. 'Okay, okay.'

'The boy can ride with you, Ash. Bree's made this special baby halter to strap him to your chest,' said Charlie. 'Harper can help cook.'

'Harper can't cook,' said Ash. 'She'd tell you that.'

'Guess that's why Harper's been having cooking lessons with Bree.'

All four men raised their eyebrows.

'It's why we'd appreciate it if you can get Bree to come,' said Ryder. 'We'll leave Harper here.'

'But if you leave Harper here, fellas, that'll be Bree's excuse to stay and keep an eye on the girl. And trust me on this, lads, we need Bree to go with us. Because once that kid makes up her mind, she'll stock up on supplies for all of us, baby gear and dogs included. Bree runs a flamin' good muster camp.'

'Right, that's settled then.' Ryder tapped on the table. 'Harper will come with us. I'll ask Jonathan for two quiet horses for Harper to ride. Do you need horses, Charlie?'

'We've got our own well-trained stockhorses getting lazy in the stables.'

'You have stables?' Dex swivelled in his seat to face the caretaker's cottage. 'How many horses?'

'Enough for me and my granddaughter to take mustering.'

'Are you sure you can convince Bree to come?' Ryder made more notes on his tablet. 'Because if we ask Bree, she'll laugh in our faces and walk off.'

'Ain't that the truth,' said Dex, with Ash and Cap nodding.

'I'll get my granddaughter to come, don't you worry 'bout that. You lads just need to convince Harper.' Charlie pointed at the house where Harper was inside Mason's room.

'Not me. I'm pretty sure the nanny wants to string me up alive,' said Dex with an evil grin. 'Ash can talk to Harper, she listens to Ash.'

'Dex is right.' Ryder plonked his elbow on the table and pointed at Ash. 'You were the one who sweet-talked Harper into working out here as a nanny, when she's clearly not a nanny. So, you can convince Harper to come on the muster. Then Charlie can convince Bree to help save our cattle, so we can pay for a legal team to help save our station.'

Nineteen

'No. And I mean no. N. O. No.' Harper scowled at Ash seated across from her at the outdoor table covered in assorted plastic containers, glass domes cut from beer bottles, thick tape, and paint. 'It's bad enough you've got me helping you do your arts and crafts session—'

'We're making fake cameras to help protect this place.'

'Is that normal?'

'No.' Ash sighed heavily. 'We've ordered more, but they won't be here for a while. I told you I want to use them for stock monitoring. I have so many ideas for this place, but it's all shoved aside for this …' He held up the painted box in his hands. 'Aren't I the lucky one,' he said sarcastically, 'delegated to making these things, cleaning troughs, or digging holes for poles to hold up these fake cameras.'

She felt sorry for Ash, who seemed to be overlooked by the older siblings. 'Have you told your brothers this?'

He shrugged. 'They look at me like I don't have the experience, but I know what I'm talking about when it comes to tech.'

'I believe you.'

He blinked at her, as if he'd misheard her.

'I can relate, too.'

'How?'

'I worked in a very male-dominated area. So when a woman, who isn't even thirty, starts telling them what to do, you should see them puff out their fat chests. Half the time I expect them to light a fat a cigar while telling the little girl to run away.' She playfully mimicked their action of shooing at a fly over their drying paintwork.

Ash's lips flickered to a grin, but only briefly as he carefully cut off the base from one of the dark beer bottles, revealing the dome shape of glass, which he lined up with the others. 'What did you do to get past that?'

'I had to earn their respect by proving to them I could do the job. If you want to gamify the station, you need to show your brothers.' She pointed to the many squares of tin foil wrapped around the timber frame to replicate a solar panel. 'I'll admit this is clever. But will these fake cameras survive a storm?'

'No. But they don't need to. It's only a temporary measure while we're out on the muster.'

'Why?' She narrowed her eyes at him.

'Nothing to worry about. It's quite normal for places to have security cameras. Especially when no one will be here, because Harper, I want you to come with us.'

'I'm sorry, do I have *I'm a gullible idiot* tattooed across my forehead?'

His laugh was a surprised rough sound, which was hot. 'You sound like Bree.'

'I did, didn't I?' She adored Bree. The sassy redhead was the ultimate fixer, from how to change nappies, fix a washer in the kitchen sink, bake a tray of shortbread, while mixing a wicked gin concoction. Bree was Harper's hero. She'd never have coped without Bree's help. 'In my normal world, I'd never meet anyone like Bree, or you, and I wouldn't be making fake cameras.'

'In your world, did you ever see a sky so big you'd feel like the only person on the planet?'

From under the lip of the verandah, she cautiously peered up at the colossally enormous sky as a wave of heaviness made her slump in her seat. 'That sounds lonely.'

Ash tilted his head, his gaze serious. 'You won't be left alone out there, Harper. I'll be there for you. I promise to keep you safe.'

Her heart stuttered at his words, making her stomach turn with a heated desire. Yet, it felt like she'd just given away her deepest secret.

She inhaled sharply, snapping her spine straight, lifting her chin to force her inner armour back in place. 'Go on, finish your pitch.' She had to think of Ash as just another politician asking for something, so he'd better make it worth her while. Big skies and horsehair weren't going to cut it with this indoor girl.

'How am I doing so far?' His lips shifted into that easy-going smile, the one with the dimple. Not fair. Why did he have to use that smile?

Again, she lifted her chin and rolled her shoulders, fighting her attraction to the dreamy guy sitting on the other side of the table. 'You haven't scored enough for the win.'

'Fine, I'd better up my game then.' He shuffled in his seat, the amusement sparkling in his eyes. 'Have you ever swum in a waterfall that's so exclusive, it's not marked on any map for the tourists to find.'

This time she rolled her eyes pretending to be bored. 'Can't swim. Plus, there are these things called crocodiles.'

'Not out there.'

His taunting tone did pique her interest.

'How about sitting in a saddle to watch an endless sunrise? Or to hear the crackle of a campfire, beneath a night sky so clear you'd see galaxies behind galaxies, where you'll catch the clear flame of a falling star.'

'It sounds like you love it out there.' She could hear it in his voice, which was chipping away at her inner armour.

What's worse was his smile. It was so soft and yet so sinfully attractive.

'It's the best thing in the world, Harper, and apparently Wombat Flats is pristine. I'm really looking forward to it. You should come and see it, too.'

'Can you take a child?'

'Charlie says Bree has something for Mason to sit with

me.' Ash then dropped his head and mumbled, 'I'm hoping we might bond, or something.'

She paused, with paintbrush dripping in one hand. 'Do you really mean that?'

His jaw hardened, as she took in the details: the straight nose, the strong jaw, his delectable mouth. The denim of his jeans tightened around his impressive thighs as he leaned back, to sip from his water bottle that he made seem so tiny in his strong hands. Then there were the tanned forearms that led to even stronger arms in a tight T-shirt that hid the perfect set of abs he had beneath it. But he kept his eyes on hers as he lifted the water bottle to his lips. Somehow, it was weirdly fascinating and kind of arousing, watching him wrap his lips around the mouth of the water bottle and drink.

She rubbed her brow, internally pushing down her desires, because she was only here for Mason. 'Going on some bush ride—'

'Muster.'

'It will be a lot of work to keep Mason contained, he can run now. Will you be there to help?' She plonked her elbow on the table and pointed her paintbrush at him. 'And I mean you. Not your brothers. You.'

He eyed her for a long beat as if waiting for her to crack. But she'd been taught the art of negotiation by her father for as long as she could remember and wasn't going to back down on this.

Finally, he gave a nod. It was small, but it was enough for her to hope for the boy's sake. She dipped her paintbrush into the tin.

'Can you ride a horse?' Ash asked.

She shrugged, brushing the paint in smooth strokes along the side of the cardboard box. 'I did pony club as a child, which went for a few hours at a time. But you're talking days, camping, with no indoor plumbing or running water.' Where was she going to plug in her hair dryer?

'Have you ever been camping?'

'I tried hiking. Once. Got talked into it because I'm not

adventurous at all. I only did it for the job.' Hiking up a hill with a politician and his staff for a photoshoot. 'I'll admit the view was good, but the effort to climb a hill … Meh.' She made sure she hired a helicopter the next time that happened. She did that to protect her shoes.

'Yeah, I hear you. I'd rather ride a horse up a hill.' He then leaned over, pinning her with his dark eyes. The intensity of them made her skin prickle and her blood pump just that little harder with heat. 'You might not think you have that sense of adventure, Harper, but you do.'

'How? I'm an indoor person who walks on a treadmill in air-conditioned comfort while the gym plays photoshopped images of the outdoors.'

'You're an Aussie girl working in Belgium. And when I met you, you were on your own driving on an outback road. Very few people have the guts to do that, but you did.'

She blinked at the realisation.

'This adventure will be special, I can promise you that. It's a story you'll tell for the rest of your life, because going on an outback cattle muster, it's the stuff people dream about. So, what do you say, Harper? Are you in?'

Twenty

The next morning, the brothers were back at the table that lived on the corner of the front verandah. Ash sat opposite Dex, with Ryder and Cap seated on either end as they worked on their plans for the upcoming muster.

Waiting for his turn to report in, Ash sipped on his morning coffee, admiring another pink sunrise chasing away the straggling stars of the night. Dex reported on his jobs of collecting horses and stockfeed, then he was going to help Ryder fix the front gate and set up the real security cameras. Cap was doing the dogs and the stable, then helping set up the real security cameras. Then it was Ash's turn …

'The poles are up for the fake cameras. I had to wait for the cement to settle overnight. And, before you ask, I checked on the troughs while doing the rounds.'

'Good.' Ryder nodded.

Yet it irked Ash, as if he'd been patted on the head like he was a boy. Why couldn't they give him something decent to do? 'I'm not putting up the fake cameras yet.'

'Why not?' Dex's typical scowl deepened behind his coffee cup.

'I'm leaving it to the last moment, so they don't deteriorate too fast with the weather—especially while we're away. Unless the new cameras show up …' He glanced at the head honcho commanding the end of the table.

'The cameras won't be here for at least six to eight weeks, minimum.' Ryder scrolled through his tablet's screen, sipping on his coffee.

'What is *that*?' Cap pointed his coffee cup in the direction of the sheds.

They all craned around in their seats to spot a bright yellow van puttering towards them. It was such a bright lemon colour it'd have to glow in the dark.

'Is that a Kombi van?' Dex wiped his nose as if he'd smelled something rotten, while Ryder arched an eyebrow.

Cap grinned. 'I've never seen a yellow Kombi van before. Not one with all-terrain four-wheel-drive tyres either.'

It was like the vintage van had been dragged into the modern world with some slick-looking rims, chrome detailing, and dark tinted windows.

It pulled up at the porch steps, where Bree hopped out from the driver's side. This time she wore no work pants, or long leather vest, with that black skull cap that barely contained her curls. Bree was in a summer dress that showed off her curves and her generous cleavage.

'Figures that the Kombi belongs to the potion-brewing hippy you are,' called out Dex, tilting his head at Bree. Even Ryder, the man colder than a snake, was watching her with keen interest.

'Dex …' Bree walked up the steps, her hair like a fiery halo, but her green eyes sparkled. 'Shoot, punch or maim anyone today?'

Dex frowned at her.

'Don't worry, stormcloud, the day is still young.'

Ash chuckled with Cap at the rarity of someone putting Dex in his place.

'Can we help you, Bree?' Ryder asked.

'I'm looking for Harper.' She knocked on the glass door before pushing it open. '*Hello, Harper?*'

'BWEEEEEEEEEE. *Bwee. Bwee. Bwee.*' Mason's little feet pounded down the corridor before he leaped into Bree's welcoming arms.

'Well, hello, little man.'

Ash frowned, with a stab of jealousy hitting his chest.

'Has that kid ever greeted anyone else like that?' muttered

Cap to his brothers, who all shook their heads.

It only made Ash frown deeper. 'Not me.' *The father!* No, wait. How many days did Ash have left for that welfare check?

He checked the calendar on his phone, where he'd marked the date. Sixteen days to go.

'Hi, Bree.' Harper strolled out in her shirt and long shorts, tightening her ponytail. 'What brings you here?'

'Is it true that you've agreed to go on this muster?'

Ash smiled, his chest rising with his posture. 'She did. Harper's going. So is the boy.' Even if he wasn't so sure of the deal he'd made with Harper, who was trying so hard to push him and Mason together.

'He has a name, Ash.' Bree held the kid on her hip while he played with one of her long red curls. 'What's your name, little man?'

'Me. Mason. Me.' The kid grinned wider.

'You bet it is.' Bree tickled his belly, and he cackled so loudly it was infectious.

It was the most Ash had ever heard Mason speak, who obviously adored Bree. Pity the woman didn't like any of the grown-ups at the table.

'It seems I've been talked into going,' replied Harper. She narrowed her pretty eyes at Ash, and he grinned like a fool, and waited.

There it was, that shy smile creeping across Harper's kissable lips. Another one of the good smiles from her smile file.

'Ash, huh?' Bree glanced back at Ash, then at Harper. 'Well then, go get your purse, blossom, and put on some shoes, we're going shopping.' She then faced the table. 'Does anyone have any food allergies?'

'Me. To all things vegetable.' Dex held his hand up.

'Well, that explains your cauliflower ears, pumpkin head … Oh, please, do keep rolling your eyes, Dex. Maybe you'll find a brain back there. But I'm talking peanut allergies et cetera.'

'No, none of us have any allergies,' replied Ryder. 'And we're not fussy eaters. But we truly appreciate you coming with us, Bree.'

'I'm only doing it for Charlie.'

'We know.'

'I don't work for you boys.'

'We know.' In a rare moment, Ryder willingly dragged out his wallet and removed a credit card. 'Here … Use this for supplies. Bring back the receipts.'

Bree fanned herself with the plastic, her evil grin widening. 'Is there enough credit on this for a ticket to Tahiti, then some VIP tickets to a private booth for the Stanley Cup?'

'The what cup?' Cap asked.

'I'm ready.' Harper burst through the front door, hair brushed, in a summer dress, her eyes brightened with a touch of make-up, and shiny lips.

Harper looked so excited that Ash sat back in his seat, dazzled by the dramatic change in her. She was stunning.

'Good, let's go. FYI, I'm driving, so it's my playlist for music choices.' Bree seemed as eager as Harper to go shopping.

'You'll need the baby seat for the car, Bree.' Ash may not have bonded with the boy, but he didn't want the kid hurt either.

Bree carried Mason to the driver's side. 'I have my own, thanks. Oh, and Ash …' Bree peeked over the roof of the bright yellow Kombi van.

'Oh, man, you're in trouble now, brother.' Dex ducked his head to avoid eye contact with Bree.

'Yeah …' Ash braced himself for it, while racking his brains for what he'd done to bear the brunt of Bree's attention.

'I'm lending my spare saddle to Harper. Charlie's getting it ready for you now. She might do with a refresher in riding if she has the right horse?'

'Good idea.' Ryder nodded at Bree, it was rare for those two to agree on anything. 'Dex is collecting our horses today.

We'll make sure Harper gets the quieter ones.'

'Outstanding. And my job is done. Now play nice and don't burn the house down, children.' She tooted the horn and the yellow Kombi van steadily churned through the dirt like an old tugboat in a red sea.

Ash narrowed his eyes at the van, taking away Mason and Harper. He ground his teeth, unable to explain the strong urge to chase after them, to tell them to be safe, to make Harper promise to come back.

He scrubbed his hand roughly over his face. This wasn't happening. He was not getting attached to any of them.

He had to remember Harper was only here on a holiday, because she lived and worked on the other side of the world. She was only here temporarily, just like Mason.

Yet, his eyes followed the van's dusty trail. Bree would bring them back. Right?

'Why would someone like Bree have a baby seat in her van?' Cap asked.

'Who cares. Bree's coming and that's all that matters, boys.' Ryder tossed back the last of his coffee, swapping his empty coffee mug for his hat. 'Let's go, we've got a muster to prepare for.'

Twenty-one

'Can we take a baby to the pub?' Harper asked Bree, pushing Mason's pram through the front doors of the Elsie Creek Hotel.

'Why not? It's a good place for lunch.'

Harper removed her sunglasses, as the aroma of assorted hoppy ales greeted her. Expecting wall-to-wall cowboys leaning over the bar, with its brass rail and glass door fridges, she was surprised at how empty the large room was, with only a few men leaning against the bar.

'Where is everyone?'

'It is a weekday, and it is working hours.'

'Are we staying long? I get hassled here.' Oh, how Harper missed the days of assistants and grouchy security guys who'd stop anyone hassling her with one look. But then she was too busy working or staring at her phone to notice or care.

But not today, when her own phone had over two hundred messages waiting for her. She'd switched it off and hid it at the bottom of her bag. She felt like Ash, hiding from her responsibilities.

But she was on holidays, too. And this was her first chance at seeing the town with a local, where Bree knew everyone and all the best places. It was so good to be out amongst civilisation again.

'This is also for work. I have cattle brands to deliver.' Bree tapped at the long heavy rods wrapped in bubble wrap. Each one, clearly labelled, and secured to the top of Mason's pram.

'Stay here, I'll get you some wine as a pre-lunch drink.' Bree hoisted the long metal rolls over her shoulder and approached the bar. She spoke with the mean-looking barmaid wearing a leather vest, with arms covered in ink. She looked like someone who'd manage an outlaw bikers' bar, not an outback pub frequented by cowboys.

Bree soon returned with a glass of wine in one hand and a beer in the other. 'This is for you.'

'Thank you.' She took the wineglass as Bree unlocked the pram's brake and effortlessly steered it across the room.

'So, you weld brands that they stick onto cows? Like a tattoo designer?'

Bree laughed. Not a giggle but a head back, riotous laugh that had everyone stopping to stare, even little Mason peeked out from behind his pram's canopy to smile.

'What did I say?' Harper shrugged her shoulders high.

'I'm a blacksmith. I shape and bend hot metals into a design that represents a station or a farmer's family name, which they then slap onto the rump of their livestock.'

'And you deliver these tools of torture to the pub?' Harper couldn't keep her face straight, not with Bree still laughing at her.

'You could say that. The pub is like the stock exchange.'

'I don't think so.'

'Sure, it is.' Again, Bree shared that evil laugh. 'We all deal with live*stock*. It's also central to where the *stock*men deliver their cattle *stock* to the train station across the road where the *stock* inspectors and *stock* agents do their thing. And then when they're all done, they'll toddle across the train tracks, to grace this bar with their presence. Where they all partake in an icy cold beverage on a hot day, to wash away the *stock*yard's dust from their teeth. Only to pause in their gossipy tall tales to listen to the mighty sounds of that big ol' train chugging their cattle off to the *stock* market.'

'Are you making that up?'

Bree winked at her. 'I've ordered takeaway for dinner, because I'm not cooking tonight and you don't cook, which means you'll have time for a riding lesson.'

'I can ride, but it's been a while.' She rolled her eyes. 'Where do I get clothes?'

'Not the designer labels you'd wear, blossom. I don't even think they'd *stock* those *brands* in the Northern Territory.'

'Ha-ha. I was talking about riding gear. I don't have the right shoes for horse riding. Or whatever it is you wear on a muster.'

'After lunch, I'll take you to the *stock*feed store.'

'Stop.' Even if Harper couldn't stop giggling with Bree. The whole trip had been fun, starting with Bree making them sing to her eclectic playlist on the drive into town. 'Now that sort of store sounds like fun. Not.'

'It's where you'll get jeans. A decent set of workboots, sun-protective work shirts, and a hat.'

'I've never bothered with hats.' She touched her tender bald spot that surrounded the scar on her scalp, brushing over her hair to hide it.

'We are not leaving town today without a hat for each of you. I won't let you two go on this muster unless properly dressed. Not on my watch. You hear that, Mason? We'll get you a proper hat and make you the best dressed stockman in the district.' She playfully tickled the boy's knee. 'Don't worry, blossom, I'm sure you'll give it that polished politician's look.' Bree led them to the far corner of the front bar where the cowboys had turned to watch them.

Bree was oblivious to the attention, even if she was stunning with her red hair and that dress. 'Oh, we've got a grog order to collect on our way out of town, too. You can pick up some wine for yourself.'

How Bree did everything without any notes, or a list, was a miracle. The redhead remembered everything, like she had a photographic memory.

She pulled out a chair for Harper, then expertly parked Mason's pram at the table so he could see the room.

Bree controlled the pram with ease, while Harper didn't even know where the pram's brake was, let alone how to erect the thing when it came out of the car, or how to steer straight. She could drive all sorts of vehicles, had an overseas driver's license and had driven in many countries, yet she was uncomfortable steering a freaking pram.

From the other side of the room, Bree carried over a highchair. 'I'll be prepping our camp meals tonight, now I have the supplies.' She effortlessly set Mason in the highchair, with his sippy cup, crayons, and colouring paper.

'You've ordered a lot of supplies.' In the supermarket, Bree knew everyone and would stop and talk, introducing Harper. Normally Harper had a memory for names, but she struggled to keep up as Bree filled three trollies full of food that the supermarket staff were packing into special freezer boxes for the drive home, for them to collect after lunch.

'The farmhouse has a big pantry that needed to be restocked.' Seated at the table, Bree handed out laminated menus.

Harper sipped her wine, which was such a simple luxury to add to this impromptu day. 'You care about the Riggs brothers, don't you?'

'Mason, you—sure. The boys? Meh. We'll see what stock they're made of on the muster. It'll be a test, that's for sure. It's Ryder's shout for lunch, by the way, so let's go top shelf.'

'I've never done this.' Harper put her cutlery down on her lunch plate.

'Done what?' Bree whisked their empty plates away, putting them on a spare table to give them room. She had one foot on the pram's footrest, rocking it gently back and forth as little Mason had fallen asleep not long into his lunch, hugging his crayons.

'Had lunch in town. Even if it is the pub.' The walls had large old black-and-white images of the town, a vintage train, and herds of cattle. Even old posters of rodeos and boxing shows. The antiquated collection gave the place character.

'I try to every time I come into town. What's your excuse, when you come from a land of takeaway stores and restaurants?'

'I was always working. For lunch I'd scoff something at my desk—if I remembered to eat. Or I'd be picking at noodle boxes of Chinese takeaway in the boardroom while discussing work with the team. But this ...' Harper leaned back in her chair, fully satiated, sipping on her wine. She wanted to be like Mason and fall asleep in his pram.

Bree narrowed her eyes at Harper. 'Don't you do anything for yourself?'

Harper shrugged.

'So, no lazing around on the couch, watching chick flicks, getting brain freeze while eating ice cream?'

'No.'

'When was the last movie you watched?'

'It was on the plane ...'

'Do you remember its title?'

'No. I fell asleep.' Until the nightmares woke her.

But a rush of feel-good warmth filled her chest at the thought of Ash leaving out her shortbread biscuits, where she'd confessed her nightmare to him. It meant a lot that he'd done that for her. No one had done something like that before.

Most of all, Ash was hoping to bond with Mason on this muster. It was the only reason why she was daring to go so far out of her comfort zone.

'Bree?' A cowboy with blond curls waved at her as he walked in through the back door. Complete with a big shiny rodeo belt buckle and a swagger in some nice hip-hugging jeans, the man was so hot, he deserved his own cowboy calendar to show off the season for summer.

Bree waved.

'Who is that?' Harper whispered.

'Cowboy Craig.'

'Isn't calling a stockman a *cowboy* an insult?'

'It is. Sweetie, they're cattle*men*, not cow*boys*.'

'But that, him, Craig …' Did she say hot?

'I'm sure it ticked off Craig at one stage. But Craig being who he is, would've claimed it as his own. Everyone knows him as Cowboy Craig, now.'

'Why would anyone want to offend that—*him*?' And that hip-swaying rugged walk of a real-deal cowboy. He was the ultimate thirst trap that would go viral on social media.

'Because they were jealous of Craig. He has a way with women, they can't resist.' Bree arched an eyebrow at Harper.

Harper cleared her throat, blinking fast, as she sat straighter. 'Like Ash.' The other player she knew. Who filled out his jeans better than Craig, and had that dimple when he smiled, and when he wasn't wearing his hat his hair would fall across his forehead. And … *Stop! Stop.* She had put boundaries in place to ward off Ash, who was only doing that for sport, not because he was attracted to her.

'Oh, honey, Ash is a child,' said Bree. 'Craig is the big leagues.'

'There's my favourite redhead.' Craig leaned over and kissed Bree's cheek. 'Keeping out of trouble?'

'Never. Craig, meet Harper. And before you start, she's with the Riggs brothers. The baby is part of that mob.'

'Hey, Harper.' Craig's hand was huge, shaking her hand firmly. 'Good shake.' He nodded at Harper with approval. He then scooped up the nearest chair, spun it around, to sit on it like a saddle, just like Ash did. But she liked the way the denim snugly fit across Ash's thighs more, and his strong hands with the deep tan. *Stop it!*

'Jonathan told me his brothers bought Elsie Creek Station.' Craig pushed up the brim of his hat allowing the lights to capture his stunning blue eyes. 'I hope you're giving them hell, Bree?'

Bree's laugh had an evil edge to it.

'That's my girl.'

The pub's front door opened, and another man walked inside, dressed like he was going to the country club in the summer. It's what Harper was used to, men in linen shirts, tailored trousers, and yacht-loving loafers, complete with a set of aviators pushing back his wild black hair.

'Oi, over here, pretty boy.' Craig waved to the new arrival.

'There you are, bubble butt. And in good company, I see.' The guy approached the table. 'Hey, Bree. Long time, no see.'

And it was another man to kiss Bree's cheek.

'This is Harper. She's with the Riggs brothers,' said Craig. 'Harper, this is the puppy-pandering, flying vet.'

'Ryan.' He shook Harper's hand. 'Good shake.'

'I said so, too.' Craig gave another nod of approval.

'Which brother are you with?' Ryan sat on the chair properly, crossing his leg over his knee, exposing sockless loafers, unlike Craig dressed like the rest of the men at the bar.

'Ash,' replied Bree, grinning at Harper. 'That's his son.'

'Oh, wow.' Craig's brow creased. 'But that dirty dog was with—'

'I'm not *with* Ash.' Harper blurted out as Bree devilishly giggled. But there was a flush of heat to her cheeks, that indicated she kind of hoped she was. *Not. No. Stop it.* This internal struggle was awful. She'd never been like this.

'Which one is Ash?' Ryan asked Craig.

'Ash is the one that's older than Jonathan, and younger than Cap.'

'I know Cap well.' Ryan nodded. 'Cap is a good man. He's saved countless canines over the years. If either of you ever need me for any of Cap's dogs, don't hesitate to find my surgery behind the supermarket.'

'I can give you my number, if you want, Harper?' Craig bobbed his eyebrows up and down.

Oh boy, Craig was a player. Big time. She peeked at Bree for help.

'Craig, your phone number is written on the wall in the women's toilets.' Bree pointed to the doors that led to the amenities.

'So, we've heard. We should take a look.' Ryan spoke to

Craig, 'But first, my friend, you can order me a lemon, lime and bitters.' He checked his watch. 'I'm still on the clock.'

Oh, how Harper remembered that feeling well. Rubbing her own bare wrist, missing her watch.

'In a sec ...' Craig leaned his elbow on the table, the smile gone and his voice low. 'How's Charlie, Bree?'

'Good.'

'Any more trouble from that prick next door?'

'Not since the brothers moved in. But Leo is after their water now.'

'I heard. New mine, huh?'

Bree nodded. 'If you hear of anything about this mine, please let me know.'

'Sure. But do you really want to bother if Elsie Creek Station has new owners?'

'Only while we're still out there, I care.'

'You do realise Jonathan's brothers are tough enough to handle anything?'

Bree shrugged. 'I only met them when they moved in with their boxes and convoy of utes.'

'I've met Dex a few times now. He's an animal in those illegal fighting pits. Underground champion three years in a row.'

'How do you know?' Ryan asked, while Harper's eyes widened at this news.

'I've been to a Riggs family Christmas. Flew down with Jonathan in their cousin Monet's plane. Their mother, Cammie, is a nice lady. You'd like her, Bree. And she'd love you.'

'Do you know Ash?' Harper had to know the gossip.

Craig's stunning blue eyes landed on her. She had to sit back and remember to breathe. 'Yeah. Ash is a gamer and a player, with a reputation for keeping a strict dating shelf-life of two weeks with the women.'

'I already said I'm not *with* Ash.'

'Are you jealous?' Ryan nudged Craig with his elbow.

'Not now, I'm not.' Craig's crooked smile offset his tan, as he sat back, keeping his eyes heavy on Harper as if touching her with his hands. She swallowed hard.

'Behave, Craig,' warned Bree. 'I don't need you breaking my friend's heart.'

Friend? It was such a warm and welcoming word Harper sat higher, as Bree gave her a sly wink as if to say *I've got your back.*

'What I want to know,' said Bree, 'is whether the Riggs brothers are good stockmen.'

Craig rubbed the back of his strong neck. 'I worked with Ash on a muster in the Kimberleys.'

'And?'

'Ash isn't as good as you, but he can hold his own. So can Dex and Cap.'

'What about Ryder Riggs?' Bree's eyes seemed hyper focused.

'Ryder's the oldest one, isn't he?' the vet asked.

Harper nodded, keen to learn the gossip as they leaned closer, voices hushed, and their blend of male colognes, divine. It was just another thing Harper missed from the land away from cattle and dust.

'What do you know about Ryder?' Bree asked Craig.

'Nothing.'

'What do you mean, nothing?' Ryan scoffed at Craig. 'You know everything about everyone.'

Craig shrugged. 'All I know is Ryder is the oldest son. He's a chopper pilot. And he's rich. But no one knows how rich, or how he made his money. Is it true Ryder paid for the station with cash?'

Bree barely nodded. 'The others chipped in, too.'

Harper's eyes widened. The station had to be worth twenty million dollars. Who had that kind of cash?

'What else have you heard about Ryder?' Bree asked.

'Well, according to Jonathan,' continued Craig, 'Ryder is the only one who'll take on Dex, and whip his arse, too.'

'But you said Dex was a champion?' This conversation had Harper sitting on the edge of her seat.

'But Ryder's got some mean military training, too. Dex is lethal, but who knows what Ryder is?'

'Are we safe out there?' Harper faced Bree. 'Is Mason safe with them?' Even if she had a good experience with the military, it had her worried that the two oldest Riggs brothers might physically fight each other in Mason's presence.

'Of course he is.' Bree put her hand on Harper's arm. 'You're well protected under the Riggs brothers' roof.'

'I agree,' said Craig.

'Here, here.' Ryan raised his finger. 'Cap is part of that family. And I know that man would do anything to protect his dogs. He'd rather feed them first than himself. Can you imagine how far they'd go to protect their family?'

Still, it didn't put Harper's mind at ease.

'Oi. Are you lot hassling these ladies?' Demanded the grumpy middle-aged chef, carrying bags of foil-wrapped food.

'No chance of that,' said Craig. 'Bree's like a sister.'

'All good, Lenny.' Bree stood from the table. 'Is that our order?'

'It is.' Lenny, the chef, handed the bags to Bree. 'Tell Charlie I'll be out in a few weeks.' Lenny's accent sounded like it was Hungarian.

'You say that all the time.'

'I'll get there when I get there,' the chef grumbled. 'But I'll bring cupcakes, when I do.'

'Aww, you know me so well.' Bree grinned as Lenny kissed her cheek, gave her a wink, then headed back to the kitchen.

'I always bring out cupcakes, too. It's the standard entry fee to the caretaker's cottage to crash on the world's greatest couch.' Craig stood tall, hitching up his belt where the light caught on the shiny champion rodeo buckle. 'Tell Charlie I'll visit when I can.'

Bree gave his arm a squeeze. 'The old man would love to see you, but he'll be busy for the next week.'

'Lemme guess ...' Craig poked up the brim of his hat. 'If

you're in town in the middle of the week, stocking up on Lenny's tucker, when you're a damned fine cook, you're going on a muster.'

'Shh.' Bree held her finger over her lips. 'Tell no one.'

'Why?'

'I'll explain it later. I promise.'

'Do you need a hand?'

'No. It's the Riggs brothers' first muster.'

'I see.' Craig nodded, with hands on his hips. 'You know me, I won't say nothing. But you know my number, all you have to do is hit speed dial and I'll be there. No questions asked.'

'I know.'

'And that's a big fat ditto from the sexiest man in the room,' said Ryan, pointing at himself.

Harper burst out laughing.

Even Craig chuckled as he elbowed the vet. 'You'll keep, puppy panderer.'

'Get over ya'self, bubble butt.'

'And on that note, we're leaving.' Bree began pushing the pram for the door.

Harper followed. 'Nice to meet you, gentlemen.'

'She called us gentlemen. Did you hear that, puppy panderer?' Craig nudged Ryan.

'She was talking about me, because she obviously doesn't know you yet. Can we help carry those bags to the car, ladies?'

'We're good. You guys go play nice over lunch. We'll see you next time.' Bree pushed the pram out the door, with Harper following.

Harper winced at the sunlight, sliding on her sunglasses. 'You know, we still got hassled in that pub.'

'Those two weren't hassling us.' Bree covered over the pram with a small blanket to shield the sleeping boy from the sun. 'But I get what you're saying. A single girl in a bar, of course you'd get hit on.'

'Why? I've sat in plenty of bars across the globe and never

got hassled.'

'I think the ratio of men to women in this town is something like twenty to one.'

'No way. How come you're single, then?'

'Why are you?'

'I've never really …' Harper shyly shrugged.

Bree stopped the pram on the sidewalk and turned to Harper. 'Do I have to tell you about the birds and the bees?'

'Nick off.'

'Finally.' She nudged Harper's arm. 'I like this playful side to you. It beats the deer in the headlights look you had going on.'

'I'm learning.'

'That you are.' Bree swung her arm over Harper's shoulders and gave her a tender squeeze. 'By the time the muster is over, you'll be a whole new you. But first, let's get you dressed for the part.'

Twenty-two

'The trick to finding the right hat is working out what it is you want that hat to do.' Bree explained to Harper as they stood before a towering wall of wide-brimmed hats of many assorted colours and styles.

'I've never bought a hat before. I usually get stuck wearing those dumb politician caps to hawk for votes. They were always ugly and flimsy things, but these are big.'

'Try one.'

'What am I looking for?' There was nothing quite like that splurge on a luxury item that maxed out your credit card, where shopping for clothes usually felt as good as a hair flick of freshly blown-dry hair straight from the salon. Right now, Harper was hoping for the power of retail therapy.

'With your skin, you'll want a wide brim. Wider the better. As you don't use a stockwhip, the brim can remain flat. So, avoid the curled sides, which will only let the sun in to burn your ears.' Bree tapped her own ears.

'But isn't that the classic design for cowboy hats?'

'In America, they're designed like that because they do a lot of roping. This is Australia and we have a harsh outback sun we try to avoid.' Bree walked before the wall of hats like a teacher giving a lecture in a classroom. 'As we're currently enjoying a fabulous winter—'

'It's summer for me.'

'This time of year, a felt hat is fine. In the summer, you'll want a straw hat, the lighter the better.'

'Like you and your vast hat collection at the cottage.'

'My skin is like yours, Harper. I burn easily, and instead of getting a tan, I just get more freckles.'

'Which is why you make your own sunscreen.'

Again, Bree nodded, sliding on a hat over Harper's head.

Harper flinched and ducked away.

'What?' Bree peered inside the hat. 'Did it have a pin inside?'

'It's not you. It's me.' She touched the bald spot at the back of her head.

'Is it irritating your scar?'

'I'm sensitive there.'

'But you're able to keep your ponytail tight.'

'I do that to hide my bald spot,' she shyly admitted. 'Normally I don't wear my hair up, except for the gym.'

'Let me see it.' She gently pulled Harper's hair out of the ponytail. 'I swear, I can't see it when your hair is down.'

'I can feel it.'

'I imagine it'd be like that tiny zit you get on your chin that feels like some massive boil festering over your whole chin.'

'Is that what it looks like?' Harper gasped, stepping back with her eyes widening in horror, her hands covering her bald spot.

'No, blossom, it's nothing like that. But it gives me an idea for finding the right hat to suit you. You'll want a taller crown to keep it off that sensitive area … Like this one.' She plucked a dark brown hat from the shelf. 'You can do the honours.'

'Can I just wear a ski mask?'

'And die from heat exposure? Go for it.'

Harper gently slid on the hat. It didn't touch the scars that lived high on the back of her scalp. There was a gap.

'Not too tight?'

'It's perfect.'

'In that case, we'll go a size bigger.'

'Why?'

'Because the inner bands shrink. It's what they do.' Bree grabbed the larger sized hat, flipped it over and slid some small sponge inside, to pad the inner lining. She then gently slid the hat back onto Harper's head. 'When breaking in a new hat, you pad up the inside. The more you wear it, the more you adjust the lining, until it eventually fits you like a glove. Then it will never come off when you're galloping on a horse into the wind. And that's what you want in a stockman's hat.'

'Where do I get a fancy hatband like Charlie's crocodile band. Or a bohemian look like yours.' She'd seen Bree's hat collection that had contrasting strips of cloth, twine or leather, feathers, lace, even a playing card and some matches tucked into the hatbands. Each hat, and each band was different.

'You can dress it up however you want later. A stockman's hat is like getting a pair of new shoes, the more you wear it, the better they fit. But its primary job is to protect you and your brain from the sun.' She turned Harper around and faced the mirror. 'Look at that.' Bree stood back from the mirror. 'Perfect. You look like a stockwoman.'

'Is that really me?' Harper lifted her chin, trying to stare at herself sideways, twirling around as if wearing a ball gown, to glimpse the back. It was just jeans, boots, a long-sleeved shirt, but the hat said it all.

'I like this hat.' It wasn't rubbing against her scar, but the brim was huge, curving down to cover the back of her neck, where Bree lifted her shirt's collar high. But the shape, the colour of the hat also highlighted her eyes, while cleverly adding some shading to her cheekbones that softened her skin. How could a hat do all that?

She'd been to milliners with her mother to find hats for race-day outfits and suffered with fascinators for fancy garden weddings, but this was something entirely different.

'Are you going to wear one of your new outfits home?' Bree put a small hat on Mason's head. 'Just like our future rodeo champion, here.'

'Can I?'

'Sure. I'm not your mother. But I recommend that you

wash your new clothes before the muster, and try to wear your boots around the house to wear them in.'

'I will.'

Mason stood beside Harper at the mirror, wearing a big gummy smile, in little boots, jeans, and an enormous hat that looked so cute. He was the perfect model of cuteness for the clothing brand. If Mason was a politician's son, she'd be taking photos to rack up social media points to boost their polls. But she took a photo with her phone, for her own keepsake. Maybe she'd share it with Ash?

'Come here, little man,' said Bree. 'I want those tags on your jeans.'

'No.' The little boy giggled. His jeans swishing as he toddled away fast, with his laughter filling the area of the feed store that held saddles, bridles, horse wash, even dog leads, collars, and dog beds.

'Mason, come back.' Bree raced after the boy.

'Gotcha.' It was a deep voice, coming from a man who had just entered the store. 'Are you running to or from trouble, young man?'

'Put down the child, Leo.' Bree's voice was deadly serious.

It made Harper rush to find Bree and Mason.

The man holding Mason was wearing a suit. A properly tailored suit, with a red silk tie, and shiny black shoes. Oh, how she missed seeing men in suits.

'Hello, Bree. Does this boy belong to you?'

'Put down the child, walk away, and no one gets hurt.'

The man laughed, passing the child to Bree.

'Here, Harper. Take him. Pack up, and let's go.' Bree passed Mason to Harper, wearing a serious expression that carried a sense of urgency.

'What are you doing here, Leo? And wearing a suit—have you just finished your parole hearing? No, wait,' Bree held up her hand and said, 'did you and your little mobster mates crash some open-mic comedy club, to really slay the crowd over lunch.'

'No. Although, I'd love to take you to lunch, Bree.' The man laughed, highly amused. He had jet-black hair with fine flecks of grey, a three-day growth peppered across his strong jawline, but his eyes had a dark, sinful look focused entirely on Bree.

'We just did lunch, thanks. Not hungry.'

'How about dinner? The jet's in town. I could take you shopping in Sydney. My treat.'

'As I've told you before, Leo, no. Or has an alien hijacked your brain for you to dare ask me that again?'

'I'm not giving up.' He stepped in real close, towering over Bree. But she never flinched, holding her spot, glaring up at the guy.

'What do you want?'

'Well, if I told you that, I'm pretty sure you'd slap me.' Leo's mouth shifted, his eyes clearly displaying a very hungry look that trailed up and down Bree's curves. 'But I don't mind a bit of rough play. You?'

'I just love how you bring violence so fast into our conversations.'

Again, he laughed, his smile handsome with that whole dark mobster vibe to him, as he loosened his silk tie. 'I'm here for a hat. Care to help me?'

'Sure. Let me fold some newspaper into a sailor's hat so you can float on outta here.'

'*Bwee, a-at*?' Mason struggled with saying the letter h, but he held out his hat to Bree as Harper strained to keep him on her hip.

'You keep your hat on, buddy. You stay with Harper.' Bree's eyes flared at Harper to leave. *Now.*

'I've got you, Mason. Let's get ready for another fun car ride.' Harper tucked him into his pram, wishing the young woman behind the counter would ring up the bill for her clothes faster.

'Is that your boy?' Leo pointed at Mason in the pram.

Bree's glare darkened, as did her tone, layered thick with maternal protectiveness. 'None of your business.'

'Come on, Bree.' Leo held up his hands. 'We're in town, its neutral territory.'

'And where is your little band of balding gorillas?'

'Where is Charlie?'

They both stared at each other, the tension thickening the air.

It was hard to tell if Bree and Leo were mortal enemies or were about to kiss. The chemical love-hate attraction was steamy.

'Can't you play nice, Bree?' His voice was deep and dark.

'You'd get bored if I did.'

His lips twitched, and he wiped his hand over his jaw as if to stop the smile. But the shine in his eyes showed how highly amused this man was. His well-tailored suit fit perfectly on his cuffs, and the length on his legs, in a rich deep blue material. A very fine Cartier watch completed the ensemble that would have Harper's suit-loving father asking for the tailor's details.

'Come on, Bree, I could really use your opinion.'

'I'm sure my opinion of anything in your world has the weight of a zebra finch fart. Wait. I meant to say that the other way around, more along the lines of: I'll write down your concerns and send it to a politician who cares?'

'I need a new hat and I saw how well you—'

'You'd been spying on us?' She waggled her finger at him. 'You do that, huh?'

'Only on what's worth looking at.' Again, his eyes slow-crawled over Bree. Harper felt naked for her friend.

'Wait, for a minute there I thought you were asking me to play personal shopper for *you*. Did I hear that right?'

'You do have good taste, and I admire your style, both on and off the station.' He held his hand over his heart, even bowing his head to her. 'I'm being sincere about the hat.'

'Fine. Let me go get you a bucket big enough to hide your entire head. With luck you'll suffocate.' Bree turned on her heels, and the man followed her, watching Bree's hip sway to the back wall.

Bree gave Harper a *hurry-up and get-out* look. Even though she seemed annoyed, there was some indication that the redhead was enjoying this game as much as Leo. It was better than watching politicians who hated each other banter with sarcastic niceties. They did that for the adrenaline rush and votes, which was just a part of the game of politics. But what was Bree's game plan?

Bree stood before the wall of hats. 'This one.' She plucked a black one off the wall.

He took the hat and slid it on. 'Too tight.'

'Well, they don't make them big enough for criminal masterminds like yourself.'

'Bree? Come on. Let's play nice.'

'Fine.' She checked the hat's inner lining, then went through the rack and selected another one. 'This one.'

'Are you sure?'

She just popped her hand on her hip and glared at him as if to say, *try me.*

Leo slid on the black hat. It was perfect, just like Bree had found for Harper.

Bree checked over the fit, the brim, then gave Leo and his new hat a nod of approval. 'And my job is done. Later, demon spawn. Please don't eat the children in town.'

'Aww, you've hurt my feelings, Bree.' Leo chuckled.

'You don't have any.'

'Do you?'

'Not for you. But you should go find yourself a gold digger and put her to work digging up that new mine of yours.'

'It's just business, Bree. And I know you're all about smart business that comes with a whole lot of outlaw attitude. It's hot.'

'Oh, please, don't make me hurl my lunch.'

'The people in your world have no idea how much of a gift you are. But I do. So please have dinner with me, Bree?'

'No. But I will agree with you that I don't think the people in my life ever fully appreciate how many lives are saved by my self-control and desire to not go to prison. So, no. I will not have dinner with you today, tomorrow, or next Tuesday.'

'I'll pay you for your time?'

'Well, for five k I'll make your eternal demise look like an accident. For a cup of raw peanuts, I'll make it look like a hilarious accident.'

He laughed so loud it made Harper pause, with Mason grinning.

Even Bree gave him a sly grin. 'Have a nice life, Leo. Enjoy your hat.'

Leo tapped his hat's brim at Bree in an old-fashioned cowboy hat tilt. It was sweet and old world gentlemanly. Even though Bree rolled her eyes at him, her lips twitched as if to control her smile.

'Let's go.' Bree pushed the pram.

Harper carried the bags outside where they copped the full brunt of the outdoor heat and the sun's glare. Harper held out her new hat like a piece of cardboard to block the sun.

'You can wear the hat, Harper. It is to be used.'

It was Harper's turn to roll her eyes, sliding on the hat. 'Who was that?'

'Leonard Travers. Leo. He's Elsie Creek Station's eastern neighbour—the man trying to steal the station's water.'

Harper gasped, turning back to the store. Inside, Leo nodded at her as he leaned his elbow against the counter while the cashier rang up the purchase of his hat.

Harper rushed to catch up with Bree who was opening the yellow Kombi van's side door. 'That's the bad guy?' In a suit.

'The ultimate bad guy.' Bree paused from loading up the van. 'If you ever see Leo, walk away, Harper. Leo is slipperier than a dozen experienced politicians on a good day. And we do not need someone like Leo learning we're leaving the homestead empty for this muster. Especially since they've just fixed that dam that Leo and his balding gorillas destroyed in the first place.'

Twenty-three

Under the thick cover of darkness, squeezed into the cab of Ash's ute, Harper had to hold the handle with both hands to stop her arm and shoulder hitting the passenger door or Mason's baby seat that sat in the middle. 'Where is the road?'

Ash pointed with his wrist casually resting on the top of the steering wheel. 'It's there. It hasn't been used in a while.'

'No kidding.' It was like they were driving over a path filled with potholes, tufts of tough grasses, and rocks. 'Where are we going?'

'We're driving to the mouth of the Stoneys first. Then we'll be saddling our horses in time to start the trek at sunrise.'

Charlie and Bree were in the Razorback, a beefy bull catcher, that was way up front with lights so bright on the vehicle it lit up the world. Behind them were Dex and Ryder in a large semi-trailer, towing a huge trailer with all the horses, churning a wall of angry dust behind it. It blended with the sounds of barking dogs coming from the back cage of Cap's old Tojo.

Ash's ute was the last vehicle on this rocky road trip to hell. It's bright row of headlights highlighted the swirling dust and assorted massive bugs that splatted hard against the windshield, making Harper flinch every time.

How did she get talked into this? It was bad enough the ute's suspension needed a complete overhaul, but she was one on one with Ash, confined to the tiny cab, where she normally struggled to make small talk. But the deafening silence was worse. 'Did all the horses fit in that truck?'

'Yep.' Ash focused on the road ahead. His wide-brimmed hat sat on the dashboard next to hers.

Oh, come on. She tried to think of something else to talk about. Anything to distract from the drone of the vehicle and the silence that was filled with Ash.

'Did you get any sleep last night?' She'd heard the men busy on the verandah.

'I never sleep the night before a muster.'

'Why?'

'Don't want to forget anything.'

'Or you're just excited.'

'That too. I love mustering.' The excitement may have barely curled his lips, but it shone in his gloriously warm eyes.

'Did you grow up on a station?'

'No.' He sniffed heavily, looking out the driver's window where the sun hadn't even made its appearance. 'We grew up in a junkyard.'

'What do you mean by that?'

'We were known as the junk brothers.'

'Excuse me?'

'It's the nickname we copped as kids, because our dad was paid to collect the rubbish lying on the side of the highway, or for towing stranded motorists. Most of the junk he collected got dumped on our property. It's odd when you see a full-sized yacht perched in a backyard that's nothing but desert.'

She straightened her new work shirt and brushed down her new jeans. 'Well, that explains the empty beer cans around the house.'

'Hey, we kept those cans for Cap.' He frowned at her. 'Cap is going to recycle them and use that cash to feed his dogs or pay for any vet fees they need.'

'And the boxes crowding the farmhouse living room?' The maze of boxes Mason liked to hide behind.

'None of us have unpacked yet. Cap can't until he finds the time to paint his place, and Dex is Dex.'

'Is it true Dex is living in a tent inside his place?'

'Dex hasn't had time to fix it up and unpack his boxes either.'

'But, it's been —'

'None of us have lived in a home for a long time, to want to settle in. Honestly, I couldn't tell you what I've got in those boxes.'

'How come?'

'We've all worked away. Chasing mustering contracts, I never needed much, just my mustering gear and my PC to play games. But now …' His grin grew as his eyes focused on the road ahead. 'We're doing this for ourselves as the bosses because it's ours. Home. I should unpack those boxes, huh? That sounds weird, right?'

'No. I'm not judging you guys about the boxes.'

He arched one eyebrow at her. 'So for once, you're actually not judging us?'

She rolled her shoulders and lifted her chin. 'I don't judge.'

'Yeah, you do, Harper. You stick that little nose of yours up in the air and look down at things. It must be your background.'

She gasped at him. 'I don't mean it that way. I'm just picky.'

'Don't worry about it, sweetheart. Growing up in a junkyard you get used to being judged.'

She reached out and touched his arm. 'I don't mean to be like that, Ash. I swear it.'

He looked at her hand, she pulled it back, curling her fingers into her palm and hid them in her lap. But the heat was felt in her ears with a twinge of shame.

'I'm not judging you about the boxes or the house, because with my job, I got used to living out of a suitcase, or moving into empty apartments with minimal items, hotels were more homely.'

The vehicle droned on, but the silence between them grew heavier. She couldn't stand it. Especially when she couldn't do anything with her hands with no work to occupy her time. Her phone was useless, and there was nothing to see out the windows, just complete darkness—except for the vehicles hidden by the thick dust ahead.

The sad thing was Harper had no friends to talk to about her travel plans. She knew plenty of administrative staff, politicians, and had all sorts of connections and contact details that would fill a phone book. But none of them were friends. Not one.

It was her own fault. She'd never bothered with small talk, never bothered to stop and ask how they were, or learn about other people's hobbies, when she did nothing except work. She'd never made the time to make friends that didn't have some hidden political agenda behind it. She had no one.

The realisation created a blanket of loneliness to drape heavily over her. She needed to say something to stop herself from drowning under her thoughts.

'What can I expect on this muster?' Besides the inhalation of red dust and the ear-hammering sound of barking dogs, not to mention her spine would need an adjustment after riding this rocky road—and they hadn't even made it to Wombat Flats.

'Dust. A lot of dust. But stick near me, and you'll get through this with a smile.' He cracked a smile, a faint one, like he'd rather not use it. But it made the world feel a little smaller and a whole lot warmer and cosier. Which wasn't hard when crammed into the front seat of his ute with a baby car seat and Mason's bags.

'When the muster is over, it'll be a story to share with your friends, family, maybe future children.' He glanced at Mason, fast asleep from the ute's sway, his smile gone as his eyes softened. It was a look that made her stomach traitorously flip.

She no longer wanted to do the small talk, she genuinely needed to know more about Ash, especially now she had the time as the ute drove deeper into the outback. 'So how did you go from junk to cattle?'

'I scored a summer job while still in school, and it went from there. Cap was the same, except he fell in love with southern winters and did sheep for a bit. Dex, he just followed the fight circuit, which meant a lot of pubs where he'd pick up jobs here and there. And Ryder ...' He sighed, his shoulders sagging.

'Ryder's a lot older than you.'

'He's almost forty. I'm thirty.'

'No way.'

'We've all got Dad's baby face, except Dex and Ryder.'

'Why do those two argue all the time?' The two oldest brothers snarled at each other like dogs fighting to be the alpha in the pack.

'They're both strong personalities. Ryder's the natural leader, and Dex doesn't like being told what to do. Me neither.'

'But he doesn't.'

'Huh?' His eyes cautiously flashed her way, then back to the dirt road highlighted by the glow of headlights.

'I get no one likes being told what to do, but Ryder gives all of you plenty of scope to say your piece. He listens.'

'Ya think?' His voice was loaded with sarcasm, creating a rigid line between his eyebrows.

'Ryder is actually doing a good job as a manager.'

'What do you mean?' The rigid line between his eyebrows deepened.

'A good manager helps to nurture and use the skills of his team to get the job done, and Ryder does that with you guys. He's got Cap looking after the dogs that make up the mustering teams, plus the security details. And Cap is good with all animals. Dex is your mechanic, driver, and part engineer. You—'

'Make fake cameras and clean troughs. Aww, man ...' He winced, slapping his forehead.

'You forgot to clean those troughs, didn't you?'

'No, I did. They were fine … yesterday-ish. Or was that the day before?' He fell silent, giving her a fleeting side glance. 'You're right.'

'About what?'

'I'm not proving myself, am I.'

She didn't want to hurt his ego any more than he was doing to himself by answering him. 'Did you bring your drone?'

'I did. I doubt I'll have time to use it.'

'I think you should *make* the time,' said the girl always chasing time.

His eyes flicked to hers, then back to the road.

She wriggled in her seat to face him. 'Can I say something, just between you and me?'

'And Mason there.' He nodded at the sleeping baby.

'Bree told me you aren't using the helicopter because it's thick country. Can't you do the same work with your drone? You'd be able to get it high enough to spot the cows, right?'

'Sure.' He shrugged from behind the steering wheel as the ute trundled through the bumpy terrain.

'Do you have a speaker on it to whistle at them, or something?'

His lips shifted as if to laugh at her.

'I'm being serious.' She crossed her arms over her chest.

'Okay, okay.'

Oomph. Her shoulder thumped into the door as they hit another bump in a road that didn't exist, making her re-grip the handle.

The twin spheres of headlights met swirls of red dust that made up the road. Occasionally, along the sides, the lights caught the tops of fluffy leafed eucalyptus trees as they drove deeper into the outback under a black night sky. 'Are you *sure* this is a road?'

'It's a track. Dex is planning on grading the roads soon. I've asked Dex to do the driveway first, to make it easier for your car.' His eyes landed on hers. It only made the space, which smelled intoxicatingly of Ash, seem smaller.

The realisation that Ash had done that for her made her stomach swirl like a ribbon that curled in various directions after being sliced by a pair of sharp scissors. He did all these little things that meant a lot to her, like keeping the pantry's light on in the farmhouse at night, or putting water bottles in the fridge for her. Leaving the shortbread on the table with her coffee cup cleaned and waiting for her.

Beneath that boyish bravado was someone who cared about keeping those who surrounded him happy. She knew that once he bonded with his son, Mason was going to be one lucky boy. If only Ash would try.

'You know …' Ash swiped back his dark hair, as was his habit. 'I could rig up something with the walkie-talkies. But what's stopping them from just standing there and staring at it? Some bulls will attack the muster choppers.'

'Can't you train them for the future? You use the drone now to check troughs, but you could also use it to move them, or do what you do with cows. Isn't that your plan? To gamify the station to save on fuel costs etc? Why not try out your drone on this muster to show your brothers what you can do—not that I have a clue what it is that you do, or what I'm to expect on this road trip.' The start wasn't very promising.

'Did Bree explain anything about what happens on a muster?'

'Only that I'd be swallowing a lot of dust. But I've been told to stick close to you, and to never wander far from the campsite. Bree also said it's better to learn on the job.' Like she'd done the moment she'd arrived at Elsie Creek Station, as a completely inexperienced nanny.

'It's how I was taught—thrown into the deep end.'

'That's what I'm afraid of. I'm not a good swimmer. I believe Bree has kept a lot from me, too. But I do know why you've asked me to come.'

'Yeah, why?' He gave her a fleeting side glance filled with guilt.

'You're trying to save the station and you need Bree and

Charlie's help to do it, by getting those cattle out of this place called Wombat Flats. Am I right?'

'We wouldn't have Charlie's help without Bree—'

'Who wouldn't be your muster cook, if I stayed at the house?'

Ash barely nodded. But the dim light from the dashboard deepened the shadows of his knife-edged cheekbones. It was an edge that tempted her to trace them with her fingertips all the way to his pretty boy lips. But that would mean crossing a boundary that neither of them were going to break—especially not with a toddler sleeping between them.

The car rocked as it hit a ditch. She struggled to keep her seat.

'Sorry.' His hand rested protectively over Mason's seat, keeping the boy in place.

She sighed, leaning against the door, holding the handle tight to keep from smacking her head against the passenger window, again. 'I liked your reason for me coming out, the best.'

'What's that? The adventure.'

'No. Because you wanted to spend quality time with your son, to bond.'

He stared at her for a long beat before glancing at his sleeping son. His eyes returned to the dark road and the massive headlights of the assorted vehicles highlighting the swirling dust.

She was clueless as to which direction they were travelling in. Some adventurous spirit, ha! Not when Harper was the fifth wheel, only here for other reasons than for her usefulness. And in this foreign world, she had no idea how to be useful.

But for the first time, she was going to try. Not just for Mason or Ash, but for herself. It was about time she started living by her own time schedules, without memos, or assistants. Maybe she could use this trip to push away the brain fog caused by that bombing, which had stolen time from her.

It was time to plan her own future—if she survived the next few days in a saddle.

Twenty-four

Charlie climbed easily into the saddle of a very fine-looking stockhorse. With a picky eye he looked over the horses and riders that made up the mustering team. Behind him the sun had barely breached the distant horizon, hidden behind the rich red escarpment that was part of Cattleman's Keep.

Beyond that were the walls of the mighty Starvation Dam, where the overflow ran downstream to weave between the thick gum trees lining the banks to barely glisten under a sky the colour of cotton candy.

Parched open fields stretched to the left of them, with only a red road that led the way back to the homestead, it was the only sign of civilisation. Beside their assorted vehicles parked nearby, half a dozen cattle dogs lay in the trees' shade line that ran along the edges of the sandy cliff face, that stretched like a wall of stone.

'*Welcome to the Stoneys,*' Charlie shouted from his place high in the saddle. '*We'll be riding down the guts. Walking only. No cowboying, ya hear?*'

'It's not our first rodeo, Charlie.' Dex rolled his eyes, sitting comfortably in the saddle. 'Let's get on with it.'

Ash couldn't wait to climb into the saddle himself. But first, he checked on Harper's stirrups, having saddled her horse. 'Is that a good length?' It looked good to him, admiring the way Harper's new jeans hugged her legs.

'I guess so.' She was very unsure of herself.

'You can do this, Harper.' He patted her knee tenderly,

hoping to give her some confidence. 'Just promise to tell me if something's not right and I'll fix it.' He gave her the reins.

'I'll do the same for Mason's harness.'

'Yeah, sure.' Ash hitched Bree's specially rigged baby harness's thick straps higher onto his shoulders, holding Mason snuggly to his chest. It made it a challenge to climb into the saddle of his own horse. But it was part of the deal.

Yet he could feel everyone watching him. And they were. 'What?' He scowled at his brothers.

It wasn't his first time in a saddle, but it was his first time carrying a child.

For weeks he'd managed to avoid getting this close to the kid, but with the kid strapped to his chest, it was impossible to avoid him now.

Fourteen days to go before the welfare visit. Thankfully, he had the ride to Wombat Flats to keep his mind occupied.

'I'll take the lead,' said Charlie. 'Bree's got the rear with our horse plant.'

'Sorry, how are we planting horses?' Harper asked with her shoulders high to her ears.

Ash chuckled. 'A horse plant is what they call a herd of stockhorses.'

'Back in the day they called the person in charge of the horse plant the horse tailor.' Charlie nodded at his granddaughter who was sliding on her riding gloves. Bree's well-worn Akubra sat low on her brow, with her red hair trailing in a thick plait between her shoulders. Just like her grandfather, she had two leather belts on her hips, one full of shotgun shells, the other for her stockwhips.

'You look like a stockwoman who means business, Bree,' Dex called out.

'I'm no stockwoman.' Bree effortlessly climbed into her saddle as if stepping up a ladder to her big black stallion that was a handsome horse. The redhead looked at home in the saddle that had not one, but two guns in holsters. A rifle and a shotgun. With one hand holding the reins, the other led a long trail of eight stockhorses carrying assorted items. Bree and Charlie's stockhorses were in excellent condition, bristling with muscles, healthy coats, and manners, compared to the horses Ash and his brothers had scored for this muster.

'Ash, you keep an eye on Harper,' warned Bree.

'I will.' Ash grinned at Harper, seated awkwardly in her saddle with stiff shoulders and a ramrod straight back. 'Relax, Harper, this isn't pony club where you lose points on posture.' He rolled his shoulders, pleased she was doing the same. The stupid thing was, it took a lot of effort to make it look effortless, considering the baby carrier's weight. 'Are you ready to do this?'

'No.' She shook her head, and for the first time he glimpsed her true fear.

'Hey.' He reached over and patted her leg. He couldn't lean too far, not with Mason strapped to his chest. 'You've got to get your new hat dirty. Just like Mason.'

He had to admit Mason's new mustering outfit was cute.

Charlie was right—Bree had shopped for all of them, from dog food, new gloves, sunscreen, neckerchiefs for the dust, spare pairs of sunglasses, she'd also decked out Mason and Harper, who were both wearing new hats. They'd all cheered when little Mason came home wearing denim jeans, boots, and a proper hat, with a swagger to match. He looked like a Riggs.

Now, kicking his little boots that swung from the baby carrier, the kid was raring to go. The cotton harness was low enough to allow his little legs to sit on the saddle, while he was still attached to Ash's chest. The city folks might not call it safe, but he knew the boy was safe there.

To have Bree on the muster, they needed Harper, who was only here for Mason, and Ash had promised Harper he'd try to spend time with Mason. He just hadn't expected the kid to be strapped to his chest like this, nor the worry he felt for Mason and Harper's safety during this muster.

'You'll be okay, Harper. You're gonna love this.' Ash gave her a reassuring pat on the shoulder. She could ride a little. But as Ryder said, Harper would have broken her saddle in by the end of this trip.

Charlie gave a whistle, and they were off. Charlie and Ryder were in the lead. Ash and Harper next, then came Cap with his entourage of cattle dogs trotting behind him. Bringing up the rear were Dex and Bree, creating the most dust with the string of horses as they entered the Stoneys.

The Stoneys were unfamiliar territory for Ash and his brothers. They'd only seen this area of the station from Ryder's chopper, even then it looked like a world of stone.

Ash craned his neck at the tall sandstone structures towering high above them in clusters as they wound through a wide gully where a small creek ambled down the centre. It was part of the run-off from Starvation Dam, with the occasional drip from the morning's dew that fell from the top edges.

Nothing grew here among the sand that muffled the sounds of the horses' hooves echoing off the walls of stone. The wind whistled as it barrelled around the twists and turns of the stony gully, which grew taller and narrower as they made their way through.

'It's like the planet Mars.' Hand on her hat, Harper's inquisitive eyes took in all the details. She pointed to the thick walls of solid stone. 'Look at those colours, the veins in that rock. It's like ripples you'd find in beach sand.'

'That's sandstone,' explained Charlie, from the horse in front. His voice echoed amid the many shallow caverns and crevices that surrounded them. 'The wind and the water cause those wavy lines. In the wet season, this whole area is mostly underwater.'

Harper leaned back, arching her slender neck to the sky. 'Amazing. It's like coarsely cemented sand.' She playfully reached out to touch the rocks, that had so many colours, from tan browns, deep reds to soft pinks, through to chalky yellows and creams like sand. 'It's pretty.'

Her slender arm stretched wide, while denim brushed against leather in the saddle, as her eyes squinted in the sun. All of her was on show, and it was as if the sun was made to shine down on her like a spotlight. The word *stunning* wasn't enough to describe her natural beauty, or that layer of peace that seemed to wash over her. But it exposed a whole new level of beautiful Ash had never encountered before, that only made his heart hammer a little quicker.

'Look.' Harper pointed to the top edges of the stone walls that sparkled under the morning sun. 'What do you call that shiny stone, Charlie?'

'It's probably quartz. Or maybe mica. Pyrite. Gold, if you're lucky.'

'Gold?' Ash removed his sunglasses and peered at the stone wall that sparkled like glitter had been sprinkled over it.

Beyond that, more walls of stone opened to deep tombs or winding alleyways that ran in a myriad of directions. 'Where does that lead to?' He pointed to the wide alley of rock on his right.

'Anywhere and everywhere. This place is like a maze,' said Charlie. 'You'd get lost in here if you're not careful. Stick to the path where the water runs. Harper, to go back home always follow where the water runs uphill.'

'Got it. Thanks, Charlie.' Her hat's brim barely dulled the shimmer in her eyes.

Finally, Ash was seeing some excitement in Harper, instead of the fear or boredom he'd seen lately. Harper now showed an open curiosity about the world around her. It was an attractive look on her.

'Did they mine gold in this area?'

'Further towards Darwin,' replied Charlie. 'Pine Creek was a gold rush town back in the 1800s. These days there are the Tanami Goldfields, or you can go fossicking west of Tennant Creek.'

'Didn't you work in the gold mines, Ryder?' Cap asked from behind them.

'Nope. Oil and diamonds.'

'Didn't you hear?' called out Dex from the rear. 'That's how Ryder made his millions, from pocketing diamonds while on the job.'

'Finders keepers, boys.' Ryder spun around to share a grin.

'Did I just see Ryder smile?' Bree pulled down her neckerchief. 'Did everyone else witness that miracle?'

The banter was casual, with no bickering, and for the first time in days, the tension had lifted. The mood grew lighter the deeper they weaved their way through the sandstone canyons.

But then the track got narrower, and Harper pulled her horse to a stop. Her mouth clamped into a knot, and she was stock-still and sombre, raising her arm to point her dainty finger. 'There is no way I'm going through there.'

Twenty-five

'**I**'m not going through that.' Harper pointed to the track ahead, that ran uphill along the edge of a cliff. Terror made her pulse pound in her ears, with a cold sweat breaking out across her skin.

'Single file from here, folks,' called out Charlie from the front. 'You right back there, kid?'

'All good, Pop.' Bree took a deep drink from her water bottle. 'Drink some water, Harper. We don't want you dehydrating.'

Harper wanted to pee. To run. To jump off this horse and run back to the farmhouse and hide behind the cardboard boxes that filled the lounge room. She was an indoors girl. Not this.

'Hey …' Ash patted her knee, concern evident in his eyes. 'You'll be okay. It's wider than it looks.'

'You know those scary movies where treasure hunters have to scale the walls on the side of the cliffs? That's *that!*' Harper pointed to the cliff. A freaking cliff. 'How did you get the cattle though that?'

'Easy …' Bree steered her big black horse alongside Harper. 'One step after the other. You can do this. Now, *go get your cowgirl on.*' She slapped the rump of Harper's horse, and it moved forward.

'I hate you right now, Bree.' Gripping the reins, Harper had no choice but to follow the road. A road made up entirely of sandy cream rock.

To stop her worry, she had to think of something else.

That's when her favourite comfort food popped into her head. Shortbread. Imagining that the smooth sandstone walls were like shortbread, and how the path was just a clever carving of beautiful shortbread biscuits.

She swallowed hard, her mouth claggy, yet her throat dry, now wishing she'd taken Bree's advice and drunk some water. But she was too scared to release the reins as she peered over the side where they were so high up, they'd fry in the sun. The deep cavern echoed their hoof steps where not even the dogs barked, as a solemn heaviness filled the air.

'You're doing just fine, Harper.' Ash turned in the saddle to show her Mason was awake. 'Wave to Harper, Mason.' His little hand waved as his smile widened.

'*Arper-Arper.*' Mason's childish voice echoed off the many stone corridors to bounce back as if there were a dozen little boy's singing. 'Bwee-Bwee.'

'Look at you go, little man.' Bree's voice was light, and with no fear. Did Bree fear anything? 'And you too, Harper. You've got this.'

Harper was too scared to look back. All she could do was trust the horse she'd just met. It made her focus on each step her horse took, with no thoughts of the future, or the past, just this present moment.

She licked her lips, trying to keep her breathing calm, tasting the sandy dust that blended with the nervous salty sweat. Her hands tightened on the reins and saddle, as her shadow stretched over the rock walls outlining her wide-brimmed hat.

The horse's steady gait made her hips sway in the saddle and there was just her, the horse, that big sky, and this sandstone trail of rich red ridges that blended into a cliffside, where rocky domes and large boulders rested like dots along the canyon's rims.

When she rode around the canyon's prehistoric wall of stone, Ash was there waiting for her, sitting proudly on his horse with a big smile, holding Mason close to his chest.

She sighed heavily from the wave of relief for having

survived. Her hands were sore, and her shoulders ached from gripping the saddle and reins.

But then Ash's smile widened, and it was directed at her, the one with the dimple that made her give in to him so easily. It was the smile that had brought her out here, only this time he was looking at her with pride and admiration.

It should be illegal for his eyes to glint like that. It was disrespectful to the laws of nature.

'You made it.'

'Barely.' Why couldn't he hold her and tell her that? She could really do with a hug.

'Well, you're gonna love this.' He beckoned her to follow, leaving her no choice. The sand muffled the horses' steps, but the men's voices echoed around her as they wove deeper into a corridor of sandstone.

At first she thought her ears were playing tricks on her, when she heard the bubbling, gurgling, gushing, rumbling roar of running water.

Behind her was nothing but rock, as she followed Ash's horse out of a honeycomb pocket. Instantly cooling down the air, a fine spray of sweet fresh water brushed against her skin. Her jaw dropped in awe at the towering waterfall, spilling over the rocky ledge to then flow down to meet the lush collection of palms and cycads, to create a hidden oasis. How could something exist like this, trapped in a rugged world of ancient sandstone walls hundreds of metres tall?

'We'll stop here and have a breather. Give the horses a chance to drink some water.' Charlie swung off his saddle and walked his horse through the powdery soft, white sand.

'What is this place, Charlie?' Harper had never seen anything like it. A few small birds whizzed past, skimming over the crystal-clear rock pool, where the water disappeared down a channel of stone.

'This is Grass Tree Creek.' He pointed to the exotic tree that had a thick black trunk topped with long-limbed branches that sprouted from the top like grass. 'We'll have lunch now, but we'll be heading for Dinner Camp Tree where we'll really put on the nosebag.'

'Here, let me help you down.' Cap held his hand out to Harper. Ash was up further, getting off the horse with Mason.

'Thank you, Cap.' Her legs were like rubber and she struggled to walk straight in her new boots. 'What did Charlie mean by nosebag?' She followed Cap as they led the horses to the glistening pool, where the dogs eagerly jumped in for a swim.

'Tucker. Food.'

'Oh, right? Charlie has some funny sayings.'

'They're Aussie slang terms that are sadly disappearing.'

She stopped for a moment to truly take in the scene. The cattle dogs wore huge grins as they paddled like puppies playing in the water. The Riggs brothers joked with each other, wearing handsome smiles that shone beneath their hat brims, while being gentle with the horses, ensuring they all got a drink.

The coiled stockwhip hung from Charlie's belt, as his spurs on the back of his riding boots clinked like coins being jiggled in his pocket. He poked back the brim of his sweaty hat with the crocodile band, and helped Bree lead her group of horses to water.

Bree removed her gloves as she approached Harper. 'So, what did you think?'

'Terrifying.' Removing her hat, Harper swiped away the dusty sweat from her forehead.

'Well, that was the worst of it. The next part has the view.' Bree pointed to the deep pass ahead that only showed the shadows of the stony trail. 'We'll be going downhill.'

'And you and Charlie did this by yourselves, with all those cows?'

'Just a walk in the park. Come on ...'

'Where are we going?'

'To find a nice quiet canyon corner to pee.' Bree held up a toilet roll.

'Oh.' She crossed her legs, in need. 'I've never ...'

'Nothing like a lesson in getting back to nature.'

It was like this trip was one big lesson, and they hadn't even made it to Wombat Flats. She peeked over her shoulder to check on Mason with Ash.

'Let his father take the reins, Harper. Ash needs to learn. Like you've been learning to ride again.'

'You're right.' She needed to take the reins on her own life, too. She'd made it this far on her own. Even if it was completely unplanned, she'd done it. Today she'd faced a new kind of terror and pushed past it to find paradise.

She gazed up at the stunning waterfall, admiring the rich colours in the rocks, and acknowledging the secrets she felt being whispered by the wind. Here, there was no ugliness in the world, just the sky, the simplicity of stone walls, fresh spring water, and the bubbling sounds of a child's laughter. It was a hidden treasure that she hadn't expected to find in the outback—it was pretty close to paradise. 'Let the next outback lesson begin ...'

Twenty-six

'Are you ladies okay back there?' Ash peered in the direction Harper and Bree had disappeared. They'd been gone for ages, and in this place of stone canyons, you could easily get lost—especially Harper, who had no sense of direction.

He dropped his head and listened hard for signs. At first, he could only hear the wind whistling and the water roaring over the brink of the falls. But then there was the faint echo of women's laughter.

He sighed, wiping his hand over his mouth where the smile grew, but the relief of hearing Harper's laugh was enormous.

Earlier, he'd seen her terror while riding through the Stoneys. It had him so worried that he wanted to pull her off her horse and make her ride with him and Mason.

But seeing Harper face her fears had been more rewarding. Each hour that passed, her inner confidence grew in the way she rode her horse and peered at the world around them. It was beautiful to watch.

'They'll be fine, lad. Whatcha need?' Charlie squinted at him from beneath his weatherworn hat.

'What do I do with this one?' He pointed at the kid strapped to his chest, who'd just woken up and was asking for Harper or Bree.

'Strip him off and let him paddle and play with the pups. The water's only ankle deep.'

'Just not too close to the falls. The torrent will knock

Mason over,' said Cap. 'I'll take him.'

'Sure.' He dragged the boy from his carrier. The air was cool against his sweaty shirt as he unclipped the contraption, freeing himself from the burden of the boy. 'Are we stopping for lunch?'

'And to swap horses,' said Ryder. 'We don't want to wear them out before we work them.'

'Here, Bree made these sandwiches. Dig in.' Charlie pulled back the lid of a large carry bag to reveal rows and rows of assorted sandwiches. Egg salad sandwiches, salty cured corned beef, ham off the bone, smoked bacon, and grilled chicken strips. They all came with assorted relishes, cheeses, and salads, creating an endless combination of flavours. 'Bree made 'em fresh this morning.'

Ash's stomach growled. He'd never had such fancy sandwiches, nor had so many choices that he wanted to stuff his face silly.

'Don't mind if I do.' He was famished. Plucking a soft buttered triangle sandwich of ham, Swiss cheese, a tarty jam, and seeded mustard, with crunchy lettuce and alfalfa. He devoured it in a few bites. What a feast!

Should he put a plate away for Harper before his brothers devoured the lot? Thinking of others … 'Mason, come and get some food.'

The little boy's eyes were enormous as he quickly sloshed through the water to grip on the sandwich with his little fingers and chow down.

Should he have fed the boy sooner? He'd made sure the boy had plenty of water to drink in between his naps, but hadn't thought of snacks.

'Tank-u.'

Aww. The boy had manners, and was chatty at times, though he struggled to say the letter H. But he was easy to please, plus he loved the outdoors with an obvious sense of adventure, he wasn't shy about peeking around corners. Just like Ash. 'Stay close, Mason.'

The boy nodded, kicking at the water, eagerly taking

another sandwich from Ash, with his little cheeks full of food.

With only the sounds of the tumbling waterfall filling the shallow rock pool, the men stood around the food bag eating, all of them watching the boy.

Nearby, the horses grazed on slender grasses growing in between the cracks and crevices in the slate-like floor. The wet cattle dogs were having a fat time rolling in the soft sand, eroded from the hard rock beds due to the wind and time.

It was common for stations in the Northern Territory to have their fair share of hidden waterfalls, but Grass Tree Creek was impressive. A hidden oasis in the middle of a towering rock garden.

'Here come the girls now.' Dex nodded in their direction.

Ash raised his eyebrows, with his half-eaten sandwich frozen in his hand, watching Bree and Harper arm in arm, giggling over some secret.

Harper's smile was so bright, as if the stress she was under was finally lifting from her shoulders, smoothing out the worry lines she'd had crinkling her brow. In its place were shiny eyes, and her natural beauty.

'I think the snooty city girl is enjoying herself,' said Dex. 'I don't think I've ever seen her smile until today.'

'Yeah …' Damn, it was pretty. Nah, Harper was better than pretty—

Dex slapped the back of Ash's head. 'Oi, stop it.'

Ash rubbed the back of his head. 'Don't hit me, ya brute. I'm not your punching bag.'

'I'm building a boxing ring at my place so we can punch up anytime.' Dex grinned, scooping up another sandwich. 'But I was talking about you going all starry-eyed at the babysitter. She's outta your league, and don't forget she's not here for long.'

'Did you remember to advertise for a real nanny?' Ryder asked, between mouthfuls of his sandwich.

Ash shrugged. 'It's on my list.'

'Did Harper say how long her holiday was?'

'Nope.'

'What does Harper do when she's not pretending to be a nanny?'

'Office something or other. Overseas.' Again, Ash shrugged at Ryder. He didn't feel like sharing the details with his brothers, he wanted to keep the conversations he shared with Harper to himself. 'Maybe if you'd bother to have a conversation with Harper, she might actually help you in the office.'

Ryder frowned. 'Charlie, if you're running a brand-making business, who does your paperwork?'

'Bree manages it all. She'd make an excellent secretary if she'd stop tellin' me what to do. Go to this appointment, eat this, drink that, don't do that, no coffee. I miss coffee.'

'Bree is only doing that because she cares,' said Ryder. 'She told us that she wants you to outlive her.'

'Yeah, I know.' The old man sighed, adjusting his hat. 'I'm lucky to have someone like her. Ol' Darcie adored her, too. Bree looked after him, too, at the end and wanted no money for it. It's why I reckon Darcie created that caretaker's caveat.'

'That's for you, right?' Dex asked, as Ryder listened.

'And Bree. That kid grew up here, too.' Charlie plonked his hands on his belt. 'Look, fellas, Bree may seem snappy with you mob, but once she learns to trust you, you'll never find a more loyal friend who'll treat you like family. I don't think you're far off now...' Charlie nodded at the food bag filled with sandwiches. 'That kid was up all night making sure you were well catered for. And believe me, there'll be times you'd tell her to get nicked, to go live a life elsewhere, which she did ...' He paused, scratching his ruddy chin.

'But one phone call from that hospital mob was all it took and my granddaughter rocked up. Then she moved her whole life, to take care of two old men and this station. Darcie's own children didn't even bother and that was his kin.' Charlie dusted his hands, then faced the four brothers. 'Let me tell you fellas, underneath that brassy red hair is a kind soul. And, if you lot bothered to talk to that little Harper, you'll find she's like that, too. Harper is a good kid, otherwise Bree wouldn't have bothered befriending her. Now, let's skedaddle before them two females give us a job, and come and get your fresh horses to saddle.' With hands full of sandwiches, the brothers left Ash.

He wasn't walking away from Mason, not near water.

Harper approached, her cheeks brushed with red, almost the same colour as the tip of her nose.

'You should put on some more sunscreen. Your cute nose is getting burnt.' Ash playfully tapped her slightly upturned nose. He hadn't meant to get that close to her, but he enjoyed being near her. Inhaling the soft fragrance that he'd come to recognise as hers.

'I will, thanks.' She gave him a shy smile. 'Where's Mason?'

'Splashing in the water.' Ash nodded at the boy.

'He's naked.' Her eyes widened with surprise.

'He'll drip dry soon enough. Go get yourself some lunch.'

'I could handle a swim.' Her smile light, her eyes bright, even her walk seemed lighter and full of energy. And that view of her high and tight arse in those jeans made his head tilt.

'She's having a good time,' whispered Bree, close to his ear.

Busted. 'Bree. Where did you come from?'

'The spinifex fairies dropped me off on their way to the pub. What do you think?' Bree giggled.

'Hey, Bree.' He grabbed her arm before she walked away. 'Thank you.'

'For what?'

'For helping Harper adapt.' Wishing he could do more to make life easier for Harper.

'You guys really dumped her in it, you know?'

'Yeah, I know.' They'd been idiots—himself mostly for not seeing it sooner.

'Talk to her, Ash. Harper is a clever woman.'

'And what do you suggest we talk about? Shopping?' Did he admit he'd been trying—but the boundaries they had were making it difficult for him to even be in the same room as Harper. Not when he wanted to tuck her close to his chest, grip the sides of her face and kiss her.

'Why not tell Harper what this mine is trying to do?'

'How? When I don't understand what they're doing.' And he wasn't asking his brothers to explain it to him, it'd only give them another excuse to look at him like an idiot. He wasn't dumb, he just didn't do legalese.

Bree got in real close, her voice low, but her green eyes were steady and sure. Ash couldn't look away. 'Talk to Harper. Not your brothers. Harper. Trust me on this, Ash.' She patted his arm and headed for the sandwiches. 'Did Mason eat all the good sandwiches ...' She scooped up the boy, with Harper beside her. His cackling little laugh echoed down the stony corridors.

Ash narrowed his eyes at Harper, taking in the details, like the way she tucked her hair behind her ear, how slender her wrists were and her long dainty fingers. Her dark hair, with that slight curl and glorious shine, was loose around her shoulders. She also looked damned fine in that hat, as if it was made for her.

Wait ... Was Bree hinting to him that there was more to Harper than he was aware of?

Twenty-seven

On fresh horses, they began the last leg of their trek through the Stoneys to head for Wombat Flats. After several hours, the trail widened where they skimmed the top of the escarpment giving them an endless view of the horizon. There the stony trail began its descent, where the walls of stone that had towered over them suddenly fell away to reveal an endless blue sky.

'Have a gecko's gander at that ...' In the lead, Charlie stopped his horse and pushed back the brim of his hat. His words echoing past them to disappear among the smooth, twisty maze of sandstone walls that made up the Stoneys.

'What did Charlie say?' Harper asked.

'Have a look.' Ash craned his neck, sitting higher in the saddle, keen to see what the attention was all about.

'Tell you what, lads, some days are like diamonds.' Charlie grinned at Ash, then nodded at the road ahead. 'Welcome to Cascades Spur, and the best view of Wombat Flats.'

Ash rode closer, his eyes widening as his jaw slackened at the sight of Cascades Spur. It was a ledge of solid rock that curved like a stockman's spur, with water cascading over it, cooling the air with clean, crisp spring water he tasted on his tongue.

It was another waterfall, many times bigger than the one they'd left behind at Grass Tree Creek. And they were standing beneath it!

With cupped hands to the curtain of water he took a mouthful. The taste of natural spring water was crisp, with a sweet, refreshing purity of rainwater blending with invigorating minerals and a subtle earthy undertone to its flavour. He could almost taste the untamed outback's wilderness.

He washed his face, then did the same for Mason, strapped to his chest. 'Good, Mason?'

The kid squealed with delight, his arms reaching for the water, with his tongue poking out for more. They splashed water at each other, their laughs blending to echo off the rocky outcrop that made up Cascades Spur.

'Try this, Harper. I doubt you'll taste water as sweet as this anywhere.'

Harper nudged her horse closer, sitting high in the saddle as her own horse eagerly lapped at the water sprays. She cupped some water and timidly drank. 'This is amazing.' Her eyes widened. 'How can there be so many waterfalls out here?'

'They're all over the Territory. But I've never ridden under one that was part of the cattle track.' He removed his hat and brushed the water over his hair to cool off, the beads trickling down the back of his shirt, but also spraying over Mason who only laughed louder, as the horse nickered with approval.

'I now understand what Charlie meant by saying *a day is like diamonds*.' With a soft smile, Harper pointed at the small rainbows cast by the curtain of fresh water that shimmered as it spilled towards a wonderland. It was a panoramic view of Wombat Flats. A hidden valley surrounded by walls of sandstone where more towering waterfalls fell from various sides.

'I get why they call it Wombat Flats.' Ash nodded at the valley, which was shaped like a fat wombat, where the sun's rays highlighted assorted flourishing ghost gums. Slender green grasses flanked the sides of the winding network of creeks that wound through to pool at the end, creating a small lake.

It was a paradise that even had Ryder stopping his horse to take in the view.

'Do we really own all of that?' Ash nudged his horse to stand beside his big brother.

'We do.' Ryder bundled up his reins in his gloved hands. 'You know what? Today, I'm glad you boys talked me into buying this place.' Ryder nodded, then rode off to catch up to Charlie on the path that widened to the valley floor.

'Are they cows?' Harper pointed, sitting more comfortably in the saddle now. Her smile, which matched the shine in her eyes, did something to his chest, making him inhale a little deeper.

'Cattle.' Ash nodded at the Brahman that were like white dots on a canvas. Hundreds of cattle. They had a herd—a big one.

'I see why you guys have such a love for this country. I get it now …' She pointed to the massive vista of pristine countryside. 'No vehicle has ever been down there. Do you know how rare that is?'

'Huh.' His eyebrows lifted. She'd made a good point.

Sharing this moment with Harper seemed special, as if something passed between them. Instead of looking at the landscape like she'd crashed onto the moon, Harper was starting to see the untold beauty of the outback. It made him want to share his entire world with her.

'*Oi, lovebirds.* You're holding up traffic.' Dex scowled at them as he and Bree led a dozen horses in the rear.

'What did he say?' Harper asked.

'Ignore the grumpy ass.' Ash frowned at his brother for ruining the moment.

He nudged his horse forward, but waited for Harper to join him. They rode side by side down the path, the rock of the saddle effortlessly putting Mason to sleep.

Mason might not remember today, but one day when he's older Ash would love to bring the boy back. They'd swim in the falls, go camping, and tell stories around the campfire under the stars, and create their own rock art, by painting directions to never get lost in the Stoneys. This place was close to heaven. No, this was better—it was a stockman's paradise.

Wait. Was he planning a future with the boy?

But then another thought hammered up his spine, making him shift in his saddle as if fighting a case of fiery indigestion.

How much water was the mine going to take? And how big of an impact would it have on Wombat Flats, where various waterfalls flowed along the escarpment?

'Hey, Harper? Have you heard about the new mine moving in next door?'

Harper shrugged, as they rode along the trail towards the valley floor. 'I know something has upset you guys, but no one's told me the entire story. Besides, it's none of my business.'

'But it's mine. Even if I don't fully understand it myself.' He paused to rub the back of his neck.

'Why? What's going on?' Even though she had a habit of looking down her nose at things, she didn't tease or judge him.

When he'd spoken to her about gamifying the station, her honesty had been refreshing. Although, at times he struggled to talk to her without his hormones getting in the way, he now had the perfect topic, that was far too close to home.

'Well, we got this letter ...' With his hand tenderly holding Mason's head as the boy slept heavily against his chest, he spoke freely with Harper, who listened and asked good questions.

Looking at Wombat Flats, it worried him that the new mine would infringe on this place, on the rest of their home. Especially when the Station Hand had told him that no cattle station had ever won against the might of the mining companies getting what they wanted—which was their water.

Twenty-eight

'Yep, I reckon this spot is good enough to swing a billy.' Charlie climbed off his sturdy stockhorse. 'Welcome to Dinner Camp Tree, you mob.'

'What did Charlie say?' Harper felt foolish asking Ash to interpret Charlie's terminology. 'I get that dinner camp is the name of the tree ...' The tree was an old and large eucalyptus tree with a salmon pink trunk and wide leafy canopy. Below its shade was a scattering of thick tree logs that formed a circle, around a circle of stones set for a campfire. '... but the billy bit?'

'A billy is a tin with a handle and a lid, like a pot,' explained Ash, while climbing off his horse. 'Bushmen use it to make billy tea. And billy tea isn't a billy tea unless it's done on the coals of a campfire.'

'What kind of tea leaves do they use?'

'Black tea leaves and freshly boiled water. Some add eucalyptus leaves for flavour or sugarbag honey. I don't mind it with lemon myrtle myself.'

'And the swinging bit?'

Ash grinned at her. 'Not the modern term for swingers. Get that out of your mind.'

'I wasn't.' But her cheeks got hot as she climbed down from her saddle to save face. But it only had Ash laughing as he held Mason strapped to his chest like a handbag.

'The reason they swing the billy is to force the leaves to the bottom. It makes it easier to pour, and it helps with the infusion process. I'm sure Charlie will show you in the morning. It's one of those things that is disappearing.'

'Because of a tea strainer?'

'No. I reckon the old bushies made a show of the billy tea, the same way the Japanese have their tea ceremonies, turning it into an art form. When an old stockman makes you a billy tea, you carve out time in your day to just sit and sip your tea while admiring the outdoors. I think it's a tradition someone like you should create for yourself.' Ash gently tapped her arm.

She grinned like a schoolgirl, even twirling a lock of her hair around her fingers. 'A tea ceremony.'

'It's got to be better than drinking cold coffee because you're too busy to ever see a sunset.'

He had her there.

Ash pointed to the scenery. 'Where do you want to pitch your tent?'

'I have a tent?'

'The only tent.'

'Where is everyone else sleeping?'

'On our swags. We thought you could do with the privacy, and Bree said it'd be easier to contain Mason, so he didn't run off.' He unclipped the harness and lowered the boy to the ground. 'Come on, mate, let's give the horses to Charlie while Harper picks a spot to sleep.' He held out his hand to Mason.

Her heart just melted to see Mason gripping one of Ash's large fingers. It was happening. It was finally happening. But she didn't want to spook Ash by noticing that the bonding had begun. 'What do I look for?'

'Make sure your tent lies on level ground that's clear. You don't want the blood rushing to your head in your sleep or having rocks sticking into your back. Go on, princess, find a spot for your palace. I'll grab the tent.' He winked at her as he led the two horses and Mason away.

Everyone was doing something, as Harper stumbled through the grasses brushing against her thighs, while her boots trod on dainty white and blue wildflowers releasing their fragrance. She was in awe of this valley that had scattered waterfalls tumbling from the escarpment that surrounded them. It was a world within a world, where even the air they breathed was rare.

Ryder and Dex carried an axe each and disappeared into the thick cluster of trees. Cap helped Bree drag out pots and pans to set up their campfire. Charlie and Ash set up a rope line to corral the unsaddled horses, leaving them to graze in the lush grasses. Yet, they all had that sense of peace, a sense of community, without any of the outside interference or stress and strain Harper was so used to living under.

'*What the flip!*' Dex came running out of the trees, knocking off his hat, waving his hands over his face, doing some weird kung fu dance.

Ryder ran towards him, axe ready to attack. 'What is it? Snake?'

'Spider. Can you see it? Is it on me?' Dex stripped off his shirt, exposing his torso of muscle and ink, slapping and pawing at his neck and face. 'It was the size of a dinner plate. Swear it.'

'Look at Dex going all Bruce Lee over a spider!' Charlie chuckled at Dex, swinging his axe at the dirt.

'You're not scared of spiders, are you, Dex?' Bree stood with hands on her hips wearing a grin that said, *I'm going to taunt you about this for the rest of your natural born life.*

'Bird spider.' With a strong arm bristling with muscles, Dex pointed his axe at Bree. 'No lip out of you, Bree. It was the size of a flipping dinner plate.'

'Dex is making that up. Spiders don't get that big.' Harper pushed through the grass to find a suitable space away from the brothers, near a scattering of trees, and looked up.

'AUGH!!!!' It was a spider, bigger than her head. Harper turned away, only to rush straight into another web bigger than her body, with a massive spider staring at her face to face.

She screamed at the living nightmare, running

somewhere, nowhere, anywhere, swatting at her face, jumping at the ground. Her screams echoed in her ears, that only made her scream more as she ran. *'Spider! Spider!'*

Oomph! She was rugby tackled to land on her back in the thick grass, with Ash on top of her.

'Harper—'

'It was a dinosaur-sized spider! It had red and black legs. A huge body. And eyes that stared straight at me. Face to face.' She wriggled to get free and run.

'Harper. Calm down.' Ash pinned her arms to her sides as he lay on top of her in the grass.

Her heart hammered loud in her ears. *'It was huge. No, it was bigger than big.'*

'That was just a bird spider. It's the golden orb spider, they're harmless to humans.'

'How can they exist? Where's Mason?' Now she understood why Dex feared them.

'With Bree. Calm down, those spiders won't hurt you.'

'I saw fangs! And their web is like a sticky string. How is that possible?' She wanted a shower. She wanted to be back indoors.

'They catch bats, birds, and even snakes in their webs, that's how strong it is. I've seen their webs knock stockmen off their horses. It's the only thing that scares Dex.'

'I don't blame him.' Her pulse still pounded. She wanted to flee. *'We have to leave this place.'*

'STOP.' He forcefully held her wrists to the ground, effectively pinning her underneath him. 'Harper, look at me. Hey …' He got so close she had no choice but to stare into his dark brown eyes, while lying cushioned in the grass, under a clear blue sky, surrounded by a wall of green grass and wildflowers.

'Take a deep breath, come on …'

She took a shallow one. Then another. Even though her heart slowed down, she was trapped by his gorgeous eyes, his care, and his heavy body weight, stirring her in ways she hadn't thought possible.

'Good. Welcome back to the living.' He rolled off her, lying beside her in the grass.

She felt cool without his body heat. And embarrassed. 'I'm sorry I laughed at Dex.' She sat up, trying to straighten her hair, pulling out some leaves.

'I'd say Dex is glad someone else is scared of them, too. Those bird spiders are big.'

'How come you're not scared of them?'

'Oh, I am. Believe me. I jumped out of a moving vehicle once.'

'Really?'

'It was on one of my early musters.' Tugging free a piece of grass, he twisted it into knots, while crossing his leg over his bent knee.

Harper leaned onto her side with her head cradled in her hand to listen, too embarrassed to face everyone else.

'Me and a mate had gone hunting to feed the stock camp. We were driving in the station's Tojo, so focused on hunting, we drove straight through this spider's web, we didn't see what was on it.'

'Oh, no.' She went to sit up.

'Ah ...' He pushed her back to lie on the grass beside him as he continued his story. 'We were young and dumb, loaded with an old twelve-gauge shotgun, keen for a hunt. All I remember was we'd wiped off the web and kept hunting until ...' He paused for dramatic emphasis.

'Until ...' She playfully shoved his shoulder.

'My worst nightmare happened. It scared the kaka right out of me.'

'Huh?'

'Think about it ...'

'Oh. Right. Like I was just before.' The rush of heat brushed her cheeks.

'But this was worse.'

'No way. How?'

'It started climbing up the side of the Tojo with the thickest, biggest spider legs I'd ever seen. I swear you could've put a saddle on this thing and ridden it at the rodeo.'

'So bigger than a dinner-plate-sized spider?'

'Bigger.' He spread his hands wide to the size of an inflated gym ball.

'What did you do?' Her voice was a whisper, with her eyes darting to the shadows between the blades of grass.

He grabbed her chin, dragging it to face him and not the scary wilderness. 'I played my part of the hero, of course.' He grinned with his dark eyes trapping hers. 'I bailed, yelling, *shoot it!*'

A giggle escaped her. 'What happened then?'

'Well, I kissed the dirt, rolling across the ground, watching the Tojo drive away with my mate still sitting in the passenger seat.'

'You were driving!'

'At that stage, no one was. But the next thing I hear is this shotgun blast, and I watched my mate jump out of the Tojo. The only problem was the vehicle kept going.'

'Let me guess, you started running after it.'

'We were like Olympic sprinters, worried we'd never catch it. Until it hit this thick cluster of saplings and I was able to knock it out of gear.'

'And that spider?'

'Gone. And the Tojo had a new hole in the floor.' His chuckle made her smile. 'Of course, we checked the car a few times before we climbed back inside.'

'I'd do the same with a shoe in one hand and can of bug spray in the other, while calling for security.'

They both lay back, laughing.

'Are you okay now?' Ash was so close, lying on the grass beside her.

'Yeah, I am.' She stared up at the sky taking a deep breath. 'Thanks for that.'

'You panicked.'

'I did.' She hid her face. 'And you rugby tackled me.'

'You were scaring the cattle, and Mason. I was worried.'

She could see it. 'I'm sorry. In all fairness, this is new to me.'

'I get it. But the good thing is with all your screaming and running around like that, I'm sure you've scared off all the snakes.'

'*Snakes?*' She scrambled to her feet.

Ash rolled around laughing at her, a perfect imitation of what Mason did when he was laughing hysterically.

'Come on. Let's go set up your tent.' He tenderly held her hand and helped her past the assorted grasses. 'Hey, at least you have your own scary spider story to share.'

'You could have warned me.'

He gave her hand a gentle squeeze. 'Why would I do that? You wouldn't have come then.'

Twenty-nine

Crickets chirped in her ear. Another insect of some sort buzzed nearby. Something crunched on the grass. A bat screamed as if it was being murdered. And a dingo howled like a werewolf. Even though she was inside a tent, it was impossible for Harper to sleep.

Meanwhile, Mason slept soundly beside her.

Frustrated, she bashed at her pillow.

'Can't sleep?' Ash's deep voice was close.

'You know, I can sleep in some hotel beside a busy highway, or I can nap near the runway of an airport, but this …' She waved at the darkness without a simple streetlight anywhere, but a silvery moonlight gently pushed back the darkest shadows, with their campfire on the other side casting a warm glow. 'I never realised it'd be this noisy.' Especially the brothers and Charlie, who were snoring heavily in their sleep. No wonder Bree was camped over on the far side.

Something cracked a twig, followed by a *thump thump thump*.

'What's that?' Her heart hammered in her throat as she sat up, holding the sheet to her chest.

'A wallaby.' Ash unzipped the tent's flynet door. 'Move over.'

'What are you doing?'

'Climbing inside. Don't worry, we'll keep Mason in the middle.'

'Why?'

'Because you're keeping me awake, jumping at every noise, when there is nothing out here.'

'Wallabies are out there. And dingoes are out there. Oh, let's not forget about the *spiders*.'

'Harper, we have almost a dozen well-trained cattle dogs that will do their best to protect this camp. And I'm pretty sure Bree's not afraid to shoot at things that go bump in the night. Now, sit up so I can slide your swag over, and let's hope the boy doesn't wake.'

She scooted to the far side, helping Ash slide her thick mattress across the floor of the tent. Mason didn't stir.

Ash dragged in his swag, zipped up the screen door, and lay down. 'What are you waiting for? Don't worry, I won't touch you.'

'I bet you say that to all the girls.'

'Pfft. No. That's the first time I've ever said that. And having a baby between us kind of kills any romance. Besides, we had an agreement. You didn't want that cliché thing. You have *boundaries*.'

'I did. I mean, I do. It's tacky sleeping with the nanny. It makes the workplace messy when a boss sleeps with their employee.' She'd seen it destroy election campaigns and promising political careers.

'Relax. I'm only here so we can all get some sleep. Consider me the guard at the door to protect you from bunyips or drop bears.'

She could practically hear his smug smile in the dark.

Fine. She could do this. And lay down on her bed.

Admittedly, having him close was soothing. 'So, this is camping?'

'It is.'

'If there was some form of indoor plumbing and hot showers, I might enjoy camping.'

Ash's chuckle was deep, making her tummy swirl with butterflies. She couldn't sleep now.

'I can't help with the indoor plumbing, as we don't have walls or doors or pipework. But I might be able to rig up something tomorrow to give you a hot shower.'

'Really? You'd do that?'

'Sure. Why not?'

'Why?' What was his angle?

She felt his shrug, the way the bed linen shifted.

'Go to sleep, Harper. We've got a big day tomorrow.'

She lay there stiff as a board as his breathing got deeper and deeper, while she stared at the stars. She was tired. Overtired. But her mind was wide awake as she watched a shooting star's astonishing long tail blaze across the night sky. It was glorious.

Surprisingly, it was the first time her mind seemed clear, without the brain fog. Did that mean she was ready to go back to work?

'Hey, Ash.' She sat up, his frame so large compared to his son's.

'Hmm ...'

'Do you think you can get me a copy of that letter? The one you got from the mines department.'

His breathing quickened and his eyes fluttered open. 'What for?'

She lay down on her side to face him. Maybe she could be useful. 'So we can work out the words together.'

He ran his fingers through his thick hair. 'I'm not dumb.'

'I didn't say that. Those sorts of letters are usually written by lawyers to trip people up.'

'So, I'm not being an idiot about this?'

'No. You're charmingly intelligent.' Oh, no. What did she just say? She quickly spoke to stop the fire-hydrant red blush flaring across her skin. 'You said the letter had some threatening undertone to it.'

'Yeah.'

'Well, I'll have a look at it—if you can sneak it past your brothers, because I doubt Ryder would approve of you sharing his paperwork with the staff.'

'That's true.' He frowned, then wiped it away. 'Don't get offended by that, Harper, it's not you. Ryder is like that with all of us. Dex reckons it's because we used to break his stuff when we were young. We were always in Ryder's room, he had the cool stuff and his own room, while we all shared.'

'Did you ever get your chance to move into Ryder's old room? I always had my own room, practically an only child.' Even if her old childhood room didn't exist anymore, she would've shared.

'Lucky you.' He sniffed. 'No. I went to work. I wasn't interested in finishing school. Our little bush school couldn't help me anymore, and I knew what I wanted to do.'

'What's that?'

'This. Working with cattle, in this industry. I knew it the second I stumbled onto that first station. I've always been happy just being a contractor, until Jonathan got Sandlot Station and the rest of my brothers started talking about buying a place together. I never thought it was possible.'

'So, this is one of those impossible dreams come true for you.' She lay facing him, with their heads resting on pillows, talking in hushed voices. Even with a small boy lying between them it was intimately cosy.

Ash nodded, rolling over to face her. 'It's more like one of those *dare to dream* kind of things. Deep down I've always wanted my own cattle station, but never thought it'd happen. But having my brothers as partners, they've made it possible.' He exhaled heavily, rolling onto his back. 'I would've freaked doing it on my own.'

'I don't think so. You're a strong guy.'

He rolled over to face her again. 'There's a lot of responsibility running a place like this. Ryder's doing it all.'

And Ash ran from responsibility.

'Do you want to help Ryder manage this place?'

'Yeah ...' He paused, blinking in the silvery moonlight where the glow of the campfire gave him the perfect silhouette. He then nodded with resolve. '*Yes*, I want to help, but I don't know how. All Ryder tells me to do is the troughs.'

'And that's where you say you'll add it to your list.' She

gently poked his chest. 'Have you ever looked over that list you're always adding to?'

He frowned.

'I'm not judging.' She held her palm open as if in peace.

'No. I haven't.'

'I bet you'll find the answers you're looking for there.' She patted his chest and her hand rested on Mason's little shoulders. 'Good night, Ash.'

'Good night, Harper.'

And she let her eyes close and soon fell asleep to the soothing sounds of Ash's deep breathing, not even realising he was holding her hand.

Thirty

The cows were enormous. They also came with massive horns and should have been classed as colossal white boulders who didn't want to move.

Not that Harper could blame them. When they had beautiful, lush green fields full of assorted grasses and grains mixed with wildflowers to tempt them.

The day had begun at sunrise where the rich layer of dusky pinks smeared across the horizon, when Ash approached his brothers over their first cup of coffee. At Harper's careful suggestion, Ash had drawn a diagram in the dirt as if giving a presentation to the board, explaining how he could use the drone for their benefit.

It was enough to give him the go-ahead.

Ash held the remote control for his drone, the dark goggles covered his eyes as he spoke over the radio clipped to a leather holster called a radio pouch.

Right beside him, Harper sat on the side of a small hill, making daisy chains with Mason, as Ash steered his drone. The aim was to muster the cattle closer, to create one large herd to then make the trek back home.

'Watch your back, Ryder,' said Ash over the radio. 'I'm bringing a bunch of cleanskins in from the scrub behind you.'

'I see them. Well done, Ash,' came Ryder's deep voice over the radio speakers. 'Dex, you with me?'

'On your ugly side, Ryder. We'll flank 'em.'

The dry season air carried a certain vibrancy with its upbeat winds ruffling old leaves free to make way for the new. From her view on the hill, the streams and billabongs sparkled like gin-clear waters. It also gave her a clear view of the show being laid out before her — the muster.

It was teamwork on horseback, but one of a rugged elegance, captivating her with the skill level and power of both Ryder and Dex as they made their horses dance, while whirling the stockwhip to gallop through the thick scrublands. From there, they'd meet up with Cap, playing the Pied Piper, whistling commands to the stocky and fearless cattle dogs who helped corral the cattle closer to Bree. With her thick plait like a red rope, that beautiful Amazon fearlessly controlled the wing of the main herd while Charlie took the lead, like he was promising them a golden ticket to paradise.

Harper understood it was for their safety, too, because this hidden wonderland was in a massive rock arena that had the potential to suffer with a flash flood either cutting off the cattle for good or …

Even with the dangers it was beautiful out here. Charlie called it utopia, and even Bree and the brothers seemed at home in this place, wallowing in the creek to wash off their sweat and dirt at the end of the day.

Then as the sun sank low, they gathered beneath the silent shadow of the Dinner Camp Tree, where Bree created an open-air feast of flavours around the campfire. From seared steaks, and crusty damper doused in a decadent dance of herbs, perfect for soaking up the rich sauces, to vibrant vegetables full of flavour, all cooked over an open flame. It was like she'd found the true taste of the Northern Territory outback within each glorious meal.

The campfire cast a red and golden glow where tiny sparks popped and crackled from the flames to float and disappear among the starry heavens. It became their place to talk, without anyone staring at a phone screen, where Charlie shared stories of his time at Elsie Creek Station.

After dinner, Harper finally got her hot shower, courtesy of Ash, where he'd hooked up a waterbag, hot from the sun.

He'd even strung up a tarp for privacy. It was heavenly.

Harper returned to the campfire to find Mason asleep in Ash's lap. In that position, you could clearly see the similarities between father and son. 'Where did everyone go?'

'They're knackered, and we've got another big one tomorrow.' Ash stood, holding the boy. 'How was the shower?'

'Brilliant. Best shower ever.'

'You're just saying that.'

'I've never showered under the stars before. It was incredible. Is that why you guys use the outdoor shower all the time?'

'We're trained to not trek dirt through the house. If you liked that shower you should try sitting under waterfalls under a full moon. Or the hot springs in winter. Charlie said there are some hot springs on the other side. I'd like to check them out one day.' Ash carried the boy to the tent, where Harper unzipped the screen door.

With hands clasped behind her back, she shyly dragged the toe of her shoe across the dirt. 'Are you staying tonight?'

'Do you want me to?'

She barely nodded, then climbed inside to take her spot on the far side of the tent, with Mason in the middle playing the part of their sleeping chaperone.

A few minutes later, Ash was lying on his swag, leaving only the crackle of their campfire.

'I don't hear any snoring,' she whispered, her head on the pillow.

'Give it time.' He sighed heavily.

'Are you okay?'

'Yeah. Thanks for helping me today.'

'Me? I did nothing. I just helped with Mason, playing the nanny.'

'For giving me that nudge to tell my brothers about using the drone. They're keen to see how we can use it in the future.'

'That's great.' She could hear the pride in his voice, and

she'd seen it in his stance that grew stronger as the day progressed. He was growing up right before her eyes. And it was hot.

'You know …'

'Yes.' She was wary of his tone.

'I've never slept with a woman like this.'

'Didn't you ever do co-ed sleepovers?'

'No. Did you?'

'No. I never had slumber parties. Not like this.'

'Can you sleep?'

She was wide awake and fully aware of his aroma, the rise and fall of his chest, and how he was lying on his back. 'No.'

'Me neither.' He rolled over to face her, his breath warm against her skin, as his hand gently stroked her hair. 'Wanna make out?'

'Ugh! Seriously.' She quickly sat up, annoyance flaring inside. 'I'm not some swag-swapping rodeo whatchamacallit.'

He chuckled. 'No, you're not. And keep your voice down, we don't want to wake up Mason.' He rolled over, turning his back to her.

Well, she ruined that, didn't she? 'I-I …' She rubbed the bridge of her nose and spilled her biggest secret. 'I don't know what to do.'

'Excuse me?' He peered over his shoulder, arching an eyebrow at her.

'I mean, I've done hook-ups, but I don't really date. I don't know how to do small talk, because I never had time to bother because of work. I don't do dinners, unless it's for work. I don't do drinks, unless it's for work. I know nothing except work. Certainly not dating or relationships.'

'And you think I do?'

'You'd know more than me—you're the guy who has the reputation of dating a new woman every two weeks. Me,' she said, stabbing her thumb at her chest. 'I only did the odd drunken one-night stand with some guy from some other department. But never in-house or with anyone I worked with, because that just made things messy. But hey, I was so busy I never got time to date—not that it mattered because I wouldn't know what to do.' Hugging her knees she sighed to herself. 'You know, I never had a boyfriend. And the only flowers I ever got on my desk were those *thank you* flowers for doing a good job.' She lay back in a huff, her hands covering her heated face. 'I've heard your brothers call me snooty. Even you said I was judgy, and I am with some things, especially with my work, because I was very particular about my job. But outside of the workplace, I'm so freaking clueless, I may as well be a born-again virgin.' For a girl who never spilled secrets, why the hell did she say all that?

'Hmph … Well, okay then.' Ash unzipped the door to their tent.

'Where are you going?'

'Stay there.'

She gasped in horror. He'd left her. After she'd confessed her deepest, darkest secret, Ashton Riggs—the notorious ladies' man—disappears in the dark.

She drew the pillow over her face to hide from her shame. It didn't last long, getting too hot. So, she lay there, stiff as a board, trying not to berate herself for stupidly sharing her secrets. Well, not all of them, she still hadn't spilled the big one, yet.

To really top off her night, the snoring singalong had begun. With no chance of sleeping, she was given no choice but to play the game of which snore belongs to who!

Charlie's snore was a snuffle. Dex had a deep trombone. Cap, no, he wasn't snoring—oh, he was just starting. And Ryder's snoring was as strong and steady as the man who barely spoke to her. It had been a big day for all of them, while Harper played tourist watching them from the hill.

She heard footsteps, then the tent unzipped, and Ash climbed back inside. 'Here.' Even with soft silverly moonlight and the glow from the nearby campfire it was enough for her make out the bunch of wildflowers he held out to her.

'What's this?'

'You said no one gave you flowers. So, this is me giving you some.'

Her heart practically doubled in size, as did her smile at the gesture. 'Thank you, kind sir.'

'It makes sense, you know,' he said, sitting back on his swag. 'The way you are. You're not snooty, you're shy.'

'No, I'm not.' She was quite fierce in her job.

'With relationships, you are.' He sat so close.

'I thought we were having a strictly business relationship.' She couldn't help but lean in closer, like they were magnets. 'You know, rules. Boundaries.'

'Normally, I keep to the rules, but sometimes you just have to push some boundaries.' His hand gently cupped her cheek. 'Because right now, I want to kiss you.' He leaned in closer, stopping barely a breath's distance away. 'Do I have your permission?'

'One kiss.'

'Sure. We can start with one kiss.' The cocky confidence that shone in that grin and sparkled in his eyes should have offended her, but it only made him all the more attractive.

She barely nodded.

He leaned in and gently kissed her top lip, her bottom lip, then reached up to run strong fingers through her hair before pulling her closer until their lips were fully flush. And then his mouth opened to hers and she found she liked the kissing. She wanted more kissing, because this was a kissing heaven that had her heart thumping loudly.

'Breathe, Harper. I won't hurt you.' His voice penetrated the haze of lust. Even if her self-esteem was at its most fragile, she couldn't stop. They had crossed a line they should never have gone near, now entering the land of clichés with the boss kissing the nanny. The same cliché that got politicians into trouble filling headlines over their sordid scandals.

But this didn't feel scandalous. It felt warm, delicious, and gloriously intoxicating. The way he kissed her, with his lips controlling hers, somehow managed to make her feel like she was the one in control. But she was so out of control, especially when his tongue got hot and demanding.

He sucked and nibbled, teased and tasted, until she found herself on her knees, pressing hard against his chest, dragging her fingers through his thick hair. Blood rioted like a swarm of bees buzzing through her ears, she couldn't tell if it was her or the crickets outside. She didn't even recognise the hum coming from her throat as she melted into him, when something squishy pressed against her leg.

It was enough to break the connection and she looked down at the small boy that slept soundly between them.

What was she doing? She was here for Mason. Not to kiss her boss in the dark. Even if it felt right, this was so wrong on all levels.

Hand to her mouth, clutching the flowers to her chest, she pulled away. 'Thank you.' She got her kiss. That's all she needed. And lay down, keeping her back to Ash, while swallowing the cool air to calm down her inner heat. She doubted she'd get any sleep now, but at least she had something sweet to think about.

Thirty-one

That one single kiss had been on Ash's mind all freaking day. Harper said one kiss. Sure, he thought, it'd just be a simple kiss—but Ash had never kissed anyone the way he'd kissed Harper.

He'd never gone to collect wildflowers in the dark for anyone.

He'd never helped a woman out of a tent.

He had never dusted a log so she could sit, to then fetch food or water like a slave, hoping for a smile. But he did for Harper, and he was willing do so much more for her. All she had to do was ask.

His mouth watered at the sight of her kissable lips, that smile, that shine in her eyes as she spoke with Bree, who was teaching Harper about mustering on horseback. He wanted to teach her, to talk to her, to just be near her. She was enough to cause his brain to short circuit.

'Are you doin' okay there, bro?' Cap rode up beside him, his assorted cattle dogs spread out around him as they effortlessly controlled the herd, heading for the trail to Cascades Spur. 'You're daydreaming, mate.'

'Didn't sleep well.' He held a protective arm around Mason, safe in his carrier, who was gripping the reins like a racehorse jockey, jabbering in some unknown language to the horse.

'I saw where you slept.'

'With a kid between us.' If Mason wasn't there, Ash was pretty sure he would have been allowed more than just one kiss with the nanny. 'Harper was scared of the noises.'

'I get it. Listen, mate ...' Cap dropped his head and lowered his tone. 'You haven't stopped looking at her.'

'Nah.' Yet, Ash struggled to tear his eyes away from Harper, riding alongside Bree.

'Look, do yourself a favour and ride up front, or get on the other side.'

'Why?'

'To concentrate on the cattle, or you'll have Dex on your back.'

'I kissed her,' he confessed, scrubbing a rough hand over his face. 'I thought, sure one kiss. But ...'

'It must have been a good kiss.'

He opened his palms up, simply unable to speak of the magnitude and power of that one single kiss.

'Damn.' Cap arched an eyebrow.

'Harper said she's never done stuff, like relationships. And she's not snooty. Harper is awkwardly shy outside of work.'

'Well, that makes sense. She's a different person, out here. I mean, you could've knocked me over this morning when she asked Bree to teach her to muster.'

'I know.' Ash was in awe of her courage and her adventurous spirit. 'But Harper said only one kiss because she didn't want to be part of some cliché of the boss kissing the nanny. So, I thought, sure. One kiss. Easy-peasy. Not.' It was screwing with his hormones. Now he was wishing he'd never kissed her. Harper was right—kissing his employee did make the workplace messy. 'What do I do?'

'You're asking me for dating advice. You?'

'I'm serious, Cap. There's no way I'd have this conversation with Dex or Ryder.'

'I don't believe this. You, the womaniser, who loves the chase and gets bored with the catch.'

'I haven't caught her.' Harper was not only out of his reach, but she was also out of his league. Even though it had never bothered him before, he knew how the world rolled.

Harper was polished—he was rough. She did business class—he was cattle class. Ash didn't own a suit or an iron to press his shirts, and he wouldn't know how to tie a necktie, but he could tackle a cleanskin bull with his bare hands and not blink.

'So maybe this is just another chase, like you do with all of those other girls?'

'Hmm …' He sat back in the saddle, with Mason trying to flick the reins, the horse patiently ignoring the boy. 'You might be right.' Most of the women Ash went with all worked in his field, they were used to mustering, and didn't mind hanging out at the pub. Harper was completely different.

'But is it worth it, bro? Breaking her heart, like the others in your past, especially when you have Mason to consider.' Cap nodded at the toddler, having a fat time in the saddle. 'Your son adores Harper.'

Ash bit his own tongue to stop himself from admitting that he adored Harper, too.

'Da-da.'

'What did he say?' Cap pointed to Mason.

'Da-da.' Mason waved the reins, showing off his gummy grin at Ash.

'Mate, your son just called you dad.'

Ash peered down at Mason's big brown eyes.

'Daddy.' His little hands cupped Ash's chin, he smiled and then pointed at the horse. 'Orsey?'

'That's right mate, horse. H-horse.' All morning the boy had been playful.

'Congrats, he's yours now, *Daddy*.' Cap patted Ash's shoulder.

Hold on, Ash had a countdown happening. Yet he couldn't remember how many days until that welfare visit, while staring down at the boy who was smiling at him.

This morning Ash woke to the boy smiling at him in the tent, tapping his nose while Harper slept, holding his flowers to her chest like a princess. He didn't want to wake sleeping beauty, so he quietly slid on his boots, with the boy copying him. They then crept out of the tent together like it was a game for Mason. The boy happily toddled alongside Ash to stand beside him and copy him as they peed near a tree. This trip the boy had become Ash's shadow, sitting beside him at the campfire for lunch, dinner, then breakfast. He'd tug on Ash's jeans when he couldn't hold Ash's hand. Even holding out flowers he'd picked for Ash. Somehow that kid had wormed his way into Ash's heart.

Now, after hearing that one little D word, it did something inside Ash's chest, releasing an inner warmth but also a fierce layer of protectiveness that washed over his shoulders, to replace that blend of fear and worry. He'd just been called *Dad*. Him. A father.

He wanted to tell Harper. Honestly, he wanted to share everything with Harper.

But he shouldn't, because in the harsh light of day, that kiss was all messed up. He should have never kissed the nanny.

'You're right, Cap.' He pulled on the reins. 'I have to think of Mason. I'll take the far side.' For his own sanity, Ash turned the horse to ride away from Harper. With any luck, he could avoid Harper for the rest of the day.

Thirty-two

The herd was massive, slow moving and almost hypnotic. Harper listened to the cattle's lowing, watched their hips sway, horns bobbing, keeping a pace that was as steady as a crowd streaming through the doors attending a classical ballet performance. All calm and collected.

This was what Bree called The Long Walk.

The pace grew slower the higher they climbed, slimming down to single file as they clip-clopped past the Cascades Spur, where they lapped at the water, to continue their slow trek to Grass Tree Creek.

This morning, with Mason hanging with his father, Harper had to focus on something else and approached Bree, who was packing up camp, tying the last of the large sacks containing their camping gear onto her horses.

'Can I help?' Harper asked Bree.

'Doing what?'

'The mustering thing?' Harper didn't want to be a spectator anymore.

'For real?'

The Riggs brothers stopped what they were doing to raise a few eyebrows. Ash grinned at her, even giving her a small nod of encouragement as if she'd made him proud. Which was odd when she was doing this to get away from him.

'Of course you can, missy.' Charlie nodded with a glimmer in his eyes. 'Bree, you can start the little miss off with the basics.' He patted Harper's shoulder. 'Good on ya, for having a go. Shows true spirit, that.'

'Ready for some girl talk?' Bree slid on her riding gloves. 'We'll be bringing up the rear for a bit. Best place to start ...' It was a slow trek, and they talked about anything and everything, and with all this time they shared, Harper finally learned the art of small talk.

From Cascades Spur, Harper took one long look back at Wombat Flats. The cattle were gone, but the place remained untouched. A paradise hidden among the sandstone. Would she ever come back?

But she was so glad she came.

By lunchtime, she was game enough to ride by herself, and shifted with the herd, making it to Grass Tree Creek.

There, Charlie approached her. 'I reckon you can ride up front with me, girlie.'

Fear had a new flavour and it was dusty sand, along with the pungent methane smell of cattle strolling down a stone corridor. It got into her hair, her ears, her sinuses, down her shirt, rubbing in her bra, and was gritty on her teeth. No one had warned her about this part.

She peered around for Ash, but he was nowhere to be seen among the sea of cattle.

Even though she'd been distancing herself from Ash, she kept remembering that incredible kiss. She may have said one kiss, but Ash only agreed because it was dark, they were in the only tent, and he was a guy who was used to being with different women.

She should never have kissed him.

Riding with Bree had kept her mind off Ash. But this was something entirely different. 'I'm not ready.'

'Bree told me on the radio you'd be fine.'

'Is that because Bree needs to concentrate?'

Charlie scratched at his grey whiskers the same colour as his hair beneath the large Akubra. 'You feelin' like the third wheel, huh?'

Harper shrugged.

'Don't worry, everyone feels like that on their first muster.

At least you can ride.' He held out the reins to her. 'If Bree reckons you're ready, then I reckon you're ready. It's you who has to believe you're ready.' With his spurs jangling, he swaggered to his horse and hoisted himself into the saddle. 'I reckon it'd be boring if you didn't do something new in your day. Always waiting for someone to tell you what to do, when you could take the reins yourself. Just look at where we are, missy? Paradise.'

Harper's eyes got blurry. She viciously scrubbed at the tears, desperate to stop them forming. Charlie had just described her life and her job, which was to follow orders, solve problems, keep to the schedules, and maintain that paper trail.

Out here, there was none of that. She hadn't seen a clock in days, let alone picked up a pen or seen a screen. Yet, well out of her comfort zone, it was like she was watching the hands of a stranger as she gathered up the reins and climbed back into the saddle.

She patted the horse's creamy white mane. She liked this horse, with its caramel-coloured hide and big hooves. No one knew its name, as it was borrowed, but she'd learned to trust it.

Charlie gave her a sharp nod of approval. 'Might have to get ya your own radio holster, for sure. Come on, missy, let's get that hat of yours dirty.'

Charlie led them down the winding canyon, where rocks and stones rolled, disturbed by the animals. Then the track widened, and Charlie waited for her to ride alongside, leading the long snaking trail of cattle.

'Charlie, where do I get a fancy crocodile hatband like yours?'

Charlie chuckled, removing his Akubra to admire the dark brown leather band that wrapped around it. The thick sturdy ridges of the leather were distinctive to the saltwater crocodile. 'Well, you go out and find your own croc, for sure. Which isn't too hard when this is crocodile country. Them snapping handbags are scattered everywhere.'

'Even at Wombat Flats?' Where they'd taken turns to splash around in the creeks.

'Not unless they're part billy goat to climb over the escarpments.' He chuckled, but then he sobered up to peer beneath the brim of his hat. 'Now, listen here, missy, trust me when I say don't go swimming anywhere unless it's a pool. Them swamp puppies are sneaky buggers.'

'Is that why you have a pool at your place?'

'That's Bree's trough. She'll dump a load of ice in there to watch ice hockey while drinking her gin. She says it's the best thing after a hot day on the tools in front of the smithy's forge. But, for me, I don't swim.'

'So how did you get the crocodile band? It's okay if you got it from the shop. Although, I like how Bree dresses up her hats.'

'That's for a purpose, missy.' Charlie was so at ease in the saddle of his surefooted stockhorse, it was like he was in a lounge chair, he was that laid back.

'What purpose?' She tried to copy his stance, shifting her bum, widen the legs and then... Oh, wow! Her spine and hips had found heaven in the saddle. Even the horse she rode nodded in agreement, giving a slight shiver across its shoulders. And everyone was happy.

'When fencing, or out in the saddle, you can only carry so much. Bree learned to tuck it around her hat. That thin piece of leather is good to tie up your swag, or if your boot starts losing its sole. That cloth band is always good to wrap a cut on your arm to stop flies finding it. I reckon she's got some wire, a match—'

'And the Queen of spades playing card?'

'I gave her that when she caught me cheating at poker. I won't play with her anymore because she knows all my tells.' He chuckled, rubbing at the dirt on his ruddy cheeks. 'But my hatband came to be because I got bit.'

'Excuse me?' She wasn't sure if the old storyteller was telling another tall tale.

'Back in the day, me and Darcie went hunting for buffalo.

When Darcie spotted this ten-carton buff—'

'A what?'

'It's how many cartons of meat you'd get once you take down that buffalo. It's measurements, like it's a two-can drive to town, six-can trek to my mate's house.'

'You measure the distance in beers?'

'For sure, mate, it's the Territory way.' His cheeky wink made her smile. 'Anyhoodle, there we were hunting after that buffalo, tracking it to where it had crossed this spring. Darcie reckoned the water was only knee-deep, and it'd be a good place to cross, he said. Little did we know that lying under that dirty water was a two-and-a-half-metre crocodile, just waiting.'

'Oh, no!'

'Well, Darcie got through fine, with me right behind him. But when I tried to climb outta that spring, it felt like a stick had jabbed me in the leg. It was only then I looked down and saw my leg was stuck inside this saltie's mouth.'

Harper gasped, hand to her throat. Her horse must have noticed, lifting its head, she patted its milky mane, which calmed her down, too. 'What did you do?'

'I froze and called for Darcie. We couldn't shoot it, coz if the croc moved it would've ripped my leg open. I was surprised it hadn't. But sure as Monday follows Sunday, I jammed the butt of my gun right between its eyes. It must've stunned it enough to let go of my leg, so I could pull the trigger, with Darcie doing the same.'

'What happened next?'

'Well, after that, my leg spasmed up something fierce. We wrapped my leg in my shirt and I drove myself to town to see the doctor. Darcie dragged that crocodile carcass back home and gave me the leather as a get-well pressie and I used it to make boots, belt, and my hatband.' He lifted the leg of his trousers and showed off the scar. 'It was my prize for surviving.'

She gasped at the size of the jagged scar in his lower calf. 'You're lucky you did survive.'

'Don't I know it.' He tapped the brim of his hat with a grin and a sparkle in his eyes.

They rode in silence for a while, concentrating on the slender, rocky path. The constant shift of hooves was like the beat of a thousand drums, blending with the low cattle murmurs.

The path widened, and they were back on the path she remembered. Hooves swapped the clash against rocks, for soft river sand and the slosh of water trickling down the middle of the Stoneys where they followed the water uphill, the direction for home.

'Reckon you can take the left and play catcher on the wing?'

'You should write a book interpreting your sayings, starting with *catcher on the what?*' Were they going to start playing baseball?

'It's where you try to block off the mob from wandering down the side tracks.'

'With what? A big baseball glove.'

'This …' He held out a rope, bound into a large coil like his stockwhip. 'You just wave it at them. They've seen enough of the stockwhip to listen up. You've got this, missy.'

The rope was coarse in her hands, like the reins she'd been holding for hours. Now she understood why Bree wore gloves. 'I'm getting riding gloves in the future.'

'If you keep this up, I might have to teach you how to swing a decent stockwhip, for sure.' Charlie nodded at her and rode to the front, the cattle following. 'Now, you wait a beat in that gap so none of them think they can play hide and seek through the caves.'

'Are you sure?'

'They're knackered now, so they'll behave. Just make some noise and your horse will do the rest. It's what they're trained to do, and that stockhorse you've got is a good one, for sure.'

She wished she knew the horse's name, as she was relying so heavily on it.

Bree and Charlie shared a close relationship with their stockhorses, compared with the horses the brothers swapped between them as they debated over fuel and vehicle cost comparisons and the benefits to riding horses. Cap was keen on keeping the horses based on the many pluses for the environment. But then the discussion shifted to horse feed and fixing the stables, in between all the other jobs they had. The to-do list for running a station seemed never-ending. No wonder the brothers were grappling with what was a priority when the list grew daily.

It reminded her of days in the office where they'd plan years in advance, down to monthly, weekly, and daily events, allowing for a change in priorities such as anti-terrorist training, or for political scandals where you dropped everything for damage control.

She was pretty sure horse riding and learning how to muster weren't part of any conventional nanny's job description. But she'd asked to try.

The nerves were still with her, a mix of fear and excitement, plus that rush of courage in her chest as she kept the cattle together, playing the catcher on the wing.

She didn't have to do much, the beautiful horse did it all for her. She occasionally gave a *yee haw*, or a *move along*, and *oi*, just like the others did, truly tapping into her inner cowgirl. The time just flew by.

Then Charlie whistled from the far end of the herd, waving his enormous hat in the air. '*Take cover, SANDSTORM.*' His words echoed down the cavern to ring in her ears.

Harper froze in her saddle.

Her eyes darted to the tower of red sand swirling like a fire to darken the sun. The wind's roar was like a hundred jet engines making the world rumble around her.

It was a dusty sandstorm that stretched like an evil cloud of doom to swallow the world and it was coming straight for them.

'What about the cattle?' Her horse shifted nervously

beneath her.

The cattle's noses flared, their eyes widened to show the whites as their lowing became more frantic, and the pace of the herd slowed down. They couldn't go backwards, trapped by towering walls of sandstone.

'Careful, the herd's gonna lock you in. Get outta there ...' Charlie disappeared with the herd that snaked around the bend. Leaving her alone with her horse and lots of cattle, as her ears ached from the sound of the roaring sandstorm.

It was like the cattle spoke in some unknown code. A few nodded their heads, with wild eyes as the herd stopped moving, the cattle lowered their heads to press against each other as if to huddle together. Leaving her with no escape.

'Harper?' It was Ash, pushing his horse through the cattle. His jacket covered Mason, keeping him safe from the wind, strapped to his chest. *'This way. We'll hide in that alley.'*

He grabbed the reins of her horse, as she hid her face from the wind, holding her saddle as he led them down the stony corridor.

The wind howled as if they were struck on the runway at an airport. The sand whipped at her skin like sandpaper, her hair blowing everywhere. She struggled to even see five feet in front of her, let alone know where Ash was taking them.

They ducked under a ledge off the main thoroughfare and into a cave, the relief from the wind instant.

'We'll stop here.' Ash jumped off his horse, helping her down. It took a few moments for her eyes to adjust to the darkness as he led them deeper into the cave, away from the wind and swirling dust outside. It was like watching the way water churned clothes during the wash cycle of a front-load washing machine, but this was sand. She'd never seen anything like it.

'Are you okay?'

She nodded, her hair everywhere. 'Is Mason okay?'

'He's fine.' Ash kept a protective hand over the boy, leading the horses away from the wind that raged outside the cave.

'We'll leave the horses here.' He secured their reins to some rope he wrapped around a rock. 'Here, you take Mason.'

'Arper. Arper.' His little fingers reached out, eager to hug her.

'I'm here, little man.' She breathed him in, getting a big cuddle from the boy. She'd missed him.

Ash dragged out his torch and a handgun from his saddlebags.

'Where are you going?'

'To make sure we're alone in this cave. I don't want any surprises.' He disappeared around the corner.

Filled with fright, she held Mason to her chest, 'It's okay, Mason.' She huddled against the wall, watching the storm turn day into night.

'Da-da.' Mason pointed at the torchlight moving against the walls and the sound of Ash's boot steps returning. 'Daddy.'

'He called you dad.' She let the boy go and he ran to Ash.

'Mason did it earlier.' Ash scooped up the boy. 'I'm right here, son. I'm right here.' He set the torch on the ground to illuminate the cave, then dragged out his water bottle and passed it to the boy.

Ash was being a father.

It was everything Harper had hoped for. All the fear and strain she'd put herself through for this trip had been worth it. The tender father–son moment brought tears to her eyes.

'What's with you?' Ash arched an eyebrow at her.

'You did it.'

'Did what?' He handed her the water bottle.

'You bonded.'

'It seems like we did, eh, Mason?' Ash sat down, pressing his back to the wall, and passed a toy horse to his son. Harper sat on the other side of Mason, as he happily played with the horse in the dirt.

'How long do these sandstorms last?' Harper hugged her knees as the world disappeared behind a wall of swirling sand, hemmed in by sandstone.

'I couldn't say. Could be anything from ten minutes up to an hour, or even longer. I went through a dust storm down south-east way, it lasted six hours. Stripped all the topsoil from the area.'

'Where are your brothers? Bree?'

He tapped on the UHF radio tucked into its pouch that he wore like a gun's shoulder holster. 'Bree, Cap, Ryder, and Dex are in a cave in the back. Charlie found one up front.'

'You were riding with Cap?'

'I was. Then moved to the other side.'

'That was in the back …' She searched his dark eyes that reflected a swirling world. 'You came looking for me?'

He'd done that a few times, dropped everything to come to her aid, from the moment they'd met when he fixed her flat tyre, then the spider incident, now this. He'd been her hero.

Ash shrugged, dropping his head in a rare bout of shyness.

'Have you been avoiding me?' she asked.

'I can't stop thinking about that kiss.' Ash scowled at her, then at the ground. Picking up a stick, he dragged it across the ground, passing it to his son to play with in the sand.

'Don't look so happy about it.' It was her fault. She should have never agreed to that kiss.

'It's not that I didn't like it.' Yet Ash rubbed his furrowed brow with frustration. 'I didn't want to mess up what you've got with Mason.'

'You're supposed to be advertising for a real nanny.'

His gaze, ink-black and serious, locked onto hers. 'What if I told you I don't want anyone else? Just you.'

She gasped.

'Would that be so bad?' He leaned closer. 'Would it be such a bad idea for you to stay?'

'I don't know what to say to that,' she mumbled, as her heart flipped inside her chest.

'Well, how about you tell me what you feel?'

She shrugged. 'This is all new for me.'

'Me too.'

'I don't believe you, because you have a reputation for dating a different girl every two weeks.' Just the thought of him being with another woman made her blood boil.

'Are you jealous?' He tilted his head, his eyes keenly watching her.

She jutted out her chin. 'No. I don't get jealous.'

'How do you know if you've never been with anyone to get jealous about?'

She ignored his question, asking one of her own. 'Do you get jealous?'

'Right now,' he said, leaning so close their noses almost touched. 'If you were to kiss some other guy, I'd turn into Dex and deck that bloke for daring to be in your breathing space. Just the thought of anyone taking you away from me scares me.'

Her eyes widened at his open sincerity. 'You saying that is so hot. No, wait, that's just the weather, and this hot cave ...' She fanned herself. Surely, she wasn't falling for his caveman routine while sitting in a cave. Come on! 'What are you grinning at? I don't like that grin.'

It was the cocky, know-it-all grin, the one with the dimple. 'You like me.'

'I kissed you, didn't I?' She crossed her arms over her chest that prickled with a tingling flash of desire.

'No, you *really* like me. Your cheeks are flushed, you're licking your lips, and your shirt is showing ...' He leaned in and whispered with his hot breath against her ear. 'Baby, you're getting turned on.'

Goosebumps exploded across her skin in a heated wave. She shuddered on the spot.

'When we get home, I'm coming for you.' His lips nuzzled into her neck as she squirmed.

'Mason—'

'Can sleep in his own room.'

'I'm not that easy.' She tried to push him away and sit straighter.

'Fine. What do you want? More flowers? Wine? Chocolates? Dinner?'

'I don't know.'

'All right then, I'll surprise you. And you will not talk your way out of it.' He held her chin and kissed her. Pressed his lips against hers so hard she felt his teeth, but most of all, his hunger. This kiss was so much deeper than the last, so much hungrier, and so much hotter, she nearly melted on the spot.

The radio squawked loudly, and Charlie's voice came over the speaker to echo inside the cave. 'Sandstorm's lifting folks. Who got the nanny? I lost her in the storm.'

But the storm in this cave was so much hotter.

'I've got her.' Ash's dark, smouldering eyes remained on hers as he spoke over the radio. 'Harper is with me and Mason. We're in a cave just off the main track.'

'Good. Where you at, Bree?'

'Stuck with the fabulous fart brothers inside this poky cave. Remind me to never feed these boys beans again.'

'It's the horses, Bree, not us,' came Dex's voice.

That's when the sand fell like a wall of rain to reveal clear blue skies and sunshine.

'Come on.' Ash picked up Mason and held his hand out to Harper. 'Let's go join the rest of the party.'

'What will they say?'

'I don't care what they say, Harper.' He pulled her closer, slinging his arm over her shoulder, and tenderly kissed her temple. 'Right now, none of them matter. I just care about you, me, and Mason. I want us to be a family.'

Thirty-three

Disappointment blended with bulldust as the day progressed. So much for her date, because when they got through the Stoneys, Ash bundled Harper and Mason into his ute, telling her to drive back to the farmhouse, while the others continued mustering their new herd towards some paddock.

That left Harper following a dirt track—on her own—with Mason tucked up in his booster seat, without a map or a blipping dot on the GPS to tell her she was travelling in the right direction. All she had was the crappy track she could barely make out after that dust storm.

When the sheds and the farmhouse came into sight, she then realised how hard she'd been gripping the steering wheel, her shoulders ached.

But it was getting *inside* the house that bothered her. She had to deal with Sarge.

Her fear fell away when she spotted the labrador, Ruby, leaping off the front porch, her tail wagging, giving them a happy dance that had Mason eager to hug his nanny dog. Scout, the beagle, did laps of joy chasing its tail, to then lean against Harper's leg and smile. Even Sarge seemed pleased to see her.

It was a homecoming she'd never expected, even though they had Cap's special five-day dog feeders and plenty of water, she was eager to spoil the dogs too.

Showered and changed into clean clothes, Harper felt human again. With Mason playing on the lawn, Ruby beside him, Harper tackled a load of washing.

At the old top-loader washing machine, she sprinkled in the powder, dropped the lid, turned the dial to wash, and the water flow kicked in, rushing through the pipes. Ah, yes, the joys of indoor plumbing.

'We should have dinner, Mason. Pity we can't order takeaway.'

Something moved in the corner of her eye as the machine shook. The washing machine was known to walk across the concrete during the spin cycle, so she checked the wood chocks were in place to keep it stationary.

When she spotted a strange brown stick lying beside the washing machine.

How did that get there?

Suddenly it moved.

She blinked, taking a step back. Her eyes widening, holding her breath as her brain finally registered what it was.

A snake.

A big one.

The washing machine knocked, and the hot water tap came on with a whoosh. The snake reared up as if covered in hot boiling water and propelled itself across the concrete, heading for the dead lawn. Straight for Mason.

'SNAKE.'

She grabbed the nearby house broom.

'*Mason, move.*' Harper tried to outrun the snake that had to be over six feet long.

Ruby pushed Mason over to put herself between the child and the snake. It reared up as Mason wailed and Ruby growled, and then struck out at the dog. Ruby whimpered.

'NO.' Harper slammed the broom down onto the snake, where it coiled around the handle. She flicked it to the nearby trees as Sarge and Scout came running from around the front of the house.

'Stop. Please stop. Sarge, Scout, *halt*. STAY!' The dogs obeyed. '*Come*.' And they did, as she dropped to her knees beside Ruby.

'Rubeeee?' Tears trickled down Mason's chubby cheeks as he crawled to his dog.

'Where is it …' Harper searched Ruby's fur for the spot. And found it. The red blood was bright against the dog's cream coat, coming from the bite mark on her lower leg.

Harper ran back to the pile of sheets that were from her swag. With her teeth, she ripped one into strips and quickly bound the labrador's leg. She wasn't sure if her first-aid training from the embassy worked on a dog, but she wasn't stopping.

She picked up Mason and ran for Ash's ute still parked nearby.

With Mason safely in his baby seat, her muscles strained as she carried Ruby to the ute and lifted her to the passenger floor. Doors closed. Her handbag dumped onto the passenger seat with a bunch of water bottles beside it. 'Stay, dogs.' She rolled up the passenger window, adjusted the mirror, and her heart squeezed at the sad sight of Sarge and Scout guarding the farmhouse that was soon hidden behind a trail of dust.

Thirty-four

Ash scowled at Ryder, seated on the other side of the campfire with Cap and Dex, Bree and Charlie had already gone to bed. Thanks to the broken fence line, they were forced to muster their herd towards the new paddock. They were hoping to sleep in their beds tomorrow. If they were lucky. 'You didn't have to send Harper away like that.'

'You weren't concentrating on the job.' The glow from the campfire only made Ryder's hard edges meaner. 'Stop thinking like an employee! Goofing off the first chance you get. We're meant to be working together, doing this for us.' Ryder's harsh voice echoed in the night air as if he was dressing down a soldier.

Ash snarled, his upper lip twitching. 'Are you saying I'm not as good as you guys?'

'I didn't say that.' Ryder exhaled heavily, rubbing his hands over his denim thighs. 'You did good with the drone.'

'I agree,' said Dex, with Cap nodding beside him. 'And you're a bloody good stockman, just not when Harper's around. Then you're too busy daydreaming, or too busy watching her, ready to play hero for her any chance you get.'

'Was not.'

'Ash, in the morning, you'll head back into the Stoneys with Charlie.' It wasn't a request, but an order from Commander Ryder, tossing the last of his coffee into the fire.

'What for?' Ash wanted to see Harper and Mason.

'Because we're missing a few dozen cattle in there after

that sandstorm hit.'

'Why me?'

'Or you can help fix fences and clean troughs with us, brother?' Dex leaned forward, his eyes taunting him to take that dare, just like he did with his opponents in the fighting pits. But Ash was supposed to be their brother.

'I honestly didn't think the drafting yards were that bad.' Cap shrugged, taking a sip from his tin mug.

'It'll take a good week—'

'Try two,' said Dex, holding up two fingers.

'—to fix it. Then we'll be ready to draft them, so we'll need that fencing done,' said Ryder. 'In the meantime, Ash, you'll go with Charlie back into the Stoneys, where you'll use your drone to chase those strays out of those tight places better than I can with the chopper.'

'Yeah, sure, okay.'

Ryder leaned his elbows on his thighs, directly opposite Ash, only their small campfire separated them. 'I am not the enemy, Ash. And I hate that I'm always riding you about your work.'

'Are you saying you'd sack me?' Ash said it as a joke, but Ryder wasn't laughing. He rarely did.

'I would've sacked you weeks ago, the first time you forgot to clean those troughs. It's only because you're my little brother, that I haven't.' Ryder showed no emotion, unlike Cap meekly shrugging, and Dex wearing his normal scowl. Ryder was as cold as a snake.

It had Ash gritting his teeth to stop his jaw trembling with rage.

'Look, we all know you were happy just being a contract musterer, so I'm happy to give you your deposit back and let you go.'

'And do what?' They were firing him!

'Do what makes you happy. Because you have to want this life, Ash. Your brothers and I are busting our butts to get this station on track. In this life, this job, there are no time clocks or suitable work hours, or lunch breaks. And I shouldn't be playing the boss to check on your work when you're meant to be a boss, too. It's what happens when you work for yourself, getting the job done, relying on ourselves to do it right the first time, every time. But you seem to want something else.'

'To be fair to Ash,' said Cap, 'He did get lumped with a kid. That'd be enough to rattle even you, Ryder.'

'It's why I've cut him some slack.' Ryder leaned forward, the dancing flames reflecting in his dark, cold eyes. 'I was hoping you'd find the drive to put in the effort, for your son's sake, to give that boy the home he deserves.'

'I'm trying—'

'No, you're not. You have to want it here.' Ryder tapped at his chest. 'You have to want it deep in your soul or you're just wasting your time and everyone else's on a daydream.' Ryder stood, towering over them, and with a curt nod, he walked off.

Ash looked at his other brothers. 'Are you agreeing with him?'

Again, Cap shrugged. 'Sorry, mate, but—'

'Stop treating this like a game, is what Cap's trying to say.' Dex leaned in, eyes blazing. 'This isn't some game where you get a thousand chances to beat the bad guys, we've only got one shot at this. Meanwhile, you're treating it like it's a bloody day care centre where you're watching the clock to go back to either kiss the babysitter or plug into some computer game to play all night. Ryder's right, your head and heart aren't in it.' Dex shuffled to his feet and dusted off the back of his jeans, shaking his head as he left.

That left Ash staring at the campfire, with Cap patting a cattle dog stretched out before him.

'What do you want for yourself, Ash?' Cap craned his neck up to the stars and then to the wide land covered in darkness. 'For me, it's this, and a kennel for the dogs. You?'

Ash didn't know what to say.

'Look, I know you weren't part of the original discussions when we decided to buy a station. You just said *okay* and tagged along for the ride.'

'I didn't want to be left behind.'

Cap patted his brother on the shoulder. 'Mate, we want you here. We do. But is this what you want, what'll make you happy?'

'I enjoy mustering.'

'I can see that.'

'I like working the stations and the whole cattle industry.' But he hated his older brothers ganging up on him like this.

'But do you like being the boss who carries all the responsibility?'

'Ryder won't share the workload.'

'He's been trying to share it with you, Ash. Yet you just treat him like the boss when he's being your partner. Just do yourself a favour and think about what you want. Write a list. Or check out that one you're always adding to.'

'Harper said the same thing.'

'Yeah, well, I can't believe I'm saying this, but ...' Cap peered around to check they were on their own, then lowered his voice and said, 'You should forget about Harper.'

Ash sat up with a frown.

'Come on, mate. Do you honestly think Harper is going to play instant family when you've never even taken her on a date? She's also on holidays with a job to go back to, so think about what's best for Mason. Sleep tight, little brother.' Cap left, his dogs following, and it was just Ash and the dancing flames of the campfire.

Fuming, he grabbed his swag and moved to the far side of the campsite. He wanted to talk to Harper, to hug Mason goodnight. He missed his family, when not that long ago he lived for the ride following the mustering contracts without caring where his next pay cheque was coming from. It was a life that used to be so free from stress. A life of little to no responsibilities.

When did life get so complicated?

He knew when … It was the day he'd met Mason.

How many days did he have until that escape clause expired?

Thirty-five

It was a harrowing ride to the small town of Elsie Creek with the dog whimpering, Mason crying for the dog, while Harper drove as fast as Ash's ute could move.

She knew the vet clinic was in town, but where? She drove past the pub on the corner, down the main street, past the hardware store on her left, then the supermarket.

That's right, Ryan had told her his clinic was behind the supermarket. She steered a hard left, then left again, and cruised down the dark street with only the lights of the police station shining behind her. 'Please be here …'

She hunched over the steering wheel, scouring the dark storefronts, where there was a council office, another business, and a little back from the road stood the veterinary clinic.

Harper parked close, with the headlights beaming brightly. She hammered her fists on the front door while pressing the bell.

Finally, a door at the rear opened, and the lights flickered on.

'*Ryan?* It's Harper, Bree's friend from Elsie Creek Station.'

Jiggling a stack of keys in his hands, Ryan approached the door. 'What's wrong?'

'It's one of Cap's dogs. It got bit by a snake.' She rushed back to the car and opened the passenger door. 'It's Mason's nanny dog. She was protecting Mason. Please help her. Please?'

'Okay, okay. Let me in there, Harper.' Ryan pulled her

back and leaned inside. 'Hello, girl. Let's see what we can do for you.' Ryan scooped up the labrador and carried her inside, with Harper carrying Mason.

Inside the clinic, Ryan laid the dog on the examination table. 'What kind of snake?'

'I don't know. I thought it was a stick, it was behind the washing machine.'

'Have a look at that wall chart, it shows the most common snakes in the Northern Territory. See which one you think it is, so I can give Ruby the correct antivenene treatment. Did you bandage her up?' He pointed to the leg wrapped in strips of sheet.

'Within a minute or two of her being bitten.'

'Good work. You've probably saved her life.'

Harper had never done a mug shot search on snakes before—terrorists yes, after that car bomb attack, but never wildlife. 'That one.' She pointed to the picture. 'The brown snake. They're poisonous, right?'

'Yes.' Ryan opened a medicine cabinet and pulled out a vial, then a syringe. 'It's not all bad, over eighty per cent of dogs recover from a snakebite, if treated quickly.'

'So, Ruby will be fine?' She patted the poor dog that had diluted pupils. Her breathing was erratic, and she'd lost her ability to walk. 'Please let her be fine.'

Ryan injected the antivenene. 'It's up to Ruby, but I'll keep monitoring her through the night. So you can leave her with me.'

She wanted to stay and hold Ruby's paw. 'Can we ...'

Ryan shook his head, guessing her question.

'Call me if—wait, they don't have a landline at Elsie Creek Station, and my phone doesn't get reception out there.'

'Bree's got a landline in the caretaker's cottage. I have her number.'

'They're out mustering.' Cap was going to kill her for getting one of his dogs hurt. Then Ash might freak out that Mason had been in danger, and who knows what Ryder and Dex would do when they found out? 'Can I come back in the morning?'

'Sure.' He held out a business card. 'Here's my number. Did you say you're out there on your own?'

She barely nodded, trying not to show her fear of being home alone.

'Did they leave you with a radio, or are they out of range?'

Again, she shrugged. 'They said they'd be back sometime tomorrow.'

'Right, well ...' Ryan took back his business card and scribbled on the back. 'This number is for the pub, and the other number is for Cowboy Craig.'

'I don't want a date.'

'Craig may be a flirt, but he'd help anyone, and he'll check over the place for any more snakes. I'd offer to go, but I can't leave Ruby.'

She gulped at the thought of more snakes infesting the place—it was as bad as those spiders that killed snakes. 'I flicked the snake into the garden.' How she did that was a miracle. 'And I have two guard dogs.'

'Sarge, right?'

'Is it true that Sarge was a riot dog?'

Ryan nodded. 'Yep. Sarge has a bullet wound in his shoulder from protecting his owner, who sadly died. Has Cap given you the command to feed Sarge?'

'Yes.' At least she'd fed the regal shepherd and his offsider Scout when she'd first arrived home.

'Which means you'll be fine with Sarge. He knows to trust you. But if you don't feel safe at all, call Craig. I swear he will be a thorough gentleman. He'll just sleep in his swag until the Riggs brothers get home. But put this little fella to bed.' He gently patted Mason's head, the poor boy was barely keeping his eyes open, and it was way past his bedtime. 'You can come back and see your dog tomorrow, okay?'

'Thank you, Ryan.' With Mason, they hugged the dog together. 'You be well, Ruby. We'll come back for you, and you'd better be here, girl.' The tears streamed down her cheeks as they left poor Ruby behind.

With a long journey back to the station in the dark, with only a small boy for company, Elsie Creek Station was proving to be a dangerous place for someone as precious as Mason. And she was only here for Mason.

Thirty-six

At midnight, the farmhouse was eerily quiet. It only made her loneliness smother over everything like an oil slick spreading across the harbour of no-hope.

Harper had let Scout and Sarge stay inside, because it was too dangerous for anyone to be outside.

To stop her worry over Ruby, and her fear of the dark, for the first time in weeks, Harper dragged out her laptop to check on her emails and let it load 762 emails. 762!

She skimmed the headlines for some international emergency. But there wasn't one. It was just the job.

Poor Ruby was an emergency, it was a life and death situation. It was enough for her to prioritise and slam her laptop shut.

Instead, she checked on Mason again. He was fast asleep, holding on to a toy dog. Normally she'd find Ruby sleeping beside Mason's bed, giving her a light wag of her tail.

She really missed that dog.

In the kitchen, she stared at the fridge. She had food, and she had wine.

Pouring a glass, she sat at the table, racked with worry for the dog, and guilt for what she was going to say to Ash and Cap.

Was her time with Ash, trapped inside the cave waiting out a sandstorm, a dream? Or was he doing that to keep his son happy, feeding her hopes of that fairytale where families were perfect?

Did she want to be in an instant family? When she was

still feeling the sting from her own.

There was no way her father would have allowed her to shack up with some cowboy in the scrub! And she hadn't factored children into her life this soon. First she actually wanted to date the guy.

What was wrong with enjoying the romance that had always eluded her? To squeal with delight as the guy dropped to his knee and proposed, where she then got to show off her engagement ring to everyone. What about showing off her Valentine's Day card, or any gift her man gave her? Where was her chance to brag about dinner dates and weekends away—just like the other women at work.

She'd always thought she'd have a wedding one day, where her father could proudly walk her down the aisle, while her mother got all teary-eyed in the front row. Now none of that was ever going to happen.

She needed to focus on something else.

Scooping up the wineglass, she leaned against the front door letting the dogs out and to do their business. She stared at the outdoor table where the Riggs brothers gathered morning and night. It was covered with dirty coffee cups, a few maps, and that large manila envelope.

She sipped on her wine, not even tasting it, and stared at the envelope.

She'd asked Ash to give her a copy of the letter from the government. She wasn't sure if she could help, but she desperately needed a distraction.

She peered around at the thick blackness that surrounded her. There were no city lights, or traffic noises, just the two dogs sniffing around the grass, again making that foul taste of fear rise in her throat. Was there another snake in the grass?

Needing something to take her mind off her fear, she pushed the paperwork off the table where it scattered to the floorboards.

'Whoops.'

She scooped up the assorted maps and papers, until she

found what she was looking for—the letter from the government. And what she read only made her frown.

Thirty-seven

Ash rode out for the Stoneys before sunrise, preferring the cold deep caverns than face his brothers. The wind carved sandstone columns, while some overhanging rock ledges were like frozen ocean waves forever rolling high on a sea of stone. No two stone corridors were the same.

'Oh Romeo, Romeo wherefore art thou, Romeo?' It was Bree, over the radio. 'You should hear the acoustics, I'm about to start a rock concert back here.'

'What do you want, Bree?' Ash was not in the mood.

'Well, good morning, snowflake. Are you ready to tackle the day, where the aim of the game is to not choke on too much cattle dust? With any luck, I'll be ending this day soaking in an ice bath, watching some hot hockey players, and knocking back some gin. But in the meantime, I'll be playing your wingman. So, where are you, my little snowflake?'

'Halfway to Grass Tree Creek.'

'Seen any cattle on the way through?'

'No, but I can hear them.' Their indistinct murmurs, and hooves clashing on rock, were echoing off the canyon walls that were a winding, twisty maze.

'There you are.' Bree rode towards him on her handsome black horse. 'Here, you left this behind.' She held out a small paper bag.

'What's that?'

'Your breakfast.'

'You legend, you.' He was practically salivating as he tore back the wrapping. 'Where's Charlie?'

'Pop's setting up some hessian wings to steer those we flush out towards that paddock. So today, you get the rare once-in-a-lifetime opportunity to tell me where to go.' She peered up at the wall of towering stone. 'Is this what they call the nosebleed section.'

'You're kidding, I get to be your boss today?' He began tucking into his bacon-and-egg toasted sandwich.

'You wish, jellyfish.' Her evil laughter bounced off the stone walls. 'But this is a good spot to start that toy of yours. I'd say the ones that are missing were stuck inside this corridor when the storm happened.' She nodded at the labyrinth that stretched on either side.

'Good point. We'll start from here and push them back.' He paused, to wolf down his brekkie in a few bites.

'You are one of the bosses, you know.'

He frowned, as he swung off the horse and set up his drone on the flat rock bed while Bree held the reins of his horse. 'Did you hear my brothers lecturing me last night?'

She shrugged, completely blasé, like normal.

'I'll take that as a yes.'

'I said nothing.'

'Do you agree with them?'

'I don't work for you guys, and Ryder made it perfectly clear I should keep out of your family's business.'

'But you have an opinion.'

'Wait, do I need to reset my mood board for this conversation?' Her eyes sparkled to match her wry grin. 'You're asking if I dwell on the little things so I can overthink *everything*? Because that's what you're doing. Don't give me that look, snowflake, you asked. And I have nothing to gain by telling you the truth, or to tell you whatever BS you want to hear. I really don't care.'

He looked at her with pleading eyes, as he gulped down some water to wash down his breakfast.

'Aww, come on.' She rolled her eyes, swung one leg up

onto the saddle and crossed her arms over it. 'Fine.' She took a deep breath and asked calmly, 'Tell me, what part upsets you the most?'

'All of it. That I'm not doing my job—'

Her laugh cut through the air, to bounce off the walls as she leaned over her saddle. 'Is this the part where I tell you I know Charlie's been doing your trough duties this past week?'

He dropped his head. 'Dammit.'

'And there is wake-up call number one. Let's aim for number two.'

'They said I'm still playing the part of an employee and treating it like a game.' Although, this felt like an awkward game show where he was the mug in the middle with no idea what the prize was if he won.

'Are you?'

'I've never been a boss before.'

'It takes time to adjust. I know I freaked out, going from someone with a steady pay cheque to suddenly being my own boss. That stress load you feel across your shoulders—that if you didn't get up in the morning, you don't get paid—gets easier once you adapt.' She rode her horse closer to point at him. 'You haven't got that yet, not like your brothers.'

'I do feel it. I just … avoid it,' he replied, admitting that more to himself.

'Why? You're a strong guy. I've seen you tackle a micky bull in the scrub. You've got nothing to be afraid of. Plus, you've got your brothers backing you up. Besides, if you fail, you can always go back to being a contractor.'

'Do you think I can do it?'

'All I'm saying is that it'll take time to adjust. You guys haven't even unpacked the boxes in the farmhouse yet. So cut yourself some slack.'

He wanted to hug the redhead wearing two stockwhips, carrying a shotgun and a rifle in her saddle, and she'd brought him breakfast.

But Bree made sense, which also gave him hope. 'My

brothers said they've been cutting me some slack, for Mason's sake.'

'And you only realised that now?' She shook her head. 'Listen, cucumber, Cap and Dex moved out of the farmhouse so Mason and Harper could each have a room, and Ryder is the one paying Harper's wages. I'm sure you've heard that saying, *it takes a village to raise a child*, and you've got one already doing their bit to help you and that boy. You just haven't realised how lucky you are.'

'Lucky? How? I didn't ask for a kid. He might be better off with someone else.' There, he'd said it. 'I didn't ask to become a father. And what am I going to tell that kid about his mother, when I don't even remember her?'

'Did you bother to find out who she was?'

He couldn't even look at her, only now realising how selfish he'd been. 'I'm afraid I'll muck it up … all of it. The station. Fail my brothers. Fail my son.'

She grinned.

'Why are you grinning at me like that? I don't like that grin.' It was positively evil.

'That's the first time I've heard you call him son.'

He blinked at the realisation.

'Seeing as how we're on the verge of swapping friendship bracelets with this heart-to-heart chat, you do realise that your brothers are the same as you. They're afraid they'll fail and lose this station, especially with that mine chasing your water.'

'I wish there was a way to help them somehow.'

'Did you talk to Harper?'

'I did.'

'And?'

'She asked to see the letter …' He turned towards home.

'Look at you …' Bree leaned over in her saddle, her green eyes narrowing at him. 'Did something happen between you two?' Her eyes widened as she pointed at Ash. 'It did, didn't it? You're pining for her. You, the guy who can't wait to leave a woman's bed is—'

'Nothing happened, just a kiss.'

'Snowflake, why are you lying to yourself?'

'Cap told me to stop seeing Harper.' But there was no escaping the truth over how deep his feelings were for Harper.

Bree just blinked at him. 'Why are you listening to relationship advice from a bunch of beer-belching bachelors? Is that because they want you to join their outback monkhood or something?'

'No. But Cap said I shouldn't expect Harper to be part of an instant family. I haven't even taken her out on a date, and Harper is not the type of lady to take to the pub.'

'Pfft.' Bree dismissively waved her hand at him. 'Harper and I had lunch at the pub just the other day. She was fine. And they have a Michelin-star chef.'

'You know what I mean …'

'Oh, you mean a *date* date. Like romance and candlelight.' Again, that grin of hers grew.

Ash shrugged. Normally he didn't bother dating, he didn't need to. But if that's what Harper wanted, he'd do it for her.

'Well, when you decide you want to take Harper out on a proper date, let me know. I'll help you with that.'

'Won't you be breaking the rules of getting involved in our business?'

'I live my life stuck under so many rules I either forget them or break them routinely. Remember, I don't work for you guys, so you can't sack me.' She sat back in her saddle and shrugged. 'If you want to date Harper, date her. I know she's got a soft spot for you.'

'Really?' Hope filled his chest.

'Snowflake, you talked Harper into being a nanny when she's never even babysat a pot plant in her life. She followed you from the supermarket when you'd just met, and you talked her into going on a muster. Do you want me to set up a billboard with flashing neon signs saying *Harper likes Ash*, as much as you like her?'

The redhead was right. 'When I get back, I'd like to do something for Harper, like go on a date. Will you babysit?'

'No. I'm not ready to babysit. Get Cap to.'

Again, he looked back in the direction of home.

'Harper will be fine. She's a lot stronger than we give her credit for. If not, it'll be one helluva learning curve for her. I have faith she can do it, otherwise, I would have gone home last night.'

'Why did you stick around?'

'We haven't finished the muster. We both know the job's only done when all your cattle are safely behind a fence that's standing.'

'We have a lot of fencing to do.' Plus, the other big list of duties to get the station back on track. 'At least we have cattle now.'

'You do. So, can we get a wriggle on, snowflake? It's your strays we're playing hide-and-seek with.'

'So they are.' Keen to finish this job, which he was actually good at, he realised he had every right to be a part owner of this station.

He just had to prove it to his brothers.

Thirty-eight

With the drone high in the air, Ash, Bree, and Charlie rode through the many twisting corridors that made up the Stoneys. Bree took the left, Charlie on the right, with Ash down the middle, as they gently mustered the stray cattle towards the mouth.

'What's that?' Ash rode up to Charlie, who was guzzling on his water bottle, and showed him the drone's screen. 'Is that some sort of machinery?'

'No machinery out here. You've seen how narrow and rocky this place gets, you can only go by horseback.'

Bree came up behind them with a calf draped over her saddle. 'This guy is exhausted. I'm thinking of adopting him.'

'I doubt management would agree to that.' Charlie nudged Ash's shoulder. 'I'm talking about you, kid.'

'Oh, yeah.' He was supposed to be the boss, and that calf was part of his herd. But this was Bree ... 'Do you really want that devouring your veggie patch?'

'Good point.' Bree's grin was mischievous. 'So, I was thinking, you should buy that cream stockhorse for Harper. It's an excellent gift for the lady.'

'Leave 'em be, kid. I wouldn't want anyone telling me what stockhorses to get.'

'You told me you liked that cream one, Pop.'

'Hush now, kid. I know what I said, coz I was thinking of getting that one to add to our horse plant.' Charlie scowled at Bree, who only grinned wider.

'I told you it was a good stockhorse way back in Wombat

Flats.'

'And I saw how calm it was during that sandstorm, and that horse has skills.'

'I know, right?'

Ash just sat on his borrowed horse, between Bree and her grandfather, listening to them talk about another horse. It'd have to be good, considering the condition of Bree and Charlie's stockhorses, they knew what to look for. And so did Ash.

How did he miss that? It was another brutal example of how he'd been too busy focusing on Harper and not on the job—no wonder he copped the lecture.

'Excuse me, before you buy out all the decent stockhorses, can you tell me what this is?' He held out the drone's screen where he zoomed in on the object wedged in a corridor of rock. 'It's a metal roof. It's not a ute or a truck, but it's big.'

'Let's go take a stickybeak.' Bree nudged her horse, taking the lead with the calf draped over her saddle like it was a blanket, but it looked comfy there. 'Did you know they used to fossick for gold through here?'

'Oi. You're not meant to tell them that.' Again, Charlie scowled at Bree as he rode alongside her.

'You and Lenny haven't found anything for years.'

'Who's Lenny?' Why did Ash know that name?

'The Hungarian chef from the pub. Fossicks for gold with Charlie once a month—if Lenny isn't too hungover.'

'Did you find any gold?'

'Nah. A few crumbs. Just enough for a good drink and a brag at the pub,' said Charlie. 'Darcie's dad used to fossick a bit. But Darcie's son had some smancy geologist come out and take a stickybeak with all this technological what-not. They reckoned there wasn't any gold here.' The old stockman craned his neck to gaze at the maze of stone that framed a clear cobalt blue sky.

'Was that the same guy that sold off all the cattle?' Ash frowned at the thought, grateful to Bree and Charlie for hiding the herd they had.

'The same ...'

Side by side, they rode beneath the cool shadows of the towering stone walls. The horseshoes became muffled under the dust and sand, until the walls opened to a tall, wide cavern.

'It's a car.' Ash poked up his hat's brim. 'How did that get here?'

'It looks old, like some vintage gangster car,' said Bree.

'No way.' Charlie swung off the saddle, tearing off his hat, his eyes wide, as the colour drained from his cheeks.

'Pop?' Bree jumped off her horse, putting the calf on the ground. She followed Charlie, concern heard in her voice. 'What's wrong?'

'It's ...' Charlie brushed off the pile of sand to reveal the number plate and a long, domed hood. He gasped with a hand to his chest.

'What is it, Pop?'

'Help me open it.' Charlie frantically dug away at the thick layer of sand that covered the car to expose the driver's door, covered with thick grime. He struggled with the door handle. '*Help me.*' Panic was clear in his voice. 'This is my brother's car.'

'What's it doing out here?' Ash asked, moving to help.

'I don't know—but he's been gone sixty years.' Charlie tugged on the car's door handle. 'It's locked.'

'And you think he's inside?' Bree asked.

'What are you doing?' Ash asked the redhead, who was removing her hat. 'Now is not the time to adjust your hat.' It had this girly stuff wound around its hatband, even a playing card, the queen of spades.

'I'm getting some fencing wire to pick that car lock.' Beneath the twine, leather, and cloth strips that held match heads she'd used to start their campfire, she unwound a thick piece of fencing wire, which she bent into a hook. At the driver's door, she pushed the wire down in the gap between the window glass and the doorframe, wiggled it around, then in a matter of moments she'd popped the lock.

Ash arched one eyebrow at the redhead. 'Done that before, have we?'

'Ask me no questions and I'll tell you no lies.' The door screeched loudly of metal on metal. It spooked the horses, with the calf skittering to hide behind them.

'What's inside?' Ash asked, with Charlie fretting beside him.

Bree poked her head in, waving her hand in front of her face. 'Besides being hot as an oven, nothing. It's empty.'

'Let me see.' Charlie climbed behind the steering wheel to sit on its long bench seat.

'Are you sure it's your brother's?' The car's interior was in immaculate condition, as if preserved in a time capsule. However, the outside had been sandblasted back to bare metal, and the tyres were flat.

'I'm positive this is Harry's car.' Charlie dragged out an old black-and-white jumper. 'This is my brother's footy guernsey.' The back of the old football shirt displayed the name *Splint* across the top.

'So where is your brother now, Pop?' Bree pointed to the car. 'Why did he leave his car out here?'

Thirty-nine

'Is Ruby okay?' Harper asked Ryan as she held Mason's hand inside the vet's surgery. They were the first to arrive.

Ryan rubbed his eyes, with his hair a mess, and clothes all crumpled. 'Well …'

'Did you get any sleep?'

'I napped.'

'Here, I brought coffee.'

'Train station coffee?'

'It is. Cool playground.' Sick of watching the clock, she'd remembered Bree telling her that the food van at the train station was a great place for breakfast. It was her excuse to leave the farmhouse early, to emotionally eat pastries, washed down with steaming coffee, and buy out all the shortbread they had. The train station had a playground, where Harper learned there was a playgroup for children Mason's age, and regular library readings by a woman who wore a ball gown and had a pet water buffalo. That she found hard to believe.

With an hour before the vet's opened, she hit the feed store again. There, she met the owners, middle-aged twins, who helped her gather a big box of childproof locks and much more from their adjoining hardware store. She also bought dog beds for Ruby, Scout, and Sarge, and some doggy treats, including toys that Mason wanted to play with more than the animals.

Then right on nine o'clock, she knocked on the vet's glass

door.

'Come this way ...' Ryan led them past his messy reception area to the back of the surgery, where assorted cages held a few dogs, a turtle, a possum, and a wallaby.

'Is that a crocodile?'

'A freshie.'

'What's wrong with him?'

'He's got a bellyache. Ate the wrong thing.' Ryan opened Ruby's cage where the labrador lay on her side. An IV was attached to her leg, but her tail wagged. 'And that's a good sign.' He patted Ruby, crouching down beside Mason.

'Rubee.' His little fingers were eager to hug his dog.

'Careful mate, she's got a sore leg.'

'Aww ...' His little hands were so tender as he patted the dog.

'So Ruby is going to be okay?'

'Well, according to her ACT test for coagulopathy—'

'Pardon?'

'It tests the clotting time in the blood. A brown snake's poison makes the blood so thin it stops clotting. Left untreated, it's life threatening.'

She gasped, blinking back tears, with her hand on poor Ruby's soft fur.

'Ruby has had no adverse reaction to the antivenene, and it has neutralised the toxins. She responded well within the first hour.'

'So Ruby is going to be okay?' she asked again.

'Well, she's happy to see the boy, showing no signs of paralysis. But she has a bruise on her leg, and with the coagulopathy she'll need to be kept calm for the next forty-eight hours.'

'I can do that. If Cap has so many dogs, should he have some antivenene?'

'It's not cheap. The treatment runs into the thousands.'

She pulled out her purse. 'I'll pay for Ruby's treatment, and any spare vials for Cap's dogs.' She had to sweeten the impact somehow when she told Cap what happened, hopefully avoiding Ryder and Dex.

Ryan raised his eyebrows at her, before shuffling files from one pile to another. 'There's a fresh box somewhere. I got a delivery sent to me by mistake. I was going to send it back, but if you want it?'

'I'll take it.' She rarely shopped for anything and held out her card that had been working overtime today.

He opened a cupboard, closed it, then opened another, as more paperwork got shuffled around.

How did Ryan find anything in this office? 'Do you work here on your own?'

'I'm looking for a part-time assistant, or an office manager, if you know of one. I was trying to talk the relief cook out at Danbunnan Station into the job, but my mate, Jake, decided to marry her and keep her for himself. Oh, there's the box.' Ryan pulled out a small foam box. 'Are you sure? We're talking five grand.'

'How common is snakebite in dogs?'

'Out here, it's more common that you think.'

'I'll take it. Not that I'd know how to do an IV.'

'Cap does. He's done the procedure plenty of times over the radio.'

'You're kidding.'

'Welcome to station living. I'm the only vet in the region.' He pointed to the map.

'That's bigger than Belgium.' She studied the map, only now realising Elsie Creek Station was almost a quarter the size of Belgium, the economic nerve centre of Europe and headquarters to NATO, crammed with over eleven million people. While Elsie Creek Station was home to less than a dozen people.

'Why do they do it? Live out here? It's so dangerous, and so remote.'

'This is all new for you?'

'I'm on holiday.'

'You'd be surprised at how many come out here for a holiday and never leave.'

'I have to go back to work.' That she'd been avoiding.

'Well, if you ever change your mind, I could do with an office manager.' He held up some files. 'Oh, there's the machine. You can pay me now.'

The machine was dusty, but the paperwork showed he was busy. 'People don't pay you?'

'People pay me what they can. I've got a freezer full of steak and fish. Cowboy Craig said I should put a tin at the pub for donations to help those who can't afford it, and for the wildlife carers.'

'Well, I can pay in full. Be sure to give yourself a tip.'

'You're kidding?' He arched an eyebrow at her.

'If politicians can raise funds for voting campaigns, I'm sure you'll find people willing to donate to your surgery. There's plenty of ways to do it.'

'Who are you?'

'I'm Harper Jamison.'

'I meant, what do you do for a crust?'

'I'm an assistant to the …' She paused at her job title that used to make her feel so proud. But it was on the other side of the world, where none of it mattered over here.

'Assistant. That makes you an office person. Want a job?'

'I have one.' Did she?

'Well, if you ever change your mind, you know where I am.' He grinned at the pay machine beeping. 'My bank is going to love this.'

'Can we take Ruby home now?'

Forty

The simple pleasure of driving her sleek black Audi back to the station, gave Harper her independence back, even if it was crammed full of goodies, a toddler, and a dog. But it was twice as quick as Ash's ute, roomier, and so much more comfortable.

She had a lot to unpack before the boys got home. Already mentally preparing for the argument to come, ready to plead her case, especially over the snake incident.

She slowed down at the main gate to the station. Digging the gate key out of the centre console, she spotted a large four-wheel drive ute parked near the front gate.

She rummaged in the driver's door pocket where she kept her taser and pepper spray handy. Having a diplomatic passport allowed her to carry such things. She just never got a gun license. And why should she? The outback wasn't a terrorist's playground.

Even so, she was alone in the country, with an injured dog and a toddler in the back seat.

The front door of the fancy black ute opened, and a man stepped out, dressed in black jeans, boots, and a check shirt.

It was Leo.

Sliding on the Akubra Bree picked out for him, he effortlessly pulled off the look. Leo may not be wearing his suit, but he still had the presence of a cutthroat business executive or a politician—the kind that only pretended to care.

Overhead, the front entrance arch that held the fancy sign

made of intricately bent metals, obviously crafted by the in-house master brand makers, announcing *Elsie Creek Station*, cast long shadows over the red dust that made up the driveway. It only served as a reminder of how quiet it was out here.

She lowered her window just a crack, feeling the heat against the cool air from her car. 'Can I help you?'

Leo's ink-black eyes narrowed at her, before he shared a smile. 'Harper, right? Bree's friend.'

'And you're Leo, the neighbour.'

'I am. I'm looking for the owners of Elsie Creek Station.'

'They're working at the moment. I'm happy to take a message.' With a lifetime's worth of experience for playing gatekeeper to diplomats, she was literally playing gatekeeper, with the locked gate in front her, only this time for a bunch of stockmen.

Leo peered inside the car where the dog growled beside the sleeping boy, before he gave an over-friendly smile. It was a politician's smile that made all the promises in the world only to flip on you in the blink of an eye.

Leo held out a large manila envelope. 'I own Blackwell Mining.'

'The mine trying to steal this station's water.' Harper never backed down in a debate—especially in her world—now that her brain fog was over.

'Straight to the point. I like that. I see why you're Bree's friend.' Leo nodded with approval. 'I'm here to apologise to the owners. It seems the local government got a bit heavy-handed with their letter. I didn't want that to happen.'

Hold up, she knew this play, having done it herself. 'And you're here to make a counteroffer.' With the hope of the bad guys looking like the good guys.

'Look, between you and me, we tried to negotiate a decent offer with Charlie.'

Was this the man who had bullied Charlie?

With Bree's warning in mind, Harper's fingertips gripped the pepper spray, well-trained to use it as part of her job at the embassy. Along with it came that familiar friend, stress, strapping itself across her shoulders. It was the same level of stress she'd endured for years while living under a constant level-four terrorism threat. Back then she may not have noticed it, but after enjoying a few stress-free weeks, she didn't like that feeling, or Leo.

'Now that Elsie Creek has new owners, we can technically argue that the caretaker's caveat over the property no longer exists. I'd like to offer the Riggs brothers the same deal we made to Clinton Darcie.'

'Who?'

'Samuel Darcie's son. The old owner of Elsie Creek Station.' He angled his head at her.

'Oh, that's his name. I only know of him as Darcie's son.'

Leo again gave that fake smile and pointed to the back seat of the car. 'Your son?' It was an obvious distraction tactic to get friendly with the enemy. Another tactic she'd used many times in the halls of parliament.

'What do you want, Mr Travers?' Her formality was cool and calm. 'I have a Skype meeting in ten minutes and a child to feed.' But there was no way she was getting out of this locked car.

'Can you give this to the new owners, the Riggs brothers?' He grinned at her, as he left the envelope on a large rock by the gate.

He then stopped and faced her. 'Do they know who you are?'

'Pardon?' Her eyes flared open.

'They don't, do they?' His chuckle was cold, sending a warning shiver over her shoulders. 'Now why would a blue blood such as yourself be hanging out with a bunch of rednecks like the Riggs brothers? What would your father say, considering the Riggs' family come from a junkyard?'

'That's none of your business.'

'Oh, that's right. I'm sorry, please accept my condolences for your loss.' Leo even removed his hat.

'Have a nice day, Mr Travers.'

'Miss Jamison.' He slid on his hat, that shaded his sinister eyes. 'Say hi to Bree for me, tell her I haven't given up on our date.' He tapped the brim of his hat and climbed into his large vehicle.

Harper waited until Leo's vehicle drove out of sight before retrieving the envelope.

How did Leo know who she was? Was Leo going to expose her biggest secret?

Forty-one

Sarge gave a deep and distinctive bark from the front porch. It was enough to alert Scout to roll off her new doggy bed and trot over to stand beside the larger dog and howl, but with her tail wagging.

Harper peered through the front windows of the farmhouse to an empty driveway, but Sarge and Scout were facing the sheds.

She pushed open the screen door as voices rose from the shed. It was the Riggs brothers.

Harper dashed inside, wiping sweaty palms down her summer dress. It was time to activate her plan.

With Leo threatening to expose her, Harper didn't know how long she had left at playing the nanny—which meant getting on the brothers' good side. Welcome to Mission Impossible.

Dex dumped his load of washing by the back door and grabbed a round of beers from the outdoor beer fridge and headed for the table. He didn't even say hello.

'Hey, who cleaned the table?' Cap asked, patting Sarge and Scout. 'It's set for dinner.'

Ryder dragged back his chair, scowling at his paperwork piled on the side bench.

Harper carried out the stew pot and put it on the table. 'This is from Bree. It's the last of her stew.' She looked for Ash, who was nowhere in sight.

'For someone who cooks on a simple campfire, Bree is a brilliant cook.' Dex eagerly scooped up a ladle full of stew into a bowl as Cap tore at the bread. 'We should have Bree come with us on every muster. That woman has some serious skills as a stockwoman. Her cooking is just a bonus.'

'Yeah, Bree was a big help. Charlie too.' Ryder loaded up his spoon with a hearty stew.

They were silent as they ate, not one of them even saying hello or thank you to Harper. *The jerks!*

'Um, so ... I put the coffee machine out here to make it easier for you guys.' She pointed to the bench, where she'd created a coffee station of sorts.

Harper still sucked at small talk, and decided to barrel though with her rehearsed speech, placing the small box in front of Cap. 'I'm sorry, Cap.'

'For what?'

'There was this snake—'

'Where's Mason?' Both Ryder and Dex jumped to their feet.

'Mason is fine. He's watching cartoons.'

'You connected the television?' Dex peered through the large open windows. 'Hey, that's my TV.' He scowled. Like scary scowled.

'You had four of them, and I picked the one I could lift.'

'So you can sit around and watch TV all day.'

Arsehole.

'Is that why our boxes are all shoved aside?'

Cap pointed. 'Oh, hey, look at the new dog beds—'

'House dogs,' complained Dex. 'She's turning the police dogs into house dogs.'

'Can I just speak without being interrupted, *please*?' She glared at Dex.

'Dex, sit down. Let her speak.' Ryder's deep voice sliced through the air, yet it only heightened the tension. Thankfully, Dex listened.

'Thank you. Now before anyone panics, it's all fine. But ...' She took a deep breath and calmly explained the snake incident.

She paused as Cap went and checked over Ruby, giving

her a nod to continue telling them about the vet's prognosis for Ruby, and the letter from the mining company. 'Don't worry, I locked the front gate again when I came back from town, in case Leo wanted to come back.'

Ryder tore open the letter and quickly scanned the page. 'Pfft. They're dreaming.' He passed the envelope to Dex, who held it out to Cap so they could both read it.

'You said they'd make an offer, Ryder. But I thought they'd at least offer us more than what we'd invested into the place.' Dex dropped the paperwork onto the table.

'It's their first offer. It won't be their last.' Cap opened the box to reveal the vials. 'That's a lot of antivenene for the dogs. This stuff isn't cheap, you know.'

'I had to get it. I hate seeing animals suffer, and the vet told me snakebite is common out here.'

'It is.' Cap nodded at her with pure gratitude. 'Thank you, Harper.'

'And I also picked up an antivenene kit and a first-aid kit for the farmhouse.' She pointed to the massive white tin box with a red cross on it. It sat beside the new fire extinguisher and fire blankets. Should she dare organise a fire drill in the future?

'I also put in a request for the landline to be re-connected for this house. And, when Ash comes back, he can put in the childproof locks, because I don't know how to use a drill. And this is for you guys.' She lifted a large whiteboard, her muscles achy from the heavy lifting she'd been doing these past few days, especially rearranging the lounge room for Mason.

'Are you gonna draw us some pictures as part of your lecture?' Dex rolled his eyes.

Ignoring the jerk, Harper continued with her plan. This wasn't her first boardroom presentation in front of a hostile crowd. 'This is for you guys to create a list for your jobs that need to be done, instead of—'

'What would you know about running cattle stations?' Dex was such a—*ugh!*

'Nothing. But I know about organising and this will help. Instead of Ryder putting it down on his tablet's list, and Ash having his separate list, you can create one big to-do list you can all see and delegate and cross off the board. I've even got a stack of colours so you can use a colour for each brother, so you'll know what everyone is doing, keeping the workload transparent. You're already having your meetings, so now you have a board.'

Dex's scowl faltered, while Cap grinned and kept on eating. But Ryder thoughtfully stroked his chin, darkened with a four-day growth.

'Where is Ash?' She'd done this for Ash, so he could see he was part of the bigger picture and a valuable partner contributing to their team.

'Ash is with Charlie. They found this old car in the Stoneys and they're using the Razorback to tow it back,' explained Cap.

'It won't take much to restore that car.' Dex picked up his fork to resume eating. 'Besides a service, a decent paint job, and some new whitewall tyres, it'll polish up nicely.'

Harper didn't know whether to sit or hover like an idiot. All that fretting for nothing.

Ryder leaned over and pulled out a chair for Harper. Giving her a slight nod, he resumed eating.

With a deep swallow, she finally sat gingerly at *the table*. This was huge. 'Um, so …' She tried to make small talk—no, she was making conversation! 'What's the deal with the car?'

'They found this old FJ Holden tucked away in some side alley in the Stoneys.' Cap dabbed his bread at the stew. 'According to Ash, the car belonged to Charlie's older brother, who's been missing for sixty years.'

Forty-two

You could've knocked Ash over with an emu's feather when he saw Harper seated at the table while his brothers ate. Just the sight of her had his pulse picking up, with a thirst to be near her. Pity he was covered in grease and dirt, and in dire need of a shower, with his stomach rumbling at the smell of food. 'Did you cook, Harper?'

He'd missed her. Like really missed both her and Mason—when not that long ago he didn't think of anyone else but himself. But now he hadn't stopped thinking about Harper, trying to come up with ways to spoil her, to make Harper and Mason happy.

'Bree, did. She said its leftovers.' Harper stood awkwardly, going all shy on him. But it had his heart doing cartwheels, so tempted to drag her into his chest to kiss her. But not in front of his brothers shovelling food into their gobs.

'Thanks, I'm starving.' He grabbed a plate. 'Please, stay.' He grabbed her dainty wrist, so soft and warm.

'I was going to check on Mason.'

'Where is he?'

Harper pointed to the lounge room and Ash peered inside the house. There were no more boxes cluttering up the main living room, a wide-screen TV sat on the shelf playing cartoons, with Mason lying beside Ruby on a bean bag with toys scattered around him.

'Harper tidied up the lounge, bro. She's getting us organised.' Cap nodded at the house. 'First-aid kit, fire blankets, antivenene, and a big whiteboard to put up our to-do list.'

'The place looks good.'

Did he hug Harper, disturb the boy for a hug, or just eat? 'How's Mason?'

Harper gave a shy shrug. 'Good— I, um, need to tell you about the snake.' She gave him a quick rundown, answering all his anxious heart stopping questions.

'Bree said you'd be tough enough to handle it.' And smiled at her, proud for her. What a woman!

'She didn't kill it,' said Dex. 'Don't worry, brother, we'll hunt it down. Unless you've got a good snake dog in your pack, Cap?'

'I don't have hunting dogs.'

'You have heelers. They've always been a good snake deterrent.'

'Is it okay if I visit for a bit, fellas?' It was Charlie, carrying his hat in his hand.

'Sure, Charlie, pull up a pew.' Ash sat dragging Harper back to her seat. Obviously he was going with the idea of food first, then shower, then a load of hugs with the boy and then the nanny—or could he just skip to the good bits and hold Harper first—even if he was filthy.

'I'll go.' Harper went to leave.

Ash gripped her thigh, keeping her in place. 'Stay, Harper. I like you seated at the table.' He didn't care what his brothers thought, Ash wanted her here. 'Do you want some tucker, Charlie?'

'I'm sure Bree's got some waiting for me back at the humpy. I just wanted to thank you for allowing me to bring my brother's car back, like you did, Ash. I know it took you away from mustering.'

'Is it really your brother's car?' Cap asked.

'It is. Rego papers were in the glove box.'

'What's the story, Charlie?' Ryder tore chunks off his bread to dab at his stew. 'For you to come over with hat in hand, it must be big.'

'Well ...' Charlie gingerly sat down, his voice laced with pain. 'My brother and I came here over sixty years ago. We were staying where you are, Dex, in the stockman's shack. While I worked here full-time, my brother, Harry, did a stint as a linesman, maintaining the telegraph line, with dreams of being a footballer.'

'Did he get that game?'

'Harry got a few games, down south. Then in the off-season he'd come back to this station and do the musters. Until he hooked up with a girl.' Charlie frowned.

'What's wrong with that?' Ash couldn't look at Harper. Yet he could feel her body heat, dying to touch her, but not with his brothers watching.

'She was married to the head stockman.'

'The scandal.' Dex gave a low chuckle.

'Happens too many times,' mumbled Ryder. 'Wrecks a place after that.'

'I didn't know. I swear it. If I did, I would've told him to quit it. But according to the coppers —'

'Why were the police involved?' Ryder dropped his spoon into his empty bowl. Cap and Dex stopped eating.

'Because of the murder. But my brother wasn't no murderer, Harry wasn't like that.'

'Are you saying your brother is wanted for murder?' Ash asked. Why hadn't Charlie or Bree mentioned this earlier? He'd been working with them all day, to drag that old Holden back to the shed.

'No wonder he ditched the car in the Stoneys.' Dex scraped the last of the stew from the pot onto his plate. 'But do give Bree our compliments on her tucker.'

'Oi.' Ryder frowned at Dex before speaking to Charlie. 'Where was this murder?'

'Um, well, here. At the station. In one of the sheds.'

'Where were you when it happened?'

'Out with Darcie. We'd been mustering when Darcie's old man rode out and told us they'd found Jack Price murdered, his wife Pen missing, and Harry and his car were gone.'

Charlie sighed, staring down at the hat he held between his two hands, showing his age in the deep wrinkles crowding around his sad grey eyes. 'My brother left without saying goodbye. I know he wouldn't do that, like I know my brother wouldn't murder anyone. Harry wasn't like that. Thankfully, Darcie believed the same, which is why he let me stay on, even if his father was deadset against it.'

He then slapped on his hat and stood. 'Anyhoodle, I thought I'd let you mob know first, before the bush telegraph kicks into overdrive.'

'Charlie, we aren't kicking you out over this.' Ash wasn't afraid to stare down his brothers. He liked Charlie, who was a damned good stockman with lots of tips and tricks he'd shared with Ash in the short time they'd lived here. 'We're not kicking anyone out.' He tenderly patted Harper's knee, hoping she got the message.

Forty-three

Later that night, after Harper finished washing the dishes, she tidied up the lounge, then turned off the TV, which unleashed a heavy silence as everyone had gone to bed.

Again, she'd failed to talk to Ash, but she needed to before Leo exposed her.

At Ash's bedroom door, she held up her fist, about to knock, but didn't. She couldn't.

Curling her fingers into a tighter fist, she started to walk away, only to turn around and stare at his bedroom door, trying to find the courage to knock. She brushed down her cotton dress, inhaled, while rehearsing the conversation in her head.

'Boo.'

She slapped a hand over her mouth to stop her squeal.

Ash chuckled, leaning a strong shoulder against the corridor wall.

'Where did you come from?'

'Bathroom.' He ruffled his hair, damp from the shower. 'What are you doing skulking around in front of my door?'

'I wasn't skulking.'

His dark eyes, laced with humour, studied her, the intensity of them making her skin prickle. 'So …'

'So,' she parroted.

Not that smile. Not the one with the dimple.

She pinched herself to focus and cleared her throat. 'We need to talk.'

'Not when you say it like that, we don't.'

'Yes, we do.'

'Not in the corridor.' He pushed open his door.

'I'm not going in there.' Especially when he was just wearing a towel. Again.

'Do you time this on purpose?' He swaggered towards her, his gaze lingering and warm on her skin.

'What?' There was no ignoring his existence, and that focus of his, and all that bare bronzed skin with the perfect set of abs.

'Catching me in my towel.' The towel that hung low on his hips.

'Why … What? No.'

His eyes were bright, and his lips twitched as if he wanted to smile but wouldn't. He was toying her with her. Again.

She stepped back, but he only stepped in closer, placing his hands flat against the wall on either side of her head. It made her stiffen. 'Ash.'

'Harper.' His fingertips brushed at her hair, to then run down the side of her face and neck, pausing on her racing pulse that matched her ragged breathing.

'Ash, we need to …'

'Shh.' He stared at her. The attention caused the heat to rush to her cheeks, as her breathing picked up so much her lips parted with a need to pant.

'I'm going to kiss you now, Harper.' He paused, and the seconds dragged on.

Did she nod? She forcefully shook her head. Only to nod.

What the hell!

'No.' She pushed him away and headed for her room. Before she had a chance to close the door, he was right behind her. 'What are you doing?'

'You said you wanted to talk. Let's talk.' He closed the door behind him, blocking her from any chance of escape.

'You should get dressed.'

'I'm fine.'

Nothing about this was fine. Not when he crossed his

powerful arms over his bare chest, that towel hanging low on his hips, and his perfect abs shaded in all the right places. No one had a set of abs like Ash.

'What are you worried about?'

She didn't know where to begin, when her eyes could only gaze over his near-naked body that made her brain switch off.

'You liked that kiss, right?'

Oh, she more than liked it, the memory making her body flush all over.

Again, he stalked across the room. She stepped away from him until her back was against the wall, where he trapped her with his hands pressed on either side of her head, while his eyes roamed across her face, seeing too much of what she'd always tried to hide.

'I want you, Harper.' His voice was like gravel, and it only lit the match, burning what little sanity she was holding on to. 'Let me take care of you.'

Her hands pressed against his chest, but he dipped down so close his lips could almost brush against hers.

She licked her lips.

His darkening eyes watched with hunger, releasing an exhale that skittered across her skin, making her arms break out in another round of goosebumps.

That's when he stepped in closer and gently—ever so gently—cupped her cheeks, where his thumb tenderly dragged across her bottom lip. 'You can say no at any time.'

She struggled to speak to this man who was taller, wider, bigger, and so much stronger. Her mind was telling her to flee, while waving a whole auditorium full of red flags. Yet her body was in charge, melting into a raging hot tidal pool of starving hormones. It was about to get messy.

'Okay.' It was barely a whisper, but it sounded louder than a starting pistol at a yacht race.

His hands firmed on her cheeks, and he leaned in. Her eyes closed as their lips met. But this didn't start with some closed-mouth peck or a sweet kiss. Oh, hell no. It was open mouths instantly connecting.

His tongue lashed against hers, his grip tightened around her chin, deepening their kiss. She moaned into his mouth and it somehow became his excuse to kiss her deeper. Harder. For a breathtakingly long time.

His hands slid into her hair, then down to her neck, gripping her, to keep her there, while his mouth crushed against hers. She could feel the desperation, not only within herself, but from the man who was about to wreck her from the inside out.

His hand slid down her shoulders, and down to her breast. There, his fingers softly ran back and forth along the top edge of her dress, before releasing the buttons.

Then he pulled back, lips wet, his eyes ablaze, to gaze down at the top part of her dress, exposing her soft emerald-green bra. 'You sexy little minx, you.' His fingertips traced the lace of her bra. 'Do these come in matching panties, too?'

Before she could respond, he swept a kiss across her lips to mumble against them. 'Doesn't matter, they won't be there for long.' That's when his mouth latched on to her breast. She groaned at the force, arching her neck, making her lips part as his hot, wet mouth busily worked from one breast to the other, with his fingers kneading her flesh, driving her insane.

She gripped his shoulders, her palms sliding over the hard, cut angles of his beautiful body, and the rippling flex of his shoulders and that perfectly muscular back. He was heaven and heartache rolled into one package. Impossible to resist. Especially when the towel fell to the floor with her panties.

Forty-four

Ash wanted to go slow. But how could he, when everything about Harper was beautiful? That sexy moan, her scent, and her taste was like paradise on his tongue. Who knew watching her body tremble just from his touch would be the biggest turn-on in his life. All he wanted to do was please her.

Her dress was gone. So too her bra, her panties, and she was beautifully bare.

There was a flash of shyness in her eyes as her hands moved to cover herself.

'Don't.' He gripped her hands and held them above her head, pinning her to the wall. 'Don't hide, not from me.' His eyes took a long, long time to admire the smooth curves of her hips, the rise and fall of her chest, and the round shape of her belly. And that arse he gripped, while dipping his head to press kisses to her smooth, flawless skin on a body he wanted to explore for the rest of his life.

'Do you want a condom? I'm clean. Just that...' He stepped back, raking fingers through his hair. 'I've got a kid.' One he hadn't planned on.

'Can you wear two?' She bit her lip.

'Stay right there.' He let her wrists go. He had enough self-control to stop, even if he didn't want to, but it was the fastest trip to his room and back in his life.

He spotted her pill packet on her bedside table as he closed the bedroom door. 'Aren't you covered?'

'I've been in hospital, so I don't trust it?'

Good call. Even if this conversation should kill the mood, it didn't, even while ripping open the packet and sheathing himself. 'Ready?'

Her nod was small, but her chest was hammering against his.

But when those eyes of hers locked on his, he had his answer before she spoke. 'Yes. I'm sure.'

Even though he was as hard as steel, pressed against her body, he had to please his lady first. That began by again catching both her wrists in his left hand to hold them above her head, pressing her against the wall. That pose exposed her delicious body that had his eager fingers admiring the soft warm skin, trailing down her inner arm, making her whimper and squirm.

Forcing her hips still, his fingers carried on their heavenly journey, down to her soft satiny thighs.

Her breathing stuttered as he skimmed his mouth across her lips, as the pads of his fingers found the softest skin in the junction between her legs.

His lips trailed over her collarbone, enjoying the flush that spread across her skin. Her whimpers created the best playlist on the planet, until she leaned her head back with eyes closed and gasped for air with the sexiest moan he'd ever heard. He'd found that nub that made her inner thighs tremble, while his fingers dove deep to prepare her.

He nipped on her earlobe as her breathing grew ragged, her body trembling beneath his hands. And just as she was about to explode, he slid inside.

Her hands flew to his jaw, their teeth clacking against each other's, as her legs lifted, and she pulled him closer. He surged into her body that stretched around him. It was so damned tight, clamping down on him from the intensity of her orgasm, which rolled on and on, he didn't know where one ended and the next began.

His grip tightened, trying to get closer, and his groan matched hers. Their mouths met as if to breathe for each other, as his strokes started slow and measured while her hands became entangled in his hair. With her ample breasts pressed deliciously against his chest, her body once again squeezed.

She was torturing him.

He was so wrapped up in her presence, her body, her arms, her gloriously deep moans, he could barely breathe. Nothing and no one could have prepared him for this moment or for her. He growled, a rumble deep in his chest, he was practically vibrating with a need to punish her with pleasure, to kiss her savagely, so that she would understand there would be no walking away from this for either of them. Not when his raw heart craved the closeness of her.

But one stroke later, he came without warning. Cheated, he roared. All his muscles contracted in a concert of emotional overload, pouring his soul into the only woman he'd ever made love to.

No way was he done, not when he had finally won the greatest prize of his life. And carried his queen to bed.

Forty-five

Asleep in a pair of boxers, Ash lay on his son's spare bed, with little Mason curled up beside him, leaving his cot empty.

There was a tap on the door. It was Harper, holding out a cup of coffee. 'Thought you might need this.'

'Thanks. What's the time?' He patted his son's soft hair. Ruby wagged her tail from her fluffy bed, with her bandage still on her leg, so he patted the unsung hero too.

'Eight,' replied Harper.

The last he remembered he'd only come in to check on the boy, take him to the toilet, then he was meant to go back to bed with Harper. 'Have my brothers gone?'

She nodded.

'Damn.' He ran fingers through his hair. 'I can't seem to win.'

'What do you mean?'

'I've been slack. Work. The boy. Everything …' He sipped the coffee rich and black, and carefully left Mason sleeping. 'Ryder's offered to give me my money back to get out of the partnership.'

'But you love mustering and this place.'

'I've been slack.'

'So change.'

'Excuse me?'

'If you want to change, change. Set an alarm, so you don't sleep in. Go to bed earlier, stop playing games all night.'

Games. Ha. He'd played with her to the brink of

exhaustion, and he would have kept going if he hadn't volunteered to check on Mason. 'Talk about a bit of tough love before breakfast, Harper.'

'Don't look at me for sympathy, when I'm not exactly playing my A-game, either.' She walked out in a huff.

He followed her, swiping a pair of jeans and T-shirt from his room.

'I'm not looking for sympathy,' he said, sliding into his jeans in the large living room with the boxes pushed against the wall, it only held a few dog beds, a beanbag, and lots of toys. 'And don't ask me what I want, because everyone else has been asking the same thing.' Did he do the wrong thing with Harper last night? Yet, it had felt so right. Where were his boots?

'Don't worry, I've been asking that same question about myself.'

'What do you mean?' He slid on his T-shirt and froze. Was she going to give him the *sorry this won't work out* speech?

'Sitting here, in this house, alone, trying to find something to do, when normally I never have time for myself, I really struggled.'

'So, what did you do, besides rearrange the house and organise stuff?'

'I tried to cook a meal. And that flopped. And—and ...' She screwed up her nose.

'What? Spit it out.' *Please don't dump me.*

'I read that letter from the government. The one you said you'd show me. It accidentally fell out of the pile of paperwork when I was clearing the table.'

'How much coffee have you had?' She was powering through her words. But he found some socks and his boots.

'One. It's cold.'

'You're the only person I know who drinks cold coffee.' He sipped his coffee, which was nice and hot. Then slid on his socks and boots and stamped the soles against the floor like normal. 'Suppose I'd better get out there. We're fixing the drafting yards.'

'So, you're just going to pretend it's all normal, then?'

'Well, my brothers won't kick me out, although Ryder wanted to fire me.'

'I'm talking about *us*.'

'Oh.' That woke him up. 'I want to take you out.'

'Pardon?'

'I'm not sure about the details yet, but I want this. You and me, I want us.' Hell, yeah.

But Harper crossed her arms over her chest. 'First, we need to talk. There are things we need to discuss.' She seemed adamant about it.

'Sure. Look, I've been planning with Bree to do something special for you—'

'You have?' She blinked, her brusque mood instantly vanishing.

'Yeah, but Bree said I had to ask you first so she could start planning it. So tonight, you and me will go on a date, outback style? Yes?'

Her shy smile came with a really sweet nod. He tenderly stroked her hair and kissed her forehead.

'Good. It's a date. And then we can pick up where we left off last night as dessert.' He dragged her close to his chest, snaking his arms around her. 'Or we can go back to bed now and get a head start.' His nose nuzzled into her slender neck, her hair like silk against his cheek. 'Hmm, you smell good.'

'Daddy?' Mason stumbled out of his room, rubbing his sleepy eyes.

'G'day, little man.' Ash crouched down, and the boy ran into his arms. It melted his heart, and the soft smile from Harper made it all worth it.

'Here, Mason.' Harper passed him his special kiddie's cup.

'I'll go see Bree first, then I'll make an appearance at the office.' No doubt to cop a dressing down from Major Ryder.

Sarge barked. It was deep.

'*Oi, it's the Coppers!*' Dex's whistle sliced through the air.

Ash, still carrying Mason on his chest, went to meet the police car pulling up near the house.

'Nice of you to show up,' grumbled Dex at the bottom of the front steps, as Cap and Ryder strode over from the sheds.

'I was asleep with my son.'

'Sure you weren't busy with the nanny?' Dex sneered at Harper standing by the door.

Ash glowered at Dex. 'Back off, Dex. I was with Mason. He had a nightmare last night, probably about the snake, so I was with him. Besides, it's none of your business who I decide to be with or not.' He may have said it to Dex, but he made sure Cap and Ryder heard him, too.

Ash was a grown man. He didn't need their permission for who he could and couldn't be with. If he wanted to be with Harper, then he would be.

'Fellas.' Porter slid on his police cap as he climbed out of the paddy wagon.

'What brings you here, Porter?' Ryder asked.

'Welfare check.'

'Has it been twenty-eight days?' Ash raked fingers through his hair, trying to remember his daily tally. 'Wait, we still have ten more days.'

'Counting much?' Dex scowled at Ash.

'Ash is right. But I'm here over an anonymous tip that the boy was in trouble. Something about a snake?' Porter tilted his head and took a long, hard look at the boy Ash held against his chest.

'Who from?' Ash asked.

Porter shrugged. 'I did say anonymous, right?'

'The boy is fine,' said Ryder in his brusque tone. 'There was a snake at the back by the old washing machine. Cap's nanny dog was bitten protecting the boy. And before you ask, I've ordered a new machine, including the materials to screen off the laundry area so it never happens again.'

'And the nanny,' Dex started, pointing at Harper hovering by the front steps.

'Her name is Harper.' Ash frowned at Dex.

'The boy's *nanny*,' said Dex with determination, 'has got us kitted out with antivenene medicine not only for humans but also for the dogs. She's also put child safety locks on the doors to childproof the house, and a fire blanket and all this other first-aid stuff.'

'You're welcome to check the house, Porter, to see for yourself,' said Cap. 'We can show you the nanny dog and her wound.'

'Porter can see the boy is fine.' Dex pointed at Ash holding Mason.

Porter kept scribbling in his notepad.

That's when it hit Ash like a micky bull's kick to the guts. 'You can't take him, Porter. *Mason is my son!* No one can take my boy from me.' It was worse than any other fear, worse than any burden of responsibility. It was the worst fear — the fear of losing his son. 'He's my son. No one is taking my son.'

Ryder's large hand landed heavily on Ash's shoulder. 'We won't let them.'

'All right, calm down, fellas.' Porter held up his hand, speaking in a tone he might use to calm down a pack of wild dogs. 'I'm just doing my job. I can see the boy is fine, and you've taken precautions. Obviously, whoever called this in, didn't know about the nanny.'

'I reckon it's that mine. That Leo,' said Dex, wearing his signature scowl. 'Didn't Leo give Harper that letter at the front gate?'

Ash peered over his shoulder at Harper, who only shrugged at him. It was the first he'd heard about her being near the enemy.

Harper was right. They needed to talk.

'Porter, what do you know about our neighbours from Blackwell Mining?' Ryder asked.

'Nothing.' Porter shrugged, taking notes. 'How long has the nanny been here?'

'Harper started the day after Mason arrived.' Ash remembered that first time spotting her on the deserted outback highway, in her business suit, running after her flat tyre. It was the same morning he'd met Mason.

Ash shifted Mason to his other side on his chest. 'Porter, what do you know about Mason's mother?'

'Eh?' All his brothers looked at him. Even Porter stopped taking notes.

'I want to contact one of Mason's mother's relatives.' Did he say that right?

'Why? They'll only interfere.' Dex's face twisted as if tasting something horrible.

'Because I don't remember Mason's mother. I don't even have a photo to jog my memory of who she was. My son will have questions about who his mother is as he grows up, and I'd like to give him something. Mason deserves that much.'

'That's fair.' Ryder nodded, then looked at Porter. 'You said Mason was here because of the mother's will?'

'That's right. Hold on, I've got the file in the car.' Porter rummaged around in the passenger seat and pulled out his laptop, flipping open the lid, he sat it on the police car's bonnet.

'We know Mason's mother was called Gemma Fallon,' said Ryder, who had a memory for details. 'How did Mason get here? Family?'

'Please don't say some foster home?' Ash hugged his son just that little bit tighter.

Porter read from his PC's screen. 'A family friend cared for Mason until they tracked Ash down, as per the request in Gemma's will that Mason live with his father.'

'Does Mason have any family out there?' Ash was doing this for Mason.

'Gemma's mother died with her in the accident, alongside her husband. Whoa, he was a federal minister.' Porter pointed to his screen. 'It says here he was a prominent figure in international trade and development. And Gemma had a half-sister, working overseas—which would be Mason's aunt. The notes show they were hoping Gemma's half-sister would make it back in time, but they found you first. Did you know Mason arrived in a private jet? Should've seen Mickey at the local airport when this thing landed, a whole jet for one small boy holding the hand of an air hostess.'

'Why? Because his grandfather was a federal minister?' Dex asked Porter.

'No. They're not blood related. According to the file, Gemma's mother, Vivian, had Gemma many years before she married the minister.'

'Name. Give us a name,' demanded Ryder. 'Who was he?'

'Richard Jamison was married to Vivian Langley. They had a daughter named Harper Jamison, who works for the Australian Ambassador in Belgium.'

Ash spun around to face Harper. 'You! You're Mason's *aunt?*'

Forty-six

Harper gulped as she stood on the edge of an abyss, from her small but terrifying perch on the front porch steps, as her entire world came crashing down.

'I knew there was something odd about you wanting to be a nanny.' Ryder's deep voice sliced through the air, matching his frown.

But it was Dex who scared her more. The professional street fighter clenched his fists as if to control his rage. 'You lied to us.'

'No, I didn't. I was …'

'OI!' Porter pressed on the police siren, blasting the air. Even the dogs cowered. 'Calm down, everyone, and let the girl explain herself.'

'I didn't lie, I swear.' Harper approached Ash.

'You're here for Mason.' Ash stepped back, holding Mason away from her. 'With those kinds of federal connections, you could take him away from me. From us.'

'Get OUT.' Ryder's voice boomed like a shotgun blast across the compound, it rang in her ears.

'But I can explain everything.'

'Dex, grab Harper's suitcase and chuck it in her car,' ordered Ryder. 'The nanny's employment has been terminated. Immediately.'

Dex bolted for the house.

'Come on guys, give Harper a minute to explain herself,' said Cap, trying to calm them down.

'No, she doesn't get a minute.' Ash glowered at her. Harper had never seen him so mad. 'You were coming here to take Mason away. When I found you, with that flat tyre, you were coming here the same day Mason arrived. It's why you stuck around in town—'

'It's why she agreed to be the nanny, when it's obvious she is no nanny.' Ryder sneered at her, it was a terrifying look.

Cap grabbed her arm. 'Come on, Harper, it's time to go, for your own safety.'

'But I—'

'Porter, if she's not gone in five minutes, I want her arrested for trespassing.' It was Ash who said it, not Ryder, not Dex. But Ash. 'Get out and never come back.'

'I didn't lie, I—'

'You deceived us. You could have been straight with us from the beginning—*with me*. How can I believe a word you say? How do I know what we shared wasn't fake?'

'It was real.'

'I don't believe you.' Ash held Mason away from her. 'Come on, Mason, let's get you inside.'

'But ...' Hot, salty tears streamed down her face, as Cap led her away from the farmhouse to meet her car being driven by Dex.

Dex left the driver's door open, the motor running, her suitcase dumped on the back seat with her clothes spilling out everywhere.

'Politician's lie for a living, so it must be in their blood, and you being their kid ...' The hatred emanated off Dex in heated waves. 'Or is this situation all about you keeping your enemies closer?'

She stepped back with that tingle of terror creeping up her spine at the potency of Dex's glare.

Harper had crossed a line and broken boundaries that were irreparable. This was why she'd always made plans and kept time schedules, because when she had no plan, it created one big mess with no time to fix it.

'Come on, Harper,' said Porter, 'I'll escort you back to town.'

She had no choice but to leave.

Policeman Porter led the way down the long driveway, and through her thick tears she followed.

With eyes on her rear-view mirror, she watched the last of Elsie Creek Station disappear behind a thick veil of dust and knew she could never come back.

This morning, she'd been invited on a first date. This morning, she had a family. Now, she had no one.

Forty-seven

Ash couldn't sleep. Instead, he sat watching Mason sleep in his cot, with Ruby snuggled in her soft dog bed nearby.

All day yesterday, Mason had looked for Harper. His room had her scent, there were still some items that belonged to her in the bathroom, her bedroom, even in Mason's room, that Ash kept expecting her to walk through the door any second.

Yet she'd hurt him in the deepest way possible.

It was a stark reminder why he never got close to any female. It's why he kept that two-week shelf-life on dating—if they made it that long. He did it for the carefree lifestyle, his lack of commitment, skipping on the responsibility. The two-week dating rule was supposed to protect him so he could avoid all the pain and drama of being in a relationship. Harper was a prime example of why he had a two-week rule, when she'd been here eighteen days.

And the thought of Harper potentially stealing his son had him grinding his teeth.

His. Son. Mason Riggs deserved to be here, because this was his home. The work Ash was doing wasn't for himself anymore. This was a legacy he would pass down to his son.

Filled with fiery annoyance, he stormed out the front door, in dire need of fresh air to calm down. Harper had betrayed him. Leaving his heart to ache as if she'd smashed it with a branding iron, it struggled to work.

Why didn't she tell him who she was from the beginning?

If Harper had said who she was then, even at the supermarket, he probably would have gladly handed the kid over—like hell he'd do that now.

At the outdoor table, he spotted the new coffee machine, complete with cups and sugar, set below the whiteboard. He rolled up his sleeves and made a pot of coffee. As the caffeine aroma filled the air, he dragged out the papers and started scribbling on the new whiteboard. He had to focus on something other than Harper. He wanted to forget she ever existed, and the best way to do that that was by tackling the mother of all problems—the issue of saving his home.

It was hours later when the kitchen screen door creaked, and Ryder's heavy boots thundered down the side verandah. 'Morning.'

'Ryder.' Ash sipped his coffee, his eyes on the whiteboard. 'Coffee's hot.'

Ryder poured himself a cup. 'That's the first time you've made coffee in the morning.'

Ash winced, rubbing the back of his neck. He'd been an idiot, not only with his slack work ethic, but to Ryder, the man who'd made their dream of owning a station a reality. 'Well, it won't be the last.' He had a lot to make up for.

'What's this?' Ryder nodded at the whiteboard covered in text and diagrams.

'I'll wait for Dex and Cap, to explain it all at once.' He pointed to Dex coming from the sheds.

Dex jumped up onto the porch, poured his coffee and took a long deep sip. 'Man, that's your best brew yet, Ryder.'

'I didn't make it. Ash did.'

Dex arched an eyebrow at Ash. 'Do you need to borrow your son's night nappies to not wet the bed in the future?'

'Did I hear right? Ash made the coffee?' Cap, with his entourage of dogs, casually strolled around the corner.

'It's good, too.' Dex even raised his cup in a salute to Ash, before taking his seat at the table.

'What's going on?' Cap, with coffee in hand, sat beside Dex. His dogs lay across the dried lawn as the sky became a soft salmon pink, where a faint yellow glow grew on the distant horizon. A flock of white cockatoos screeched, and the fresh aroma of outback air carried on the breeze.

Ryder leaned back in his chair at the head of the table. 'Ash has something to say.'

Ash stood at the other end of the table and faced his brothers. 'First, I want to say I'm sorry. I wasn't pulling my weight, I was being slack, and unfocused. But after nearly losing my son …' he said, patting at his constricted chest, '… the fear of Mason being taken away from us, our home —'

'It hit home at what we're doing?' suggested Dex, without any malice.

Ash nodded. 'I wasn't committing myself to anyone or anything. I was being irresponsible because it was just me, and if I got into trouble, I didn't care. But that all changed.' In the biggest wake-up call of his life. 'I want to change, not just for you or me, but for my son's sake. It's time I put family first and stopped being so selfish.' It was time for Ash to grow up.

'So, this is my wish list.' He pointed to the whiteboard. 'This is what I know I can do, that will save us time and money. I suggest we start by modernising some of our processes, using precision agriculture technologies, involving the use of drones, sensors, and GPS systems. I know these technologies, I've used them extensively, and have seen firsthand how they can optimise our crop management, effectively monitor our livestock, and enhance the station's overall efficiency, including cutting down on our fuel costs and saving us precious time.'

'Who are you, and what have you done with our baby brother?' Dex grinned.

'Don't listen to him, keep going,' urged Cap.

'I know I've said this before, but I've never explained it properly …' Ash paused for a beat, to gulp on his coffee. 'I want to build an automated system for watering our livestock, ensuring a more efficient use of our water resources in a way that those mining pricks can't point at us for any environmental issues.'

'How do we do that?' Cap asked.

Ash dragged out a map of the station, along with the diagrams he'd been working on all night. 'We'd use sensors for not only the water levels, but also water quality, all remotely controlled. Without wasting a single drop, we can repurpose the water I normally flush from those troughs into our new paddock to become crop feed or—'

'Wildlife corridor.' Cap held up his arm.

'Anything is possible. With my tech background, and Cap's knowledge of renewable energy, and Dex's mechanical skills, we could create our own solar farm, to provide plenty of sustainable power for this station. It would slash our operational costs—'

'Giving us higher profits.' Dex nodded. After all, Dex and Ryder were the money men.

'As for the security cameras, I'd like to create an intranet.' His heart squeezed at the thought of Harper, who'd been there as his sounding board listening to his ideas. 'We can use them to monitor our watering points, the stock, so if there are any health issues, we can send out the drone for a closer look.'

'Or just get in the ute and drive out there,' said Dex.

'Or use my dogs to move them,' said Cap.

'All of it, or we can create self-mustering gates to do it all for us,' said Ash. 'There are only four of us. We each have certain specialised skills and experiences, we just don't have the manpower or enough hours in the day to do everything. But with these things,' Ash said, tapping on the board, 'we can make it manageable by using technology to our advantage. And that,' he said, dragging out the letter from the government, 'answers points three, four, and five, regarding the environmental impact we'd have on our water on this station.'

That made all his brothers sit back to think long and hard over what he'd said. Ash waited patiently, hoping he had shown them he was determined to save his home for his family.

'I may only have one drone, but I know how to use those sensors, and I've built solar plants for other stations. I can do that here.'

'I know you can,' said Ryder. 'I've just been waiting on —'

'My list.' Ash held out his shopping list. 'This is what I estimate we'll need as our first investment in the troughs, as a test to show you guys how it's done. And I'm sure once you see how it works, you'll want to expand this to our next paddock.'

'So one paddock at a time, is that what you're saying?' asked Cap.

'Yeah, we'll start small. Isn't that what you said, Ryder?'

Ryder nodded as he read over the wish list. 'Do you want to test out all of your ideas in the one paddock?'

'That's a great idea.' Cap sat on the edge of his seat, leaning his forearms on the table. 'We should all pick our own paddock to run our own experiments. I'm sure we all have our own ideas, and now we can test our own theories. That way we can see what works and what doesn't, to then expand across the station as our herd grows.'

'I'd second that.' Ash nodded as he tapped on the top edge of the shopping list. 'I can scrounge a lot of stuff from what's in the sheds to make a start today. But this is a list of items we can't cut back on to make it effective.' He then dropped into his seat and picked up his coffee. 'Questions?'

'BREE! *Bree-Bree*.' Mason pounded on the screen door.

When did the boy wake up?

In her leather apron and gloves, her skullcap barely containing her red curls, Bree waved from the yard as she carried over a shopping bag.

'Here, go say hi to Bree.' Ash lifted his son over the child safety gate.

Mason's little legs ran fast to Bree, who scooped him up in

her arms for a hug. 'Morning, little man.' Bree carried him towards the house. 'Morning, boys. I'm dropping off these cooking utensils I borrowed for the muster. Is Harper around? I'm doing a trip into town later and I want to see if she'd like to come.' She placed the bag on the edge of the porch.

'*Arper?*' The little boy wriggled as Bree put him on the ground and he climbed up the porch steps. '*Arper …*'

'She's gone.' Ash scooped up the boy. 'I'm sorry, mate, but Harper isn't coming back.'

'Oh.' Bree took a step back. 'Well, I'd better get to it then.'

'Did you know?' Ryder stood from the table and glared at Bree.

'I know a lot of things, cupcake, but as I haven't polished my psychic's crystal ball in a while, how about you tell me what we're all talking about?'

'That Harper was Mason's aunt.'

'Duh. It was obvious.' She pointed at the boy. 'They have the same ears, same chin, and so many other familial similarities. Oh, let me guess, you guys were too busy being so self-centred to notice.'

'Why didn't you say anything?' Cap asked.

'Why didn't you tell me?' Ash frowned at Bree.

'Because Ryder told me to stay out of your family's business!' She glared at the man. 'Remember that conversation, cupcake?'

Ryder's jaw ticked as he glared down at Bree. 'I do.'

'See, I listen. Even though you *had to* include me on the muster, I stayed out of the family business, as you requested. So, my job is done, and now I'm leaving.'

'No, you're running away,' said Ryder. 'And you never run from anything.'

She spun around, her eyes like fire. 'Because I don't want to get lumbered babysitting and will not put up with the way you all treated Harper.'

'We were nice,' said Cap, offended. 'Harper and I got on well. She spoiled the police dogs, who adored her. And I trust my dogs—they have a good sense about people.'

'You were, Cap. But you, Dex, you were the worst. Who was she?'

'Who are you talking about?' Dex crossed his arms over his chest.

'The woman that made you hate all women.'

'Rack off.' Dex sneered.

'And you, Ryder, just blatantly ignored her.' Bree pointed at Ryder. 'Not once did you ever hold a conversation with Harper. All of you, shame on you. When she was only here for the boy—'

'*She was going to steal my son!*' Ash's voice echoed around the porch, as he protectively held his son to his chest.

'The view from Mount Stupid must look good from where you lot are sitting.' Hands on hips, Bree fearlessly faced them all. 'Did you even bother to ask Harper why she was here in the first place?'

'Did you?' demanded Ryder.

'Why would I? When you told me to stay out of the Riggs brothers' business—'

'Okay, okay, you win.' Ryder ripped off his hat. It was that, or he was going to blow his stack. 'The next time something involves this family you tell us.'

'Are you giving me permission? All of you.' She narrowed her eyes at them. 'To tell the truth and the whole truth, as much as you'd hate to hear it?'

'I have nothing to hide, but if it affects us like is does with Harper, heck yeah,' said Cap.

Dex just gave his death glare, but nodded.

'You could have told us, Bree,' Ash said in a calmer tone. 'You were helping me to plan a date with her.'

'Where I was giving Harper and you the opportunity to really talk. I know she was trying to talk to you.'

Ash remembered how he kept brushing Harper off. How he had distracted her the last time she'd asked to talk to him.

'Look, I honestly don't know the details,' she said, 'but I purposefully chose not to ask, because Ryder said it wasn't my business.'

'Hmm ...'

'Did you just growl at me, Ryder?'

A vein ticked in Ryder's temple. Tight-lipped, he continued to glare at the redhead.

'Pfft. I'm outta here. It's too early in the morning for this much testosterone.' Bree turned on her boot heels. 'It's not my fault you fell in love with the nanny, Ash.'

'I did not.'

'Denial is not a good look on you, snowflake. And don't forget, Harper is part of Mason's family. At least you now have a way to find out more about Mason's mother.'

'Why don't you crawl back to that cottage where you belong?' Dex's voice was full of fury. 'We don't need you preaching to us.'

'Dex is right,' said Ash, holding his boy. 'He's my son. Not yours. Find your own.'

Bree then did the weirdest thing. She daintily picked up the skirt of her leather apron and gave a proper curtsy as if standing before royalty. 'Your wish is my command, your lordships.' She then kissed her middle fingers, flipping them a double bird, then walked away.

'Why do I have a feeling that's going to come back and bite us on the arse?' Ryder pointed to Bree walking away.

'Bree-Bree?' Mason held out his hand to her, clearly upset. It was heartbreaking.

'It's okay, mate, Bree's busy. She's got to go to work.' There went his idea of a babysitter. But he didn't need one. 'Let's get you some brekkie, mate. Come on, you're hanging out with me today, we're going to clean some troughs.'

Forty-eight

Harper rested her chin on the back of her hands, which lay across the thick, cool brass rail that ran along the entire front of the bar. She stared at the tiny trail of bubbles rising in the amber liquid to become part of the creamy foam that made up her glass of beer. This particular ale had a rich malty aroma, with a hint of fruit, and was apparently brewed by a local mango farmer. So far, it was the only beer she liked.

It had become her mission, her personal tourist's tour from the front bar of the Elsie Creek Hotel, hassling the poor barmaids as they tried to find the right beer for Harper's picky palate.

Some beers were dark and yeasty, and some so thick you could stand a spoon in them, while others smelt like vomit, or earthy grass, even a dark caramel. It had kept her amused for hours, getting a crash course on beer while drowning out all background noises in the pub.

'Well, aren't you the saddest-looking thing I've seen in here for a long time.'

Harper barely moved her head. 'Oh, it's you.' Cowboy Craig.

'Well, that's not the normal reaction I get from the ladies.' With a chuckle that shone in his blue eyes, he pushed up the brim of his hat, which highlighted his blond curls. He leaned against the bar beside her. His cologne was crisp and invigorating, but it was nothing like Ash. There was no one like Ash.

'How's the dog doing?' Craig asked.

That made her eyebrows lift, but her chin remained resting on her hands.

'Ryan told me about the snakebite. He also told me to expect your call, in case you were in trouble.'

'Would you have really helped? Someone you'd just met.' What was his angle? Because everyone had a hidden agenda. Heck, she should know.

Sipping on her beer, she wiped the back of her mouth with her hand like a sun-parched stockman! Yee haw.

Craig gave her that cocky grin, his bright blue eyes almost twinkling.

'Stop. Please. Don't bother flirting with me.' Not while she was learning how to breathe with a broken heart, with loneliness as her new best friend. Great, she was heartbroken and homeless!

Craig shrugged. 'I wouldn't have, you know.'

'Wouldn't have what?'

'Made a play.'

'Not good enough, huh?' Typical. Men only spoke to her about her job. While she was too busy to hold a conversation, or know the art of small talk, because she'd never had time. But today, she had all the time in the world to sit on this stool and drink beer. Hooray.

Sculling back her beer, she pointed to the world's greatest barmaid for another one. 'Pourer's choice. Can we make a note that this is a good one.'

The barmaid grinned as she opened a few fridge doors. 'I have a list.'

Just like Ash had a list, the thought making her sink in her chair.

'What are you doing?' Craig asked.

'I'm making my way through the beer varieties. I didn't know there were so many.'

Craig signalled the barmaid to order a beer for himself. 'Why?'

'I'm on holiday. Isn't that what people do when on

holidays? They drink some sort of alcoholic beverage ...' For breakfast.

'Where are your chaperones from the station?'

Harper shrugged, again resting her chin on her hands to watch the bubbles rise in her new glass of beer. She didn't even have Bree's number. If she did, though, what would she say when she struggled to understand it herself? 'Aren't you a mate of the Riggs brothers?'

'I'm a good mate of Jonathan's, the youngest one.'

'He owns Sandlot Station, right?'

Craig nodded. 'I've even been to their parents' place for a feed.'

'What are they like? Mr and Mrs Riggs?'

'Landon and Camilla Riggs are great people. Cammie loves her knitting, she's obsessed with photographs of her family, and she's always got something cooking on the stove. Nothing fancy, but enough to feed her tribe.'

'I heard she liked photos.'

'Big time. Only of her family. You should see it—next to her stove, Momma Riggs has plastered all of her children's school photos for every year they went. It covers her entire kitchen wall.'

Harper sat up and sipped her beer. It was nice. Or was she getting used to the flavours? 'Are you talking about Ash and Dex's school photos?'

'All of them, in this big collage. She even wallpapered their entire hallway with all of their favourite childhood drawings. Some are really old.'

'I've never heard of such a thing.' Her parents' house had specific artworks, investment pieces, with only a few of her school photos kept in special frames, like her graduation. 'You mean there is a mug shot of Dex in a school uniform, suffering with teenage pimples?'

'Wearing one of the goofiest smiles, back when Dex did smile.'

'No way.' It was enough for her to smirk—not smile— smirk. 'I'd love to see that.'

'Well, now you're living with the Riggs brothers, I'm sure you'll see it soon.'

'No.' And she dropped her chin back onto her hands, holding the rail, to stare at her beer. 'I got kicked out.' And it was all her fault.

'Oh, I'm sorry to hear that.' Craig's smile disappeared. 'If you're stuck for somewhere to stay …'

'I'm a guest at the pub, and I've even got a beer tab.'

Yesterday, after crying an absolute river of tears, her entire chest ached as if punched by the tactical squad's hammering arm they used to break down doors. She'd struggled to breathe.

But Policeman Porter had been an absolute gentleman. He'd made her pull over to the side of the dirt road, handing her tissues and a water bottle, waiting patiently while she howled and hiccupped for air.

It was the same uncontrollable flood of emotion, the heartache she'd suffered when she'd learned her parents and sister had been killed, leaving her alone to grieve all over again.

Thankfully, Porter had booked a room for her at the pub so she could avoid talking to anyone. He'd helped her upstairs, left her his business card, and closed the door behind him, leaving her to cry herself to sleep.

Today, she was emotionally drained and just numb.

But she'd found the energy to walk down the stairs and stare at her beer and to befriend the world's best barmaid, Mean Rene. With arms full of ink, ear plugs, a tight leather vest, skin-tight jeans, and some seriously sexy head-kicking black boots, Mean Rene had become Harper's well-tipped bodyguard, blocking any cowboy from coming near her.

'Hey, can I ask you something?'

Harper didn't have the energy to nod. 'Sure.'

'Have you heard any more about that mine trying to take the water from Elsie Creek Station?'

'Why? Do you have a station that'll lose their water, too?'

'No. But my best mate owns Danbunnan Station.'

She shrugged. 'I think Ryan mentioned it?'

'Danbunnan Station is the largest family-owned cattle station in the Territory, and they're about to sell their fancy bottled spring water to the southern markets.'

Didn't that tug on her memory strings, along with the pain of missing Ash and Mason, because she knew how amazing the water tasted out here, especially at Grass Tree Creek, and then at Cascades Spur. And that amazing time they'd shared together. Ash had been right, that muster was a story to share for the rest of her life, one that would bring tears.

'My concern is, if they can claim a stake in the water from Elsie Creek Station, what's stopping them from doing the same to all the other stations in this region?' Craig wasn't being flirty, he looked worried.

'Oh, wow.' She finally found her spine to lift her head from the brass railing, to face Craig.

She glanced around the bar where other groups of stockmen were busily talking, showing the same look of concern that Craig had. And she'd been oblivious to it all, when she used to have such a well-trained ear for reading the room.

Maybe there was a reason she was here.

She'd read that government letter, then emailed a stack of queries as research back when she'd been so worried about poor Ruby. Again, her heart ached, pushing back her tears, missing Mason. Missing Ash.

She hadn't opened her laptop to see if there had been any responses.

She dug around for her phone in her bag and switched it on. She had to do something to fix this mess.

It wasn't just Elsie Creek Station involved, this involved an entire industry that included all the people of this town. She had to do something.

The phone came alive, and it dinged, and kept dinging — not with phone messages but emailed responses. This was a good start.

'Hey, Craig? Do you know any water specialists? Someone who'd know where to find the historical data concerning the water for this region?'

'I reckon I might …' Craig adjusted his white hat, giving her a smile filled with hope. 'It just so happens Ryan and I are best mates with the Federal Government's leading water analyst in charge of the Top End's extensive artesian water basins.'

'I need to speak to him. Today.'

Forty-nine

'Boys, I brought this over.' Charlie lumbered up the front steps with a child's booster seat for the car, dumping it on the spare chair at the table where the four brothers had sat down for the evening. 'Where's the lad?'

'Inside, watching TV.' Ash pointed to the open doorway where the childproof gate gave him a clear view of his son, happily playing with his toys. He'd just fed and successfully bathed the boy, who was now ready for bed.

It wouldn't take much for Mason to fall asleep. He'd been outside all day with Ash as he worked on his new ideas for his paddock, working on the troughs, then helping his brothers work on the drafting yards.

He was proud to have survived day one as a single dad doing it on his own, without … Her.

'Where did you find this car seat?' Ash checked over the chair that looked well used. 'I could have used it today. Harper stole mine.'

'She did not. None of you gave Harper a chance to take it out of her car.' Cap effortlessly flicked off the caps from the four beer bottles and handed them out to the brothers. 'Charlie?'

The old stockman shook his head.

'Stop sticking up for her.' Dex scowled, taking his beer to lean back and rock in his chair. Dex then pointed his beer at Charlie. 'Did you know Harper was Mason's aunt?'

'No. Swear it, fellas.' Charlie stood firm. 'I'd wondered if she was something to the boy. She might not be a nanny, but she truly cared for that kid like he was her own.'

'That's what I keep telling them.' Cap rubbed at the lines across his forehead. 'Just that these morons won't listen.'

'Stop sticking up for Harper. She betrayed us, the deceiving little wench.' Again, Dex scowled.

'Or you didn't give her a chance to talk. None of us did.'

'Enough.' Ryder slammed his beer bottle down on the table. 'She's gone. That's that.'

'Anyhoodle, this is the baby seat from Bree's Kombi van. She doesn't want it anymore and thought you might need it.' Charlie nodded and stepped off the porch.

'Thanks, Charlie. Can you please tell Bree thanks for me, too.' Ash hoped to make amends with the redhead.

'Hey, why did Bree have a baby seat in her Kombi?' Dex asked.

'Oh, that.' Charlie stopped with hands on hips and a heavy head dropping to his chest. 'That was my great-grandson's seat,' he said, his voice filled with sadness. 'Bree's son.'

Dex swallowed hard, sitting forward in his chair with a heavy thud. They all felt it, like they'd been sucker punched in the guts.

Ryder spun around in his seat, to face the old man. 'Bree had a son?'

'Liam. He was a good lad, a real spitfire like his mother. He kept Bree on her toes, that's for sure.'

'What happened to him?' Cap asked, the rest of the table listening.

'Liam got this rare form of leukaemia, where there was nothing they could do for him, just take his pain away. But he was a tough lad, smiling to the very end.' The old man sniffed, wiping the tip of his nose.

'How old was he?' Ryder's voice was low, soft even.

'Two. Just a little older than your boy, Ash.' Charlie faced them squarely. 'Treasure that boy, because when they're gone it's heartbreak like I've never felt before and Bree … Well,

Bree ...' He adjusted his hat on his head and looked back to the caretaker's cottage wearing sorrow heavily across his shoulders. 'Just know, that young lad brings a lot of joy not just to you mob, but to us, too.' Charlie gave a curt nod and left.

Ash felt like he was standing underwater as he struggled to process the news of Bree losing a son.

Ryder stood from the table and snatched his bottle of Wild Turkey. The *other* bottle he used for celebrations or commiserations, and he poured a full round, sliding the glasses across the wooden tabletop, leaving the bottle standing on the table, uncorked.

Ash had never guessed Bree was a mother. He couldn't fathom the pain she'd gone through.

It was Bree who'd helped a wailing Mason on his very first night. She'd known he was teething and how to help him. She'd made icy pops, supplied sunscreen, cooked meals, and had given Harper countless tips on how to care for Mason. She'd even supplied the cot, the special baby carrier for the muster, and the highchair! Not once did Bree ever let on that she was a mother who'd lost her child.

'Bree told me once that it takes a village to raise a child, telling me how truly lucky I was.' Ash licked his lips, tasting the bourbon. 'I thought she was joking, like she does.'

'No wonder Bree said she won't babysit.' Dex swallowed down his glass, hissing as if it was bitter.

'Do you blame her?' Ryder gripped his bourbon glass tightly and tossed it back. The man, who normally savoured each drop of his bourbons, slammed it down and poured them another round.

'Excuse me.' Ash got up from the table.

'You okay, bro?' As the most sensitive of the brothers, Cap was the peacemaker, placing a brotherly hand on Ash's shoulder.

'Yeah ...' No. He wasn't. 'I'll be with my son.' Ash headed inside, his stomach in knots, sickened with the fear of losing someone who had become such a deep part of his soul it scared him. All he wanted to do was hold Mason, while ignoring that part of him that wanted to hold Harper, too. She was gone. Even though she'd deceived him, he missed her terribly.

Fifty

In the back corner of the bar at the Elsie Creek Hotel—which Harper had commandeered—it had been dubbed chaos central. She had her phone and laptop plugged into the wall. Paperwork covered four bar tables she'd commandeered as her desk, with charts, maps and diagrams covering the corner wall where she interviewed farmers, fishermen, storekeepers, the publican and her staff, plus lots and lots of stockmen. Thanks to Cowboy Craig, who'd brought these people over to meet her, all in the name of research.

Harper didn't even recognise herself.

Once fearful of people hassling her, where her staff sent people away, now, it was Harper who engaged these strangers with small talk before getting into deep conversations with them over how the new mine's proposal for water rights would affect this region.

Thankfully, the wheels were turning in her head again, the ones silenced by the bomb blast, were now powering at full steam. Pausing her *round the world beer tour*, she was back to cold coffee, and had befriended the cranky Hungarian chef, named Lenny, who made decadent pastries. She was in sugar-rush heaven, while calling in favours from across the globe.

'Well, I was expecting you to be hugging it out with a box of tissues.' Bree stood at the table, tapping on the empty plate of crumbs. 'Lenny's pastries?'

Harper nodded.

'He makes a mean cupcake … So, why haven't you called me?'

'I don't have your number.'

'Liar.' Bree pinched Harper's phone from the table and tapped away at the keys. 'You could have just said that you'd cracked your phone in half like an FBI agent gone rogue. But Cowboy Craig knows my number, Lenny the chef knows our number, and it wouldn't be too hard to search master brand makers and beautiful blacksmiths to find our number.'

'I'm sorry, you're right. The truth is I didn't want to bother you.'

Bree plonked one hand on her hip with a *don't give me that crap* look. 'I'm well aware that you're new to the world of friends, but in times like this you call a friend. See, it says so.' Bree held up the phone that now had an entry that read: *In case of emergencies call this friend.*

'Listen, blossom, I'm the kind of friend who'll get drunk with you, help you clean up a murder scene, supply you with ice cream, or buy you every packet of shortbread off the supermarket shelf.' Bree upended her shopping bag, allowing over a dozen red packets of shortbread to spill across the table. 'See, the darkside does come with cookies.'

Harper wanted to cry at the kindness, and the feeling of guilt. 'I'm sorry.'

'Oh, honey, stop saying sorry. I don't even say sorry for being snappy when breaking in a new bra.'

'Okay…' She shrugged, trying so hard to not say sorry.

'So, Mean Rene and Craig both said you've been fine, and that you went on a round the world beer fest?' asked the redhead, whose mere presence commanded the room.

'You know the world's greatest barmaid?'

'Blossom, how many brain cells did you fry yesterday?' Bree held up her hands. 'I'm not judging on the beer binge. Believe me, I get why we drink to blur life's many nightmares—it's why they invented gin. But you don't look like rock bottom.' She glanced over the wall charts. 'When did you get your attention span back?'

'Um, today. No, it started clearing when Ruby was bitten by the snake.' Harper flicked at the paperwork.

'I hope you're proud of yourself for saving that dog. I know I was when I heard the story.'

'So, how did you know I was here?'

'Well, I was waiting for your homing pigeon to deliver a message, telling me what part of the galaxy you'd absconded to. But thankfully, this little honey in a uniform knew how to pick up a phone and dial *my* number.'

'I swear to always call you first. I promise. But can we please skip the guilt trip.'

Bree's grin was positively evil, but full of fun.

'So, who told you I was here?'

'Policeman Porter. He is a friend of the family, and he was worried. Said he saw your car still parked at the pub on his way to work. I'm just sorry I couldn't get here sooner, but I'm here now.' Bree picked up a spare chair, carried it around the table to sit right beside Harper, giving Harper her full and undivided attention. 'How are you doing?'

Harper swallowed, her bottom lip quivering. 'I'm sorry I didn't call you … I got …' The tears started again.

'Come here, blossom, I've got you.' Bree pulled her into her arms and held her.

It's just what Harper needed, a hug from a friend, and she quietly wept, clutching her packets of shortbread like a teddy bear.

After a while, Harper sat back, wiping at the tears, and began stacking her packets of biscuits. 'How are they?'

'Mason misses you. Ash too, but he won't admit it. Cap told them they're idiots for what they did.'

'They threw me out when they found out I was Mason's aunt. I should have told them sooner. Or at least told you.'

'Pfft, I already knew who you were. We do get google, that's a little faster than homing pigeons, and I do know how to make a few phone calls.'

'Leo knew, too.'

'How?'

'I don't know. But I was trying to tell Ash, but we just kept putting it off, or something else got in the way. And ...' She looked at her hands. 'I didn't want to ruin the moments we had. I was happy out there. Somehow Elsie Creek Station helped me heal.'

'I get it.'

'You do?'

'Yeah, when you move to the country, you somehow learn to relax, not just with the place but into yourself.' She patted over her heart. 'Everything about you becomes weirdly, calmly, okay. It's magical when you discover that under all that red dust there's this hope that eventually everything is going to be okay. You learn to smile again. It may be crooked or bleak, but it's the start of a smile.'

Harper grimaced, couldn't help it.

'I've been there too, blossom. I've learned through my many, *many* mistakes that there are always new ones to make, but that's okay—it's just the death part that sucks the most. You are grieving, Harper.'

'I called it my brain fog.' She tapped the side of her head. 'It got so thick, and I let it, to help me forget that my parents, my family were gone. I got so lost that all my plans got thrown out the car window.'

'What were you planning to do?'

'To come back to Australia, close up my parents' house. I was supposed to put the car in storage and catch a plane to meet up with Mason. But when I learned that Mason was coming here, and that my father had slipped in his own caveat for Mason's welfare, offering Ash twenty-eight days, as a choice.'

Bree leaned closer. 'You mean Ash was given an escape clause? That if he didn't want the boy—'

'I stayed in case Ash rejected his son, my nephew.' She'd been keeping a tally of the days. 'Today is day nineteen. We're just nine days shy of the twenty-eight-day agreement.'

'Wow.' Bree sat back. 'So you drove here...'

'To be close. I've been living in limbo ever since. If Ash

didn't want Mason, I had to think about work, day care, where we would live, everything. I have plenty of job offers. My boss, the Ambassador, even offered to let me work in Canberra, until I got Mason a passport. But ...'

'You can't do anything until the twenty-eight days is over.'

Harper nodded, even though the stabbing pain rolled around her ribcage, and an anxious sweat brushed across her skin. The fear of missing out on time, or losing time, created a sickening stomach squeeze.

Harper was a fixer, but she couldn't fix this. She couldn't turn to her parents for advice, nor ask her sister questions about Mason, her work, or living arrangements for a child because it would always be the same answer. Complete silence. The weightlessness of silence from those you'd loved and would never hear from again, was like floating in space with the earth and the moon rolling past, like tiny stars stuck in an endless galaxy of silence. It was depressing.

'Have you ever lost someone?' Harper asked.

Bree nodded, but remained expressionless. 'I could give you all the *nice* words that they'd say at funeral homes, but ...'

'The funeral home said some words, but I didn't hear them. Have you got any words of wisdom?'

'Far from it.' Bree shrugged. 'Only that life happens. Life hurts. Life sucks. And you'll have days where you'll want to chug down a jug of gin —'

'I did beer.'

'Good. Which means you're stumbling down the path the overpaid shrinks call the healing process.'

'What did you do to get over your grief?'

'Oh, I got freaking mad.' Bree even chuckled. 'I wanted to burn the world. And I did for a time. But then I learned to let go.' She leaned closer, patting Harper's hand. 'As you are the queen of watching time, let me tell you that time does something as part of this process. Some say time heals as it passes, and it does get a little less painful. I think time helps to make the memories blur a little around the edges, and the guilt of not being there, or not doing enough for them, starts to pass. But you also have to think of what your parents would have wanted you to do with the time you have today.'

'They would want me to be happy.'

'And Mason's mother, your sister?'

'To watch out for Mason, to make sure he was happy.'

'Which is what you've been doing. And you found your happiness out there at the station, didn't you? Not just with Mason, but with Ash, too.'

She licked her lips, pushing down another spate of tears that went with the heartache of missing Ash. 'I'd never planned to, you know, with Ash. Believe me, I tried to push him away. It just happened. But none of the brothers will let me explain myself, and I swear I never lied to them.'

'But you were playing politician, cleverly deflecting the truth.'

Harper couldn't lie now. 'Because I didn't want to ...'

'Leave.'

Harper nodded at the truth she'd only realised now.

She'd loved the station's mornings, even if it had taken her a while to find the courage to step outside, to peer at a strange and foreign world. But once she let that screen door shut behind her, to stand beyond the farmhouse's shadow, she fell in love with the sky. The way that colossally large sky would change colours continuously throughout the day, from soft pinks, cool grey blues, to arctic blues so deep it was like looking for secrets in the deepest ocean. There were the blazing reds, scorching oranges to vivid magenta and mauves, where the sunset surrendered to the galaxy of stars that lowered over the earth, putting the red dust to bed and the outback world was quiet once more.

There were no terrorist threats out here. No peak-hour traffic, no sirens screaming, no phones ringing, no *click clack* of the many shoes across the pavements, no crowds bundled in big coats hiding from the weather.

Her time at Elsie Creek Station had been an adventure,

from the moment she'd arrived. And those days, when she'd climbed into the saddle to ride through the Stoneys, had helped her to see the beauty in a world that had once seemed so desolate, where beneath that harsh shimmering scorched surface, she saw paradise.

She'd never forget the flavour of the spring water at Cascades Spur, or her shower under the stars at Wombat Flats. Sure, she had her own scary tales of the bird spiders, the tussle with a snake, and her own high-speed trip into town. But there were the cuddles from the dogs, the giggles of a child curious to learn a new word. There were her cooking lessons with Bree, lingo lessons with Charlie, or those conversations with Ash about his plans for the station, long after dark.

She missed the station and the family that felt like hers.

When her phone beeped alerting her to an incoming message, she peered at the screen. Her eyes widened. Her fingers shook as she quickly tapped on her keyboard and opened her emails.

'Good news?'

Harper pointed to her laptop screen. 'I think I know how to save the station.'

Fifty-one

Sitting high in the saddle, holding the reins with one hand, Charlie leaned over the neck of his horse to push open the front gate. He tipped his hat to Harper as she slowly drove under the tall archway holding the sign with its intricate metalwork proclaiming *Elsie Creek Station*. She used to admire it, now it made her sweaty hands tremble as she struggled to grip the steering wheel.

The nerves just got worse, churning her stomach into sour butter, the further she followed Bree's yellow Kombi down the long dirt driveway.

She was about to face the Riggs brothers.

The sun sank lower, creating a splashy display of fiery reds and oranges across the sky. It was glorious. But it also meant it was time for the brothers to sit at their outdoor table, knock back a beer or three, to then argue over whose turn it was to cook dinner.

Bree had said Harper owed them an explanation. So, she prepared herself for a frosty reception, hoping that the Riggs brothers had the patience to listen to what she had to say.

The simple weatherboard farmhouse came into view, with the four brothers gathered around the table. It made her want to spin the car around and escape.

Yet with Bree in her Kombi, and Charlie riding on horseback, Harper had her own private security detail, normally given to politicians about to front a hostile crowd. But those politicians had never met a more hostile crowd than the Riggs brothers, who now stood on their porch ready to defend their home and family.

'Come on.' Bree opened Harper's car door. 'You can do this.'

'What is she doing here?' barked out Dex, coming down the steps.

'STOP. All of you.' Bree blocked off Dex, who started stepping away from the fearless redhead. 'Harper is here to explain herself, and you all owe her the decency to listen. You told me I had the right to get involved with your family business. You all agreed to this. So this is me stepping in for your family. So, *trust me* when I say you'll want to hear what Harper has to say.'

Ryder looked at Bree for a long beat, then gave Harper the nod to go ahead.

But it was the angry glare from Ash that had Harper struggling. It was Ash she needed to speak to most, but it was obvious she wasn't going to get that private one-on-one conversation, she had to do this in front of everyone.

So, with a deep breath, she stood before the brothers towering over her from their place on the verandah. 'I'm sorry I didn't tell you who I was.'

'Why didn't you?' Ash scowled like Dex, with his arms crossed over his chest.

'Because I didn't want you to look at me like you do now, filled with hate.'

'Are you here to take Mason away?'

'You being a senator's daughter, you'd have enough political connections to take him away, right? They said Mason arrived on a private jet. Where were you?' Dex was scary angry. Harper stepped back, but Bree was at her side.

'One question at a time, and she can answer you all.' Bree gave Harper an encouraging nod. 'They deserve to know everything.'

Again, Harper took a big breath and spilled the one answer Ash needed to hear. 'I would never take Mason away, I swear it. I came out here to make sure he was okay, especially when I'd learned about the twenty-eight-day caveat.'

'What caveat?' demanded Dex, with Cap arching his eyebrows, both looking to Ash.

'That if I didn't want Mason, I could give him back,' Ash replied to Dex, but he never took his eyes off Harper. 'And that will never happen.'

'Good.' And she meant it.

But Ash stood firm and was as expressionless and cold as Ryder.

'We were told you were overseas when your parents died? Why didn't you come back?' Cap spoke next. His face was the only friendly one out of the brothers, as if trying to help her, somehow.

'I had been a victim of a car bomb from a terrorist attack in Belgium. My team had died, and I'd suffered a severe concussion. It was when I was in the hospital that I learned my parents had died. *My. Parents. With my sister.*' Her words echoed with her grief shown for all to see. She couldn't and didn't want to hide it anymore. Bree had been right, she was grieving and had the right to grieve.

But she also had the right to fight for what she believed in. Her story.

'Before I could get medical clearance to fly back to Australia, arrangements had already been made to bring Mason here as per Gemma's will.'

'You could have stopped it,' said Ash.

'I didn't want to.'

'Why not?'

'From the day Mason was born, we promised Gemma that if anything happened to her, Mason would go to his father.' Even though the tears welled up in her eyes, she stared at Ash.

'Why should I believe you now, when you told me you were practically an only child?'

'I was. I never lied,' she implored. 'My mother' had Gemma when she was sixteen and put her up for adoption. I knew nothing about Gemma's existence until I was fifteen. I'd just come home from school when Gemma knocked on our front door and introduced herself. Her adoptive parents had died and she'd tracked Mum down. As an only kid, it was the best thing to suddenly have this older sister. And my parents, especially my father, quickly accepted Gemma into our family. Gemma never knew who her father was—Mum never talked about it—but she did have a wonderful father–daughter bond with my father, like I did. Gemma wanted the same for Mason … You should know Gemma was coming to see you.'

Ash blinked fast in a flutter. 'When?'

'Soon after Mason was born, Gemma and I started planning this road trip together, but we had trouble finding you. You kept moving around.'

'You were after him for the maintenance,' said Dex with a snarl.

Dex was such a dick!

Harper spoke to Ash, ignoring the others. 'We were never after money because we were doing it for Mason. Ash, you said yourself, you wanted to know who Mason's mother was for your son's sake. Gemma was doing the same with you as Mason's father.'

'Gemma talked about me?' Ash's brow shifted, his cold stance starting to defrost.

'I have a photo of you two.' She pulled out her purse. 'You two met at a B&S ball in Longreach.' Her hand trembled as she held out the photo.

Ash's eyes widened at the photograph. 'I remember that.' He took off his hat to rake his fingers through his thick hair. 'We spent the entire weekend together and had a blast. And then the weekend was over. I headed west, Gemma headed south. She said she was on contraception, so I thought we were protected.'

'Gemma said the same. She didn't realise she was pregnant until I came home for Christmas and found her being sick in our bathroom. She suffered badly with morning sickness, but she always said it was worth it the day Mason was born. Gemma loved Mason. Mum and Dad did, too. They built him a nursery and everything. They adored their grandson.'

'Where was this?'

'Adelaide. But they did build this playground for Mason in our summer house on the beach in Queensland. But not in the ski chalet at Thredbo, Gemma said Mason hated being cold and refused to go outside and play in the snow.'

'Coz, he's half Territorian, missy, where it's summer every day.' Charlie winked at her, while patting the mane of his horse, it somehow eased the thick tension in the air.

'How did your parents, and Gemma, die?' asked Cap.

Harper swallowed, allowing the tears to fall. She had nothing to hide. 'They were in the city centre of Adelaide. My mother and Gemma, with Mason, were meeting my father for lunch. Dad had been in some heavy negotiations at Parliament House, so said the guys from ASIS—'

'Who?' Cap asked.

'The Australian Secret Intelligence Service—ASIS.' Ryder spoke for the first time. 'They're Australia's equivalent of the CIA or MI6. Why were they involved?'

'ASIS said threats had been made against my father over his position on a NATO international war trade agreement. Given my parents' deaths occurred at about the same time as the car exploded in Belgium, landing me in hospital, ASIS had to investigate. But it turned out their deaths were just a tragic accident.'

'How were they, um …' Ash asked softly, the empathy shining in his eyes, as his stance softened even more.

'My family, along with a dozen other innocent people, were waiting for the traffic lights to change to cross the road when a car ploughed into them. The news reports all say that the driver just lost control.'

'Mason?'

'Gemma had pushed Mason's pram out of the way, he was safe and unharmed. My father,' she said through the tears, 'he copped the full impact trying to shield his family.'

Ash patted his hand over his chest, his eyes sullen as his voice softened, 'I'm so sorry for your loss.'

She faltered at his sincerity.

'When did you find out that they'd…'

'A few days later, while in hospital on the other side of the globe. A family friend took care of Mason and set about trying to find you. They also arranged for my parents' house to be packed up.' When she finally made it back to Australia two weeks later, the house had been empty. She'd hated the house being so quiet, expecting her mother to walk through the front door with her father, trying to work out their time schedules for a dinner date.

'So why did you come here?'

'When they told me they'd found you and they were going to fly Mason out to you, I just started driving. Once I realised I was in the middle of nowhere, that there was no turning back, I began writing this speech that I practised as I drove. The plan was to introduce myself to you, Ash, and to see my nephew again—'

'To take him.' Dex scowled.

'No.' She ignored Dex, focusing on Ash. 'I was going to tell you, that my parents had set up a trust for Mason.'

'For what?'

'For school fees, university fees. Or, I don't know, medical fees for braces or something. I wasn't planning to take him away. Come on, I've never even babysat a pot plant before I came here. But Mason is the last of my family and I'm doing what my family wanted. I've always been here for Mason to ensure his safety.'

'That's why you bought the fire extinguishers, the first-aid kit for the house,' said Cap.

She nodded, never looking away from Ash. It was Ash she had to convince. 'Ash, you told me how unsure you were about keeping Mason, from the beginning. You said that if it turned out that you wanted to give him up after the 28-day period, then I would have taken him, but not unless that happened. I was never going to take him without you making that decision first, all I was doing was trying to protect Mason. Remember the reason for me agreeing to go to Wombat Flats?'

'Yeah...'

'Well don't leave us in suspense. What was it, besides playing tourist,' demanded Dex.

'Harper went because I told her I was going to use the trip to Wombat Flats to bond with my son.'

And he did.

'Is that true, brother?' Cap asked. 'Were you thinking of giving Mason up?'

Ash rubbed his eyes, sighing heavily, then opened them to focus on Harper. She felt them stab straight through to her wounded soul. 'I was. But not anymore.'

Good. It's what she'd hoped for Mason's sake.

But she understood his brothers were being protective, and they'd fiercely fight for Mason, too. It's what she'd always hoped for Mason's sake.

'But you have the political weight to take Mason away from Ash, any time.' Dex was such an arsehole, stirring the pot.

'Dex, do you know what the first rule to déjà vu club is? Oh wait, she's already told you all this!' Bree was Harper's hero, giving her a nod of encouragement to continue.

Harper turned and removed a box of paperwork from her car. She took another deep breath, wiped away her tears, straightened her shoulders, and squarely faced the brothers. 'Because Mason *lives here*, and because this is *his home*, and to prove to you all—' she glared at Dex with determination. 'I am not here to take Mason away, instead I've learned how to save this station.'

Fifty-two

'**G**ive Harper a chance to explain, fellas. Trust me, you'll want to hear this.' Charlie leaned against his stockhorse where they stood in the shade of the farmhouse.

Ryder looked at Ash. 'Your call.'

Ash kept his arms crossed over his chest, all calm on the outside. Inside he was a mix of jumbled emotions. From seeing Harper looking so sad, hearing her story, seeing the photo of her sister—Mason's mother—in his hand, it had his head spinning. But now Harper had a way to save their home?

'I'll clear some space on the table.' He turned his back on her.

'Where's Mason?' Harper asked, carrying the box of paperwork.

'Sleeping.' He showed her the baby monitor clipped to his hip.

She gave him a soft smile, as if proud that he'd learned to use it. When she shouldn't be proud of him for finally doing what a parent is supposed to do. And he shouldn't want to smile back at her. But it was hard when he could smell her perfume, that soft aroma he wanted to inhale deeper. Her nervousness made him want to put her at ease, like the first time she rode the horse, or that spider incident. But he'd been hurt, too.

'What were you going to show us?' Ryder asked, as Cap and Dex cleared the table of empty plates, beer bottles, and glasses.

'This.' Harper took a set of maps out of the box she'd dragged from the back of her car. 'These are satellite images of the property for the past fifteen years, right up to yesterday.'

'Why do you have these?'

'To show how Starvation Dam came to be. According to the federal water analyst, Starvation Dam was a run-off pocket carved out of the soils from the wet season rains. It just got added to over time to become a dam that still allowed for the natural run-off to occur, like it does to trickle down through the Stoneys and to the waterways that the mine is requesting.' She showed them all the maps of the past and the present. 'Starvation Dam has always been part of Elsie Creek Station and these historical images can prove that. Charlie, you'd know all about Starvation Dam during your time here.'

'Yeah, that'd be right.' Charlie loosely wrapped the reins of his horse around the rail, poking up the brim of his hat, while his boots with their thick Cuban heels clomped up the front steps to join them around the table. 'It was always a big watering hole, and when they put in the irrigation, we made the walls higher.'

'These show the first major excavations to the dam in 1961.' Harper showed them an old black-and-white image. 'The archives images aren't that crash hot, but they're good enough to show the changes, and the dam being built.'

'I remember using the ol' Massey backhoe. We called it the widow-maker. It gave us a heck of time.'

'What has this got to do with saving the station?' Who else would ask but Dex.

'Because it proves this dam was here a lot longer than they claim in the government letter—'

'How do know about that letter?' demanded Dex, with Ryder also scowling.

'I forgot,' blurted out Ash, with that need to protect her. 'I said Harper could read that letter, to help us.' And here she was helping, even giving him a slight smile.

But then her eyes focused on the paperwork, and she was all business. It was hot.

'The Territory Government's wording states *new works*. However, this dam is considered an improvement upon existing infrastructure on a naturally occurring waterway.'

'So they have no claim?' Ryder asked.

'None. And I also discovered something else,' she said, unrolling another map. 'Someone is approaching other properties along the river with offers to buy their land.'

'The pricks who hassled my grandfather.' Bree looked ticked, and ten times scarier than Dex or Ryder ever did. 'And they work for Blackwell Mining.'

'They're buying out farmers for mining?' Ryder asked.

'I think it's more to do with water rights,' replied Harper.

Ash and Dex shrugged. They didn't know anything about water rights.

'Oh, no ...' Cap moaned as if in pain, dragging a hand down his face, going all doom and gloom. 'Trust me, brothers, the sale of water rights is big business. We're talking billions of dollars. Am I right, Harper?'

She nodded.

'For water?' Charlie scratched his head. 'That falls from the sky?'

'Water is a rare commodity, especially down south. And where the water entitlements are owned by foreign investors, the water is typically used to grow food, or used in mining operations—'

'Like Blackwells.'

Harper nodded.

'And they want to do that here?'

'Well, they can try ...' Harper grinned in a way that had them all leaning back. 'Do you guys know the local zoning regulations?'

'We know of the zoning areas for cattle-tick regulations and when we need to move our cattle to different areas. All stockmen do.' It was part of the job.

'I'm talking about the zoning for land that defines the legally permitted uses for a specific property or area.' Harper dragged out another map of the Northern Territory. 'The government allocates areas of land for sporting and recreation areas, housing, industrial, and zones for agriculture, Aboriginal sacred sites, national parks, and mining. Now, all this area, everything on this side of Elsie Creek, is under an agricultural zone. It includes Elsie Creek Station, your brother's station, Sandlot, and the many other cattle stations along this region.' Harper tapped on the map, explaining that the green zone was for agriculture, and the red for mining. And Elsie Creek Station, and all their closest neighbours were all in the green zone.

'That means they can't mine out here. Not on this side of the highway?' The excitement shone in Cap's eyes as he tapped on the map, eager to show his brothers. 'They don't have the zoning for it. It's all agricultural land, for farming, not mining.'

'But how long will that last?' asked Ryder.

'That what I wondered,' said Harper, in a rare agreement with Ryder. 'From what I can gather from my research, Blackwell Mining is buying up land, hoping to put forward a submission to change the zoning to allow for mining.'

'Can they do that?' Cap's excitement died.

'Not now we know about it.' Harper grinned one of those grins that was both smart and sexy.

'What do you know?'

'The Northern Territory isn't a state. It's a territory. They don't have full constitutional powers of self-government and are effectively under the Federal Government's control. It's the Federal Government that funds the Territory's roads, housing, and mining. Which means, that even though the Territory has a Water Act, it doesn't hold much ... water.' She grinned at herself for the pun. 'And that letter from the government ...'

Ash dragged it out of the pile and passed it to Harper.

'This letter should never have been written.'

'But it's official, right?' Dex pointed at the letter. 'It's got the official letterhead, and they had that government courier drop it off.'

'They never conducted a property inspection on your neighbour's property for the mine about their uses of water.'

'How do you know?'

'Craig's friend, the water analyst. He was the one who showed me how big of an impact that mine would have on the waterways for this entire region. It was enough for me to speak to the mines department—'

'You did what?' Ryder wasn't happy.

'Settle down, cupcake, she's not done,' said Bree, stepping closer to Harper's side.

'How did you speak to the mines department when they were ignoring all of our calls?' asked Ryder. 'My lawyers couldn't get through.'

'I skipped the local government and went straight to the Federal Minister of Mines,' replied Harper. 'He was the best man at my father's wedding, and we had Christmas dinners with his family.'

'You used your father's connections?' Ryder arched an eyebrow at her.

'And mine, through my job. For the first time, too.'

'Why would you do that?' Ash asked, stunned at all of this.

'Because this not only affects all of you—it affects Mason. The stress you're all living under is not healthy. I should know, after living under a level-four terrorism threat ...' She touched the back of her head, the place that hid her scars.

Ash knew why she liked wearing hats so much, it was to hide and protect that sensitive area. It made his heart melt for her, he wanted to hold her, to take away that pain, but he couldn't.

'I may have used my connections to get in the door, but I had to show logical proof. Which I did with the water reports, satellite imagery, interviews, and historical research.' Harper flicked at the maps spread across the table. 'I collated all the data I could get my hands on to present my case to the Federal Minister. It was my job to show both sides of the argument.'

'And?'

'I could prove this new mine would have a severe impact on the environment, including the underwater artesian basin. Effectively blocking any mining works in this area without an extensive environmental impact report based on their mining methods—which Blackwell's never did. The Territory Government should have never granted them that mining permit. And the Federal Mining Minister's office is asking them why that permit was allowed.'

'Are you saying they're done?' Ash held his breath.

'Well, you should have received an email from the Territory Government retracting that letter, with an apology because they should have never legally sent it. So, someone in that office is about to lose their job.' Harper checked the watch strapped to her wrist. The watch Bree had made her take off to stop clockwatching. 'I warned them that if they didn't send that email to you, by the close of business today, I was sending in a team of environmental lawyers and the Cattlemen's Association's team of lawyers to create a class action to sue their arses off.'

Ryder pressed his thumbprint on his tablet, waking it up. His eyes moved as he scrolled over the emails.

'Well? Don't leave us in suspense,' demanded Dex.

Ryder held up the tablet and read, 'It is with deep regret that we inform you of an interoffice error over the water rights for Elsie Creek Station ... any previous correspondence pertaining to this matter should be disregarded, effective immediately. We are sorry for any inconvenience ...'

'Does that mean it's over?' Cap asked.

In a rare moment, Ryder nodded and smiled. 'It's over. We won. Harper, you did it.'

'*Yes!*' Dex high-fived Ash, Ash high-fived Cap, then Ryder, then back to Dex.

'I say we pop some bubbly and celebrate, you mob.'

Charlie patted the brothers' backs. 'You lads won. Elsie Creek Station is safe.'

'Hey, you guys should know that they can change the law and—'

'Let them enjoy this victory, blossom.' Bree put her arm around Harper's shoulders and squeezed. 'Today, they won the battle, tomorrow they can focus on the war.'

Cap, Ash, and Ryder re-read the email, while Dex came back to the table with arms full of beers. 'Who wants one? Because I plan to party.' He flicked open the lids and handed out bottles.

'Hey, you'll wake up Mason, you lot.' Ash turned to talk to Harper, but she was walking away.

'I'll get the little man. In the meantime, snowflake, you go speak to Harper before she drives away.'

'I'm sorry, Bree, for what I said about—'

'Let's not ruin the party mood. Go.' She pushed him towards the front steps. 'Don't let her get away.'

Fifty-three

arper juggled her keys to the sounds of a celebration behind her and opened her driver's door. She needed to leave before she collapsed and howled in misery at losing everything.

'You've had a really rough few weeks, haven't you.' It was Ash, right behind her. 'What with your parents, your sister, but also how me and my brothers treated you too, which was rude of us and not fair to you.'

She couldn't respond or even look at him.

'Where are you going?'

'Back to town.' She inhaled deeply, and forcefully turned to face him, trying to pretend that everything was okay.

'Then what?'

'I don't know. Maybe I'll go back—'

'To Belgium?'

'I quit that job.'

'Why?'

'After being out here, and speaking with the locals, I saw a whole different side to life. I learned to step off the hamster wheel of politics, away from the stress of my job, and the anxiety that went with it.'

'What are you going to do?'

'I don't know.'

'But you usually have a plan.'

'And I learned how plans change and to just go with it. You taught me that.' She gazed at the large horizon and at the simple farmhouse with a horse parked out front like a car.

Most of all she saw the family who worked, lived, and celebrated life together in this place they called home.

'Did you honestly enjoy living out here? Away from that busy world and the shopping?'

She gazed at the beauty of the sunset and colossally enormous sky and smiled. 'Yeah, I did. I missed this place. I missed the freedom you have that comes with this lifestyle. I missed not clockwatching.' She lifted her wrist, tapping on her watch.

'Even Dex?'

'Meh.' She rolled her eyes. 'Mason, absolutely.' But she didn't think they'd let her see him just yet. It would take time. And time was finally becoming her friend, as she learned to work with time and not against it.

'And me?' He tilted his head. It was impossible to avoid his bright, all-seeing gaze and untrusting scowl. She'd done this to Ash.

Where was her gorgeous, smiling stockman now?

'I am truly sorry, Ash, for not telling you who I was when we met in the supermarket, and I should have. But, when I first met you, with that flat tyre, I had no idea where Mason was or if you knew about him yet. But then you seemed so unsure about keeping Mason, when I wanted more than anything for you to bond with him, so he could have a home with his father.' But that cheeky, smiling, tanned, and gloriously beautiful stockman had been her hero. Honestly, he'd dazzled her. 'And then, after we got closer, and you did start bonding with Mason, I wanted to tell you, but I didn't want you to hate me.' But he did now.

'So, what now?'

'Well, maybe you could send me photos of Mason growing up, like the ones you send your mum. And I'll send him birthday and Christmas presents. Then, maybe, when Mason is older, and you trust me again, I'd fly Mason out to join me for summer holidays or something. It's what I'd always planned with Gemma. I was going to be the fun aunt—who'd hire a nanny. Not be one.'

'Do you still want to be part of Mason's life?'

'Absolutely. I can tell him about his mother. I have photo albums and things that belonged to Gemma that I've kept for Mason.' She sighed heavily. The burden of saying goodbye and losing something that felt like a home was horrible. 'I never wanted to cause trouble. And I never meant to ...' She paused, licking her bottom lip.

The pause just got longer.

His eyes narrowed at her. 'Go on, what were you going to say.'

'Oh, what the hell ...' She had to say it, or she'd regret it for the rest of her life, even if she knew she'd lost him. 'I never meant to fall in love with you.' There, she'd said it.

Ash's brow crinkled as he stepped back.

'I know, bad timing as public enemy number one. Right?'

'Harper, you come from a fancy political family who has a ski chalet. You can't mean that.'

'But I do.' She stepped closer, facing the only man who mattered to her. 'Sure, if my father was alive, he'd hate you. But in time you'd win him over, when he'd see what I see.'

'I have faults, Harper, plenty of them. But I am growing, I am working on it.'

'But you also have this inner wealth at the way you look at the world, and where you live, how you live and who you live with makes you far richer than some kings I know.'

'See, look at your list of contacts. And I'm just ...' He removed his hat, raking fingers through his hair.

'You didn't think like that before you knew who I was, did you?'

He slid on his hat. The sexy way it shaded his eyes made her heart ache that it was over. 'No. But I know now.'

'You know I'm not like that. I'm the girl who'd rather eat a packet of shortbread that I shared with someone over a cup of coffee, like we did, than eat caviar or truffles. Where I come from none of those people are my friends. Not like Bree, who was there for me without any hidden agenda. You were there when I was scared or in danger, and you also taught me about friendship and family, too. My father had this mantra: *there are no friends in politics, you only have family to rely on.* You have that, Ash, and you have no idea how lucky you are.' She nodded at the table full of people celebrating the victory for their home.

'It still makes little sense. You. Me.'

'Why should it? I may not have the experience you have with relationships, but I can honestly say that I am thankful for all the heartbreaks, trials, failures, angst, and misery I went through before I found you, in this amazing place you call home. Without it, I never would've found you or appreciated the genuine gift you were to me, I just didn't realise how deep it went until you threw me out—'

'Harper.'

She held up her hand. 'I wish I could rewind time for so many things. But if I was to rewind back to one time, it would be to that moment we first met. I would have done things differently, even at the risk of your rejection, but I would at least have that memory of meeting you. So, this is the last time you'll see me—'

Ash stepped towards her, gripping her chin, he kissed her, hard. His warm lips pressed against hers, his hand cupped the side of her face where he controlled the kiss, consuming her completely. All she saw, felt, heard, and tasted was Ashton Riggs.

'There is no such thing as the last time not when it comes to us,' he murmured, holding her close to his chest, leaving her to swim in his warm eyes as a fingertip tenderly stroked her cheek. 'These past few days, I have felt fear on so many levels. The fear of failure, the fear of trying, the kind of fear that tried to cheat me out of the best thing in life—my son. And the fear of losing my home. But my greatest fear is losing you, because I love you.'

'You do?'

He sighed, but it was there in his eyes, the same love she felt deep inside. It might not have made sense, but it made sense to her soul.

'Hearing you love me, even though our story started with the wrong time, wrong place,' he said, 'and I know this is a new world for you, but you are the right person for me. You make me want to do better. You have this gift for giving me the confidence to try and be better, helping me realise I could be a father. You helped me pull out all those plans I wanted to throw away, while listening to my crazy ideas, where I finally found the courage to share them with my brothers.'

'You did?' Her eyes widened with hope surging inside for Ash.

He tenderly held her arms as if to keep her in place. His head lowering as he stepped in closer, with a hint of smile spreading across his lips. 'It's starting, all those ideas are starting because of you. I want to plan a future for us, where we'd never need to look back at the bad, but only at the good memories we create together. I want you to stay, because I love you, Harper. Because you belong here, with me. And I want you to move back into your old room.'

'And where will you be?'

His lips bent into one of those delicious grins. 'I plan to prove myself to you and try to move in there.'

'Yeah-nah, mate, I'm not that easy.' She grinned at his arched eyebrow, sounding like a long-time local in the pub. 'You haven't even taken me out on a date.'

'I plan to fix that. We'll have weekly date nights, where we can talk freely away from any other influences, where we'll be free to just be us because I'm only ever like that with you. I love you. You're family to me, to Mason, to us. That includes my brothers.'

'Even Dex.' She screwed up her nose.

'After what you did for this station, you've earned their respect. But most of all, you won me.' He then lowered his voice, and said, 'Do you realise how sexy hot you are when you get all businesslike?'

'Stop it.' She dropped her head, the heat brushing her cheeks.

'Hey?' He lifted her chin, making her face him. 'You're not

going anywhere, because your place is here with me and Mason. This is your home.' With his lips pressed to hers, he pulled her against his chest. His hands slid around her body, bringing her closer, where her heartbeat matched his and there was nothing more perfect in the world than kissing him right now, in a kiss that was better than any first kiss, because kissing Ash—kissing the man she loved—was like kissing heaven.

'Breathe, Harper. I won't leave you and I'm not letting you leave me.' His voice penetrated the haze of lust. Even if her self-esteem was at its most fragile, she was no longer the nanny, she wasn't someone's daughter, she wasn't some assistant or office worker, she was part of something truly fabulous. She was with Ash, and he was with her. And it was a warm, delicious, and gloriously intoxicating world that only held the two of them, that tasted of eternity, and of that deep soul-fulfilling love, that once-in-a-lifetime kind of love she'd always dreamed of was now a reality.

'Oi, that's enough, you two. There are children present,' called out Dex.

It was enough to break their kissing connection. Ash's darkening eyes matched the hunger she had for him as his thumb dragged over her bottom lip. 'Can we ignore him, and just go inside, to your room?' murmured Ash, his nose tenderly rubbing hers, while their arms wrapped tightly around each other, oh so deliciously close.

'Oi, you two,' this time it was Cap speaking. 'We just got an invitation to pizza night at the caretaker's cottage.'

'Yeah, it's party time at the neighbours,' said Dex. 'I'll even find you some wine, Harper.'

'ARPER, ARPER. *H-H-Harper.*'

'Mason?' Harper whispered, with her heart tight in her throat, as the tears welled up at the sight of the small boy, holding Ryder's hand by the front door. Did she dare move? 'Who taught Mason to say H?'

'I did. When we were out doing the troughs.' Ash gave that beautiful sexy grin with the dimple, the grin she loved.

'Go see your aunty.' Ryder helped the boy down the front steps and his little legs raced across the red dirt.

'Mason!' Harper ran to scoop up the toddler and squeezed him tight, breathing him in.

'*Harper home?*'

Ash slid his arm around Harper's shoulder to kiss her forehead, while she held his son between them. 'Yes, Mason, Harper is home to stay.'

Fifty-four

'Why are we out here?' Harper complained as Ash led her by the hand to her car, parked under the cool shade of the back shed.

'If you're going to drive to town—how many days a week?' Ash pulled back the dust cover he'd bought for the Audi to protect its black polish. Parked beside it was his old sunburnt ute covered in a layer of red dust, in the long car shed of sorts filled with assorted vehicles, tractors, and a truck. Dex had his fancy sleek ute at the far end, black of course, parked closest to the rundown stockman's shack. Next was Cap's mustard-coloured Tojo with the large dog cage on the back. There was Ryder's big beast of a fancy vehicle. The crazy and fun Razorback. And the latest addition—the 1957 FJ Holden, the car they'd found hidden in the Stoneys after that sandstorm.

'Three days. Monday, Wednesday, and Friday to help Ryan with the vet clinic. Don't forget, on Fridays, Mason has his playdates at the train station and the school library.'

'That leaves me to play daddy day care when you're at work. Are you sure you want to work at the vet's? And not the council office?'

'I'm not going anywhere near any government offices. No more politics for me. And it's only part-time, so I'll still get my cooking lessons from Bree. We're making regular lunch dates. Oh, and horse riding, lots of horse riding.' Her smile was nothing compared to the inner joy threatening to burst from her chest, because Ash had given her a horse. A beautiful horse. 'Did I say thank you for my horse.'

'Many times. Have you got a name for your horse, yet?'

'Shortbread.' It suited the cream horse she'd ridden during her first muster, the horse she'd survived the sandstorm with. 'Can we go riding now?'

'We'll do this lesson, first. By then Bree will have finished making us our hamper to take on our ride.'

'Aww ...'

'Date night, baby.' His kissed her nose. 'You know, you don't have to work. You could stay home.'

'I like being in an office and having my independence. I want to put on make-up, be near shops, and hear my shoes on concrete at least once a week, or this city girl will go through withdrawals.'

'You're so weird. But you're my kind of weird. But you in that tight office skirt, hmmm.' His eyes, laced with hunger, slowly walked over her body in her muster clothes—boots, jeans, long-sleeved work shirt and hat.

No need for make-up or fancy dress for her date on this station.

'Besides, poor Ryan needs the help sorting out his surgery. I'm doing up his website and I'm going to create an online campaign to help raise funds for all the animals he saves.' She had so many ideas.

'Don't forget that promise you made me.'

'To have a life outside of work.' She grinned, looping her arms around his neck to lean against his chest. 'Hell yeah, I'm good with that promise.'

'Good.' He kissed her nose.

'So, why are we here? Cap has Mason for the afternoon, we should do something other than hang out in the shed.'

'Because I want to give you a lesson.' Ash juggled her car keys, pressed on the button and the Audi's boot popped open, where he dragged out the tools.

'A lesson about?'

'Changing a car tyre. I'm not having some other bloke

come to your rescue.'

'Everyone knows that ...' She trailed off, biting her lip.

'Go on, say it.' He stood close, their noses nearly touching, daring her.

'We're a couple.' She slid the toe of her shoe across the dirt. It was so new to her.

'We're family, Harper.' He kissed her lips as if never tiring of kissing her. 'Now, this is called a lug wrench, also known as a torque wrench ...' Ash patiently explained the name and purpose of each tool, as he showed her how to change a car tyre.

Nearby, Charlie and Dex worked on the Holden's large engine. The vintage car they'd found in the Stoneys, was massive, and despite its rough condition it looked cool, like an old gangster's car.

'It's a good skill to learn there, missy,' called out Charlie, wiping greasy hands on an old rag. 'Which reminds me to check out the toolbox for this beast. Did you order them tyres, Dex?'

'Yep. Whitewalls to really make this thing look schmick. And the local mechanic can get us the paint—the original Brookmere Green—for the body.'

'Where did they score that?'

'Not sure. But we can use our brother's spray booth out at Sandlot Station. Jonathan's got all the spray guns and buffers to give it a professional paint job,' said Dex. 'He reckons he could sell this car for you today, as is.'

'Nah, I'd like to keep this old girl in the family. My brother and I had some good times in this car.' The lid of the boot creaked as he opened it to rummage around inside. 'I'll be buggered.' Charlie dropped the old toolbox with a clang.

'He's not having a heart attack, is he?' Ash whispered to Harper.

Harper approached. 'Are you okay, Charlie?'

Charlie's hands shook as he dragged out a long package from the boot of the car.

'What did you find?' Dex followed Charlie as he laid it

out on the workbench and unwrapped the old, oiled cloth.

'Is that a branding iron?' Harper shrugged at Ash. 'Bree's been giving me the basics. Did you know they're a family heirloom?'

'She's right. And this here …' Charlie held up the metal rod, with letters shaped on the end like a brand. 'This was my father's branding iron. He gave it to Harry the first time he moved on.'

'Not you?'

'I was making them. I got the one I wanted, the Elsie Creek Station brand. But this is the Splint family brand. A legacy brand made by my grandfather, that my father gave to Harry, so he'd always remember who he was on his travels.' He poked back the brim of his sweat-stained Akubra, with its distinctive crocodile leather hatband as the creases deepened around his grey eyes.

'Harry would never leave this behind. The guernsey, sure. The car, maybe. But never this. This brand meant everything to Harry. He wouldn't have run off and left this behind. Something must have happened to him …' Charlie turned to face the direction of the Stoneys where the breeze scattered fine red dust across the outback, where many secrets were buried from a past that has yet to be discovered.

To be continued in

STOCKMAN'S STOWAWAY

I HAVE A GIFT FOR YOU!

Learn more about
ELSIE CREEK STATION
The family tree
Behind the scenes
Plus so much more

Free & Exclusive!
Simply go to:
https://melarowe.com/the-stockmen-series-gifts/

Want more from the Elsie Creek World?

Binge-read all the bestsellers found in:

The Elsie Creek Series

&

The Station Series

Find them at your favourite online bookstore.

ACKNOWLEDGEMENTS

Welcome! I'm so glad you're here.

Can you believe that this is only the start of a series that is a few hundred thousand words long, filled with twists, turns, dog hair, and the occasional misplaced semicolon!

Thank you to all those who helped me on this amazing journey to get here, I wish I could name you all. I'd like to say a special thanks to the amazing Territory stockmen and stockwomen, to all those retired ringers, the crazy bull catchers who have their own Razorbacks, to the cheeky drovers who make the pub messy, the rodeo cowboys with their dazzling smiles, and the keen campdrafters and their entourage. Thank you all for being a part of the real-life outback story, I am truly humbled to share some of our adventures within The Stockmen Series.

Thank you to the amazing Handbrake, who'll be sighing with relief that this book is over—until my next book. (*Buckle up, kid there's four in this series!*)

Thank you to the fabulous first readers team of amazing arc readers, your reviews make me want to hug you all. Thank you to the epically incredible and patient editing Deb team at DP Plus, you ladies deserve medals, a few grand parades, and statues raised in your honour. Or I could just say: 'love your work!'

Lastly, to you, dear reader, thank you so much for giving up your spare time and for the courage to start this epic adventure romance series. It means the world to me, and I look forward to sharing more with you in that romantic *'Escape to Happily Ever After'*.

Until next time,

A. ROWE

ABOUT THE AUTHOR

Australian bestselling author, Mel A ROWE, creates romantic escapes for today's busy readers to enjoy from the comfort of their home.

Delivering stories with a dash of drama, witty humour and quirky family units, Mel is known for reinventing romantic versions of home, taking her common characters on uncommon journeys that lead from boardrooms to billabongs as they try to find their own HAPPILY EVER AFTER.

Living in Australia's Northern Territory, Mel enjoys random outback road trips, fumbling with her camera, annoying her family with her bad singing, and making new friends in the middle of nowhere—except for water buffalos. She's been chased by a few.

Find Mel at

MelAROWE.com

Receive exclusive insights, book gifts, and news
of upcoming releases by joining:
https://melarowe.com/newsletter/

Also by MEL A ROWE

THE STOCKMEN SERIES:
Stockman's Sandstorm
Stockman's Stowaway
Stockman's Stormcloud
Stockman's Showdown

ELSIE CREEK SERIES:
The Art of Dust
Diamond in the Dust
Caked in Dust
Xmas Dust
Muster in the Dust
Rolled in Dust
Written in Dust
Doctoring Dust
Buffalo Dust

OASIS OF THE OUTBACK DUOLOGY:
The Station, Volume One
The Station, Volume Two

STANDALONE STORIES:
Avoiding the Pity Party
Unplanned Party
The Football Whisperer
Winter's Walk
Run Beautiful Run
The Sister Trip

For story exclusives & more visit MelAROWE.com